Praise for the novels of Allison Brennan

"[Brennan] keeps readers guessing whodunit to the
end." —*Publishers Weekly* on *The Wrong Victim*

"An intense, pulse pounding thriller from start to finish.
There were so many suspects, not to mention surprises
and twists." —*The Reading Cafe* on *The Wrong Victim*

"It's always such a pleasure to review an
Allison Brennan novel! She knows how to write
absorbing, twisty thrillers with plenty of heart and
sense, and The Sorority Murder is no different."
—*Criminal Element*

"Allison Brennan is always good but her latest and
most ambitious work ever...is downright spectacular...
A riveting page turner as prescient as it is purposeful."
—*Providence Journal* on *Tell No Lies*

"Bestseller Brennan's intriguing sequel to...
The Third to Die...[has] fast-paced action...[and a]
well-constructed mystery plot."
—*Publishers Weekly* on *Tell No Lies*

"A lean thriller starring a strong and damaged
protagonist who's as compelling as Lisbeth Salander."
—*Kirkus Reviews* on *The Third to Die*

"Leave all the lights on... You'll be turning the pages fast
as you can."
—Catherine Coulter, *New York Times* bestselling author
of *Labyrinth*, on *The Third to Die*

ALLISON BRENNAN

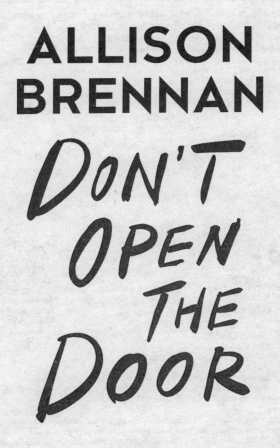

DON'T OPEN THE DOOR

mira

Recycling programs for this product may not exist in your area.

ISBN-13: 978-0-7783-8650-6

Don't Open the Door

For questions and comments about the quality of this book, please contact us at CustomerService@Harlequin.com.

Mira
22 Adelaide St. West, 41st Floor
Toronto, Ontario M5H 4E3, Canada
www.Harlequin.com

Printed in U.S.A.

There are few people who embody friendship, honor and humor as Bill Saracino, a good friend of the Brennan family, and especially of Dan. Together they could keep anyone laughing all night. Now Bill is keeping the angels in good humor with his wit and charm. Bill will be missed by all who were lucky enough to know him. Requiescat in pace.

Don't Open the Door

MONDAY

One

Tommy Granger awoke with a start, the remnants of a disturbing dream fading as he struggled under his twisted, sweat-soaked sheets. As it was with most nightmares—at least for him—he didn't remember details. A vague sense that he'd been at the office, but Regan was still a marshal. They were suited up in full gear, preparing to track a fugitive, but as dreams were tricky, he was then alone in the woods at night, deep in the Shenandoah National Park, tracking a predator who was elusive and dangerous, his heart racing, pounding, an unfamiliar feeling because his training taught him to keep his fear in check.

The break of a branch behind him and he was awake, not knowing if the sound was in his head or in his yard.

He fought to untangle himself from his bedding as he sat up, rubbing his bare feet on thick carpet, grounding himself. The panic was brief, fleeting. Training and control were hard to break, even in a deep sleep.

The faint numbers of his bedside clock told him it was 4:51 a.m. His alarm was set for 5:30, but he always woke a few minutes before then, as if his body was trained to anticipate the irritating buzz. He hit the off button; he had a busy day.

He was finally prepared to share with his office his off-book investigation into the murder of Chase Warwick.

It was all about money, Tommy thought with disgust as he pushed himself out of bed. Money and greed and what corrupt men were willing to do to keep their secrets buried. The killer may have been apprehended, but Adam Hannigan's motives had never sat well with Tommy. And then Hannigan was dead and the case closed.

He paused at his bedroom window. The air was still, but he couldn't get the sound of a cracking branch out of his mind. It had sounded crisp, sharp. Real. But he saw nothing out front, no jogger, no passing car, still too early for Mrs. Benson down the street to be walking her friendly golden retrievers or for Richie Luna, his neighbor to the east, to leave for work—though he noted the faint light in the kitchen, signaling that Richie, like Tommy, was an early riser.

Dreams and nightmares were deceiving, which was why he was having a hard time shaking this one.

The hot water cleared the remnants of fog from his brain. He shaved, dressed, the morning ritual comforting. Downstairs, he brewed a pot of coffee and stared out at the large kitchen window into the side yard, running through his head how he was going to lay out the case to Charlie and then his boss.

Knowing *why* Chase Warwick had died was only one piece of the puzzle. He knew Adam Hannigan, the man arrested for murder, was only a pawn—used or hired—but Tommy couldn't prove who he suspected was behind everything. If Tommy could convince his boss that he was onto something—that the murder of Chase Warwick was a small piece of a bigger conspiracy—they would then be up against high-priced lawyers, big name corporations, and even their own government.

Bring it on, he thought. He was itching for a fight. Itching to get to the bottom of this conspiracy. He'd only recently realized that he couldn't do it alone anymore. There was information he couldn't access without a warrant.

Regan deserved to know why her son was dead. Chase deserved justice for his murder. And those responsible must pay for their crimes.

And maybe…just maybe…Regan would come back.

Don't be a fool. She made it clear she was done with the Marshals Service, that she wasn't going to return to duty, that she wanted to be with her friends and family. Far, far away from the pain and heartbreak she'd left behind here in Virginia.

He'd go anywhere for her, but Tommy wasn't naive. Regan was her own woman, and while he was confident of his feelings, his greatest fear was that she didn't love him like he loved her.

And he wouldn't follow a woman who didn't want to be followed.

When the coffee was done, he pulled out the carafe and poured a cup. He walked to his office, a comfortable room with built-in bookshelves and cabinets, two comfortable leather chairs facing the original brick fireplace, and his massive antique desk he had painstakingly refinished years ago. It was his favorite room in the large house, but since he started this investigation, he couldn't relax and drink Scotch while listening to a ball game or watching the news. Not when he was so close to the truth.

Tommy packed up his laptop, notes, and the evidence he'd collected. No smoking gun, but ample circumstantial evidence. The government had opened cases with less. He needed an unbiased eye, someone who hadn't been eating and sleeping Chase Warwick's murder for the last month. Tommy needed to talk through his theory with his most trusted colleague, put everything on the table, then ask Charlie to help Tommy present the entire case to their boss in the DOJ.

While the US Marshals were not generally an investigative federal law enforcement agency, they did have a special operations unit that would undertake certain criminal investigations, and Tommy had to make the case that *this* case deserved their attention. He could already hear the objections—that the FBI had jurisdiction, that they would be causing friction with their FBI colleagues if they took the case—so he needed to be clear and compelling in his presentation—including his reasons for not trusting the local FBI office. No way was he sharing his information with those jokers—not until he could identify the bad cop among them.

Someone in the FBI was rotten to the core.

Once he double-checked to make sure he didn't leave anything important behind on his desk, he went back to the kitchen, put his briefcase down, topped off his coffee, and went upstairs to retrieve his gun. After he'd holstered his service weapon, he pulled his phone from the charger on his nightstand. Hesitated.

He'd almost called Regan a half dozen times this week while assembling the facts in preparation for his talk with Charlie, but Tommy managed to stop himself. Now...dammit, he wanted her *here*.

Tommy wasn't certain he could trust the information Regan's ex-husband Grant Warwick had given him. Not only did Tommy dislike Grant, but in the past the man had lied to him. Regan was cool and methodical, she'd be able to assess Grant's information without bias. It's one of the many reasons Tommy loved her—the clear way her mind worked.

Not that he could tell her yet. He didn't want to jeopardize their friendship by telling his former partner that he'd been half in love with her for years.

Regan knew that he was looking into Chase's murder. She didn't want to be part of it, but she hadn't told him to stop. In fact, she'd told Tommy to get back in touch with her when he had something concrete. Now he'd assembled solid facts…he just didn't know how they fit together. Would they be concrete enough for Regan?

Before he could talk himself out of it, he hit her name on his contact list. He almost hung up when he realized it was 3:00 a.m. there in Arizona, but then her voicemail picked up.

He waited for the tone, then said, "Regan, it's Tommy. I'm close to the truth about what happened to Chase. I'm laying it all out to Charlie this morning, but I wanted to talk to you as soon as possible. I think I have a good case for the DOJ. Call me when you get this message. I—well, just call."

Tommy ended the call before saying *I love you*. He couldn't put that weight on her right now, and definitely not over the damn phone.

It was just after six o'clock and he wasn't meeting Charlie until eight, but Tommy was antsy. He had toast and a banana, considered how he was going to lay the case out.

Adam Hannigan was a hit man hired to kill the Warwick family.

Charlie would ask him how he knew that. Tommy didn't have proof, which was one of the problems—to get the proof, he needed a warrant. He had an inside man in Grant

Warwick, but even Grant didn't have the hard evidence they would need, and he wasn't exactly a reliable witness. Tommy bent a few laws in the pursuit of justice, but he was confident he didn't cross the line.

Tommy would also have to explain why they couldn't trust the FBI. His reluctance wasn't based on hard facts, but he'd seen enough to at least cast doubt—especially with how they handled the Hannigan investigation.

Though it was early, Tommy was too antsy to stay. He poured the rest of his coffee in a to-go cup, topped it off. He'd get to the office early and poke around, start catching up on things after his month's leave. He was ready and motivated to return.

What if you can't sell this investigation?

Tommy had thought about that a lot—if he laid all his cards on the table and his boss still said no, they weren't getting involved. He didn't know what he would do at that point. He didn't want to consider failure. He'd been a Marine, dammit—failure was not an option.

Resolved that he had enough to make his case, he grabbed his keys, set his security system, and stepped out the front door. There was a small garage behind the house, but between his tools, home renovation supplies, and ample Christmas decorations—his neighborhood went all out every year—he had no room for his truck.

He hesitated when something caught his attention. A movement, a slight reflection, something in his yard that he didn't expect. Dawn was just breaking to the east, and his porch light was still on—it automatically turned off at eight and back on at six. Between the dim morning and the bright white light, he saw nothing in his yard, yet the memory of the breaking branch that had drawn him from sleep had him wary.

Tommy had been in the Marines for three years and the US Marshals Service for sixteen. His instincts had always been good…but he knew in that instant he'd hesitated a second too long.

He reached for his gun while he dove to the right where there was some small cover behind the laurel bushes. Nothing solid to stop a bullet, but maybe enough to give him time to fire back. He had just put his gun in hand when the *whoosh* of a sniper rifle echoed in the still morning.

The bullet hit his left thigh, and he grunted as he stumbled off the small porch into the bush. The shooter was in the tree—in the fucking *tree*!—in the middle of his front yard. He couldn't see him in the faint light, the yard still dark. He immediately turned his gun on his porch light and fired; glass shattered, dark fell. He didn't need to make himself an easier target.

He fumbled for his phone as blood flowed down his throbbing leg. His vision blurred as the unrelenting pain flowed through his body.

Focus, soldier!

He'd never been shot before, not in the military, not in the Marshals Service. He was trained in how to handle being wounded, under attack, learning to take cover, to call for reinforcements, to survive until help arrived. He dropped his phone, couldn't unlock it, hit the emergency button, then refocused in the direction of the shooter.

He could see nothing in the near dark, he couldn't see the tree through the bushes. He scrambled up, put too much weight on his leg and grunted. The blood was coming out too fast; his head felt light, woozy.

He heard a bullet hit the brick behind him. Another.

He couldn't fire at what he couldn't see!

Where are you, you bastard?

A bullet ripped into his shoulder, another into his neck, and he knew then that he was a dead man.

Nelson Lee didn't hesitate: as soon as Granger shot out the light, he'd reached into his small bag and retrieved his night vision goggles.

The distance was child's play; he could have hit a target twice as far back when he was ten and shooting cans in his backyard. Granger had moved suddenly, surprisingly quick, diving for the only potential cover.

But leaves couldn't stop bullets.

The clean one-shot kill eluded him, but Nelson hadn't lost. Granger was wounded, bleeding, and Nelson had the high ground, training, and patience.

He adjusted the goggles, looked into the bushes. Saw the large man stuck between the house and the hedge. He fired. Saw flecks of brick when the bullet hit the wall. Adjusted his sights, fired four times in rapid succession, moving the barrel down slightly to compensate for the different angle.

The third bullet hit the target, shoulder. The fourth in his neck. His body slumped and Nelson didn't have a clear shot of his head.

Granger would bleed out in less than a minute, but Nelson left nothing to chance.

He descended from his roost in the tall oak tree, collapsed his rifle, put it in his case, then slung the case over his back as he walked across the driveway and up the short flight of stairs to where he could better view the body behind the hedge. He had on a Kevlar vest, neck gear, a helmet, goggles. Not only to avoid being identified by a neighbor, but Granger was a marshal; he might have fired back.

He was dead; Nelson was certain as he stared at the body

slumped against the house. But he put a bullet in Granger's head on the off chance that he wasn't. He hadn't known the man; it was better that way. Nelson didn't like killing men he knew personally. But he had learned Granger's routine, schedule. He knew the man was well trained, and had to wait for a successful kill. He'd had two previous opportunities where he'd walked away because they weren't perfect. Nelson didn't want to be caught or killed.

Nelson heard a faint noise, listened more carefully, realized it was a phone. He looked carefully and saw Granger's phone under the bushes, the screen up, dimly lit.

Dammit. The man had called 911. Nelson didn't have much time.

He grabbed the briefcase that Granger had dropped on the doorstep, then ran down the steps and around to the bush. He had to get on all fours to reach under and extract the phone. Immediately, he ended the call, cutting off the voice of the dispatcher. Working quickly, he shut off the phone, pulled out a faraday bag, and slipped the phone inside to block all tracking. He would turn the device over to his employer for analysis. There might be information from the phone that they could use, once they removed GPS tracking.

Nelson walked briskly away from the house. The man was dead; he had the documents and his phone; as soon as he turned them over, he would be paid the second half of his fee.

A hefty price because of the tight deadline.

"He has to be dead by eight Monday morning. Any means necessary. Collect the documents."

And so it was done.

When his money was in hand, Nelson would return to

his South Carolina retreat and wait for another call, another job. That might be a day or a month. Could even be a year.

But inevitably they'd call, and he would come. Nelson Lee owed his life to his employer; they owned him until the day he died.

Two

At eight that night, Jenna Johns ended her shift at the hospital. For a blissfully busy twelve hours, she had focused solely on the hectic routine of emergency room triage. Most nurses wouldn't call the ER blissful but compared to the last couple weeks of her personal life, Jenna was grateful for the organized chaos of her vocation.

She loved being a nurse. The last few years had been difficult, to say the least, but the trying times had made or broken hospital staffs across the country, leaving behind the best of the best. Jenna had learned that not only was nursing her calling, she actually thrived in the fast-paced bustle of the ER. The highs were amazing, and the lows she dealt with as they came. Lucky for her she had a great group of friends who, like Jenna, loved their jobs.

She stayed a bit after her shift because she wanted to check on Mrs. Reynolds, a sweet elderly widow who had been brought in via ambulance with a broken hip. Mrs. Reynolds reminded Jenna of her grandma Jeannie, whom Jenna was named for, who lived in an assisted living facility thirty minutes away. Jenna visited her at least once a week and wished she could have taken care of her. Unfortunately, her grams needed full-time help because she couldn't walk, but her mind was sharp and witty. She was a whiz with her smart phone and sent Jenna funny memes every day, plus shared all the gossip at the care facility.

It seemed all the white-haired women over a certain age reminded Jenna of her grams.

Mrs. Reynolds's daughter lived in Boston. Jenna had talked to her a few hours ago, and the daughter booked a flight for tomorrow morning. Mrs. Reynolds was trying to keep a brave face, but Jenna could tell she was scared.

She glanced at the info board outside Mrs. Reynolds's room, noted she was scheduled for surgery first thing in the morning with Dr. Varma, one of the best orthopedic surgeons on staff. Good. The X-ray showed a clean break below the femoral head, which meant they didn't have to do a full hip replacement, but they needed to put in a rod down the marrow of the femur and anchor it with screws.

Jenna entered the room with a smile. "Hello, Mrs. Reynolds," she said brightly when she saw that the patient was awake, watching a game show on the small television in the corner.

Mrs. Reynolds looked away from the TV. "Are you my nurse tonight? Don't you get time off?"

Jenna laughed. "I'm off duty but wanted to check on you. Did your nurse tell you I spoke to your daughter?"

The woman smiled. "Yes. Melanie will be here in the morning, but they say I'll be in surgery when she arrives."

"You're in good hands." She glanced at the board in the room listing the nurses assigned to Mrs. Reynolds. Tami was the floor lead, and Lance Martelli was assigned to her for the overnight shift. "My best friend is taking care of you," said Jenna with a wide smile. Maybe too wide— Lance always made her smile.

"The handsome young man?"

"Don't let Lance hear you say that! It'll go straight to his head," Jenna laughed. "Don't let his good looks fool you, either; he's as smart as they come."

"*Ah*, the perfect entrance line." Lance walked in right then, saying to her, "You're never living that down, Jenna." He poked her in the ribs and she stifled a giggle.

She winked at Mrs. Reynolds. "Don't you worry. By the time you're out of surgery, your daughter will be here."

"She's been wanting me to move to Boston to be close to her, even found me a place that seems nice, but I love my little house. Herb and I moved in to it right after the Korean War. I was eighteen, he was twenty-one. We raised two kids in that house, had thousands of meals, we laughed and cried. Now…she'll probably use this stupid fall as a reason to try and force me to come."

Jenna lightly squeezed her fingers. "She loves you and is worried about you."

Lance chatted with both of them as he took Mrs. Reynolds's vitals, asked her about her pain level, swapped out her IV, and made sure she was comfortable.

Jenna told her, "You're in good hands with Dr. Varma, so don't worry about anything, Mrs. Reynolds. You'll probably be out of here before I come back on shift Thursday, but if you're still here, I'll stop in to see you."

"Thank you, dear, you have been so kind."

Once Jenna and Lance were out at the nursing station, he turned to her. "This is what, the two hundred, sixty-seventh old person you've adopted?"

"I can't help it," said Jenna, slightly blushing. "I can't stand seeing them alone and scared when they come in. Thank goodness her daughter is on the way."

Lance stood at the computer and typed in the information he'd just collected. "I miss having the same shift as you," he said.

"Ditto. But I'm sure the nighttime bonus is nice."

"It's not so much the money as that it's the only way I can go back to school." Lance was studying to get a certificate in trauma care. He shouldn't have to, Jenna thought—he'd been a medic in the army for three years; he'd seen plenty of trauma. They'd met last year when he did his clinical in the ER on a shortened nursing program because of his army training, but he still had to go back for the certificate in trauma. He already knew more than most of the nurses Jenna worked with.

"Well, it's not forever," she said.

"Nope," he said, logged out, and grinned at her. "Now go home—get some sleep. I'll text you when Mrs. Reynolds gets out of surgery."

Home. That was the last place she wanted to go right now. Because then she'd start thinking about going in to the Marshals office this week, giving her statement, reopening all the emotions about her sister and everything surrounding her sister's death. She'd successfully put it out of her mind because of work; now she couldn't avoid it.

Lance eyed her suspiciously. "What's wrong?"

"Nothing."

He tilted his head and kept his mouth closed and tight, his eyebrows rising just a fraction.

"Really," she reiterated.

"Nothing," he repeated flatly.

"It's personal."

"Not that jerk you were dating who wouldn't get lost when you kicked him to the curb."

"No, he hasn't bothered me in months—I *swear*," she added when Lance looked skeptical. Yeah, she was sometimes too nice and yeah, she sometimes had a hard time saying no when she didn't want to go on another date. But she was getting better about standing up for herself. "It *is* personal. My sister…" Her voice trailed off.

"Sister? I thought she died."

She nodded. "It's complicated, but…well…dammit."

She was getting weepy. For more than twelve hours, Jenna had focused on her job, putting everything that was going on in her life aside. But now that she faced going home alone, the emotions and worries and fears came rushing in.

Lance took her by the arm and led her to the small break room at the end of the hall, which was fortunately empty. "Tell me," he said, crossing his arms and leaning against the wall. He was so handsome with his dark Italian skin and bright green eyes. She always felt chunky around him because he was so fit. She was fit, too—she was all muscle. Her grandma called her "sturdy" but Jenna didn't really take it as the compliment that Grams intended.

She caught herself playing with the end of her long dark-blond braid, a nervous habit. She pushed her braid off her shoulder.

"I can't—it's a long story."

Again he waited, patient but insistent. Lance never had to press, and she always relented and told him whatever he wanted to know. Maybe because she trusted him.

"It *is* a long story," she repeated. "And I'll tell you everything when I know *exactly* what happened. But. Okay. Short version." Deep breath. "It turns out that my sister, Becca, might have been involved in something illegal before she was killed two years ago. I mean—she might have been involved in something illegal *when* she was killed. And now it seems like it's going to all come out."

"Do you think that anyone here, who works with you, would care at all about something your sister did years ago?"

"Maybe not, but *I* care. Becca was my big sister. She became my guardian after our parents died. She moved back home, commuted to college instead of living in her sorority. She really stepped up for me. I know she made mistakes, but I don't want people only remembering her mistakes."

"Hey, what matters is what *you* think. And you know your sister better than anyone. Honestly, I don't care what she was doing." He cocked his head. "What happened to her? She was killed in a bank robbery, right? A hostage?"

"That's what I thought." Then it all came out. Maybe because not only did she trust Lance, but she needed to tell someone. Ever since Deputy Marshal Tommy Granger came to her last month she'd been on pins and needles wanting to talk to someone, but not knowing how. "Two years ago, almost to the day, my sister was taken hostage and killed in a bank robbery. Potomac Bank, in Arlington. She was a teller, had been cooperating with the gunman, but he shot her anyway. At the time, that's all I knew. The FBI investigated, but because the guy was killed by police, it was pretty much a closed case.

"Then, at the end of last month, a marshal came to me, asked me a bunch of questions about Becca, and showed me a picture of her and a guy—the guy who killed her. He said he thought Becca was in on the robbery, that she knew the guy—Michael Hannigan—and he wanted to know what I knew. Which was nothing. At least—I thought I didn't know anything. But as we talked, I realized I knew a lot more than I thought."

"Like?"

She shook her head. "I shouldn't talk about it. I might have to testify and give a statement and stuff. But—well—I guess I can tell you that Becca had been acting odd around that time. She talked about a possible second job where she'd make a lot of money, maybe enough to quit her job. All stuff I never thought was that important, though I always had this feeling that Becca was involved in something…I don't know, sketchy. It bothered me, but she was my sister, and every time I tried to talk to her about anything it was like *don't worry, Jenna! Everything is great, you're such a worry wart.*" Jenna frowned. "With what the marshal knew and what I knew, yeah, I think she was involved in the heist, too."

"No one deserves to be killed in cold blood."

"Thank you," she said, and meant it. Jenna still felt the hole in her life where her sister had been.

"Why now? I mean, why did the police come to you now about your sister?"

"New evidence that the robbery was part of a bigger crime. Deputy Granger was bringing all the evidence to his superiors today. There was a lot going on with Becca back then… Anyway, I might have to go in and give a statement, though he hasn't called to tell me what happened. I'm anxious about it. So…" She shrugged, looked down. What else could she say?

"Jenna—" Lance put his hands on her shoulders "—whatever happens, you have friends—me especially, I'm the cream of the crop." He grinned, trying to lighten the mood. "And there's Josie and Nat and Chris. We'll all be there for you, you know that, right? No matter what happens, we'll stand by you."

She blinked back tears, hugged him. "Thank you. Do you still have Wednesday through Friday off?"

"Yes. I have class Wednesday afternoon—but after that,

a late dinner maybe? You can tell me anything. I'm not going to judge you or Becca—I'm on your side."

"Wednesday then. I'll cook?" she asked more than told him.

"God, yes. I'm so tired of takeout. I'll text you. And—if you need to talk sooner, call, okay?"

She nodded. "I will."

When she walked out of the hospital, Jenna felt a million times better. It helped knowing that she had friends to lean on, no matter what happened with Deputy US Marshal Granger and his investigation.

Jenna was still upset that he hadn't called or at least texted her about his meeting this morning. They'd been talking almost daily for the last three weeks, and he knew how anxious and worried she was. It wasn't just her being concerned about Becca's reputation—though she didn't want anyone thinking bad about her sister, if Becca committed a crime then she committed a crime. But Jenna knew things that Deputy Granger thought might put her in danger—people Becca had met, things Becca had said to Jenna.

Deputy Granger promised if that was the case, he would protect her. But right now, as she walked into her dimly lit house Monday night, that assurance didn't ease her fears. She wished she still had a dog, but her longtime golden Labrador Ginger had died last year and she hadn't had the heart to adopt another. But right now, a dog to sit with was just what she needed.

There had been no phone or text messages from the marshal, but she had avoided checking her email at work. Now she sat on the couch and flipped through her phone to her email app.

No email from Deputy Granger. Everything was spam or junk or not important.

It was ten now, but she wouldn't be able to sleep if she didn't talk to him, even if he didn't have any real news yet. She called him.

After the fourth ring she expected it would go to voice-mail, then a voice said, "Ms. Johns?"

It was a deep, gruff, unfamiliar voice. Definitely *not* Tommy Granger—he called her Jenna, not Ms. Johns.

"I'm calling for Deputy Granger, is he available?"

"He can't come to the phone."

She felt very, very cold. Something was wrong.

"What can I help you with?" the man asked.

How did he know her name?

Caller ID, you idiot.

Why would the marshal give his cell phone to someone else?

"Where is Deputy Granger? I need to speak to him."

She heard a click, a beep, and then the man said, "Deputy Granger has been working on an unauthorized investigation, and it seems he brought you into it. Perhaps it would be beneficial for both of us to meet and discuss the matter."

Every warning bell went off in her head. She ended the call.

She would never forget what Tommy told her last week, when he informed her that he was going to his superiors.

"I don't know how deep the conspiracy goes, Jenna. I'm keeping your name out of it for the time being, but you might need to come in and make a statement. If that is the case, I'll put you in protective custody. Until then, you're anonymous. So don't be scared. No one knows you're help-ing me."

Her phone almost immediately rang with the caller ID "Marshal Tommy Granger."

She didn't answer, but the voicemail the deep-voiced man left gave her chills.

"Ms. Johns, answer your phone. We need to know what you know, for the safety of everyone involved. You understand, don't you?"

The caller waited a few seconds, then ended the call.

This could *not* be happening. Was that man working with Deputy Granger? Why wouldn't he identify himself as a marshal? Why wouldn't he let Jenna talk to Tommy?

She didn't know who to call, but now she was no longer anonymous. Because she'd called him, someone else had her name. They might be able to find out where she lived. Tommy had promised if her name became public, that he would protect her. Now…he wasn't answering his phone.

She couldn't stay *here*. When Tommy Granger knocked on her door three weeks ago and asked for her help in putting together pieces of information about the weeks leading up to the bank robbery that ended Becca's life, Jenna had trusted him. He's been straightforward and kind and she appreciated both.

Now, unable to reach Tommy, Jenna worried she wasn't safe at home. Half-panicked, with no idea where she was going, Jenna packed a suitcase.

Until she talked to him, she might never feel safe again.

She left, heading west, and hoped she was doing the right thing.

TUESDAY

Three

Carry-on in hand, former US Marshal Regan Merritt waited for her lone bag to appear on the carousel. She'd taken the red-eye out of Phoenix, landing at Dulles Airport in Virginia at 7:55 a.m. She'd never been comfortable sleeping on planes or in the presence of strangers so she'd downloaded a book on tape and hoped the story would lull her into a half sleep, but she couldn't stop thinking about Tommy. Her former boss, her friend, her...well, damn. Trying to blank her mind and suppress all the memories had given her a headache, which throbbed as she stood to the side, waiting for her bag at the customer service counter.

Tommy was dead.

She hadn't wanted to believe it. Hadn't the last year been hell on her? Hadn't she suffered more than anyone should with the loss of her son? Now Tommy, too?

She called Tommy immediately after listening to his voicemail. No answer. She then called her old office. Maggie, the office manager, had been crying and immediately forwarded her call to Charlie's cell phone. He didn't hedge, he didn't lead in with platitudes.

"Tommy was shot and killed outside his house this morn-

*ing. Not more than two hours ago. I'm sorry to tell you
like this."*

Regan needed to find out if his death had anything to do
with his investigation into her son's murder—an investigation she should have told him to drop but didn't.

While Regan had told Tommy she couldn't be involved
in his efforts, she also didn't tell him to stand down. She
wanted the truth.

*You didn't have the courage to help Tommy. Now he's
dead, and you're going to bury the one person who shared
your belief that Chase's death had nothing to do with your
job. Tommy was the one person who supported you from
the beginning of this god-awful last year.*

Regan grabbed her bag as soon as the clerk called her
name. She tore off the bright orange firearm tag and tossed
it in the trash; no use advertising to the world that she was
carrying a weapon. She walked outside, pulling on sunglasses as she stepped into the morning glare. She followed the signs to the shuttle that would then take her to
the rental car lot. Fifteen minutes later, she drove away in
a large comfortable sedan.

She had sent Charlie a message that she would come by
the US Marshals office in Alexandria as soon as she could,
but first Regan was heading to Tommy's house.

Regan wanted to see where Tommy had died. To grieve,
fast and hard now instead of letting it surprise and sabo-
tage her later.

She would never forget the last time she'd seen Tommy.

When you left someone, you never thought it would be
the last time.

It was just six weeks ago. She'd flown from Arizona to
Virginia. A quick, twenty-four-hour trip to visit her son's
grave on what would have been Chase's eleventh birthday.

From the cemetery, Regan had driven to Tommy's. She planned to stay in the guest room.

Instead, she'd stayed with Tommy in his bed.

It was not expected, but it happened. Maybe she'd known that it would happen because she and Tommy had always been close and at that moment after leaving Chase's grave she had been desperate for a real human connection, something that would make her feel alive and whole, even just for a few hours.

She didn't regret sex with Tommy, but she also didn't know what to feel about it. Their relationship hadn't been sexual for the nearly fourteen years they'd known each other. Suddenly, it was—partly awkward, partly interesting, partly exciting. Whatever it was, it made her self-conscious. Regan didn't generally overanalyze or romanticize relationships—possibly why her marriage had failed—but she couldn't stop thinking about what might have been had her life not gone sideways.

Now her closest friend, her mentor, confidante, and one-time lover—was dead.

What did you find, Tommy?

She'd been thinking about their last conversation almost nonstop since she heard his message on her voicemail. He'd told her he was meeting with Peter Grey, the man who killed Adam Hannigan. The man who stole justice from Regan when he shivved Chase's killer in prison.

Adam Hannigan was the only person who had the answer to her question: *Why.*

Tommy's house was on a quiet tree-lined street of older homes on the outskirts of Reston, thirty minutes from where they had worked together at the federal courthouse in Alexandria. He'd bought the house years ago when the market was in the tank and over time had painstakingly renovated it. The sanding and painting and extensive maintenance had been his release from the pressures of their job. A few times over the years Regan had worked for the US Marshals—the first eight as Tommy's colleague, the last five as his subordinate after his promotion to assistant chief deputy—she'd joined other members of her team to help out when Tommy needed extra hands for a specific improvement, but he'd truly enjoyed the work himself.

A towering oak tree stood in the center of the circular drive. It was in that tree, shielded by thick foliage, that Tommy's killer had waited for him to leave his house yesterday morning. Seventy feet away, thirty feet high, hiding in a tree, waiting for his target. As soon as Tommy closed the front door and started down the steps, the sniper fired a bullet.

Charlie had told her before she left Arizona that an analysis of the crime scene showed that Tommy had evaded his attacker after being shot in the thigh, that based on the angle of the blood spatter he'd been moving into the bushes when he was first shot.

But the shooter shot him three times more, including once through the head. Took his phone—Tommy had called 911, but at 6:09 a.m. the call had disconnected and GPS could not be traced. Because Tommy was flagged as law enforcement and dispatch couldn't reach him, they sent out a patrol and found his body ten minutes after the call disconnected.

Why did the killer take his phone?

Regan's chest hitched. Tommy was a former Marine and a trained marshal. He'd fought back, did everything he could under the circumstances, but the shooter had defeated him. Had Tommy suspected a threat? Was he on alert? Or did he leave the house expecting nothing, until a sliver of an instinct had him diving into the bushes?

The shooter was a trained sniper. Former military? Cop? The FBI—who would most likely be investigating Tommy's murder—would be asking the same questions.

Regan pulled her rental car behind Tommy's truck, which was parked in front of the stairs leading to the small porch fronting the brick house. She stared at the oak tree for a long minute before getting out of the car. Charlie had sent her crime scene photos. She knew where the killer had staked out his spot.

She breathed in the spring air. Mild humidity hit her first—maybe because she'd come from the dry, crisp, fresh mountains of northern Arizona she noticed it more. Then came the scents of honeysuckle and pine and fresh-cut grass.

The house was grand—far too big for one person, but for Tommy it had been a therapeutic project as well as his home. She walked up the five steps and stopped at the door. The smell of bleach hit her. Someone had recently, perhaps even this morning, cleaned the remnants of biological matter off the porch and the door.

She looked down. Blood had soaked into the brick. That would be next to impossible to remove. If someone didn't know what it was, they'd think it was just spilled paint.

But Regan knew. It was Tommy's blood.

The bushes that Tommy had dived into were cut away so first responders could retrieve his body and collect evidence. She couldn't see the blood that had soaked into the earth, but some of the leaves were stained dark, and she knew that, too, was Tommy's blood.

"Tommy," she murmured, "what got you killed? What

did you find out? Who…" The million dollar question. *Who did it?*

She turned, her back to the door, and stared again at the oak tree. The leaves easily hid the shooter. It had been dawn, so visibility would have been poor. One shot could have killed him; but Tommy had sensed or heard or seen something and tried to escape.

No tire tracks had been found, but faint shoe prints—an average size eleven—led to the street, a point between Tommy and his neighbor to the west. Not clearly visible from Tommy's house because of the neighbors' hedges on both sides.

The killer could have parked there; he could have been picked up. Whatever he'd done, he was gone before the first sheriff's unit rolled up less than ten minutes after the 911 call went through.

Kill a man and disappear in minutes.

The killer retrieved his phone. The killer saw his handi-work, walked right up to Tommy, and stared at his dead body.

Tommy didn't deserve to die like that, killed in cold blood.

Regan watched as a white Volvo pulled into the circular drive behind her rental. It was Terri Granger, Tommy's sister, right on time—nine sharp.

She stepped out and approached Regan. She wore slacks, a blouse, little makeup. She was five years older than her brother, which made her more than a decade older than Regan. She didn't dye her light brown hair, which was now liberally streaked with gray. Her pale blue-gray eyes matched Tommy's.

Regan walked down the steps to greet her. She didn't want Terri to see the bloodstains.

"I would have met you at your place," Regan said after

pulling Terri in for a close hug. The two women exchanged half smiles.

"Grace and I were talking to our pastor about Tommy's memorial service," said Terri. "She stayed to work through some of the details, I needed to leave. It's been—well, Tommy has always had a dangerous career. We knew this could happen, but—I wasn't expecting it."

"No one ever expects it. Even when you think you do."

"Tommy—because of his job I'm sure, or because it was just how he was—had already taken care of everything in the event of his death, so there's not much for me to do. The only thing he left for me was the memorial. He said I believed more than he did, and he wanted *me* to find peace." Tears filled her eyes. "Damn. I'm going to cry again."

"Do you want to go in, sit down?" Regan asked.

She shook her head. "I need to check on a patient at the hospital, then pick up Grace at the church." Terri was a pediatric surgeon at the children's hospital in Arlington. Her wife, Grace, was an administrator in the same facility.

"If you want to talk—anytime—I'm here."

"Later—it would be good for both of us, I think." Terri reached into her pocket and pulled out a familiar key ring with a USMC emblem. "Here's my set of his keys. Charlie said Tommy's are in evidence."

When Regan had spoken to Terri yesterday, she'd asked for access to the house because there could be clues to Tommy's death in his notes or computer. Terri had said—insisted even—that Regan should stay, that Tommy would have wanted her to.

"Do you know who's handling the investigation?" Regan asked. "The FBI?"

The Marshals Service didn't usually investigate homicides, but there were always exceptions.

"That's what Charlie told me yesterday," Terri said.

The FBI had investigated Chase's murder and come to the wrong conclusion. Regan had pushed, and the bureaucracy had not budged. Killer was dead, after all. What could they do? Regan didn't have any love lost with the FBI.

"Did you know Tommy was looking into my son's murder?" Regan asked Terri. Guilt seeped in; it seemed likely to her that investigation had led to his death.

"I knew, but he didn't talk about it much," Terri said. "He wanted answers. For you, and for him."

"I—" Regan's throat hitched. This was going to be even harder than she thought, and she'd already thought it was going to be very hard.

Terri took both of Regan's hands into hers. Terri wasn't a large woman, but she had strength, inside and out. "You and I both know that my brother did what my brother wanted to do. He was stubborn that way."

Terri was right.

But there was more to it, Regan suspected. She had begun to think that Tommy wanted to solve Chase's murder so she'd return to Virginia, and they might get together. But Regan knew she never would have come back. This was her past. Her present was in Arizona. Her brothers and sister were there. Her dad. Friends. She didn't know about the future, but she thought of Flagstaff as her home, and it was there she'd found peace after she lost everything.

Regan said, "If you need help with anything, answering emails or returning calls or organizing the service, call me."

"Thank you, but Tommy's instructions were clear, and you have other things to do."

"No—"

"You do. I have Grace. She's my rock, she'll be by my side, do anything I need. She and Tommy didn't always see eye to eye, but they both love me, and I love them. The memorial service will be early next week, I'll send you the details when they're finalized."

"Thank you."

Terri tilted her head, looked squarely at Regan. "You're going to find out what happened to my brother, right? Charlie will let you help."

"It's an FBI investigation," Regan began.

Terri raised her eyebrows, but didn't say anything.

Why else had she rushed out here? She knew the funeral wouldn't be for several days. She came because she needed the truth—as much about Tommy's murder as her son's. She owed it to Tommy, to herself. "Yes, I will," she said. "I can't believe he's gone."

"He was larger than life. I keep expecting him to walk out that door and ask me to look at paint colors for the living room...or hold his ladder while he replaces a light fixture. He loved this place."

Terri looked at her with red-rimmed eyes. "Find out who killed my brother, Regan. He'd do the same for you."

"I will, Terri." And she meant it. Staying in Virginia meant revisiting her son's murder—reliving the pain that Regan had tried to bury these last eleven months—but she wasn't leaving until she saw Tommy's killer in prison.

Four

Regan Merritt walked into the US Marshals office for the Eastern District of Virginia at eleven that morning. She'd tried to nap at Tommy's, but after thirty minutes knew that sleep wouldn't come; too antsy, too many questions. She called Charlie, made sure he was in the office, then drove to Alexandria.

She'd officially left in October, but her heart left on June 30 when Chase was killed. Shot in his own home, where he should have been safe.

Not much had changed. Administrative assistant Maggie Crutcher still manned the main desk. She was fifty-five and could retire, but Regan knew she wouldn't until mandatory retirement age. Six semiprivate cubicles faced the center of the room where there was a large table for morning briefings. Two of the cubicles were occupied; four were vacant. Three glass-walled offices: one for the chief deputy, one for the supervisory deputy, one for interviews and meetings.

The office for supervisory deputy Thomas V. Granger was dark.

"Regan?" Maggie jumped up from her desk and ran over

to embrace her. Hugging the diminutive woman felt like hugging a child. "Oh, Regan."

"Don't cry," Regan said, but it was too late. Maggie stepped back, wiping tears from her eyes.

Charlie North heard Regan's voice and rose from his cubicle, strode over, and hugged her tight. Regan was nearly five foot nine; Charlie towered over her. He didn't let her go right away. The US Marshals office was small: they normally housed between five and six marshals, the supervisory deputy, and the chief deputy. But positions were slow to fill. It looked like they had only four deputies now, with the chief deputy retired and Tommy dead.

She stepped back and looked into Charlie's sad face. His dark eyes were red, showing the emotion she felt deep inside. She said, "I wish—"

"Yeah. Me, too." He touched her chin. "We've missed you here."

If only things had been different. Regan had tried to work the month after her son was murdered, but she couldn't do it. Her world had fallen apart and there was no going back. If she wasn't reliable, wasn't one hundred percent focused on her job, she could have put herself or her team in danger. She resigned.

Everyone understood—Charlie had three kids. He and his wife, Sharon, had been there for Regan whenever she needed anything. She would never forget that. But even with all the support from her colleagues—from Tommy, Tommy's sister, Charlie, her own family—Regan couldn't put Chase's death from her mind. She couldn't find a way past it, not until she left and moved back to her childhood home two thousand miles away.

Yet here she was: in her old office because of another death. Only she no longer wore the star.

She glanced at the empty office of the chief deputy. "Steven's position hasn't been filled?"

Chief Deputy Steven Mortimer had retired three months prior—Regan was supposed to attend his retirement dinner, but it had just been too close to Chase's birthday and her emotions were raw. She'd sent Steven two dozen cookies from his favorite bakery and a gift certificate for two tickets to a Nationals home game. Her former boss loved baseball as much as her son had.

Charlie shook his head. "Tommy was acting chief. Let's grab some privacy."

He motioned her into the interview room, closing the door behind them. She glanced back at the only other person sitting at a cubicle: a female marshal she didn't recognize.

She sat in Regan's old cubicle.

Charlie followed her gaze. "That's Anna Lujan. Rookie, joined us three months ago. She'll be attached to me for three more months. Good instincts, graduated high in her class. Right now Carl and Doug are transporting a prisoner. Another agent transferred in from up north—I doubt you know him, he has courthouse duty today."

She sat down across from Charlie. "What happened to Tommy?"

"I told you everything we know on the phone. I'm waiting for the autopsy report, but the FBI's preliminary forensics report confirms that the sniper was perched in the big oak tree in his front yard, took at least one shot from there—maybe more. But they believe the gunman also shot Tommy at close range, in the head."

Cold flowed through her, a darkly familiar sensation that she'd only felt one time before. When she was told Chase was dead.

"The shooter fired when Tommy was leaving. To meet with you," she added.

Charlie nodded. "What do you know about that? You know he took a month's partial leave. He was still handling the administrative work in the office, but from home—and no field cases."

"I didn't know he had taken leave," she said quietly. "I would have told him not to do that, but…" She assessed her old friend. She wasn't certain how much Tommy had told Charlie, but they trusted each other implicitly. If she wasn't upfront with Charlie from the beginning, they might never find the truth, and she would damage one of her best friendships. "This has to be between you and me," she said.

He didn't say anything. Waited.

She raised an eyebrow at him. "I need to know, just for the next five minutes, that we're talking as friends only."

She was relieved when he nodded his consent.

"I was here six weeks ago," she said. "I would have called, but… I came to visit Chase's grave." She cleared her throat.

Charlie reached out and took her hand, held it. "It had been his birthday."

"Yeah." Nothing got past Charlie, but she had forgotten how empathetic he was. She stared at their clasped fingers, her Arizona tan still very pale against Charlie's black skin. She took a moment, pushed down the pain of discussing Chase. She realized that it was easier now—nearly a year after his murder—but still brought back bad memories she struggled to suppress.

Finally, she said, "I saw Tommy, after. You know that neither of us were satisfied with the FBI investigation—first Chase's murder, then Adam Hannigan's murder."

"Yeah, and Tommy continued to look into things after you left. I thought with your blessing."

"Yes—and no. I told him I couldn't be involved, not until he had something substantive. I couldn't do that to myself again."

"You don't need to justify yourself to me, Regan. It wasn't healthy for you to keep all that pain front and center."

"Well." She cleared her throat. "Tommy told me he had a meeting scheduled with Peter Grey. He'd been trying for months, but Grey put up a wall." By the look on Charlie's face, he knew.

"He never told me what Grey said," Charlie said. "All I knew was that they met, and Tommy took a leave of absence. He didn't tell me why specifically, but I knew he'd come to me when he needed my help."

Neither of them stated the obvious: that Tommy had scheduled a meeting with Charlie, and now Tommy was dead. It was very likely that his murder was related to something he learned in the last month.

"I didn't want to be involved." Her voice cracked. The guilt seeped in. She couldn't let it, or she wouldn't be of any use to Tommy now.

"Anyone would understand why, Regan. Dammit, you can't put this on your shoulders. Tommy was a big boy, he knew what he was doing. I talked to him nearly every day about the office, I should have pushed him to share more. But I didn't."

"So we either both should feel guilty, or neither of us," she said.

"No—this isn't on you, on me, or even Tommy. No matter how many secrets he was keeping, he had a reason for it. This is on the shooter. One hundred percent. Okay?"

He waited until she nodded.

She *was* angry at herself because she had turned her back on Tommy when she left in October. Yet…she'd made the best decision for herself out of a group of mediocre options. She didn't regret leaving. She regretted that she hadn't had the strength to stay.

"It was a dark time for everyone, but it was hell on you, Regan. You did everything you could to find out what happened. But with Hannigan dead…" His voice trailed off. He didn't need to finish his thought. With Chase's killer dead, the truth died with him. Regan's divorce followed. The soul-destroying grief gutted her, left her hollow with a perpetual fluttering of butterflies in her stomach.

Charlie understood. He was a father. He had been here when Chase was murdered; he'd helped in the manhunt for Adam Hannigan. The evidence was overwhelming, but during his arraignment, Hannigan pled not guilty. The statement he made to Regan may or may not have been ruled admissible by the judge—they hadn't gotten that far in the pretrial proceedings before his murder.

"I didn't mean to kill the boy. I'm sorry."

A year before Chase's murder, Adam Hannigan's brother Michael had attempted to rob Potomac Bank in Arlington. In the process, Michael had killed one of the hostages, Regan had been part of the team that responded, and she had killed Michael when he didn't immediately drop his weapon.

There seemed to be no reason for Michael to have killed the hostage—the teller had done everything he wanted. As soon as he had turned the gun on the teller, Regan got the green light from the FBI negotiator in charge to take the first clean shot. It was a clean kill. They saved the other eight hostages, and she hadn't lost any sleep over shooting Michael Hannigan.

Until Adam Hannigan avenged his brother's death.
Allegedly.

On the surface, it made sense—he killed her son like she killed his brother. Only nothing in his personality, background, or current life suggested that Adam Hannigan would have been so angry or grief-stricken that a full year after his brother's death he would go after her child.

"I didn't mean to kill the boy..."

Regan and Tommy had never believed that Adam Hannigan killed Chase out of vengeance. They didn't know *why* he'd targeted Chase or the Warwick family, but Hannigan's comment after he was captured told Regan that Chase wasn't the target. Maybe Grant—which the FBI considered. But their conclusion was the same: the motive for the shooting was the same.

And for a time, Regan believed it. That her lawful actions as a US marshal had made her family a target. But she kept coming back to *why.*

Regan had finally convinced the FBI to let her talk to Hannigan, and he agreed. The night before she was to sit down with the man who shot and killed her son, he was stabbed by convicted killer Peter Grey in a room full of witnesses.

She and Tommy had gone around and around with the FBI about that, but they were unswayed. A coincidence, the lead agent said.

She didn't buy it. A coincidence that Hannigan wanted to talk to her, to tell her something, and then turned up dead? Tommy was nearly positive that Hannigan had been hired to kill Grant—but they found nothing, not a shred of proof, that he was a hired gun. And when the FBI closed the case, that was it—every investigative lead dried up.

Regan's marriage was falling apart. She couldn't sleep

more than an hour or two a night and her mental health was in the balance. So she put it all behind her and went home, to Flagstaff, Arizona, and moved in with her dad.

"He called me yesterday morning," Regan said after the silence lasted just a few beats too long. "Three in the morning, it went to my voicemail. I now know that he was dead less than ten minutes after he left this message."

She pulled out her phone and played Tommy's message to her.

"Regan, it's Tommy. I'm close to the truth about what happened to Chase. I'm laying it all out to Charlie this morning, but I wanted to talk to you as soon as possible. I think I have a good case for the DOJ. Call me when you get this message. I—well, just call."

Hearing Tommy's voice now that she knew he was dead broke her heart all over again. She didn't know how many pieces she had left to break.

"I need to talk to Peter Grey."

"That's going to be tough," Charlie said. "You're not a marshal anymore. He's in maximum security."

"You can make it happen."

"We can't force him to talk."

"He talked to Tommy."

"Regan—"

"He took time off to investigate. The only reason he would do that is if Tommy believed him. Neither of us bought into the revenge theory of Chase's murder that the FBI ate up hook, line, sinker."

Charlie grunted at the mention of the FBI. He didn't like them any more than Regan did. The US Marshals didn't always play well with other agencies. Most marshals thought the FBI were a bunch of lazy bureaucrats, and the FBI thought the marshals were a bunch of arrogant mavericks.

There were some truths to both stereotypes, but Regan always sided with mavericks over bureaucrats.

There were of course exceptions. Regan had more or less liked FBI agent Lillian O'Dare the few times she'd worked with her—until she investigated Chase's murder. Then they'd butted heads to the point where O'Dare had threatened to write Regan up for impeding an investigation and Regan had nearly decked her. It had been an unpleasant scene.

Charlie said, "You know the FBI has Tommy's homicide."

"Of course they do," she grumbled.

"It's O'Dare. She's the SSA—she's taking lead."

O'Dare had no imagination, no ability to see all the possibilities. If something wasn't right in front of her, the FBI agent declared it irrelevant. She was competent, Regan supposed, but not much else.

"We should talk to her," Charlie said.

"I don't like her."

"That never stopped you from doing your job."

"This *isn't* my job." She paused. "Tommy's entire investigation was predicated on what Peter Grey told him."

"Not necessarily," Charlie said.

"What else?"

"Tommy never let it go, Regan, even after you left. I agree—something Grey said or didn't say helped Tommy, gave him a clue to follow—but he was following a lot of threads and there's no way of knowing what yielded results. If Tommy had a smoking gun, so to speak, he would have left something more for us, wouldn't he? Something beyond a vague phone message?"

She didn't know the answer to that so she changed course, asking, "Any suspects? It's been more than twenty-four hours."

"The FBI thinks it's related to an old case of his. Asked me to compile a list of all his cases, threats, the whole nine yards. They'll identify recent parolees, track their whereabouts."

"It's not a parolee," she said. Of course the FBI would need to look at that angle, but Tommy was killed *right before* he was going to tell Charlie everything he knew about his investigation into the murders of Chase and Adam Hannigan. That was not a coincidence. "Wait—did you tell them about Tommy's investigation?"

"No," Charlie said slowly.

"Why not?"

"Because I have no details. He planned to talk to me, then he was killed. I don't know where to point them."

"We need to tell her. As much as I detest turning this over to the FBI, they have the manpower and resources."

"I hear a *but* in your tone."

"In my experience, they're going to dismiss everything we say and we won't know if they're pursuing this avenue of investigation or not."

"And then?"

"I'm going to find out who killed Tommy and why. It's connected to my son, therefore it's connected to me." She might end up butting heads with the FBI, but she would deal with that when and if it happened. "In the meantime, we need to find out what the FBI knows, what they're doing, and whether they'll take my theory seriously."

"So we're going on recon?"

She shrugged. "Pretty much."

"I'll call over there," Charlie said.

"Let's surprise her at the office. Bet you twenty bucks she's not in the field."

"No way I'm taking that bet," Charlie said.

Five

Regan asked Charlie to stop for coffee at a cool little indie coffee shop that she frequented back in the days she worked out of the Alexandria courthouse. It was the lunch rush, so the two of them waited in line. Charlie convinced her to get a sandwich, though she said she wasn't hungry.

"Then for the drive back," he said.

It was also the end-of-lunch rush over the Potomac. Charlie ate his sandwich as they drove, and it looked good, so Regan ate half of hers. They drove to the Washington, DC, field office, which handled all the FBI's cases in Northern Virginia.

It was just after one o'clock when Charlie presented his credentials to the guard at the FBI parking garage.

"I definitely don't miss this traffic," Regan commented.

"Leave your gun in my glove box," Charlie told her when he pulled into a visitor parking slot.

"Shit," she mumbled as she unclipped her gun from her holster and slid it inside. "Sometimes I miss being a marshal."

"I'd take you back in a heartbeat."

Tommy had been trying to get her back since the day she resigned, but when Regan left last year, she'd left for good. She didn't know if she'd lost her edge, maybe, maybe not, but mostly she no longer had the heart for the job. And Virginia itself held too much pain. Every landmark, every park, every road reminded Regan of Chase.

At the main entrance, Charlie showed his badge and ID; Regan had to show her driver's license. Then they waited. And waited.

"What's friggin' taking her so long?" Regan muttered.

"Maybe I should have taken the bet," Charlie said.

"It would have been an easy twenty bucks because I thought for sure she'd be happily riding the desk."

The door opened and Lillian O'Dare emerged. Regan thought there was a fifty-fifty chance she'd heard her comment, but she just smiled and said, "Agent O'Dare."

"Marshal," O'Dare said with a nod to Charlie. "Regan. I don't have any news. I was surprised to hear you had come into the city."

"Do you have a few minutes?" Charlie asked politely. "It's important."

O'Dare made a point to look at her watch, which irritated Regan. She tempered her frustration.

"Just a few," she said. She led them down a long hall and into a small conference room, motioned for them to sit, then offered coffee or water.

"We're good," Regan said, not giving Charlie the opportunity to ask for something. He'd do it, not because he was thirsty, but because Charlie could sense that Regan was already on edge and the delay might calm her.

She was calm—well, calm*ish*. O'Dare had the information she needed and she wasn't in the mood to play games. Regan always preferred people when they were straightforward and to the point. She was about to lay it out for O'Dare when Charlie said, "We were hoping to get an update from you on the progress of your investigation into Tommy's shooting."

"You could have called and saved yourself the drive." It was the tone that grated on Regan—arrogant, dismissive.

"Tommy was my boss and friend," Charlie said.

"I know," O'Dare said flatly, then offered him a look of sympathy. "And I'm sorry." She turned to Regan. "I didn't know you were back in Virginia."

Regan gave a brief nod. O'Dare hadn't asked a question so Regan didn't see the need to provide an explanation.

"But you're not back with the Marshals?" O'Dare asked.

"No."

Charlie said, "I emailed you a list of Tommy's major cases. As you know, my office expects to be involved."

"I told the deputy director yesterday, in person, I'll be copying both your local office and headquarters into all my reports. We don't have much to go on right now."

"But you have the autopsy report—the coroner said he'd have it this morning."

"Preliminary," she said. "Nothing you don't already know."

"I'd like to see it."

"I'll send it over. It'll be there before you get back to your office. But to summarize, Granger was shot first in the left thigh, then in the shoulder and neck. The neck wound was fatal. He bled out."

"He was also shot in the head," Charlie said before Regan could.

"Yes, and the coroner believes that the head shot was postmortem, close range, as you indicated at the scene yesterday. We confirmed that three shots missed completely, hit the house. Our crime scene technicians have retrieved the bullets, both from the brick and from his body, and we're running full ballistics. We released the property to the next of kin last night. The shooter didn't go inside, the house was locked, and his security system was on." She paused. "The FBI knows how to investigate a homicide, Charlie. We have the best lab in the country at Quantico."

Was she being deliberately antagonistic, or was Regan projecting her own dislike onto her?

The door opened, and a skinny young agent of about thirty walked in and handed O'Dare a file. "You wanted this?"

"Thanks, Don. Please sit, you're more familiar with the crime scene analysis and I'm sure Deputy North and Ms. Merritt have more questions." She said to them for introduction, "This is Don Portman, who's assisting me in the investigation. We *are* prioritizing Granger's case. Anytime a federal cop is killed it takes its toll on everyone. We want answers as much as you do."

A good line, but Regan didn't buy it for a minute.

Maybe that wasn't fair. O'Dare was a longtime agent, older than Regan, and had the respect of her superiors and subordinates, from what Regan had learned of her in the past. It could be just a matter of her style that rubbed Regan the wrong way, or their serious disagreement about the motive behind Adam Hannigan killing Chase. Regan could admit that she had tunnel vision with regard to that issue.

"Don, you supervised the canvass? Results?"

"We processed the crime scene," Agent Portman said. "The shooter collected his brass. We have four bullets from Granger's body, two in good to excellent condition—we sent them directly to our lab for processing. The one that went through his neck shattered on the wall behind him, and the one in his thigh was fractured. The three bullets that we extracted from the brick are unusable. .45 caliber."

".45? A handgun?"

"Possibly," Portman said. "I don't think we can make that determination, I'll leave it to the lab and ballistics analysis. There are some rifle hybrids that shoot a .45. It's not my area of expertise. The tree has also been processed, but there is no trace evidence—no DNA, no hair or fiber. We know exactly where he was sitting—there were some broken and cracked branches, and gunpowder residue on one of the branches and some of the leaves.

"We talked to the neighbors. The neighbor to the east," Portman glanced at his notes, "a Mr. Luna, fifty-four, was awake and he didn't hear gunshots, but thought he heard a faint popping sound. Said it almost sounded like a champagne cork, but not quite. We suspect there was a suppressor on the rifle, which you know doesn't completely silence the gun. He was geographically the closest neighbor. The family across the street was awake, but in the back of the house. Didn't hear anything until sirens. One witness, a neighbor from the street to the west, stated that he was jogging at approximately five fifteen that morning and passed a dark-colored truck, either a Ford or a Chevy, small SUV like an Explorer, two houses down from Granger. He didn't really make note of it, just that it wasn't usually parked there. Tall hedges blocked the vehicle from the neighbors, though we asked everyone on the street about the vehicle—no one owns it, no one else had seen it. The owners of the house in question stated that they'd come in late the night before, at approximately one in the morning, and that there was no car or truck parked in front of their house. We deduced that this may be the killer's vehicle, and that he arrived after one in the morning and left immediately after the shooting.

"Nine minutes passed from Granger's 911 call and the

arrival of the first unit to the scene. No SUV at that location. We fully processed the area where the car was parked and found nothing of use, but I'm going to have the lab review every piece of trace evidence in case our team missed anything. We assessed that there is no Ring or security camera in line of sight to the house or the car, but we're broadening our canvass to include streets leading from the neighborhood to the highway."

"It sounds like you're on top of it," Charlie said. "But we know the killer took his phone. Were you able to trace it?"

"Either off or the battery is dead," O'Dare said. "We haven't been able to ping it."

"Have you attempted to track it since?" Regan asked.

"Yes, the lab is working on it. But criminals are getting smarter and there are programs that can prevent tracking."

O'Dare glanced from Regan to Charlie. "I don't mind keeping you in the loop," she said in a tone that implied anything other than what she said, "but my time is valuable, and these impromptu meetings take away from what I should be doing. This *is* an FBI investigation, as you well know."

"My office is at your disposal."

"I already received your list of Tommy's cases, which you helpfully prioritized, I don't know how much more you can do."

Charlie said, "As I told you yesterday, Tommy took a partial leave of absence."

"Yes, I have that note in the file."

"I also told you that he was coming in Monday, the morning he was killed, to talk to me about something he was working on."

"And this is relevant why?" O'Dare gave her a suspicious sidelong glance as if she thought Regan was the instigator of this meeting.

Regan refrained from commenting, though it was getting more difficult to ignore O'Dare's attitude. She kept her hands tightly in her lap and let Charlie continue to steer the conversation.

Charlie said, "Tommy was investigating the murders of Chase Warwick and Adam Hannigan."

O'Dare reddened. *"What?"*

"He interviewed Peter Grey three weeks ago."

"For shit's sake, Charlie! I can't believe you guys are still pursuing that dead end! Those are closed cases, closed *FBI* cases." Agitated, she narrowed her eyes at Regan. "When did you arrive in Virginia?"

Regan didn't answer. "You need to consider that it was no coincidence that Tommy was killed the day he planned to share information about his investigation with Charlie and their boss. That maybe, Tommy's murder has nothing to do with his cases and everything to do with what he uncovered about the murders of Adam Hannigan and my son."

O'Dare put her hand up. "Stop right there. Your son's case is closed. *Closed.* It's *over.* Adam Hannigan was the shooter, not only did he confess, but we proved he did it, and you know it."

"Yes, he pulled the trigger. There's no doubt about that."

O'Dare shook her head, sighed as if Regan was a rookie and she was explaining the rules to her. Every sentence further irritated her. Regan had always controlled her temper well, but now she felt her control slipping.

"I get it, Regan, I do," O'Dare said, her voice edging toward condescension with just enough sympathy that Regan couldn't call her on the disrespect. "You have to let this go. As I told you then, and I'll tell you now, you and Granger were barking up the wrong tree about Hannigan's murder. Peter Grey is a *psychopath*. He killed three people for no reason other than they irritated him. He's in prison for life. Hannigan looked at him wrong, and Grey doesn't like child molesters."

"Hannigan was not a child molester," stated Regan, determined to hold in her building fury. "Who told Grey that he was? If that was, in fact, his motive."

"We can only work with the facts and statements we have, and we have Grey and others stating that the word inside was Hannigan was a pedophile. What can we do about that? Honestly, there were people around here—not me—suggesting that *you* put the word out about Hannigan."

Before Regan exploded, Charlie said, "That is a blatant lie, and I hope you put an end to that rumor the first time you heard it."

"Of course," O'Dare said without seeming concerned, "I'm sure no one *believes* such a thing, but no one would lose sleep over it, either."

"I had a scheduled interview with Hannigan," Regan snapped. "I wanted that meeting. I didn't want him dead—not without a conviction in a court of law."

Charlie cleared his throat, was about to speak, but O'Dare cut him off. "He killed a *kid*," she snapped. "Close enough for a vengeful nut like Grey. Maybe Grey put a hit out on Granger from prison. I'll look into that, but that's *my* job—definitely not yours. In fact, I expect you to turn over any and all evidence about whatever Granger was doing while he was on leave. This is my case."

"Why would Grey want Tom dead?" Charlie asked.

O'Dare shrugged. "Makes as much sense as any of the theories your former colleague here tossed around last year." O'Dare continued with clearly feigned compassion,

"No cop wants their family targeted because they do their job, but it happens."

The FBI agent knew Regan's vulnerable points and hit them hard.

Regan stood up and walked out, leaving Charlie behind. It had taken all her strength to leave without screaming. O'Dare pushed all her buttons.

Portman followed her out. "Um, can I direct you somewhere?"

She whirled on him. "I don't know you, but I will do everything I can to find out who killed Tommy, and I don't think O'Dare has the desire or, frankly, the skills to do so. So stay out of my way."

He looked nervous, glanced around at the people who may have overheard. "I promise, we're keeping the Marshals fully in the loop. The assistant director—our boss— told us this morning that this was our number one priority. If you know what Deputy Granger was doing during his leave, that might help us."

She stared at the young agent, assessing him. His eyes were sharp behind his glasses, his attitude alert, eager to please. But he wasn't in charge, and he wouldn't be able to do anything without O'Dare's explicit approval.

"That's between O'Dare and Charlie. I'm not a marshal anymore. But I'll tell you this: I'm not sitting back and watching her screw this up like she screwed up my son's murder investigation. You weren't here then, so get up to speed and maybe you'll be able to help this time."

She walked to the elevator, punched the button for the lobby. She had to get out of this building. She had to think, to just *breathe*.

She shouldn't let O'Dare get to her. The woman had done more to rile Regan than almost anyone. It was because of that FBI theory that Grant blamed her for Chase's murder. It was *her* job that got their son killed. She should have backed off, known the threats, done more to protect them. Regan didn't know what she was supposed to have done! But that FBI theory, and Grant's accusation that her job had meant more to her than her son, had been the final nail in the coffin of their marriage.

On the surface all the dots connected, which was why the FBI considered the case closed. And Regan even believed it for a time, believed that Chase's death was her fault, that she *should* have known, *should* have protected him.

Once she could put aside the emotion of what happened, she realized there were too many unanswered questions. Threads the FBI never followed up on—like Adam's nearly nonexistent relationship with his brother, Michael Hannigan. Why did Adam wait a year before coming after her? Why were there no threats, no letters, emails, phone calls, *nothing* that suggested he was angry with her for his brother's death?

Mostly, it was the fact that Peter Grey killed Adam the night before he was going to talk to her. He didn't have to talk to her, but he'd contacted her through a guard at the jail, not through his lawyer. Why? What had he planned to tell her?

O'Dare insisted that Hannigan wasn't going to tell her anything she didn't know, and in fact would probably want to rub salt in the wounds, make her feel worse. But Regan didn't see that. He'd shown remorse for killing Chase when he was caught.

It was all these unanswered questions that created holes in the FBI theory.

Maybe they were right. But the questions should still be answered.

That's what Tommy was doing: finding answers. And now he was dead.

What did you learn, Tommy? What answer got you killed?

Regan walked out of the lobby, tossing her visitor's pass on the guard desk without saying a word. She went through the door that led to the underground garage, and jogged down the flight of stairs. She leaned against Charlie's SUV and kept her face as blank as possible. There were security cameras all over the place, and if O'Dare looked at them, Regan didn't want to give her the satisfaction of knowing she'd gotten under her skin.

Of course she knows. She did it on purpose. And you responded by walking out.

Usually, Regan was in full command of her actions and words. But now, her emotions were raw. Being back in Virginia. Listening to the clinical recount of Tommy's murder. Not being in charge of the investigation or anything else that could help them find answers.

Maybe if she hadn't quit her job last year, she could have found the answers Tommy had died for.

But her grief had been too dark, all-consuming, exhausting…and the only place she wanted to be was home, back in Arizona where she'd grown up. Her dad was there; she was closer to her brothers and sister. So she went and almost healed…as much as any mother could after the loss of her child.

At what cost?

Was the cost her soul? Tommy's life? Could she have stayed, hardened her heart, done her job, found the answers?

She didn't know.

Ten minutes later, Charlie exited the stairwell and walked over to his car. He remotely unlocked it and said, "She's a bitch."

Regan agreed.

She climbed into the passenger seat. Charlie used the small key to unlock his glove box. Regan retrieved her gun. The weight felt good in her hand. She holstered it. Once Charlie pulled the car out of the parking garage, he asked, "What are your plans?"

"I'm going to find out what Tommy knew. Go through everything in his house, his notes, figure out what got him killed. Because you know his investigation into Chase's murder is the reason he's dead. That O'Dare won't even consider it has me seeing red."

"For what it's worth," Charlie said, "I suspect if we find something connective, she *will* listen."

Regan grunted.

"She has a narrow investigation style, but she's also thorough. If we show her evidence that something's there—she'll look at it."

"Then I'd better do a damn good job so there's no doubt."

"You find something solid, we'll take it to the Marshals Special Operations Group."

The bold move, coming from Charlie, surprised her. "Do an end run around the FBI?"

"I suspect," Charlie said with a slight grin as he backed out of the parking space, "that was Tommy's plan. Present the evidence to the deputy director and ask him to put SOG on it."

They drove in silence for a moment, then Regan said, "I'm going to talk to Peter Grey, find some way to convince him to tell me what he told Tommy." She knew Charlie wouldn't like the idea, but he didn't comment. "I'll need your help to get into the prison."

"As soon as I get back to the office, I'll start the process.

I don't know how fast I can make it happen, but I'll move heaven and earth to get us in there."

"Thank you," she said, and meant it. She was relieved she didn't have to do this all alone, and told him as much.

"I will do everything I can to get to the bottom of this," Charlie said. "I'll go through this forensics report, see if the FBI missed anything. Go through the cases I sent over to see if something pops. I'll call O'Dare five times a day if I have to."

"As well as run the office and supervise staff and chase fugitives and protect the courthouse."

He chuckled. "We'll be getting help soon, and the other divisions are picking up slack."

"Meaning, I don't know how much time you'll have. Are you assistant deputy chief now?"

"Yes," he said. "The director called me last night, asked me to take it. Actually, he asked if I wanted deputy chief, that he'd put my name up for consideration, but that's a political appointment and I don't want that headache. I just want to do the job. He understood."

"So are they going to get someone to replace Steven anytime soon?"

"Hell if I know," Charlie said. "I suspect they'll put our district at the top of the list—there are still dozens of vacancies—but I don't know when."

There were ninety-four chief deputies, all appointed from ranks of the US Marshals Service, one chief deputy to head each of the ninety-four jurisdictions, which coincided with the federal court jurisdictions.

He glanced at her. "You're a smart woman, Regan. While there's a slim chance that Tommy was killed by someone he apprehended, neither of us believe that's what happened— which is exactly what I told Lillian O'Dare. But they're going down that path because it's the most logical, and I can't disagree with the approach based on the limited information we have."

"Which means what I find out could put me in danger, just like Tommy. I'll take precautions."

"Tommy was one of the smartest cops I knew. He didn't see what was coming."

"This isn't on him," Regan said. "We don't know *what* happened." When Charlie didn't say anything, she added, "Charlie, Tommy was doing this for *me*."

"You're missing the point, Regan! He found something that put a target on his back and *he didn't know it*. He *should* have known. *He should have fucking known!*"

There was grief in his tone; anger; accusation; guilt. Violent death was cruel to the dead, but even more to the living, the survivors, the grieving. They both felt an overwhelming emptiness.

When Charlie stopped the car at a light, she put her hand on his shoulder. He was tense. She took solace that she was not alone in her grief, but she wanted to help him as he was helping her.

"Everything is a potential threat," she said. "I will be cautious."

Charlie smoothly maneuvered the vehicle through heavy traffic across the bridge back into Alexandria. Regan was grateful they didn't feel the need to fill the silence with small talk. She needed to collect all the relevant facts and formulate a game plan—though that would start at Tommy's house.

They passed the Washington Sailing Marina, where she and Grant had often rented a boat to take Chase out for long, lazy, wonderful days on the water.

Grant had wanted to buy a boat, but Regan thought it was

an unnecessary luxury and she'd been raised to be frugal. The expense of storing and maintaining a boat would far exceed renting a boat a few times a year. They'd argued about it, but Regan won because she laid out the cost/benefit analysis—clearly, without emotion.

It had been small disagreements like that that had put little wedges in their relationship during their twelve-year marriage. She wasn't wrong. Neither was Grant. They just looked at the world differently.

As they went by, she caught a glimpse of a young couple taking out a boat from the marina. Regan could almost see Chase sprinting along the dock, wearing an orange life vest, a grin on his lightly freckled face as he hurriedly climbed aboard the boat, ready for an afternoon out on the water. Chase had been so full of life.

"I'll ride the line as hard as I can, but there are some lines I can't cross," Charlie said several minutes later, jerking Regan back into the present.

"I appreciate that." Her voice sounded odd, trapped in the emotions of the past. "And I won't put you in a compromising position."

"If you're in trouble, call me. Even if you cross that line, call me. You saved my life, Regan. I will never forget that."

"I'll never pull that chit, and you know it."

"That's not what I meant. Damn, you're prickly today."

She rubbed her eyes, squeezed them shut, opened them. Everything looked brighter. "I haven't slept much since I heard about Tommy."

"What I meant, what I should have said, is that we've worked together for a long time. Hell, you trained me when I was wet behind the ears."

She laughed, which felt surprisingly good. "You didn't need much training, and you're older than me." Charlie had spent five years in the army before joining the Marshals Service. He was older, but she had seniority. Charlie had been assigned to her for field training when he graduated the FLETC.

Charlie said, "You've always had terrific instincts, and you *did* save my ass when we were tracking Bonnie and Clyde." Not the real Bonnie and Clyde, of course, but Regan had given the nickname to two young lovers who'd gone on a killing and robbery spree in Virginia seven years ago.

"You've always been made of Teflon, that's what Tommy used to say," Charlie continued. "You're calm under pressure."

"That's how we're trained."

"Tommy was as good or better than you, with more years experience. And he was caught in the crosshairs of a sniper. I don't want the same to happen to you."

"Tommy found the truth," she said. "The *why*. Maybe from Peter Grey, maybe from someone else. If I had been here right beside him as I should have been, I could have saved him."

"Or you could be lying next to him in the morgue." Charlie pulled into the Marshals' assigned parking at the courthouse.

"I should get going," she said, gathering her things.

"Come up for a minute. I asked Maggie to create temporary credentials for you so you can park here and access the building whenever you need to."

She nodded her thanks. "I appreciate it, Charlie."

He said, "Do you have the code to Tommy's gun safe?"

"He told me once years ago, unless he changed it."

"Doubt he did. You only came here with the one gun, so make sure you can access additional firearms, just in case."

Six

Regan stopped by a grocery store before heading back to Tommy's house in Reston, one of the many communities in Northern Virginia, this one more rural than suburb.

Tommy's truck blocked one of the circular driveway's exits, so she backed in. If for some reason Regan had to leave quickly, she didn't want to be trapped. From the driver's seat, she stared at the oak tree that had been a sniper's roost. She imagined herself in a gunman's sights. Her eyes canvassed the street, yard, house.

It was late afternoon. The neighborhood was quiet, peaceful. She cracked the window to listen, hearing laughter and the shouts of kids playing in a backyard not far away. Their joy and abandon should have made her smile; instead she was on the verge of tears.

You're okay. You're going to be okay.

If she repeated it enough, maybe one day she'd believe it.

When she was certain there was no immediate threat, she got out of the car, two bags of groceries in one hand, her dominant hand free.

She walked to the front door and again glanced around, eye out for danger as she unlocked the door. The alarm system beeped, and she closed the door, turned off the alarm, then reset it for home. It was a good residential alarm system, but it hadn't saved Tommy.

In the kitchen, she put down the two bags and let out the breath she'd been holding. She then inhaled deeply, exhaled, getting her bearings. These last two days had been emotional. Regan had been even-tempered since she was a kid, and that had helped her learn to remain calm in stressful situations. Charlie was right; she was good in a crisis. But being calm and rational made these complex memories and emotions more difficult to deal with, because there was nothing *rational* about any of this. She'd much rather be in the middle of an active shooter situation where her training and muscle memory would kick in, than standing in Tommy's kitchen with memories of him, of her son, of her ex-husband, of her previous life, all punching her skull, fighting for attention.

And Regan, standing there alone, was unsure how to fix anything.

She smelled coffee, saw that there was half a pot in the carafe, cold. Tommy would have made it yesterday morning before he left. He loved coffee even more than she did.

Regan unloaded the groceries. She noticed a New York strip steak that hadn't expired. Tommy loved to grill. There were fresh vegetables. She would eat them, think about Tommy, about their friendship and what might have been had life dealt them a different hand.

She closed the refrigerator as if closing her emotions. She couldn't find the truth if she allowed the past to creep in and drag her down.

Then she saw a picture of her, Tommy, and Chase, taken a few years ago at a Marshals family picnic. She stared at it, trying to feel that past happiness that had been her life—

content, satisfied, successful in her career. Her marriage wasn't perfect, but it wasn't bad. She had many friends, a home, a son. Her family. Imperfect, but hers.

Now gone.

Tommy had turned forty-two at the beginning of the year. He should not be dead. He was in his prime, had a great career, had a sister who loved him, and lots of friends.

Chase had been ten. He shouldn't be dead, either. He'd had his entire life ahead of him.

She swallowed the emotions, but the burn rose up and she knew if she kept it bottled it would come out later when she least expected it. She gave herself the moment, this moment, to just grieve.

She turned into his den, not so much a cozy den as a book-filled library with dark shelves original to the house, more than a hundred years old. Thrillers and history books and a full collection of Westerns that Tommy had enjoyed the most. The den looked out into the fenceless backyard. She stood in the threshold and smelled Tommy. Bay Rum and pine and leather. This was where she would have to start, but not yet. She needed a few minutes to gather her thoughts, regroup, settle her emotions. She turned from the room and headed upstairs.

She remembered when Tommy had refinished the staircase. It had taken him weeks to sand, repair, treat, and stain the original wood. The result a deep brown with a hint of red. To protect the finish, he'd installed a carpet stair runner in navy down the center; the result was classic and stately.

He'd told her time and time again that to do anything well, you had to pay attention. Renovating his house or chasing a fugitive. To Tommy, the devil was in the details. Skip a step, and you would have to start over on a project, or you'd lose your convict. Everything he did, he was methodical and disciplined.

He had answers. Maybe not all the answers, but he had enough where he felt he could lay out his theory to her, to Charlie, to the deputy director in DC. And someone killed him to prevent him from sharing.

She'd stowed her bag in the guest room earlier, but now walked into Tommy's room. It smelled like him, a subtle scent from basic Dove soap. His bed was made; the room tidy, uncluttered. Large, chunky furniture that fit the large, square master suite. Custom cabinets and drawers filled the closet. Tactical gear took up one wall—marshals were provided basic protective gear, but most upgraded their vests at their own expense and had other equipment for drills and games and training. He had a gun safe installed. She thought about what Charlie had said—to make sure she had guns accessible, just in case. She verified she still knew his code.

It worked.

Closing the safe, she walked back to the bed, stared at it for a moment debating if she should stay here, in this room. Then she lay down upon it, her head on his pillow. Closed her eyes.

She didn't cry. She wanted to, but tears never came easy to her. Instead, she let the emotions she'd been repressing since yesterday morning, which had given her this dull throbbing headache, roll over her.

She hadn't loved Tommy. She wanted to, but she wasn't certain she could love anyone after her failed marriage and son's death. She and Tommy had been friends. Nothing romantic between them, but a good working chemistry and solid friendship. When Grant cast blame on her for Chase's death, it was Tommy she went to, Tommy she cried with.

And then six weeks ago.

* * *

Regan flew to Virginia the morning of April 2, Chase's birthday. She hadn't told anyone that she was coming— only her father knew—and until she boarded the plane, she wasn't certain she could go through with it.

Chase had been dead for nine months. He shouldn't have been. He should have been celebrating his eleventh birthday at Nationals Park, watching his favorite baseball team play.

The grief she felt—grief, guilt, deep sorrow—filled every cell of her body. She thought she'd been handling it after quitting the Marshals and moving back to her family home in Arizona. She had always been close to her family, and she needed them—especially her dad—during those dark days. She'd reconnected with her oldest friend. They went for walks and hikes. Regan made a conscious effort to be active in the community.

She still didn't know what she wanted to do with the rest of her life, but that was okay—living day-to-day, regaining her center. The grief was still there, but it wasn't debilitating. She thought of Chase a lot, but not every minute of the day. And when she did think of him now...when she passed a baseball field or an elementary school or saw anything that reminded her of him...it wasn't pain that hit her first. She'd begun having memories that made her smile rather than filling her with loss. She could look at his picture and not want to scream. She could even talk about him, about the fun they'd had both together and as a family, without wanting to run away from her feelings.

But as his birthday crept closer, the old grief returned and she felt the overwhelming need to say goodbye again.

She no longer lived in Virginia; she had visited his grave often when she did, always leaving it filled with anger and deep pain. But it had been five months since she moved to Arizona; she needed to...hell, she didn't know. She just had the overwhelming urge to remember her son, to mourn him, to sit with him.

So she flew out on the red-eye, rented a car, and drove to where he was buried, at a beautiful site near the Blue Ridge Mountains.

She'd been there an hour, sitting against his headstone, her head between her knees, unable to get up even when it started to rain. The rain was light, almost welcome, as if God wept for her. Then Grant arrived with flowers. He did not seem surprised to find her there at Chase's final resting place.

He sat next to her in his thousand-dollar suit and they just...sat. He invited her to his townhouse for a late lunch. She said no, but for the first time she didn't look at Grant with grief and anger. When they talked, it was bittersweet. They remembered the good times, and there had been many. But if they had too much time together, one of them, both of them, would eventually speak words that hurt the other.

When they parted in the parking lot, she drove to Tommy's house. Waited until he came home and when he saw her, he knew why she was there. He fed her, didn't talk about Chase, or Grant, or her dry, red eyes. She had planned to check in to a hotel. He asked her to stay.

Did he know, like she did, that if she stayed, they would end up in bed together?

She stayed.

She loved him, but she wasn't in love with him. There was too much...stuff...clouding her emotions. But that night, she let herself be in the moment without guilt, without grief, without overthinking every damn thing.

She and Tommy had sex, and it wasn't awkward. Two

friends who knew each other well—who could joke around, talk, laugh, and satisfy each other. They didn't sleep much. Maybe they both knew this was the one and only night they would have together, so they wanted to make it last, make the sex memorable, an emotional and physical connection that grounded Regan, reminded her that she was solid and whole and could reclaim her life.

Not her old life. Maybe not a better life. But for the first time, she believed that she could live fully again.

Yes, she loved Tommy. But she knew then that their relationship would go no further.

Seven

Jenna Johns had scoured the news all day, but it wasn't until six o'clock that she found out that Deputy Granger had been murdered.

The newscaster didn't have much information about the crime but revealed that the victim of a shooting at his home in Reston on Monday morning was a US marshal out of the Eastern District, Thomas V. Granger the third.

The FBI is investigating the murder of assistant deputy chief Granger as a possible revenge killing. A sixteen-year veteran of the US Marshals Service, following a decorated three-year career in the US Marines, Granger had worked several high-profile cases, including the apprehension of nineteen escaped prisoners. Three years ago he led a team of highly trained marshals into the Shenandoah National Park to apprehend four violent fugitives who'd escaped Cumberland and taken two women hostage. While there are no suspects at this time, the FBI is asking anyone with information to contact the Washington field office at...

Jenna started shaking. The deputy was *dead*. Monday morning...that was the day he was going to talk to his boss about the bank robbery—the bank robbery where Becca had died.

Jenna didn't want to be scared, but she was now even more terrified than when she left her house yesterday. She knew far too much about the robbery—and what Becca may have been involved with. She also knew the real target of the heist and that the bank robbery was just a cover... she'd told Tommy Granger all of it, not realizing how important it was until he told her that Becca had known Michael Hannigan before the heist. And then everything else had clicked into place.

While she had only one piece of the puzzle, it was important—Tommy had told her it was the final piece he needed that made "everything make sense." Without her testimony about what Becca had told her and who Jenna had seen Becca with before the robbery, he didn't have a case...and without proving that Becca was involved, he couldn't prove who the real target was.

"You'll need to testify under oath," Tommy had told her last week. *"And I'll protect you. As soon as the truth is out there, you won't be in danger anymore."*

The man who picked up Tommy's phone last night wasn't Tommy, and he wasn't a cop. Not the FBI, not the Marshals, no one she knew.

Now he had Tommy's phone, and her name, and Jenna didn't know what to do.

She paced the warped floorboards of the small cabin she had rented outside Hagerstown, near the Pennsylvania border. She had been so exhausted last night after working a twelve-hour shift. But she'd been scared, too, so she'd driven as far as she could until she got to a motel she'd stayed at as a kid with individual cabins that catered to families. She felt safe.

Today she'd stayed inside, not even enjoying the beautiful countryside. Mindlessly watched television. Paced. Slept. Ordered delivery and ate inside. She'd left her phone at her house because she didn't want anyone to be able to track her, but now that seemed foolish. She *needed* a phone. What if something happened on the road?

It was late, but there was a Walmart twenty minutes away. She would get a prepaid phone, and call the FBI first thing in the morning. Tell them what she knew about Deputy Granger, what he planned to do on Monday—and they might be able to help her. They'd tell her what she should do, if she should go home or stay here in the cabin. Maybe she'd need to go in and talk to the police.

She desperately wanted someone to tell her what *exactly* had happened to Tommy and whether it was because of the information she had given him or a random accident.

He'd sought *her* out, but she still felt awful that what she knew about Becca might have somehow gotten a US marshal killed.

A chill ran down her spine. Maybe she had been paranoid about fleeing in a panic after the stranger answered Tommy's phone. She told herself that there had to be a logical explanation. But no matter which way she turned it around in her head, she knew something was very, very wrong with that phone call.

Still, after she returned to her cabin from buying the phone and snacks, watched even more boring television, then turned off the lights, it took her many hours before she tumbled into a troubled sleep.

Eight

When Regan opened her eyes, the light had changed. She'd fallen asleep; it was nearly dark. She looked at the clock on Tommy's nightstand—6:49 p.m. She'd been out cold for nearly three hours.

No surprise there; she hadn't slept on the plane, she hadn't given herself time to nap this morning.

She got up, went to the guest room, showered, and changed. Focused on the process and cleared her mind. Went down to the kitchen and made a sandwich, then brought the sandwich and a bottled water into Tommy's office, flipping on lights as she went. Made sure all the blinds were closed; the house was a fishbowl at night.

It was time to get to work.

Sitting at his desk, she booted up Tommy's computer. The FBI hadn't taken it, which was good for her. They clearly were focused on Tommy's past cases—who he had apprehended, who had been released from prison, who had a beef with him. Regan would go through everything she could before O'Dare decided to flex her muscle and take her and Charlie seriously.

She wasn't holding her breath.

Tommy hadn't changed his password—SemperFi followed by the year of his sister's birth. Not smart, but easy to remember. Now that Regan was logged on, she could access any of his files. Tommy had embraced technology as a tool, but wasn't particularly tech savvy, and while he used his computer, he still preferred to keep his notes in longhand.

She opened the drawer and smiled; some things never changed. She pulled out a notepad with Tommy's familiar block printing and flipped through his notes. She understood his unique shorthand. He used only a few words and phrases when he wanted to remember things, and would star important items, liberally use question marks and underlining, and often box information he wanted to specifically remember.

Unfortunately, most of the information was vague without substance or reference. Relevant names and events that she already knew.

She noted that he had completed deep backgrounds on both Adam and Michael Hannigan. He'd confirmed everything that they'd known last year: the half brothers hadn't been close. They'd been raised by different mothers and saw each other infrequently while growing up. They'd attempted to be friends when they reached adulthood, but their social media circles were vastly different. It appeared that Tommy had reverified everything, including their criminal records—which were clean up until Michael had robbed Potomac Bank and Adam had killed her son.

At the top of one page Tommy had written and circled:

Brock Marsh Security—paid under the table?

He didn't indicate which brother the note referred to, though Regan assumed it meant Adam Hannigan, who had been employed by Brock Marsh for three years in his early twenties, a decade before he had killed Chase. Did Tommy have evidence that Brock Marsh was still paying Adam? If so, why under the table? Why was it important?

Everything is important until you know that it's not.

Unfortunately, she found nothing more in Tommy's notes about Adam or Michael Hannigan, or any affiliation with Brock Marsh.

On another page, he'd written *Becca Johns* with two stars next to her name.

Becca was Michael Hannigan's victim in the bank robbery. A teller, he'd used her to access the bank deposit boxes and then killed her, seemingly for no reason.

Tommy noted he planned to do a full background on Becca, that he intended to reinterview all witnesses, and then he wrote:

Contact Jenna Johns—sister.

He didn't list a phone number or email, but he'd circled and starred her name and added a notation:

Jenna—Becca's employment history, debt, boyfriends.

Debt was a signal in many investigations of possible motive for crime, especially white-collar crime. But there had been nothing in the FBI records that pointed to Becca—a victim—as being an accomplice.

She put a star next to Becca's name on her own notepad and wrote down *Jenna Johns.*

A few pages near the end of his tablet, on a page flanked by several blank pages, Tommy had written five names and businesses. They seemed familiar to Regan, but she didn't know why. She tore out the page and clipped it into her own notepad.

Turning to Tommy's computer, she reviewed his most recently accessed documents, then frowned. He hadn't created or opened any documents on his computer for weeks. Would he have committed everything to hardcopy? That struck Regan as out of character.

She stood, walked around his office, thinking. If Tommy was preparing a report or presentation for Charlie at headquarters, he would have the information in writing. Print, PowerPoint, something. He wouldn't rely solely on handwritten notes.

Suspecting that he had another device, she looked around the room, in cabinets, drawers. She didn't remember Tommy having a laptop or tablet, but she supposed it was possible. Leaving the library, she walked around the house, flipping on light switches as she went, looking for anything out of place.

Then she found it.

In the butler's pantry that bridged the dining room and the kitchen was a laptop charger, plugged into the wall next to a small built-in desk. No laptop, no case. Maybe Tommy had taken it with him—that would be logical—and now it was in the possession of the FBI.

Regan needed to see what was in it, and Charlie should be able to at least access it in evidence. It might even be considered personal property, so the FBI would return it forthwith. At a minimum, Charlie should be able to look at the contents.

One mystery solved, she returned to the den and sat back down at his desktop. He hadn't been working on his main computer. Why, she could only guess. Still, there might be relevant information in his email.

She opened his email, pushing aside the guilt at invading his privacy. Scanned the inbox. Scanning various messages, she found nothing that referenced Chase, Adam Hannigan, Becca Johns, or Peter Grey. In fact, Tommy hadn't used his personal email for much of anything.

Why would he have a secondary account?

Where was Tommy's cell phone? Had the killer taken it? Why?

She called Charlie as she retrieved Tommy's search history. Swearing under her breath, she realized that it auto-deleted every time he shut down his computer. She did the same thing, but it was infuriating when she wanted information. There were ways to recreate the history, but that went way beyond her skill set.

"Hello," Charlie answered in his deep baritone.

"Charlie, it's Regan. Tommy wasn't using his computer much while he was on leave. He has no recent files, he regularly deletes his browsing history, and nothing of import is in his emails. Did you know he owned a laptop?"

He thought for a moment. "I might have seen him with a laptop case a few times, but he didn't usually carry one around."

"It's not here. Could it be with the FBI or with his personal effects at the morgue?"

"Hold on, let me look at the evidence log. Give me a sec."

"I'm sorry it's late—I didn't mean to disturb you at home."

"You can call me anytime, day or night. Just takes a minute to log in to the system…okay. Let's see…"

His voice trailed off. A moment later he said, "No laptop in evidence."

"And no phone, either," she said.

"No phone, no laptop, no briefcase, nothing. You're

thinking, if he was going to talk to me about what he learned, he'd have something to show me."

"You must be thinking the same thing," she said.

"It's suspicious."

"The killer must have taken his laptop along with his cell phone."

"Does Tommy have a cloud account?"

"No—I checked on his home computer. If he has one, he didn't access it from his desktop."

"I have access to his work computer and files—I'll see if he saved anything to our network."

"Thanks, Charlie. Best to Sharon."

She had another idea. She went to Tommy's email again and found the automated emails from his cell phone provider. She then went to the browser and as she suspected, the login information auto-populated as soon as she clicked in the box.

Most everything was digital these days, and bills were no exception. She clicked on his last bill—the cycle had ended eight days ago. She printed out a list of all the calls to and from his phone. It wouldn't give her text information, but at least she had something to follow up on.

She printed out the calls from the cycle before the last, to cover the entire four weeks he'd been on leave, but the last eight days were unavailable until the end of the billing cycle. Law enforcement could request the data with a warrant.

For now, she took the pages and scanned the numbers, making notes. Her own phone number appeared a few times, but only once in the last six weeks—the day after Chase's birthday, when Regan had called Tommy after she landed in Phoenix to tell him that all was well between them, and she'd talk to him later.

And she hadn't called. That bothered her now.

She would call all the numbers in the log to find out who they belonged to, if possible. There were at least two calls a day to the Marshals office, but that wasn't surprising. There were calls to his sister—she crossed those off.

A number jumped out at her.

555-703-7880

She knew that number: her ex-husband's cell phone.

An outgoing call that lasted three minutes on April 29. Three weeks ago. The day after Tommy had his visit with Peter Grey, per his calendar.

Why the hell had Tommy called her ex?

Tommy and Grant had never particularly liked each other. They got along well enough when they had to, but Regan had always felt tension between them. She didn't understand it, generally ignored it, figured it would work itself out. She dismissed it as two strong-willed, intelligent men who had dissimilar backgrounds and interests. Tommy had grown up in a lower middle-class Baltimore neighborhood with a single mom, raised more by his sister Terri. Grant had grown up in an upper middle-class Boston neighborhood, moving to Virginia when he graduated law school to work for what Tommy had once called a "stuffy" law firm. Tommy was former military, barely passed high school, got into the Marshals Service with an AA instead of a bachelor's through a military-to-federal service program. Tommy wasn't unintelligent; he was more tactical and kinetic than book smart. Sitting at a desk for hours was his version of hell. It was something that Regan and Tommy had bonded over. The only difference was she'd taught herself ways to combat the need to escape a classroom.

She itched to call Grant but wanted to talk to him in person. They hadn't spoken since that day beside Chase's grave. Maybe Tommy's call had been irrelevant to the investigation. She didn't want to speculate, but the timing was suspicious. She'd track down Grant tomorrow.

She circled several other numbers she planned to call, then printed out his calendar, which fortunately was synced between his phone and his computer. She saw a meeting with Grant on his calendar. April 30. *Grant Warwick, here.*

The day after their phone conversation, and two days after his meeting with Peter Grey.

She flipped through Tommy's notepad, searched his desk—no notes on their conversation.

Odd. Again, she almost called Grant right then...but decided her original instincts were best—reach out to him tomorrow in person. She hadn't called or texted him to let him know she was in Virginia—she'd hopped on the first flight she could get after she heard about Tommy's murder.

She cut and pasted the phone numbers from Tommy's account into a spreadsheet on the computer so that she could add information, search and sort data as needed. She tabulated incoming and outgoing numbers, plus the total number of minutes between Tommy and the caller. The first three weeks of April, before his leave, he'd called dozens of different numbers, few numbers more than once, other than his sister, Terri. But in the last three weeks—since his meeting with Grey—there were several calls both incoming and outgoing to Grant, and another number that popped up a half dozen times. She tried that number just for kicks—it went immediately to voicemail.

A computerized voice started up then a female said "Jenna Johns" before the computer continued that she was unavailable and to leave a message.

Regan left a message with her full name and number and a brief explanation. She hoped Jenna would return her call, but if not Regan would try again tomorrow.

She made a note on her spreadsheet and then looked at the other numbers. A few were familiar—using the reverse telephone directory, she identified most of them.

The prison where Grey was held.

Several private numbers that didn't seem to hold any relevance.

Potomac Bank of Arlington.

She brought up the bank's website and realized this number went to the same bank that Mike Hannigan had attempted to rob two years ago.

There was a note on Tommy's calendar for a meeting with Stuart Van Horn, scheduled the day after the phone call he made to that specific branch. Regan remembered the bank manager.

She didn't have time to contemplate why Tommy had met with Van Horn because her cell phone rang.

It was after ten. She'd been hunched over Tommy's notes and computer for three hours. She stretched as she answered the call.

"Hi, Dad."

"You settled in okay?"

"I texted you when I got here." She was too tired and sore to be humored that her father was checking up on her. She got up and walked the room, rolling out her stiff neck and shoulders.

"You're staying at Granger's house?"

"Yes."

"Do you think that's safe?"

"He has a basic home security system to alert me if there's an intruder. I'm being careful, Dad."

Her dad had wanted to come to Virginia with her, but she said no. He didn't push, but she could tell he wasn't happy about her decision. Former sheriff John Merritt rarely had people tell him no. She had considered letting him join her—she appreciated and welcomed her dad's insight and experience—but her gut told her that he didn't want to help her investigate: he wanted to watch *her*. She didn't need or want a babysitter.

"Will you check in regularly?" he asked.

"I will."

"I assume you're staying until the memorial service."

"Yes."

"Longer?"

"Maybe." It wasn't like she had a job or anything else to do. That had been grating on her for a while. She didn't *need* to work yet—between her savings, her half of the proceeds from the sale of the house, and the fact that she was living almost free with her dad—there had been no rush to find a second career.

"If you need me out there, just say the word."

"I appreciate that, Dad. I mean it. And if I need to bounce around theories, I'll call."

"Anytime, Regan."

"I *am* fine," she reassured him.

"I can't help but worry. You're too much like me. I know that you're suffering, and you won't let anyone see it."

Yep. She and her father suffered in silence, as her mom used to say. Regan hadn't really understood what it meant until her mother became ill with cancer and died a year later. Her father had been a rock, but he didn't cry—at least not around his children—and he didn't yell or complain or curse God. He just *did*.

For the most part, that was Regan. Instead of crying, she

took long walks or hiked. Got out of the house, got out of her head. It worked, for her.

She rarely spoke about her feelings of rage over how the FBI handled Chase's murder, and when she did speak of the situation to her family or her former colleagues, she was matter-of-fact. Removed from the details. When Peter Grey killed Hannigan in jail, she had demanded answers— and when she didn't get them, she didn't scream or knock heads together. She had no answers—and had no way to get answers. Staying had become untenable. So she left.

"I'm not going to lie to you and say it's easy being here," she told her dad. "But it was harder six weeks ago than today."

Silence. Some things really didn't need a conversation. Her dad really did understand her.

"I love you, Dad. I'll call you later."

She appreciated her dad reaching out to her, but right now she needed to think about Tommy. Talking to him had just brought back all her feelings of being unsettled.

She thought she had been moving on from Chase's murder. She'd been living at home since October. She and her dad were gutting the small apartment above the barn— where her granddad had lived for years before he died— so that she would have her own space. But truth be told, she didn't mind sharing a house with her dad. Maybe that wasn't healthy now that she was thirty-five, but there was a deep comfort in being able to go home and grieve.

Yet, she had been indecisive on what she was going to do for the rest of her life now that she quit the Marshals. Despite having had months to think it over, Regan had yet to make a decision.

That was unlike her.

She was about to go to bed—it was late, and she wanted

to get started early in the morning—but she was still flummoxed that she hadn't found any of Tommy's files or notes related to his conversation with Peter Grey or Chase's murder. She really didn't want to read about Chase's murder—she knew every detail—but if Tommy had learned something, he would have had notes, ideas, theories. *Something* she could use to find his killer.

She sat down at his desk and closed her eyes. Remembered the single worst call a parent can get.

It was a Saturday night. She wasn't supposed to be working, but she and Charlie had been called to transport a prisoner from upstate New York down to Virginia.

They were two hours from the prison at eight thirty at night when her cell phone rang. It was Grant.

"Chase was shot, Regan. He was shot. Chase, my boy, he's dead. Oh God, he's dead."

The sobs filled the line but she was in shock. She couldn't have heard him right. How could Chase be dead? He and Grant were at home.

"Where are you? Are you at the hospital? What happened? Chase is going to be okay. What hospital? I'll be right there."

She said it even as the cold rolled through her at what Grant had said; believing he was wrong, that he was scared. Something happened...but not what he said. Right?

"Grant, where are you?"

An unfamiliar voice came on the phone. "Mrs. Warwick?"

"This is US Marshal Regan Merritt. I'm Grant's wife. Where is my son?"

"I'm sorry, I didn't know he was going to tell you like that..."

"Where. Is. My. Son."

"There was a shooting, we don't have all the details, but your son was shot while in your sunroom. The shooter was in the backyard, we're still investigating and—"

"What hospital? Where was he taken?"

"I'm sorry, Marshal. He was killed instantly. The coroner just arrived and..."

There was a commotion over the phone and she heard yelling in the background, but she couldn't distinguish who was speaking. Then a familiar voice came on. "Regan? Regan? It's Tommy."

"Tommy. What is going on? Tell me. Please." Her voice cracked, but Tommy wouldn't lie to her.

"Come home, Regan."

"Is Chase— God. No. Please. Tell me."

"Just come home. I'll be here."

Regan opened her eyes. They felt heavy, as if she had been sleeping or crying; she'd done neither. Memories had weight, and she felt the past drag her entire body. She knew she needed sleep.

She got up and was about to turn off the desk lamp when her eyes focused on the cabinets below the built-in bookshelves. Though she believed Tommy had taken everything important with him—and therefore the killer now had the information—maybe he had copies or notes in his files.

She opened cabinets and looked inside—four doors concealed two shelves each. Inside were magazine holders, the kind you might see in a library, labeled with cases. He kept files on all his major cases at the Marshals Service, mostly his own personal notes, his copies of the files. He had dozens labeled by date. She went to the end.

There she found it.

No date, but the label read: WARWICK.

Her heart skipped a beat.

She pulled it out of the magazine holder that housed only a few files, but based on the telltale bulge of the thick cardboard, there had been much more here.

She sat on the couch and took the remaining files out.

The first was the crime scene report for Chase's murder. She didn't look at it—she'd read it before, far too many times, and didn't want the deep sorrow that went with reading. The memories were already almost too much to bear.

The next file was Adam Hannigan's murder investigation. She had read it before, but maybe she'd see something new. She put it aside to review. He also had a file on Peter Grey—his rap sheet, but no notes from his recent conversation.

One file was empty—though clearly a thick stack of paper had once been enclosed. It was labeled FRANKLIN ARCHER.

The name caught her by surprise.

Archer was Grant's partner at the law firm. His father had started the firm more than forty years ago, but Franklin took it over fifteen years ago around the same time Grant had started working there as a junior partner. She knew Franklin well, he and Grant had been friends as well as colleagues.

Why the hell did Tommy have a file on Grant's partner? And where was the information now? Had it also been taken by the killer?

She opened one last file so thin she expected it to be empty; inside was a lone photo. Mike Hannigan and Becca Johns. It had been downloaded from the internet, looked like it had been printed from social media. No date, no location, no indication where it had come from. Written on

the bottom was the name *Jenna-sister* and a phone number. Under that: *Ask what Jenna knows about Hannigan.*

Her head pounded as she struggled to put together all
the confusing pieces.

Her ex-husband Grant had been talking to Tommy. He
must have answers.

She would talk to him first thing tomorrow.

WEDNESDAY

Nine

Regan planned to catch Grant at his townhouse before he went to work, so she was in the car by 7:15 a.m.— fifteen minutes later than she'd wanted, but she was dragging after so little sleep.

Before leaving Tommy's house, she looked out windows in every direction to ensure that no one was watching the house. Most of the lots were between one and two acres, and several people had horses, including the neighbors to the rear.

Once she was confident that no one was outside, she set the alarm system and left.

While driving toward the main road, she checked for a tail or anyone suspicious. A couple kids were walking together to the bus stop; a mom was fast-walking a double-wide stroller. All good. Yet, she kept feeling like the other shoe was going to drop.

Regan dreaded Northern Virginia commuter traffic, which seemed to start earlier in the morning and last later in the evenings as time marched on. She always forgot how bad it was until she was in the middle of a slow-moving caravan. She kept the local news on low, paying half attention to the traffic and weather reports. When a call from Charlie came at 7:35, she muted the radio.

"I hope I didn't wake you," he said. "I know you're still on Arizona time."

"I'm already on the road."

"The FBI are holding on to all of Tommy's personal effects as evidence. I double-checked, however—and they don't have his laptop or any papers. All they have are his wallet, service weapon, backup weapon, the to-go coffee mug he'd been carrying, and his clothing."

"His laptop isn't at the house. I went through everything in his office and there are some rough notes, but nothing he would present to you."

"The killer could have taken everything," Charlie said.

Which confirmed her belief that Tommy was killed because of his investigation into Chase's murder.

Charlie continued. "I'm going to let O'Dare know, keep her in the loop, but I don't think she's interested in our theory."

She didn't comment on that; she had nothing nice to say. Instead, she said, "I have another favor?"

She said it as a question because she knew Charlie was already overextended. She didn't want to put too much on his plate.

"Okay, but it might have to wait. I'm on court detail this morning, won't be out until noon."

"How fun," she said dryly.

No one liked boring court duty. Only once in Regan's thirteen-year career with the Marshals Service had there been an actual serious situation in the courthouse—the husband of a defendant had taken a judge and jury hostage and demanded his wife be released. The six-hour standoff had ended without bloodshed. Prison transport wasn't fun either, but at least you were out of the building doing something.

Fugitive apprehension—that was the best gig, in her opinion, though other marshals disagreed.

"What do you need?" he asked.

"The Michael Hannigan file. Tommy had some notes about Mike Hannigan and the Potomac Bank robbery, as well as his victim, bank teller Becca Johns. He thinks that Hannigan and Becca knew each other, has a photo of them together that appears to be from social media, but other than that I don't know how he made the connection or why he was looking there. I need to refresh myself, I don't remember the details. Other than we had to go in when he killed Johns."

"Regan—"

"I know what you're thinking. I'm not feeling guilty about shooting Mike Hannigan. It was justified."

She had complex feelings about the case after the fact because it had indirectly led to Adam Hannigan killing her son—allegedly. Though neither she nor Tommy had bought into the motive that the FBI put forward, the whole thing made her feel...*off*. Off-kilter, off-center.

She had to be in the right frame of mind if she was to figure out what Tommy had learned and why he had been killed.

And find his killer.

Because whoever killed Tommy may have orchestrated the murder of her son.

"Regan," Charlie said softly, interrupting her thoughts as her car crept forward.

"I'm okay," she said. She cleared her throat. "Tommy wrote down the name Jenna Johns, Becca's sister. I found her phone number in Tommy's records, tried to call her last night but the call went to voicemail. I'll try again later today if she doesn't return my call."

"Physical copies of reports plus any physical evidence would be with the FBI, but you can swing by our office and access the digital reports from our system. Have Maggie log you in. If you need hard copies, it'll have to be after lunch."

"Thanks, Charlie."

"Watch your back." He ended the call.

She didn't reach Grant's townhouse near Founders Park in Alexandria until close to eight thirty. She knocked; he wasn't there. She looked through a small garage window; his sporty Mercedes wasn't there, either.

She shouldn't have been surprised. Like her, Grant had always been an early riser and would likely have left for work before eight. His law offices were in Arlington, fifteen minutes without traffic, but nearly twice as long in the morning.

She parked in the courthouse parking lot, but before going up to her old office, she walked two blocks to her favorite coffee shop for much-needed caffeine. It also gave her more time to go through Tommy's phone records and make a plan for the day.

What she found most odd was the empty Franklin Archer file in Tommy's office. Where were the papers that were supposed to be in there? Could something about Franklin have piqued Tommy's interest, and that's why he contacted Grant?

The coffee shop line was long, even now that it was after nine, but she waited then ordered black coffee and a blueberry scone, then sat at a table by the window where she had a view of the door and the street.

Some habits never die.

She called her ex-husband. Best to get the conversation out of the way and set up a time to meet.

He answered on the second ring.

"Regan?"

"Hello, Grant."

She didn't know why it was still awkward talking to her ex-husband on the phone. They'd been married for twelve years before their divorce was finalized in March. It hadn't been a perfect marriage, but they'd had good times. And they'd had Chase. She wondered if they had really loved each other if they would have been able to survive his death.

But they hadn't loved each other, not anymore, and Chase's death showed it.

"*Um*—Regan? Is everything okay?"

Of course he would ask that. She never called him.

"Tommy was killed on Monday."

"Oh—God. I—*wow*. I hadn't heard. Was it on the job? Are you coming out here?"

"I'm here." She refrained from telling him how Tommy had been killed.

"In *Virginia*?"

"Yes. We should meet. Lunch?"

"I can't—I have a meeting. It's important, work." Why did she think he was lying? Avoiding? "I'm—I'm so sorry about Tommy." He sounded genuine.

"When can we get together?" she asked.

"I don't know. I'm prepping for a civil trial— How long are you going to be here?"

"Grant, I'd like to talk today. Tonight, after work?" She almost brought up his meeting with Tommy but resisted the impulse, decided to wait until they were face-to-face. Grant could be cagey at times, even when he *didn't* have a secret. He was always thinking about *why* someone wanted information.

"Must it be tonight?" he asked.

"I don't know how long I'll be in town." Make it sound casual. Grant had often said her conversations with him sounded like interrogations. She was simply straightforward.

He relented. "Dinner?"

"Sure. Great. Your place?"

"Remember that Mexican food place we loved in Chantilly? Buenos Gatos?"

"Of course." It was thirty minutes out of town, but it had been one of their favorite restaurants. When they were first married, they'd lived in a small two-bedroom house in Chantilly—it was all they could afford. But after Chase was born, Grant started making more money, she got a raise, and they moved to a two-acre ranch-style property on the edge of Fairfax. A much bigger house, back when they'd been considering having another baby. If they'd had a second child, would they have stayed together after losing Chase? She didn't know. But now, with perspective, she realized that a loveless marriage wasn't good for anyone.

"I'll meet you there at seven," Grant said. "I really must run now." He ended the call before she could say anything else.

She frowned at her phone. Grant didn't sound himself. She had half a mind to show up at his office, but that seemed drastic. Tonight she would get the answers.

At the coffee shop, she finished her drink, then looked over Tommy's phone records again, ran a reverse telephone directory on Jenna Johns's number and found her address. It didn't take long to identify her social media profiles. Jenna didn't post much, but Regan learned that she was an

ER nurse at a busy hospital in Bethesda. She had a small but active group of friends, all of whom appeared to work with her. On November 1 of last year, she had posted an old picture of herself and her sister with a caption, *Becca, you would have been thirty-one today. I can't believe you're gone, when you always had so much life and joy in your heart. I'll love you forever.*

Jenna stated that her favorite things were piña coladas and any cookie that had coconut in it. Based on a limited number of pictures, she had a gym membership, but she admitted that she didn't go as often as she should. Two men popped up in numerous pictures but didn't seem to be boyfriends. They were tagged—one, Lance Martelli, had a private account; the other, Chris Fielding, was a nurse where Jenna worked and seemed to be a practical joker. On March 20 she had multiple posts about her birthday, when she turned twenty-six. Her friends had taken her out to a country music bar, and she thanked them profusely because apparently she was the only one among them who liked country music.

Jenna seemed a normal, average, busy twenty-six-year-old who wasn't obsessed with social media, appeared to love her job, and had a solid support group.

Regan hoped she heard back from her today. She had questions for her, chief among them: Why did Tommy think that Becca had been Michael Hannigan's accomplice in the botched robbery of Potomac Bank?

Ten

Grant Warwick was unsettled after talking to his ex-wife.

He stared out his office window. Downtown Arlington was still buzzing with traffic below his perch on the sixth floor. His was the second-best view in the building, but he didn't mind. He had large windows and natural light and a comfortable office. He had staff and respect and was a partner in a moderate-sized corporate law firm. He specialized in contract law; the senior partner, Franklin Archer, specialized in civil litigation and negotiation. His theory was if the case went to trial, they hadn't done their job.

Franklin was outstanding at negotiation. Trials cost more than dollars.

What happened to Tom Granger?

Grant felt alternatively hot and cold. He admitted to himself—now—that he had been worried about Granger because he'd failed to call him Monday night, as Grant expected. But because this entire mess was driving Grant a bit crazy, he didn't reach out, hoping that Granger's boss told him that he was wrong, and pointed out all the flaws in his reasoning.

Grant didn't like Granger, the mightier-than-thou marshal who thought he understood Grant. The man who looked down on him because he thought Grant wasn't right for Regan. Grant suspected that Granger had been in love with his ex-wife—when they'd still been married—but for all of Regan's faults, infidelity wasn't among them.

She was too fucking honest about *everything* to cheat on him. Sometimes her bluntness made him angry.

But when Granger told him he had evidence pertaining to Chase's murder, all the little nagging doubts Grant had for the last year resurfaced. So he answered Granger's questions, got him needed information, and waited.

You should have called.

What would calling Granger on Monday have done? Tell him sooner the man was dead? He hadn't wanted to make waves, knowing Granger would reach out when he needed Grant's official statement. And in the back of his mind, Grant hoped that everything Granger believed was wrong. Because if he was right? Grant's life as he knew it was over.

It never occurred to him that Granger was dead. Maybe it should have. After all, Tom was investigating Very Important People, all of whom had their own reasons to shut him up.

Grant should never have helped him. Ethically, professionally, personally. He'd overstepped and would be disbarred.

If anyone found out.

Granger was dead. Maybe Grant was next. Someone cleaning up loose ends.

A chill ran down his spine. There was so much at stake.

Tom Granger had come to him three weeks ago and turned his life upside down. There was no going back, Grant knew.

* * *

"One of these people had your son killed."

Tom Granger—Tommy to his close friends, of which Grant was not one—had called Grant and asked— ordered—him to come to his house in Reston. Then he laid out a conspiracy that seemed so wild, so bizarre, so improbable that Grant had laughed. Until Granger lost his temper and told him that he—Grant Warwick—had been the target the day his son was killed last summer.

"No," Grant had said, not certain he spoke out loud.

"Right in front of you. You were the target, but Chase got in the way."

"Shut up!" Grant pounded his fists on Granger's desk. "Do not mention his name."

"Dammit, do you think I wanted to come to you for help? After what you said to Regan? After how you treated her at the worst time of her life?"

Through clenched teeth Grant hissed, "Chase was my son, too."

"Which makes it worse. Help me, Grant. I've gotten as far as I can on my own, but I need you to get me files from your office. Names, payments."

"I'll be disbarred."

"Peter Grey was jerking my chain most of our meeting, but he told me one thing that I believed. One of your clients wanted you dead."

"What? What the fuck did that bastard say?"

"He said maybe I should be looking at who wanted you dead, not Chase. That one of your clients wasn't happy with your work."

"People don't kill lawyers when they're not satisfied; they fire them. You and Regan were the only ones pushing

that insane theory—if Hannigan wanted me dead, it was because of Regan!"

Tom was angry, but Grant didn't care; it wasn't because of him that his son was dead. Regan had the dangerous job, not him.

"Peter Grey wasn't lying," Tom said through clenched teeth. "I don't know which of your clients—he wouldn't say—but he was clear. The FBI got the motive flat wrong, and you're going to help me prove it. Regan deserves the truth. Even you deserve to know what really happened the night Chase was killed."

"You believe the word of that killer? Grey killed four people!"

"All of whom he killed for Brock Marsh Security. Including Adam Hannigan."

"Brock Marsh?" Grant had been confused. He knew that name. He knew that business. He'd worked with them from time to time. They were primarily an investigation firm, though they started with personal and corporate security. They did a lot of work for Archer Warwick Bachman Law Offices. Why would Peter Grey even know about them?

"But—would that have come out? Wouldn't the FBI have investigated Brock Marsh?"

"Grey sold them on his motive for killing Hannigan, and the FBI had a nice, neat closed case. Why go the extra mile and do their fucking job?"

"You're pulling this out of your ass. You don't know—"

"Did you know that at one time Adam Hannigan had been employed with Brock Marsh?"

"That can't be."

"A friend of mine in Treasury pulled some strings. I can't get the files, not without a warrant, but she verbally confirmed my suspicions. Both Adam Hannigan and Peter

Grey had at one time been employed by Brock Marsh—and they almost exclusively work for your *law firm."*

"How certain are you?" Grant asked, his mind twisting as to what this all might mean. He didn't want to believe it...but he had questioned some of the tactics of Brock Marsh over the years. But because nothing they did appeared to cross the legal line, Grant ignored their questionable ethics.

"I'm a hundred percent certain that Brock Marsh paid Peter Grey—sending money to his only living relative, his daughter—to kill Adam Hannigan because Hannigan was a weak link. Hannigan felt guilty for killing Chase. He had intended to kill you. *When Hannigan agreed to meet with Regan, they thought he would talk, tell her what was going on, that something you did or knew or, fuck, whatever you're into—got Chase killed. So Hannigan was a liability. We just have to figure out who wanted you dead—and why they didn't follow through and kill you." Granger stared at him, all cop, all military, all hard edges. He was bigger than Grant in every way, and at that moment, Grant felt smaller than he was.*

In the back of his mind, he thought Tom Granger might be right.

Granger softened; his voice quieted. "I can't do this without you, Grant. Please. I need your help."

Grant had wanted to believe everything Tom Granger told him was a lie or a coincidence, but the more files he pulled, the more he realized Granger might be onto something. It wasn't any one thing that caught Grant's eye. It was the fact that he knew far more damning or proprietary information about some of his clients—and Franklin's clients—than he realized. He'd always tried to stay firmly on the right side of the line, even when he knew that his partner sometimes crossed it. He felt plausible deniability was the right approach—don't ask, don't tell.

Now he wondered if he knew too much about a corporate crime. Or a personal crime. He knew a lot of nasty shit about his clients. But ethically, unless he knew of a crime about to be committed, Grant could do nothing about their transgressions. And he didn't know what, specifically, would have made him a target.

He passed everything he had over to Tom, but Tom didn't return with answers. He just had more questions. About BioRise Pharmaceuticals, a West Virginia mining company, and Senator Clarence Burgess primarily.

Grant had questions of his own, but Tom never gave him answers—until last Saturday, when they met again at Tom's house.

Tom told him that he would present all his information to his colleagues on Monday and see what happened. If they were going to proceed with an official investigation, Tom wanted to put Grant into protective custody—Grant and Grant's girlfriend, Madeline, a junior partner in Archer Warwick who had helped Grant find the files that Tom needed.

Grant didn't want to believe Tom, but he said one thing that really stuck with him. *"There is a clear path between Brock Marsh Security and Adam Hannigan. Brock Marsh works almost exclusively for your law firm and three of Archer's clients. I also have evidence that Brock Marsh paid Peter Grey's daughter a hefty sum two months after Hannigan's murder—for no obvious reason. Everything else—I need warrants. And I think the Marshals Special Operations Group will take this on."*

Grant couldn't imagine that someone would want him

dead—he didn't know anything that was worthy of killing him for! Except…he had gone through a dark period after Chase's murder and admitted to Tom that he didn't remember anything that he had been working on during that time—even in the weeks before Chase's death. Franklin had taken over all his cases until Grant could get back to work.

Franklin Archer—Grant didn't want to believe that his best friend, who had been best man at his wedding, who had been part of every important event in Grant's adult life—could be involved in *anything* that resulted in the death of Grant's son.

And until Granger had proof, Grant *didn't* believe it.

Except now Granger was dead.

A knock on Grant's office door interrupted his thoughts. The door opened and his assistant Jeffrey Lange stepped in. "Grant, your ten o'clock is running late, and Senator Burgess has moved lunch from one to twelve thirty so Mr. Archer can join you."

"Thank you, Jeff," Grant said.

Grant had known Senator Clarence Burgess since he started working as a junior partner for the law firm when it was known as Archer and Archer. He didn't particularly like the man—after all, Grant had negotiated and written several nondisclosure agreements between Burgess and his staff that weren't exactly favorable to the staff—but could the senator have hired a hit man to kill him? Why?

The only reason Grant remembered that he'd been in the middle of a settlement between Burgess's youngest son, Hank, and Hank's ex-girlfriend last year was because Tom Granger had forced him to look at his calendar and all his cases during the months of May and June leading up to

Chase's murder. Franklin had ended up finishing the deal because Grant took weeks off to grieve and bury his son.

"Is everything okay, Mr. Warwick?" Jeff asked. "You seem preoccupied."

"Sorry, I'm fine. Preparing for the Zarian depositions. Can you make sure all legal names and addresses have been verified, and that all certifications have been returned?"

"Of course." Jeff closed the door and Grant breathed easier. He didn't know why he was starting to become suspicious of his assistant. Jeff had been with him for three years, a top graduate from Georgetown in business administration and prelaw, who decided to become a legal secretary instead of a lawyer. He was the most efficient, sharpest assistant Grant had ever had.

Yet...

Grant shook his head. He was getting paranoid. Maybe he had reason to be—Tom Granger was *dead*. He needed to find out exactly what happened. Maybe it had nothing to do with his investigation into Grant's law firm and Brock Marsh Security.

He *wanted* to believe that, but he didn't.

Grant felt nauseated. He didn't want to admit to Regan that he'd been an idiot. Even worse, he had laid all the blame at her feet. He had hurt her when Chase's murder may actually have been related to *his* work.

Grant had loved them both so much, though he had never quite felt like he lived up to Regan's expectations. She'd never belittled him, but she was so damn *dispassionate*. And every time they argued about something, she never actually got angry with him. She was the epitome of calm when he just wanted to see that she *cared*.

Hindsight, of course. Regan was who she was. She cared, but she didn't get emotional. He didn't realize when they married that he needed that emotional connection, the passion that told him that she loved him as he loved her. She compartmentalized and analyzed *everything*. It was annoying and frustrating and made him question everything about them. She was a rock. She was dependable and loyal and smart. But sometimes he had wanted...hell, he never knew how to tell her he felt more like her responsibility and less like her lover.

Tonight he would tell her everything he knew, explain that he had never in a million years thought that one of his clients could have hired Adam Hannigan to kill Chase. To kill *him*. Ask her forgiveness. When he'd seen her six weeks ago at Chase's grave, something shifted inside him.

He missed her. He never expected her to return to him— she was right, they had fallen out of love with each other somewhere along the way. But they'd once shared something special. Together, they had an amazing son. Chase might be gone, but neither of them could forget him. He was theirs, their boy they had created together, and that was an unbreakable bond.

He wished he'd realized that last year.

Grant owed it to Regan—and even to Tom Granger—to help her finish what Tom started.

Eleven

As Regan walked to her old office in the courthouse, she expected a sharp wave of loss as the nostalgia hit; instead, the dull, steady ache that she had learned to live with continued. Was this progress? She couldn't point to one specific moment in time when the grief had shifted, but she feared returning to Virginia, to the remnants of her old life, would bring back the pain. She was relieved it hadn't.

The office was quiet when she walked in, though it was after ten in the morning. Maggie was at her desk, one of the marshals Regan didn't know was on the phone at his cubicle, and a clerk was busy filing along the narrow hall that barely complied with fire regulations. So much in law enforcement had switched to the computer, but there were still reams of actual *paper* in the paperwork.

"Charlie called," said Maggie. "I already pulled up the files that you need. Do you mind working in Tommy's office?"

"Thank you, that's great. Can you do me one other favor?"

"Anything."

"I was hoping you could dig up any information available on Jenna Johns. Here's her address and phone number and her employer, but if you can confirm?" She handed Maggie a slip of paper. "I know it's asking for a lot."

"Nonsense. I'll get what I can."

"Thank you."

Regan took a seat at Tommy's desk, but she left the door open. It didn't feel right being here with him dead. In some ways, it was more uncomfortable than sleeping in his house.

She moved the computer mouse and the screen woke up. Maggie had already brought up the files for her. Regan dived in and started reading.

Some law enforcement reports were entered directly into the computer, others were scanned or uploaded—such as field notes, forensic reports, photographs. But she remembered the case even though there was nothing special about it. She'd responded to multiple hostage situations throughout her career, most that ended without bloodshed. But more than a few had ended with one or more dead or wounded—like the Potomac Bank heist.

In fact, if the perpetrator's brother hadn't killed her son a year later, Regan wouldn't have remembered the event at all.

Just over two years ago, Mike Hannigan had taken nine hostages during a bank robbery. He had acted alone, which was unusual—most bank robberies that went beyond a bad guy handing a teller a threatening note had two or more people involved: one who was responsible for watching the hostages while the other collected the money. Hannigan— armed with a semiautomatic rifle and two sidearms—had forced the manager, Stuart Van Horn, and the teller, Becca Johns, to take zip ties that he had brought and secure the hostages at the wrists and the ankles; then he told Becca to tie up the manager. Except for Becca, each hostage had been restrained, their phones taken, and ordered to lie facedown on the floor. The victims were told if anyone moved, they would be shot in the back. He gave one warning to a male customer who attempted to fight back by shooting him in the leg—he told the group there would be no further grace given.

No one else fought back.

Hannigan forced Becca into the safe deposit vault at gunpoint. He used a cordless drill to cut through the lock's core on five safe deposit boxes, but the FBI suspected he knew exactly which box he wanted, and that the others were a diversion. It was possible he only knew the general area of the box, but either way, the FBI believed he was targeting *one* box.

The marshals were first on scene because they were physically closer to the bank, but the FBI took over when they arrived minutes later. Their lead negotiator soon made contact over the phone with Hannigan, who seemed amicable at first. But ten minutes after first contact, Hannigan shot and killed Becca Johns.

Regan and Charlie had been first inside during the breech. She took out Hannigan when he didn't respond to commands to drop his weapon and put his hands behind his head. No one else died.

She wished that there had been CCTV footage, but Hannigan had disabled it and all they had to go on were witness statements. At the beginning, Hannigan had seemed in control and focused. After returning from the safe deposit vault, he'd acted frustrated, agitated, and angry.

One statement was repeated by multiple witnesses: Hannigan said something to Becca before he shot her. No one heard what he said.

When the FBI searched Hannigan's backpack, they

found nothing. The FBI interviewed the five box owners, and they all stated that nothing was missing from the boxes.

The list of the five box owners looked familiar to Regan; she printed it out and put it aside to review.

Hannigan didn't have any money, jewels, bonds, gold, *anything* on him when he'd been killed. His phone was clean: a burner, untraceable. No photos or phone numbers. No outgoing calls during the time he'd been in the bank.

If Tommy was right and Becca was Hannigan's *accomplice*, why would he kill her? Had Becca deceived him somehow? Was she supposed to identify the correct box and made a mistake?

It was all speculation, and with both Hannigan and Becca dead, they couldn't prove anything. Except…maybe that was why Tommy had been in communication with Becca's sister, Jenna. Perhaps Jenna had information that led Tommy down this particular path.

Because she was a victim, there would have been no reason for the FBI to review Becca's cell phone data or do more than a cursory look into her background. Regan found nothing in the reports that suggested the FBI had done anything beyond processing the scene and trace evidence, interviewing the hostages, and talking to the five box owners.

The whole robbery stunk, Regan realized. She hadn't considered it at the time because she wasn't involved in any follow-up, other than the mandatory interview, investigation, and subsequent psych eval from the shooting. She'd been on mandatory two-weeks' administrative leave. Jumped through all the hoops, was cleared and back on duty. Didn't give the robbery a second thought.

Now, reviewing the files and witness statements, there seemed to be no clear reason for Mike Hannigan's actions. The final FBI report concluded that he had targeted the five boxes because he believed there was cash inside. When he learned that all the boxes had only documents or personal items, he became angry and volatile, lashing out at Becca because she was the closest one to him or because he equated her with his failure.

Hmm. It might have made sense at the time, but…

Documents *could* be as valuable as cash, Regan thought. She grabbed the sheet she'd printed and looked at the names of the box owners. There were three businesses and two individuals. They were familiar.

Tommy had these five names listed in his notes.

Tommy had been looking into these people, Regan realized. The revelation gave her pause. Did he think there was something more here than a botched robbery? Why? What triggered his interest?

First things first. Time to talk to bank manager Stuart Van Horn.

Twelve

Regan arrived at the Potomac Bank of Arlington not far from Alexandria at quarter after eleven that morning. The bank was on a side street off Fairfax Drive with limited street parking, so she pulled into the small lot behind the bank that serviced the row of businesses on the block.

It wasn't a bank she would have chosen had she been a bank robber: there was only one public entrance, the street wasn't well traveled, it was blocks from the metro, and didn't have much parking. Not to mention it was less than ten minutes from the courthouse, eight minutes from a police substation, with narrow side streets that were easy for law enforcement to block off.

That further bolstered the FBI theory that Mike Hannigan had been targeting a specific security box in this branch.

When Regan walked into the bank, she noted some differences. First, the security guard was younger and more alert than the older rent-a-cop who had previously worked there. Second, the formerly open, high-ceilinged bank had walled off three offices, with lowered ceilings, for the manager and two loan officers, and the tellers were now behind thick plastic shields. That wasn't unusual; many banks had converted to such protective dividers over the last twenty, thirty years—even a neighborhood bank like this that prided itself on personalized customer service.

A pedestal with a sign-in sheet stood sentry next to a comfortable grouping of four large leather chairs and circular coffee table stacked with financial magazines and a lone kids' book. The manager, Stuart Van Horn, stood chatting with a customer outside his office door.

Van Horn was tall, slender, and impeccably dressed. Midforties, dark graying hair, wire-rimmed glasses, large hands.

Another staff member—by her name tag, the loan manager—approached her.

"May I help you, ma'am?"

"I'm waiting for Mr. Van Horn."

"Do you have an appointment?"

"No. But I need to speak with him," she said, preempting any attempt to convince her to sit with the loan officer.

"Of course. May I tell him who's waiting?"

"Regan Merritt." She didn't want to explain the reason for her visit twice, so she didn't give the loan officer any additional information.

As soon as the customer Van Horn was speaking with left, the staff member approached him, spoke quietly, and he looked over at her. He tilted his head slightly as he approached. "Ms. Merritt, I don't believe we have an appointment. Do we know each other?"

"I was one of the marshals who responded to the bank robbery two years ago."

"Yes, I do remember you now. How may I assist you?"

"Do you have a few minutes?"

"Of course." She politely declined his offer of coffee or water and followed him into his office.

He sat behind his desk—highly polished dark wood, clear of all paperwork, only a computer and keyboard in the corner. A framed picture of his family was on the credenza behind him: wife, three kids under ten, two dogs. Her eyes lingered just a moment on the lone boy, the youngest of the three, about four or five. He looked both sweet and mischievous. Her heart ached. She tore her eyes away and sat in the chair across from the manager.

"Thomas Granger came to see you three weeks ago. You may not have heard, but Tommy was killed on Monday."

"I'm so sorry to hear that," he said sympathetically. "In the line of duty?"

"No. He was murdered," she said bluntly. "I'm helping to recreate his activities in the weeks leading up to his death. He had a meeting with you on his calendar. Did you contact him, or did he contact you?" Jump right in, don't give him time to think about why she, a *former* marshal, was asking these questions.

"Deputy Granger called me to set up a meeting."

"What did you discuss?"

"Mr. Granger had follow-up questions, I suppose you could say, about what happened during the bank robbery. He showed me a copy of my sworn statement, we went over it again. He said he wanted me to refamiliarize myself with what I stated at the time, then asked if I remembered anything else, which I didn't, and said as much. Had I thought of something new, of course I would have contacted the FBI."

"But Deputy Granger had additional questions," Regan probed. "About Becca Johns."

He raised an eyebrow. "Yes, that's correct. He did."

"He had her name in his notes, but no details as to why." Slight fib. "What did he want to know?"

"I admit I was shocked by his questions. He asked if I knew that Becca personally knew Mr. Hannigan prior to the robbery. The thief who—who killed her," he added, though it wasn't necessary. "Mr. Granger implied that the information had just been discovered, and he said that he was considering reopening the investigation."

She remembered the printed photo of Hannigan and Becca in Tommy's file. Was that all he had been going on, or had Jenna Johns provided more information? And if Jenna had known, why hadn't she told the FBI?

Regan wondered if Tommy had been serious about reopening the case or was just using that as an excuse to reinterview Van Horn.

She was glad she'd reviewed the case file before coming in. "After Hannigan secured the hostages, he took Ms. Johns to the safe deposit room and drilled into several of the boxes to access the contents. You provided a list of those boxes to the FBI."

"Yes, and the FBI contacted the customers. We also followed up after the fact, when the FBI cleared us to, because they were our customers and we wanted them to know of additional security protocols that we were taking, in light of the robbery attempt."

"Nothing was taken."

"Correct. Each individual came in and verified such. I confirmed that with Deputy Granger."

She looked at the list she'd written down from the files. Not for the first time, she wished Tommy had left clearer notes. She asked, "Did Tommy have specific questions about the safe deposit boxes that were accessed?"

"Nooo," he said slowly, "though he did ask if we had records of the last time each box owner accessed their boxes."

"And?"

"We do, but I couldn't share that information without a warrant. I would have been happy to give it to him, but the original FBI warrant had expired. He said if he needed the information for his investigation, he'd return with a new warrant. As you know, we are happy to work with federal law enforcement in any criminal investigation, but documentation is critical to protect all parties."

Banks were always forthcoming, but the rules were there for a reason.

She asked, "Did Deputy Granger tell you why he concluded Hannigan and Johns had known each other?"

"No specifics, just that he had uncovered evidence that they'd known each other prior to the robbery. I told him I was surprised because the FBI never told me anything about such a relationship."

She wondered how closely they'd looked two years ago. Bad guy dead, they'd search his house, business, talk to his friends, co-workers. Cross the *t*'s and all that jazz. But nothing was missing—the robbery was a failure—and if they didn't find something specifically incriminating that Hannigan was part of an organized network, then they'd close the case.

"Was there anything else?" she asked Van Horn. She hated open-ended questions because they rarely yielded anything, but she was scrambling.

"He simply confirmed my statement, and he had other statements from the witnesses and wanted to know if anything was missing. I couldn't say—I mean, I don't know what people recollect in a stressful situation."

She understood the unreliability of witness statements.

Fear messed with memories—it could heighten a specific memory, or someone might completely block out an incident.

Yet it was odd that Tommy would ask Van Horn about the *other* witness statements. She needed to print them out and study them. Did Tommy think that one of the hostages was lying?

She handed Van Horn her card. Well, not *her* card, but one of Tommy's where she had crossed out the front and written her name and cell phone on the back. Probably not kosher, but he had a box in his desk at home, and she'd grabbed a few in case she needed them. "If you remember anything else that you and Tommy discussed, please call me. That's my cell phone."

He took it. Stared for a minute. "One thing seemed a bit…well, no one had asked me the question before, and I had to think on it."

She motioned for him to continue.

"Deputy Granger asked if Hannigan had approached any of the customers after he returned from the vault. I couldn't say. I didn't *think* so. When I reread my statement, I had indicated that Mr. Hannigan had paced the premises after he returned from the vault. He was agitated. I recall him walking back and forth in front of where the customers were tied up. My staff, and myself, were against the teller wall. The customers were forced to lie in front of the main doors— I assumed that was to make it harder for you all to enter."

It was a standard bank heist tactic—put the hostages in the line of fire. But Regan had entered through the fire door in the back with her team. Some criminals didn't know that law enforcement had special tools to access doors that appeared to have no way to open from the outside.

"And?"

"The gentleman, Brian Thompson was his name, the customer who was shot in the leg, he was lying on the floor, where the sitting area is now. He was separate from everyone else, I suppose, halfway between us staff and the other customers. Hannigan kept pacing back and forth between Mr. Thompson and the staff."

Hannigan had shut down the security cameras so they had no visual of what happened in the bank for the twenty-seven minutes that Hannigan held everyone hostage before he was shot and killed.

"Do you personally know Mr. Thompson?"

"By sight. He'd been a customer for about a year."

"You know that off the top of your head?"

He shook his head. "I learned more about the customers who'd been hostages with us after the situation ended. I felt it was my duty to see if there was any way myself or the company could help them after their ordeal. We offered a lifetime of waived checking fees, though I wish there was more that we could have done."

"And Mr. Thompson came in regularly?"

"A few times. I recognized him, didn't know his name. You probably know this from your files, but he was in the middle of financing a gym—which is why he had an appointment with our business loan officer that morning."

"Did he qualify for the loan?"

"He would have, but he pulled it. He said he needed to rethink his plans. He'd been shot, after all. I think the experience traumatized him."

"Have you seen him since?"

"No—Mr. Granger asked the same thing. Brian Thompson closed his accounts, but he went to a different branch to do it. We were closed for a week after the incident."

Regan thanked him and left.

Had Becca Johns been the accomplice? Or Brian Thompson? Tommy had been interested in both Becca *and a second partner*—Thompson? That meant Regan was, too.

Within thirty seconds of leaving the bank, Regan knew she was being followed.

She reflected briefly on how she'd picked up the tail. The bank was close enough to the courthouse that they could have followed her from there or they might have had a tag team that she didn't notice. Unlikely, but possible. She'd been at the bank for more than twenty minutes—someone could have called in her presence. Van Horn didn't have enough time after she left, and he hadn't been on his phone or computer when she walked in.

Two men, dark SUV that looked official, but had no government plates.

She considered confronting them, even trapping their vehicle down an alley or dead-end street, but that would be foolhardy to attempt alone. She was one person without backup, and she didn't know the threat level.

She had planned to drive straight to Tommy's place to go through his records again. Instead, she drove to the courthouse, there was a greater chance of getting the SUV—now keeping pace two cars behind her—on one of the many cameras outside the building. If they were legit and this was a coincidence, they wouldn't care about the camera. If they weren't legit, they'd peel off a block away from the courthouse—assuming they were aware of the higher security there.

Still, she decided to go the long way back, just to see if they followed. She hopped on the highway that cut across Arlington, then exited south of Alexandria.

The SUV kept pace, alternating between two and three cars behind.

When she called Charlie, his phone went straight to voicemail. Likely still in court. She left a message. "Black SUV followed me from the bank. No front plates, no government tags, two unidentified males. I'm heading to the office, meet me there when you're done with court." She ended the call.

As Regan neared the courthouse and turned right to access the parking garage, the black SUV kept going north.

No rear plates. Illegal, and should a cop encounter them they'd be pulled over. But no plates made the vehicle impossible for her to trace.

Dammit.

If anyone followed her again, she would turn the tables, find a place to trap and confront them.

The tail confirmed to Regan that she was definitely on the right investigatory trail.

Thirteen

As soon as Regan entered Charlie's office, he said, "Did you get their plates?"

"No plates, front or back."

"Where'd you pick them up?"

"Outside Potomac Bank in Arlington. I talked to the manager, Van Horn, who confirmed that Tommy suspected that Becca Johns was an inside accomplice to the robbery. Based on the other questions Tommy asked him, Tommy also suspected that Hannigan had a second partner inside the bank that day."

"Another teller?" Charlie said, eyebrows dipped in confusion.

"One of the customers. Brian Thompson."

"The guy who was shot in the leg?"

She nodded, sat at Charlie's computer. "Do you mind?" She motioned for him to type in his password.

He punched it in. "What are you looking for?"

"I want to talk to Brian Thompson. His name wasn't highlighted in Tommy's notes, and he had no meetings with him on his calendar, but he could have talked to him." She typed in the name, and a record popped up.

Reading over her shoulder, Charlie said, "He's dead."

Thompson had no criminal record, but they had access to the death record. "He was killed in a car accident six months after the robbery," she said, reading the notes. A weather-related three-car crash, and Thompson had been the only fatality when his car spun off an icy bridge. He'd died instantly, per the ME report. No drugs or alcohol in his system, but signs of sudden cardiac arrest. He'd been thirty-six, not overweight, worked out daily, yet a heart attack may have contributed to the accident.

"Brian Thompson was shot during the attempted bank heist," Charlie reminded her. "If he was working with Hannigan, why shoot him?"

"So we didn't realize they were working together. It's an old gestapo trick."

"Quoting classic movies now?"

"Doesn't mean it doesn't happen."

"Still," Charlie said, "a long shot. Almost to the point of being unbelievable."

"Maybe. Yet… Hannigan went into the bank with allegedly no partners. He used Becca Johns—who Tommy learned had known Hannigan prior to the robbery—to break into five safe deposit boxes. Nothing was taken, per the box owners. He then shot and killed Johns for no apparent reason."

"He didn't plan it through. Criminals aren't always the smartest tacks. What he wanted wasn't in the boxes and the guy freaked out. Maybe our response time was faster than he expected."

"What if—" she began turning over possibilities in her head "—it was *information* that Hannigan was after? He could have taken photos of something and passed it off to Thompson. Or he really did take something from the box, but the owner didn't want to acknowledge it later. Thompson was taken to the hospital right away—not interviewed until hours after the situation was wrapped up. He would have had plenty of time to hide or pass off a document or flash drive or extra cell phone—something he could fit in his pocket."

"I see where you're going with it, but it's still an out-there theory. And why kill Becca? All the witnesses stated that Hannigan was agitated, upset. That suggests that whatever he expected to find wasn't in those boxes. Why kill his accomplice?"

Thompson was dead; he wasn't talking. Could he have been working with Hannigan? Maybe, she thought. But there was no evidence to support the theory, and Tommy had left no notes regarding Thompson. Unless she found more evidence that Thompson had been involved—or knew either Hannigan or Becca—then she had to shelve the theory.

"There's something else I learned since we talked yesterday. I pulled Tommy's cell phone records from his billing information on his computer. He'd been talking to my ex-husband, Grant, several times over the last three weeks. According to Tommy's calendar, they had a meeting days after he talked to Peter Grey. Speaking of Grey—did you get through to the warden? When can we meet with him?"

"I put in the call. Told the warden's office exactly what we want. If I don't hear back by the morning, I'll call again."

"I appreciate it, Charlie." She picked up the files of the safe deposit box owners. "Tommy had these names listed in one of his notepads, and he asked Van Horn about them. I'm going to head back to Tommy's house, do some more research."

"He didn't have any more detail?"

"No. Whoever killed him took his phone, took his laptop— He must have had any notes with him."

"That is a far more plausible theory than Johns *and* Thompson both being accomplices."

"Both things can be true," she said. "But either way, I'll find the truth." She had to—for Tommy.

Fourteen

Jenna woke up Wednesday morning in the cabin she'd rented feeling disorientated and out of place. She'd left her house for two nights, no plans, no idea what she was going to do or who she was going to call. Last night she had been positive that the only answer was calling the FBI with the information she knew about Deputy Granger…but what did she really know? She didn't know anything about his murder! She only knew what he had been investigating.

Still, the news report was clear. *Any* information about Deputy Granger or his murder would be important for the police to know.

She weighed all this as she walked the short distance from the one-room cabin to the small lodge where they provided breakfast and coffee. After her restless sleep she needed the coffee, and after not eating much of anything yesterday she realized she was starving. She filled a plate with eggs and sausage that had sat on the warmers for a little too long. Orange juice, coffee, toast. She ate, not really tasting the food, and after her third cup of coffee, Jenna walked back to her cabin determined to find out what happened to Tommy Granger. She called the FBI phone number that had been on the TV news report about Granger's death.

For the next three hours, she talked to three different people—the intake interviewer, that interviewer's supervisor, then an actual agent after she'd been on hold for nearly forty minutes. She explained *three times* how she knew the marshal and what she knew about his murder—which really wasn't *anything*, she realized—and she was *still* waiting for a call back after the agent said yet *another* agent would be contacting her. The entire process cost her another night in the cabin, because she was supposed to check out at eleven.

Jenna didn't think the worst of people, but she also wasn't a Pollyanna. She might be a bit paranoid, but she had no family left outside of her grandmother, who was in a care home. She wanted to go home, but she was scared. The indecision and growing fear coupled with the sense that she was being ridiculous gave her an intense headache.

She needed to talk to someone she trusted—someone who knew her, who knew she wasn't crazy. She considered Lance—he was her closest friend and she trusted him. But she didn't want to put this on his shoulders. It was her problem, her paranoia.

You're not paranoid! she told herself. After all, Tommy had told her to be cautious, to call him if anything out of the ordinary happened.

She hadn't expected his murder to be the "out of the ordinary" event.

Finally, after taking three Tylenol, she called her grandmother. She needed to hear her voice, remember that she had someone who loved her unconditionally. Maybe she could gain some perspective.

Grams answered on the fourth ring. "Hello?" Her voice was bright and Jenna almost cried.

"Hi, Grams. It's Jenna."

"It is so good to hear your voice! This isn't your number, I almost didn't answer. Do you know how many of those telemarketing calls I get every day? What do they call them?"

"Spam."

"Yes. Spam calls. But I just had a feeling I should answer... Do you have today off? Are you coming for a visit?"

She sounded hopeful, and Jenna realized she needed to see her.

"Yes," she said, making the decision right then and there. She'd call the front desk and see if she could still check out today, maybe pay a fee or something for the extra hour. "I was going to swing by this afternoon, wanted to make sure you didn't have a hot date."

Grams laughed, her voice lilting and sounding younger than her years. "Maybe someday I will. A new gentleman moved in down the hall from me. His name is Rock Jameson. Rock! Can you believe that name? I thought for certain it was an alias, and he told me his given name was Richard, but he'd been called Rock since he was five years old when he had an accident and his doctor said his head was as hard as a rock or he would have been dead." She laughed again, and Jenna joined in.

"I can't wait to meet him," Jenna said.

Her grandmother's assisted living facility was only twenty minutes from Jenna's house, but more than an hour from the cabin.

"I'll come by between two and three this afternoon?" She knew her grandmother napped after lunch.

"Perfect. I should be back from my walk with Misty around two."

The home was one of the few in the area that allowed residents to have a small dog or cat. Jenna was thrilled when they'd found it, because there were many studies that proved the elderly lived longer, happier lives when they had a pet.

"Does Rock have a dog?"

"No, he doesn't. But Misty seems to like him just fine."

"Oh, introducing the new man in your life to Misty! It must be serious."

Grams laughed again. "I love talking to you, but it's eleven thirty and if I don't bust my butt and get to the dining hall, Dottie and Flo are going to nab extra lemon squares and I won't get even one."

"Walk, don't run," Jenna admonished jokingly. Her grams had a scooter, but could get around short distances with her walker.

"Already have my scooter charged and waiting for me."

"If you get another speeding ticket, I'm not bailing you out."

"I'll go the speed limit," she giggled. "I love you, sweetie. Can't wait to see you!"

"Love you too, Grams."

Jenna felt so much better after talking to her grandmother. She called the front desk and they said if she was out by noon, they wouldn't charge her.

She didn't have much with her—she'd only packed an overnight bag. But she made sure she hadn't left anything in the room, then checked out two minutes before the deadline and headed to her car. She didn't know what she planned on doing after her visit with her grandmother, but anything was better than pacing the small cabin waiting for a call that might never come.

Her phone rang just as she started the ignition. The unfamiliar ring of the prepaid phone made her jump. She answered.

"Hello?"

"Is this Jennifer Jeanne Johns?" a woman asked.

"Yes." No one called her Jennifer. "Jenna. I go by Jenna."

"Ms. Johns, I'm FBI special agent Natalie Wexford in the Washington, DC, field office. I understand you may have some information regarding the murder of US Marshal Thomas V. Granger."

"Not exactly, but—"

"This morning, you called the tip line and told Agent Richardson that you knew Deputy Granger."

"Yes, that's true."

"Based on your statement, you do not have firsthand knowledge of Deputy Granger's murder, correct?"

"No, but I explained everything to Agent Richardson." *And two other people*, but she didn't say that.

"It would help if you could be concise and start at the beginning."

So Jenna went through everything yet again, starting with how Deputy Granger had contacted her about her sister's possible involvement in the Potomac Bank robbery two years ago and everything she had given Tommy— Becca's tax returns, pay stubs, banking information, and more. "Tommy—Deputy Granger—called me on Sunday and said he had a meeting Monday morning and would be laying out his theory that my sister was involved in the robbery—that she had been an accomplice—and that the robbery may be connected with a series of other crimes. When I called him to find out what happened—he hadn't called when he said he would—a stranger answered. When I saw the news report, I realized this was *after* he was killed. And…that scared me."

She sounded paranoid *and* stupid. She cleared her throat.

"So if I understand," Agent Wexford said, "you do not have firsthand knowledge about Deputy Granger's murder, but someone else answered his cell phone *after* his murder, correct?"

"Yes. I think—well, I mean, it has to be the person who killed him, right? He didn't tell me who he was and he said that Deputy Granger *couldn't come to the phone*! I mean, he had his phone, and Deputy Granger was already dead, why would he say that?"

"Perhaps he didn't want to share information over the phone."

"So the FBI has his cell phone?"

The agent didn't answer her question.

"Do you have anything else to add to your statement?"

Jenna was even more upset than at the beginning of the call. "Aren't you at all concerned? I mean, the stranger said that Deputy Granger was working on an *unauthorized investigation* and that he wanted to talk to me. I hung up. I'm scared."

"I think you may have let your imagination run away with you. If the FBI is not in possession of Deputy Granger's cell phone, they would have run a trace on it."

"So you can find it!" That gave Jenna hope.

"I'm not able to share any details about our investigation into Deputy Granger's murder."

Jenna was now confused. "Can I come in, maybe talk to someone in person? I can explain what Deputy Granger was working on, and what I knew about it. It was a major investigation, and he said I had important information. I mean, I didn't know I had information until he started asking questions." She was rambling and sounded like a total airhead. She took a deep breath. She was smarter than this. But somehow, the fear that had nagged at her for the last thirty-six hours had intensified and was making her testy.

Plus, she didn't like this woman's tone. As if whatever Jenna said wasn't important or relevant.

"My files indicate that Mr. Granger was on an official leave of absence with no outstanding investigations."

Jenna realized the woman knew nothing important about Deputy Granger's murder. Maybe she should call the Marshals directly. She had thought she was doing the right thing by calling the FBI. That's what the news said to do.

"Ms. Johns, are you there?" Agent Wexford asked.

"So you're not taking my report seriously?" She didn't mean to sound snide, but that's how she felt.

"We take every report seriously, Ms. Johns." Agent Wexford paused, then said, "This is what I think we should do. I'll send two agents to your residence so you can give an official report, and they may have additional questions."

"When?"

"I couldn't say. I'll put it in the system, and tag the lead investigator on the case. I would say in the next day or two. Probably tomorrow, it depends on their workload. They'll identify themselves with badges and photo ID."

"So not today?"

"Possibly late this afternoon, more likely tomorrow or Friday."

"I work tomorrow. Eight in the morning, a twelve-hour shift."

She heard clicking over the phone, typing on a keyboard.

"The main hospital, emergency room?"

"Yes."

"I've made a note of your schedule. Please don't worry, Ms. Johns. If you feel unsafe or threatened, contact 911."

"That's it?"

"For now."

Jenna thanked her, though Agent Wexford had not been

much help, and Jenna still didn't know *what* she should do. Would the Marshals office give her the same runaround?

What if whoever killed Tommy thought *she* knew something? She didn't want to go home…but she didn't want to stay here, either. She couldn't stay with her grandma. Jenna could sleep on her couch, but then Grams would ask why, and Jenna didn't want to worry her.

First things first. Visit Grams. Relax. *Think.* Likely the FBI agents would be coming to her work tomorrow, which made her feel a bit better. Not just because she could show them in person that she wasn't some lunatic, but she could show them the emails and text messages that she and Tommy had exchanged, to prove she wasn't a paranoid twenty-something idiot. There were also people there at the hospital, she'd feel a lot safer. Friends, colleagues, security.

Lance.

How could she have forgotten that Lance was coming over for dinner tonight!

She really didn't want to bring him into her problems, but maybe—*maybe*—talking to him about this would help. Lance was smart and clearheaded.

She texted Lance to confirm dinner.

He responded: Who's this?

Jenna. Sorry, temporary phone. Dinner?

Lance said: Yep! 6:30 ok?

He'd also included an emoji, but it came through on the little flip phone as an asterisk and line. She really needed her smart phone back.

Great, she replied.

She felt a million times better just knowing that Lance was coming over. First Grams, then she'd go shopping, then home in plenty of time to whip something up. She loved cooking, but not just for herself, so this would be fun.

If she could only get rid of this awful feeling that something was very, very wrong.

Every call into the FBI was logged and catalogued. Every case had a unique identifier, and every action on a case was attached to that unique identifier.

So when Special Agent Natalie Wexford pulled up the Thomas V. Granger homicide investigation and logged her conversation with the potential witness, Jennifer Jeanne Johns, everything Jenna said to the agent, as well as her up-to-date contact information, was in the file.

Including an internal push to the office manager to schedule two agents to interview Ms. Johns: priority low. Copied into the routing was the agent in charge of the investigation, supervisory special agent Lillian O'Dare.

Wexford doubted the woman had anything more to add to the conversation, but in a case like this, an in-person interview was nevertheless warranted. Unfortunately they were short-staffed and for this particular case they had pulled four agents to review all of Deputy Granger's past cases and threats. The US Marshals office had wanted to take the case but the FBI reminded them that the FBI was the primary investigative unit and thus solving Tom Granger's murder fell to the FBI.

Once Wexford finished updating the information, she returned to the other calls. She wasn't working the hotline as the intake agent, but instead reviewed all calls to determine what was potentially viable and what was irrelevant. Multiple pranks, the habitual confessor, several nosy citizens who knew nothing but wanted information. One potential witness—a neighbor who may have seen the suspect's

vehicle in the neighborhood the day before the murder—
Wexford automatically forwarded all information to the
field agents for follow-up.

Now, back to the calls. She sighed, stretched, rolled out
her neck. She really detested this part of the job.

While Wexford went back to her phone to follow up on
other potential witnesses, another agent in another squad
on another floor saw the update to the Granger file via an
alert he'd set up on his computer.

He quickly scanned the information, frowned. Glanced
at his watch, then told the squad secretary that he was taking a fifteen-minute break and left the building.

Ten minutes later he walked back in, accessed the file,
wrote down Jennifer "Jenna" Johns's contact information—
and new phone number—and left again.

No paper trail, no phone calls in the building, no chance
of being caught. He knew how to cover his tracks.

He damn well hoped.

Fifteen

Grant Warwick was seven minutes late to his lunch with Senator Clarence Burgess and Franklin Archer.

He was never late to any meeting, especially with such an important and busy client. He apologized as he sat in the booth at the overpriced steak and seafood restaurant that the senator preferred.

The senator represented a northeast state, but he lived in Arlington, had raised his kids in Arlington, and owned a house in Arlington. It didn't seem to impact his favorable rankings in the political polls, as he had been handily reelected two years ago.

Clarence brushed off Grant's apology. Grant didn't tell them why he was late, or that he had almost canceled. After talking to Regan, he was out of sorts. He'd tried to talk to Madeline, but she was in a meeting all morning. He wanted to run everything by her, because she was as invested in this situation as he was.

If she hadn't helped him quietly procure the files that Tom Granger wanted, he would never have believed Tom's accusations that a client of Archer Warwick had hired Adam Hannigan to kill him.

Grant ordered a Scotch. He didn't often drink during lunch meetings, but it wasn't so out of the ordinary that it raised a red flag. Burgess's own preferred drink—a dry martini—was half-empty. He'd drink two at lunch, never three.

Franklin, however, recognized that Grant was edgy. He didn't say anything but raised an eyebrow after the waitress walked off.

Grant ignored Franklin's unspoken inquiry and instead, smiled at Clarence. "Congratulations on the appropriations bill. I heard it was a ball-breaker."

"Damn senator from Kentucky thinks the government runs on goodwill and elbow grease. Never wants to spend a dime. Can't run a country without resources. This time he almost convinced enough of my colleagues to join him on his fool's crusade, but clearer heads prevailed. Had to make some side deals on other bills, but it came together in the end, at least until this time next year."

They chatted about people in the building—conversations Grant usually enjoyed because information was king inside the Beltway—but today his heart wasn't in it.

It wasn't until they finished lunch and Franklin took care of the bill—which Clarence would end up paying when it was billed to him next month—that Clarence said, "Hank got himself into another pickle."

Hank. Why hadn't Grant expected this at the beginning of the conversation? Hank was *always* in a "pickle."

"Do we need to contact Cheryl?" Franklin asked. Cheryl Campanelli was a colleague who handled criminal investigations—she specialized in representing the wanton offspring of successful men and women. It was amazing what wealthy parents paid to keep their brats out of jail.

"Oh, no, nothing like that," Clarence said, but in a tone

that suggested to Grant, at least, that it might *become* something "like that."

"It's a paternity claim," Clarence said. "Hank says the kid isn't his."

"Easy to prove," Franklin said.

"The baby isn't born yet. We're months away. The woman is not, shall we say, reputable."

"Not reputable" could mean any number of things.

"Is there a chance the baby is Hank's?" Grant asked.

"Hank says no."

That wasn't an answer. Grant detested men who didn't live up to their responsibilities. Especially men like Hank Burgess who had the means to support a kid, whether he wanted one or not.

"She's likely a gold digger," Clarence said. "I would prefer that she make the only wise decision in this situation."

"How far along is she?" Franklin asked.

"I couldn't say, but approximately three months."

"How much are you willing to offer?"

"The cost of the procedure, of course. Plus ten thousand. If she pushes back—which she might—I'll go up to twenty-five, but that is the maximum. It needs to be made clear to her that if she doesn't take the money and take care of the situation, that the cost to her will be far greater than she can afford. Lawyers and court costs. I need this agreement to be airtight, and nothing leaked to the press."

"Of course," Franklin said.

Grant ignored Franklin's glance. He didn't like this at all. He liked Clarence for the most part, but his situational ethics disturbed him. Clarence had four children and three grandchildren—all from his oldest son, a decorated military officer. CJ Burgess could do no wrong in the eyes of his father—but his two daughters and his youngest son were problems that Clarence was determined to protect from their bad decisions. How long would that go on? Hank was thirty-five! How long was Clarence going to pay for him to "get out of trouble"?

The kid was Hank's, no doubt in Grant's mind. Otherwise, Clarence wouldn't want to spend up to twenty-five thousand to have the woman "take care of it." Did that make it worse? Maybe, Grant thought. Maybe it did.

"Grant, do you have concerns?" Clarence asked.

"No."

After all, he'd written up NDAs for exactly this type of situation multiple times. Why was it bothering him now? Because he had been thinking in the back of his mind that Hank Burgess had another type of problem last year at the time Chase had been murdered? Grant had a problem because Hank had been drunk driving and injured another party. Grant and the senator had argued about the NDA back then, but ultimately, Grant handled it because it was his job. He convinced the senator to tack on an additional ten thousand for pain and suffering—not that they called it that in the NDA—and Burgess relented.

Would Clarence Burgess want to kill Grant because he'd made some critical remarks about his son? It made no sense that Burgess—of all people—would have someone killed for something so little. Burgess was the type of man who would have Grant fired—after paying a handsome severance. To men like Senator Burgess, money was the answer to *every* problem.

The more Grant considered this as a motive, the more he realized he was being foolish. Tom Granger may have been right—that an Archer Warwick client wanted Grant dead—but that client wasn't Clarence Burgess.

Carefully, Grant said, "We need to know any mitigating

circumstances. Whether the woman in question has gone to authorities, whether sex was consensual, whether drugs or alcohol were involved. The more we know, the better we can protect you."

He didn't say *protect Hank*. Grant didn't care about Hank. He did, however, consider it his fiduciary responsibility to protect the senator. He was Grant's client, not his irresponsible son.

"They had a consensual relationship, but the woman was also seeing other men in her capacity—well, there's no way to sugarcoat. She's a call girl. She should have taken the necessary precautions."

Grant wanted to say that maybe Hank should have been wearing a condom if he was going to pay for sex, but he didn't.

Franklin spoke up when Grant didn't. "You're absolutely right, Clarence. Grant will write up an airtight NDA and we'll present it to her, with your terms. I would also suggest we bring in our investigatory team to follow up."

"Yes." Clarence sighed, finished his coffee. "I would love another grandchild. If Hank would find a good woman, settle down. Until he was thirty, I gave him leeway, didn't expect him to follow in CJ's footsteps. Who could? God doesn't make many men like CJ. But now? Hank is *thirty-five*. He needs to knock it off. This *is* the final straw."

Grant doubted it. If paying off a kid he'd hit while drunk driving didn't turn Hank Burgess around, why would knocking up a prostitute? He would continue to get away with his bad behavior because his father would never cut him off. And his father wouldn't cut him off, because Hank's crimes and moral failings would be very public if the senator didn't pay to sweep them under the rug.

"Let us know how we can help," Franklin said.

Archer Warwick also handled wills and trusts—that was another department, run by their third partner. They had prepared the Burgess family trust, had the wills for all the members.

Hank had never been cut out of the will. There were no conditions to his inheritance. And Grant knew that Clarence wouldn't add any. He didn't have it in him.

All talk.

Clarence excused himself, said he had another meeting, and left. Grant got up to leave, but Franklin waved him back down.

"You're not on your A game. Is everything okay?"

What could he say to that? Just come out and ask Franklin if he'd hired a hit man to kill him? If he was responsible for killing his son? A *child*?

"I've really had it up to here with Hank Burgess."

Franklin shook his head as he said, "I know, I know. The kid will never grow up. But Clarence doesn't pay us for parental advice or moral judgment."

"Can I just be frustrated?"

"Of course. You can always talk to me, about anything."

Grant wanted to. Because in no world would he have ever believed that Franklin Archer could have someone killed...especially him. Especially his son.

Not until three weeks ago when Tom Granger came to him.

Grant still didn't *want* to believe it, but the doubts were there. Nothing he could prove. And now Tom was dead and Grant didn't know if his investigation into Brock Marsh Security had been the trigger.

"What else," Franklin said. A statement, not a question.

His friend and partner knew him well, and Grant wasn't ready to accuse him of murder—an accusation he couldn't come back from. So he said the first thing he could think of, the other thing on his mind.

"Regan is back."

"Oh. For good?"

"No. A friend of hers was killed. I assume she's here for the funeral."

Some fib. He knew why she was here and what she was doing and what she wanted to know from him.

"She called me this morning, and it threw me off. I haven't talked to her since Chase's birthday." His voice cracked. His son had been dead for ten and a half months and he still couldn't talk about him without getting emotional.

Franklin reached out, his pale blue eyes moist with concern, compassion. How could this man, the man who had held Grant when he broke down after Chase's funeral, be involved in his death? The man who bought Grant a box of Cuban cigars when Chase was born, the man who was his best man in his wedding, the man who made him a full partner? Grant had been to his home for dinner more times than he could count; Franklin's teenage daughters had babysat Chase; they'd gone on vacation together, their families! It just couldn't be. It just couldn't.

"It's difficult to have a conversation with Regan," Grant said.

"I can imagine. After…everything."

"Anyway, I shouldn't have allowed my personal life to bleed into my professional life."

"It happens, Grant. I mean, you're no CJ Burgess."

And they laughed. They were friends, they were colleagues, and Tom Granger had to be wrong about Franklin Archer knowing anything about Chase's murder. Maybe Tom was right that it was one of Grant's clients. While he couldn't imagine that Senator Burgess could hire a hit man—the thought seemed ludicrous—it seemed far more likely than Franklin Archer.

There were other clients. One of them could be responsible.

Yet Grant had doubts.

He had many doubts.

Sixteen

Regan arrived back at Tommy's at three that afternoon. Since she'd skipped lunch, she cut up some cheddar cheese and an apple, then sat at Tommy's desk. She had the owners list of the five safe deposit boxes that had been accessed by Michael Hannigan. Tommy clearly felt they were important; he'd had them listed in his notes. If only he'd written down why.

"What did you see in these people?" she muttered as she worked at Tommy's computer.

Two of the owners raised no red flags. One was a retired couple married for forty-two years. Their FBI interview revealed basic information, and they offered that the only items in the box were their passports, marriage and birth certificates, insurance records, and savings bonds. All the savings bonds were accounted for. The other individual was a divorced mom of three, a Realtor who had not even remembered that she had rented the box—inside was her wedding and engagement ring from a failed marriage that she didn't want in the house but didn't want to sell, plus all the legal paperwork from her divorce, some financial documents, and bonds for each of her children that she'd bought at their birth that would mature when they turned twenty. Again, all was accounted for.

People were…odd, Regan thought. As if papers from the divorce could curse someone or project bad karma if they were under the same roof. Maybe she'd been too matter-of-fact about her own divorce. She hadn't wanted it—but not because she had been in love with Grant, not anymore. The two of them had loved Chase, though, and that would never have changed. But without their son, they didn't have a foundation. Without a foundation, the marriage crumbled.

Grant had always been more romantic and passionate than her. He'd planned every vacation or anniversary dinner. In the beginning, he'd asked her out. He'd pursued her. She liked him, was attracted to him, they had some great conversations. He was the first to say *I love you*; he remembered important days while she relied on her calendar.

She'd always seen things clearly, and never felt the need to overanalyze anything, especially relationships. She enjoyed Grant; therefore, she must love him. Regan had been content in their marriage, but Grant had wanted more than contentment and mutual respect.

They went to counseling; that helped for a while. They were united in their love for Chase and wanted to make their marriage work. Grant worked hard at it. She didn't. In the back of her mind, she didn't understand how she could constructively work on something when she couldn't identify the problem. Grant said that just once, he'd like her to be spontaneous, to surprise him with a romantic dinner while Chase was at a sleepover. He seemed to find fault with her because she didn't think of these things herself.

She countered with the truth: he had known she wasn't spontaneous when they met. She had always been methodical. Surprises unnerved her. And she wasn't romantic—she was too practical, she supposed, to find whimsy or love in flowers or food. She felt that time was the important component—she gave Grant her time, and that said *I love you* better than a dozen roses.

Her job was part of the problem, as was his. At first he seemed to be proud of her position in the Marshals Service, but Grant didn't like when she moved over to fugitive apprehension, which sometimes necessitated overnight trips. Chase was in preschool at the time. Then Grant's work hours started to keep him away from home. He was a lawyer: he left the house by seven in the morning and was rarely home before six—but if he worked on the weekend, he did it at home. She'd made sure her schedule matched his, because *time* was valuable. But then he started working nights…then weekends…and it got to be finding time together was difficult. The last year of their marriage had been particularly rough, and they argued far too much about it. Well, *he* argued. She didn't. She laid out the situation in a matter-of-fact tone that he once told her grated on him more than fingers on a chalkboard.

"Don't you care? You stand there, talking as if you're in a fucking negotiation, never raising your voice, never showing me that you actually care that we fix this!"

"Why is yelling equal to caring? I care, Grant. I want to solve the problem. But I have to understand the problem first."

It wasn't until after their divorce that Regan finally understood why their marriage had failed. Grant sincerely believed that passion—anger, lust, spontaneity—equaled love. She didn't have the passion, she didn't raise her voice, she didn't *fight* for their marriage. That's what Grant wanted; she couldn't give it.

It was over before Chase was murdered. They simply hadn't acknowledged it.

"Stop it," Regan told herself. She wouldn't wallow in the past just because she was back in Virginia where her life had been destroyed. Being here…all the feelings, the anger, the pain, the regret…yes, she could acknowledge the past. But she could not fix it and she need not relive it. It wasn't productive. Especially now, when there was a killer to find.

She would grieve her loss for the rest of her life, but after Chase's birthday six weeks ago, after she'd sat at his grave and let herself just…*be*, her heart didn't feel quite as heavy as it had. Moving away from Virginia had been the right thing to do to steady herself, but coming back to say goodbye *again*? That put her one step further on her journey to…she still didn't know where. Though she remained in limbo, she felt like she was also moving forward. Slowly, but steadily. She had yet to figure out what to do with her life without her son.

But you will.

That's what changed six weeks ago. She believed that she would find a new path.

Regan got up from the desk chair, stretched, made a fresh pot of coffee. She couldn't help Tommy if she was thinking about herself and her losses.

Once she had a mug in hand, she returned to the library and refocused on the list of bank box holders. She put aside the retired couple and the single mom. The remaining three boxes were rented by businesses.

Novak Brothers Construction was a luxury residential homebuilder that had been around for more than a decade. Its home office was in Alexandria, not far from the Arlington bank.

Delarosa Equity, LLC, was a small investing firm with

no physical street address and no public contact name. A listed PO box was in Arlington. Regan would have to request public corporate filings to get a name and phone number, but the information was public record. She made a note.

The third business was an accounting firm in DC doing business as Legacy CPA. Why would a DC-based business have a safe deposit box in a small Arlington branch office? Perhaps one of the principals of the company had a home nearby. Or they might have been a local business that had grown. It raised a red flag to Regan; perhaps it had done the same for Tommy.

She made a list of priorities—starting with Legacy, followed by the equity company, then Novak Brothers Construction.

Were one or all three businesses targeted? And if nothing was physically taken, had there been information inside valuable enough to steal? For an equity company, it could be financial. Ditto for accountants. Maybe for all three.

Regan rubbed her head. She was getting a headache. Her phone rang and she grabbed it, glad for a break.

"Regan, it's Charlie. You'll never believe it."

"I'll believe almost anything."

"Peter Grey was transferred from Cumberland to Lee Penitentiary."

"When?"

"April 29th."

"That's the day after Tommy met with him at Cumberland," she said. "That's no coincidence. Why?"

"The warden gave a nonanswer—for his safety. I pushed, and I honestly don't think he knew the reason. The order came from the court. I asked for the documents, he's sending them over in the morning."

"We need to get in there."

"And I made a call down to Lee. I'll tell you when I know anything."

Lee Penitentiary was as far southwest in Virginia as you could get and still be in the state. It would take six hours or more to drive.

"Thanks, Charlie."

"I'm heading home, but call me if you need anything."

"Appreciate it."

She ended the call and looked at the time. Five. Time to get ready for her dinner with Grant.

Seventeen

Jenna had made the right decision to visit her grandmother. She stayed longer than she planned because she honestly didn't want to go home. She was trying to time arriving home not much before Lance said he'd be there.

At four, she drove back across Bethesda to Trader Joe's and bought a few things for dinner. When she saw the fresh bell peppers on display, she decided chicken fajitas were in order. She bought what she needed, headed for home.

Maybe the FBI agents would show up today, tomorrow, next week, but she wasn't holding her breath. Agent Wexford didn't sound all that interested in what she had to say and didn't seem to think that what little she knew about Deputy Granger was relevant to what happened to him. They probably knew far more than she did, anyway, so that was a good thing, she figured. He was likely killed because of some other case. She felt bad about it—she had liked him, even if he was a bit on the intimidating side. He had genuinely seemed to care about what she had to say, and sympathized with her conflicting feelings about her sister—that she loved her sister, even if she may have committed a crime. She appreciated that he didn't pass judgment on Becca, or her.

She'd tell Lance everything over dinner, and if he thought she should talk to the US Marshals directly, she'd do it. Maybe he'd come with her for moral support. She'd like that—this whole thing had put her on edge.

As she drove, she realized how foolish it was to disappear for two nights. She hadn't told anyone where she'd been, she hadn't brought her phone, and she'd spent nearly four hundred dollars on the cabin, gas, and food. The house was hers free and clear—it had been her parents', and their insurance had covered the mortgage in full—but she was paying off her student loans and had her car payment. She couldn't just go throwing money around like that.

It was nearly five by the time she pulled up in front of her small house on a charming tree-lined street. Her parents hadn't been rich, but they had bought the three-bedroom, two-bath brick house near the Silver Springs border of Bethesda shortly after they were married—thirty-four years ago. Today it was worth well over what they paid for it.

Over the years, the house had caused friction between her and Becca. Becca had wanted to take money out of the house—she and Jenna were both listed on the deed. Jenna didn't want a mortgage. At one point, Becca had demanded to sell the house, that they should each take half the money and do what they wanted. Jenna refused. They hadn't talked for months after that, but Becca finally apologized and admitted Jenna was right, having the house was better than having the cash. Of course, Jenna forgave her—Becca was family and Jenna loved her.

But maybe Becca's constant struggle with money had contributed to whatever mess she'd gotten herself into with Michael Hannigan.

Not that she deserved to be shot in cold blood. Nothing Becca had ever done warranted being killed.

Jenna turned up the long, steep driveway and stopped at the garage door in the back. The single-car garage was cluttered with Christmas decorations and stuff she couldn't part with. A big cleanup was one of those projects she always had on her to-do list. It would be nice to have a garage to park in, especially when it was snowing.

She had two bags from Trader Joe's, and she carried them in one hand with her overnight bag slung over her other shoulder. She walked up the back stairs to the deck, then entered the door that opened into a large, bright laundry room. She'd filled this space with hanging plants and colorful artwork. If Jenna had to do chores, she wanted the space around her to be appealing.

The kitchen wasn't large—perhaps the house's only drawback—and she put her bags on the counter. When she turned around, Jenna screamed, then grabbed her mouth as if trying to push the sound back in.

Her house was a disaster.

Every drawer in the dining room hutch had been opened, some only partially closed. The cushions in the living room were pulled out. The den, on the other side of the living room—where she had a desk and floor-to-ceiling bookshelves and a rocking chair—was the worst. Papers and books littered the floor. Her computer was gone.

She didn't look through the rest of the house or even go upstairs. Instead Jenna went outside and called 911.

"I've been robbed."

Her hands were trembling, and she almost couldn't breathe.

"Please hurry, I don't know if they're still here and I'm scared."

Someone had gone through her house, her sanctuary, and destroyed her things. Tears burned in her eyes. Why?

Because of Deputy Granger's investigation?

Someone answered his phone. They know your name. They know where you live.

Jenna feared she would never be safe again.

Eighteen

Regan arrived at Buenos Gatos several minutes before seven and gratefully accepted the chips and salsa the waitress brought out. She would have enjoyed a margarita, but instead she ordered light beer. Regan loved tequila but wanted to be alert for her conversation with Grant.

She had written down several notes she wanted to address, mostly to keep them straight in her head, then pocketed her notepad so Grant didn't think she was interrogating him.

He'd accused her of that, too, whenever she had a list of questions. She hadn't seen anything wrong with keeping a running tab of things they needed to discuss—they both had busy jobs and sometimes only had an hour or two alone together in the evening—but Grant had seen it as a sign that she treated their marriage as a job or chore.

She'd reflected a lot on her marriage over the years, even before they lost Chase. Her parents had been married for more than twenty years before her mom died of cancer when Regan was in high school. Her dad was a cop, her mom a nurse. They had argued on occasion, but Regan never doubted they loved each other and their kids. They showed their love through the little things they did for each other, like when her mom would get up with her dad when he had early shift and make him breakfast, or when her dad would cook the nights her mom had a long shift. They balanced household chores in a way that seemed effortless, and Regan often caught them kissing in the kitchen or on the porch swing, holding hands, smiling at each other in a way that said they were the only two people in the world and they were happy.

Regan had never been overly demonstrative growing up—her younger brother and sister had always been far more emotional and exuberant. The ups and downs of their lives drained Regan, which could be why she shunned such behavior in her own life. Her older brother JT was more like her, though prone to being a hothead that had, fortunately, tempered once he became an adult.

Regan had always assessed a situation before acting. This made her well suited for the US Marshals Service. Experience and training had taught her to read almost any situation immediately. She didn't discuss, she acted.

She remembered a time, years ago, when Chase was four or five. Grant was having a dinner party for the partners and junior partners and significant others at their home. He was anxious about it because he'd just been promoted to full partner—with his name on the building—and he wanted the dinner to be a great success. He asked her to help.

Regan asked Grant a few questions about what he wanted from the event, who was coming, and what image he wanted to project, then she made all the plans. She hired a cleaning service, a caterer, selected the menu based on what she knew would accommodate the variety of dietary preferences, went with a "rustic elegance" theme based on the advice of the catering company, who then brought in the tables and decorations for the party of forty.

Grant was livid. He had wanted to be involved, expected her to run everything by him, not just do it herself. She asked him what he would change, and he said nothing, but that wasn't the point. She had not understood at the time, especially after the success of the event—and while she understood *now* that he had wanted *them* to make the decisions together, she knew what he wanted and had acted accordingly.

Regan now recognized the difference between walking into a hostage situation, assessing the best action for the best outcome, and planning a dinner party. But she was so used to *knowing* what to do that playing a polite game of this or that or what-if grated on her. It struck her as a waste of time. She didn't fret; she wasn't indecisive.

At least she hadn't been until now when she was no longer a marshal and had no idea what she wanted to do with the rest of her life.

She glanced at her watch. Grant was twenty minutes late, and she suspected he wasn't coming at all. No text, no message.

She called him, and he didn't answer. She left a message.

"Grant, I'll wait here for ten more minutes unless you let me know you're on your way."

Almost immediately, he texted her—too quickly for him to have listened to her message.

Sorry, I can't make it, I'm stuck at the office. I'll call you tomorrow.

She almost got up right then and drove to his office to confront him. Instead, she responded to his text, finding it suspicious, or at least odd, that he'd texted her instead of calling.

We need to talk in person. Tonight, your place.

He answered: I'll be late. I promise I'll call you tomorrow morning. I'm really sorry.

Regan didn't know what was going on, but Grant was irritating her.

Hungry, she ordered dinner. The Mexican food in Virginia was nowhere as good as the Mexican food in the Southwest, but the tacos at this little hole-in-the-wall that she and Grant had discovered early in their marriage could almost compete.

Alone at her table, Regan pulled out her notes that she'd planned to discuss with Grant—a timeline of his calls with Tommy, the empty Franklin Archer file, the questions about Brock Marsh Security, and of course the big one: What were he and Tommy working on together?

She'd planned to show Grant the three businesses and ask if any of them were familiar. She needed to know what Tommy had shared with Grant—Grant might know what information Tommy's killer had stolen. Maybe Grant knew what Peter Grey had told Tommy that led him down the rabbit hole.

That led to his murder.

Grant may, at least, get Regan to the point where Tommy had been so she could solve this…or he, too, may be in danger.

That gave her pause. Was Grant scared that he was next? If so, why wouldn't he immediately seek protection? From her…from someone else? He was a white-collar professional, hardly someone who was well versed in personal security.

But Regan's biggest question remained: Why had Tommy contacted Grant in the first place?

She finished her meal, still irritated and suspicious over Grant's cancelation. She decided to pay him a visit.

Grant didn't want to see her tonight? Tough. Regan drove straight to Alexandria—forty-five minutes from Buenos Gatos at this time of night. She was going to ask him questions. Too many facts were missing, she thought as she drove. Tommy had taken everything relevant from his files, leaving her with disconnected notes.

Her head hurt thinking about everything. Lack of sleep, grief, frustration, anger. Grant had answers, and he would damn well tell her.

When she arrived, she knocked on the door; rang the bell. She looked in his garage: his sporty Mercedes wasn't there. Maybe he'd told her the truth about working late.

She doubted it. He'd texted her because a call would mean speaking, voice inflections, stress levels. She would know whether he was lying if she heard him, and he knew that.

Could someone have responded to the text for him? That seemed unlikely, but she didn't completely discount it. She would find out tomorrow.

She almost drove by his law firm, but if he was there, she wouldn't know unless he allowed her to come up to their suites. She wouldn't be able to access the parking garage after hours, and since it was after hours, she wouldn't be allowed up without being cleared.

Frustrated, she drove back to Tommy's.

As Regan turned into Tommy's rural neighborhood, she saw bright lights in the direction of his house. She sped up, rounded the corner, and spotted two police cars and Terri's car in the driveway. Regan pulled up and slammed the car into Park, turning the ignition off at the same time. She jumped out and hurried to the front door, where a deputy stood sentry.

"I'm Regan Merritt. I'm staying here. Where's Terri?"

The deputy called into the house. "Ms. Merritt is here."

"Let her in," a male voice called.

When Regan entered, she saw Terri and her partner, Grace, standing in the foyer, speaking to another deputy. Terri saw Regan and looked relieved.

"I was so worried about you," she said.

"What happened?"

"The alarm company called—both the door wires and motion detectors went off. They called me and the sheriff's department was dispatched automatically. But whoever broke in was gone before anyone arrived."

Terri put her hand on Regan's arm. "I am so glad you weren't here."

Regan couldn't very well tell Terri she wished she *was*. She could have apprehended the intruders and maybe learned what the hell was going on.

Regan introduced herself to the deputy who identified himself as Craig Sheridan. "What was the response time?"

"Eight minutes" Sheridan said. "Alarm company has a two-minute control time—the time they attempt to notify the owner unless the panic button is hit. So ten minutes from first alarm to arrival. No one was here when we rolled up, but there is evidence of a break-in." He motioned for her to follow.

Regan glanced at Terri, but she waved her to follow the deputy, while she and Grace headed for the kitchen.

The back door was down the hall, behind the staircase. The glass had been smashed, and an intruder had entered through there. "I called in a crime scene tech, they're en route," said Sheridan. "Ms. Granger couldn't tell us if anything was missing. We did a quick walk-through. No evidence that the safe in the master closet has been tampered with. It doesn't appear as if anyone went upstairs. I found a sidearm in the nightstand: a .45 Sig Sauer."

"It belonged to Tommy. His personal firearm."

He nodded toward her holstered gun. "Is that your only weapon?"

"That I brought with me, yes. I live in Arizona."

"Ms. Granger said you're staying in the house?"

"Until Tommy's memorial service next week." She led the way to Tommy's office, worried more about information than anything valuable being stolen.

The lights were on in the office and hall; she had turned them off when she left. "Did you turn these lights on?" she asked.

"Yes, except the desk lamp was on when we arrived."

"Your crime scene people will need to dust that as well. My prints are on file. I'm former law enforcement, but I can provide them for comparison purposes."

He made a note.

"What do you think they were looking for?" he asked.

She wished she knew. She had a theory, but not something that she was confident about.

Regan walked to the desk, didn't touch anything but peered closely at the stack of paper and files on the corner of the desk—the printouts she'd brought from the Marshals office. They appeared to all be there, but the stack was askew. Someone had rifled through them.

"Is this break-in connected with Mr. Granger's murder?" Sheridan asked.

"I couldn't say for certain," she said. "But that's my hunch."

"Do you notice anything missing?"

"I don't think so. I'd have to look in his desk to make

certain." She pointed to the papers. "Someone went through these—it's likely they went through his desk. Perhaps just for information, or to take pictures of documents. I really couldn't say."

"What do you think they were after?" he asked.

She shrugged, though Regan damn well knew that whatever the intruder had been after was related to Tommy's investigation.

"I need to call the Marshals office," she said.

"I was under the impression that the FBI took jurisdiction over Granger's murder," said Sheridan.

She didn't comment. The last people she wanted to talk to were the FBI, but she might not have a choice. First things first: she pulled out her cell phone and called Charlie.

Nineteen

Madeline McKenna had thankfully convinced Grant *not* to meet with his ex-wife.

It had taken every argument in the book—and tears—to keep him at her condo with her. When he finally relented, agreed that she was right, they fell into bed together and now—after intense sex—he had fallen asleep and was blissfully unaware of what she was about to do.

She slipped out of her bed naked, pulled on a silk bathrobe in the dark, walked barefoot into the living room after silently closing the bedroom door. Grant desperately needed sleep, and he seemed to only sleep well here after sex. She would do anything for Grant; she loved him. It was as simple—and as complex—as that.

Grant should never have talked to that marshal three weeks ago. Ever since, he'd been paranoid, jumpy, tired. Grant had, of course, told her everything—how the marshal thought that he, Grant, had been the target of the assassin who'd shot and killed his son, Chase. That Granger suspected that the shooting incident was connected to the law firm based on what Madeline told Grant was the thinnest of reasons—that Adam Hannigan had once worked for

Brock Marsh Security and Brock Marsh worked primarily for Archer Warwick. That certainly didn't mean that anyone at the law firm—or one of their clients—was involved!

It was ridiculous to even think such a thing, though she couldn't say that to Grant. He had, after all, lost his dear little boy, his only child.

But she'd helped Grant because she loved him. She'd pulled all the files that he wanted, even though she knew she shouldn't. She'd hoped that the information would prove to Grant once and for all that Tom Granger was barking up the wrong tree. She even looked at the information and didn't see anything untoward, but Grant said the files may be in code.

In *code*. Like some sort of spy game. Certainly *that* theory had also come from the marshal.

Madeline felt strongly that Tom Granger had used Grant's grief, played with his heartstrings, to convince Grant to commit what really amounted to corporate espionage, of sorts. To extract files from the law firm—confidential records!—to bolster Granger's weak theory that Grant was the actual target. All on the word of a convicted killer.

A hot flash washed over her. She was guilty, too—she had retrieved some of the information for Grant. She could, ostensibly, explain it away—she was a junior partner; Grant was technically her superior. But she knew she'd done it because she wanted to show him he was wrong.

The opposite happened. Grant became *more* anxious and paranoid.

She ached for her lover. Losing his son had been awful, had nearly destroyed him. She'd been there for him, to help him pick up the pieces because his wife—now *ex-wife*—couldn't be. Not in the way he needed. And everyone believed that Regan Merritt was to blame, anyway—after all, she'd shot and killed Adam Hannigan's brother.

A tragedy all the way around. Madeline felt sympathy for Regan, though she'd never particularly liked her. After Grant's marriage to Chase's mother fell apart, he and Madeline had acted on mutual feelings. Feelings she had kept buried for years because she didn't want to be a home wrecker.

Grant needed perspective, and only she could give it to him. Tom Granger was a US marshal. He had a lot of enemies. It wasn't because of this...*investigation*, for lack of a better word...into the law firm and the private security company they hired that he ended up dead. The FBI would find Granger's killer, and when they did Grant would realize that Granger had seen conspiracies where there was nothing but a few shady clients. Nothing that would warrant murder.

Still, she was worried about Grant, especially now when his ex-wife was here, dredging up all the drama and bad feelings from last year. She wasn't concerned that they would rekindle whatever they had; Grant had told her enough about his failed marriage and ex-wife that she was secure in her belief that she was far better suited to the man than Regan Merritt had been.

Though it was close to midnight, Madeline poured a glass of white wine and sipped. She nibbled on cheese and crackers while thinking about all she could do to protect the man she loved. She'd told Grant to talk to Franklin about Granger's suspicions.

Grant didn't want to.

"Franklin is my closest friend. He gave me everything I could have dreamed of at the firm. I can't possibly accuse one of his clients—one of our clients—of using Brock

Marsh to hire Adam Hannigan unless I have proof. Such an accusation could destroy his father's legacy, the law firm. It would destroy our friendship, our business relationship, if Tom was wrong. I need more...something solid. Then I can go to Franklin, show him hard evidence, and together we'll go to the authorities."

But Franklin had perspective Grant did not. He had distance to analyze the big picture. Madeline understood why Grant was emotional; it was his son who was dead. But she was his rock. She would do what needed to be done, for both of them.

She went back to the bedroom, made sure that Grant was sleeping soundly, then closed the door and walked back down the hall to the living room, where she called Franklin's cell phone. It was late, but she knew from experience that Franklin rarely went to bed before midnight.

Franklin answered on the fourth ring, his voice quiet, and she worried she had woken him up.

"Madeline? Is something wrong?"

"I'm sorry for calling so late."

"I wasn't in bed, but Isabelle is sleeping. I'm walking down to my office."

She winced. She shouldn't have called this late.

"I wouldn't have called if it wasn't important."

"Of course, Madeline, it's fine. Is it about Grant?"

"Why do you think that?"

"He's been preoccupied the last few weeks. And our lunch with Senator Burgess today—he was off. Not his usual professional self. I almost sought you out this afternoon, but it didn't seem appropriate to discuss personal issues in the office."

She then knew she had made the right decision to call Franklin.

"I'm worried about him," she said. "He's exhausted and stressed, and I think you can help."

"Of course. Please tell me what's going on."

Madeline had thought long and hard about exactly what to say, because Franklin didn't need to know *everything*, especially about how Madeline retrieved confidential files for Grant. She didn't want to lose her job *or* her lover.

"Grant has been looking into some of the activities of Brock Marsh. He seems to think that they are more than a traditional investigative and security firm that we hire, but might be more of, what do we call them...*fixers*."

"There's nothing illegal about fixers. They solve problems. They don't break laws."

He sounded perturbed, and that was the last thing Madeline wanted.

"Of course, that's not exactly what I meant. Grant has been looking into our clients who have hired them *separate* from the law firm."

"Why would Grant be doing such a thing?"

"Deputy US Marshal Tom Granger approached Grant three weeks ago." She glanced down the hall to make sure her door was still closed. She kept her voice low. "Granger cast aspersions on Brock Marsh, enough to make Grant suspicious of their activities. I think I have dissuaded Grant's fears, but in light of Deputy Granger being killed the other day, Grant has become paranoid. Granger had a lot of enemies in his line of work, but I worry that if his ex-wife talks to Grant—" She let her voice trail off.

"What are you worried about?"

She bit her lip. She didn't want to betray Grant, but at the same time, she was *really* worried about him. "Do you remember last year when Grant's ex was positive that

Hannigan didn't kill Chase because of her job? That there was another reason?"

"Vaguely," he said. "But the FBI determined that bastard killed Chase out of revenge."

"Right. And Grant agreed with them. But I think it's always been in the back of his mind that there might be something more. Regan just wouldn't let up. When she moved it was the best thing for everyone involved."

"What are you getting at, Madeline?"

"Just—I don't think Grant should be talking to Regan. He's already on edge, and she keeps calling, wanting to meet, and I can't help but think it all has to do with Deputy Granger's murder. She's going to twist Grant all up again— that could very well be why he wasn't himself during the meeting with the senator today."

When Franklin didn't respond, Madeline feared she'd said too much.

"You're his best friend," she pleaded. "I'd hoped you might talk to him, maybe listen? See what he has to say? Alleviate his fears? I've listened, but he needs more than I can give him right now. It pains me to say that, but it's true."

"I understand the sensitive situation, and it was very kind of you to call. I sensed that Grant was struggling with something, but I had no idea he still had unresolved questions about his son's murder. Thank you, Madeline. I'll certainly speak to him tomorrow and put this matter to rest."

Twenty

Regan was pleased with how thorough the crime scene techs and sheriff's deputies were at Tommy's house. They didn't leave until after midnight. Terri and Grace were long gone, and Charlie had stayed with her until after the police left. Together they secured plywood over the broken window.

"Are you sure you are comfortable staying here alone?" Charlie asked, not for the first time.

"Yes. I'll set the alarm to alert me if anyone attempts to break in. I'm not a heavy sleeper. I know what you're thinking, Charlie, and you're right—they could return. But I won't be caught unawares."

"You must have rattled some cages."

"They seemed to be looking for information—perhaps wanting to know what *I* knew. The police dusted, but I don't expect them to find anything suspicious, the intruder—or intruders—most likely wore gloves. They checked the perimeter. The perp didn't drop his wallet or a cigarette butt or anything else that might lead to him."

"You're being sarcastic," said her longtime friend.

"I'm being realistic." She motioned for Charlie to follow her into the office, where she now started to clean the fingerprint powder with a dust rag. "There's nothing here except Tommy's computer—which he wasn't using for this investigation. I took my notes with me to dinner tonight. All that's here—well, it's not important information, but could point to what I'm looking at." She gestured to the file copies she had on the desk.

"Maybe it was a standard B and E."

"And not take his television? Electronics? He had a couple twenties in the top desk drawer; still there."

"What do you think?" Charlie asked like he knew the answer.

"They wanted to scare me *or* find out what I knew, that's why they only searched the office. They didn't take anything—there was nothing here that they couldn't have found through other means, so yeah—I think someone wanted to rattle my cage."

"They clearly don't know you."

"I know you're working on this, Charlie, but we need to talk to Peter Grey sooner rather than later. Whatever he told Tommy led him down this path, and we need that information."

"If I don't get answers in the morning, I'll go straight to DC. It may be the only way we can get in to talk to him, but even then it's a long shot."

She agreed. "You're going to tell the deputy director everything?"

"I already did. He doesn't like that Tommy was working this off-book, but he didn't ask questions that he didn't want the answers to."

"This has put you in a difficult position."

He shook his head. "No. This is about doing what is

right, and I'm with you one hundred percent—but I have to follow the rules."

"I don't expect you to break them. I'll take the heat, Charlie—not you."

"Don't worry about me. Remember, you always told me I was the diplomat." He smiled, sat down. "You need anything else? You want me to stay here tonight?"

"No. I'm fine. Really."

She sat across from him, glad to get off her feet.

"How was dinner with Grant?"

"He canceled. After I was already in Chantilly."

"Jerk," he said, then added, "Sorry."

"It was a jerk move," Regan agreed. "I'm going to see him tomorrow. At his office, unannounced. I don't know why he's being difficult about this, why he's avoiding me. Might he actually have an idea who killed Tommy? I don't know!" She leaned back into the leather chair and closed her eyes. "I don't know *what* my ex is thinking. Sometimes, I don't think I ever did."

They sat in companionable silence for a long minute. Regan considered that the two attacks against her—being followed and the break-in—were passive. No one confronted her; in fact, they intentionally *avoided* confrontation.

She worked through a rough theory in her head, then said, "The killer took whatever was important when he killed Tommy. His phone, his laptop, the files. All this?" She waved her arm around to indicate everything that had happened to *her* in the last day, "is just making sure there's nothing else that will come back on them. That's my guess."

"Them," Charlie repeated. "There's more than one person involved."

A group of people, a *conspiracy*, making sure that the truth stayed buried.

"I'm going to find the truth, Charlie. It's here, somewhere. I'll find it and I'll find Tommy's killer. And learn what really happened the day Chase was murdered—and why."

THURSDAY

Twenty-One

Nelson Lee sat on his deck, looking out at the Atlantic Ocean. The moon was rising, the ocean was calm, and he was filled with serenity as the night turned to morning. Sleep eluded him, but he didn't need sleep when he was here, at home, refilling himself with a sense of peace.

He didn't think about all the men and women he had killed, guilty or innocent.

He didn't think about the wars he had fought.

He didn't think about his past, the family that disowned him long before he started killing.

Nelson Lee didn't think about much of anything, his mind blank, only some stray thoughts about what he would pick up at the farmer's market this weekend in town. He would enjoy fresh strawberries, but last time they weren't sweet enough. Apples were good almost all year, and he thought of baking an apple pie. A classic. Or if there was a decent variety of fruit, perhaps a tart. One of his past lovers had been a chef, and he'd learned quite a bit from her.

He didn't miss Sherry. He had no regrets leaving when he did; he'd only been involved with her because of a job that had kept him in San Francisco for three months. But he did miss her cooking. Being a good student, he was now almost as good as she, though Sherry had a gift, an added *spark*, that made her desserts especially heavenly.

His phone vibrated on the table next to him. He never expected a call, but he always had his phone with him. It was 12:22 a.m.

He answered. "Yes."

"We have another job. It's urgent."

"Send me the details."

The call ended. Seconds later the details came through. Two photos.

A man and a woman. He knew them both.

After the photo was a list of addresses, prioritized. Schedules for the next twenty-four hours.

He was surprised at the targets, and little surprised him anymore. But perhaps he had expected this turn of events. Things had gotten out of hand of late, and no one liked the unpredictable.

The phone rang again. "We need this done right away. Twenty-four hours, double your fee. Murder-suicide would be ideal, but it has to be airtight."

Twenty-four hours meant Nelson should be back in time for the farmer's market on Saturday.

"Agreed," he said and ended the call.

Twenty-Two

Regan tried calling Jenna Johns again Thursday morning; again, she didn't answer. She didn't leave a message this time. She might have to drive out to Bethesda and track her down. But at this point, her best bet for information was Grant, followed by Peter Grey—provided that Charlie could get them a meeting.

She pulled into the parking garage attached to the building that housed Archer Warwick Bachman Law Offices, grabbing a ticket on the way in and tossing it on her dashboard.

She'd been here many times over the years. It was an open building and if you knew where you were going, you could go right up because the elevators were open to the public from 7:00 a.m. until 6:00 p.m. Two guards monitored the lobby and a reception desk managed package deliveries and general information. Since it was already eight in the morning, she went straight up to the top floor. Grant's law office took up the entire penthouse suite of offices.

The elevator opened into a small lobby surrounded by glass. Potted plants—real—stood sentry in each corner. Double doors straight ahead were etched in gold. Regan opened them, approaching the receptionist.

Regan recognized the thirty-something blonde. It took her just a few seconds searching her memory before saying, "Hello, Barbara. I'm here to see Grant."

If it was someone she didn't know, she would have given her first and last name. But Barbara clearly recognized her.

"Mrs. Warwick—I mean, Ms. Merritt. You're looking well. Do you have an appointment?"

"Not on the schedule, but he knows I'm coming."

Not exactly true, but he *should* have known after he didn't show at the restaurant last night.

"Of course. Let me buzz him and see if he's free."

She picked up the phone, spoke briefly and quietly. A few seconds later, she said, "Mr. Warwick's assistant will be out momentarily to escort you back."

She would have preferred to surprise Grant, but this was the second-best option.

It didn't take long before Jeff Lange, Grant's legal secretary and admin, came out and smiled. "Ms. Merritt, it is so good to see you."

She took his extended hand, shook it. Jeff had been with Grant for several years, had been over to the house when she and Grant were married. He was in his late thirties and had a wife who did something in biotechnology for a university, no kids.

"Jeff. As always, call me Regan."

"I didn't know you were in town. Grant didn't mention it."

"It was a last-minute trip."

Jeff escorted her through the maze of cubicles to the last office in the row. Grant, as one of the partners, rated a large office with two dedicated staff—Jeff and a junior legal assistant—and an office full of windows. Jeff knocked on the door but opened it without waiting for an answer.

Grant knew she was here, it wasn't like she needed to be announced.

"Thank you, Jeff," Grant said.

"Coffee? Water?" he asked.

"No, thanks," Regan said.

Jeff smiled at Regan, then closed the door behind him.

"Hi, Grant."

He stared at her for a moment and she took in the changes. Grant looked tired and he'd lost weight, at least ten pounds, and he'd never been overweight. Still, he was a handsome man. His chiseled features, dark hair graying at the sides—he would be forty next year, but it wouldn't matter. Grant had the timeless good looks of men like Cary Grant and George Clooney, the kind of man who took care of his mind and body and would turn heads well into his seventies.

Being tired wasn't unusual, especially if he was working on a complex and timely legal matter. The weight loss was out of character. Even if he was busy, Grant made a point of eating right, going to the gym three times a week, and being active on the weekends—golf, a friendly basketball game, biking, sailing. His love of the outdoors had attracted her, even though she preferred camping and hiking and Grant refused to sleep in a tent.

Now that she was here, Regan didn't know how to begin. Grant looked as uncomfortable as she felt. This was the man she had once loved, the man who had fathered her only child, the man who grieved as much as she when their son was killed. She walked over and hugged him.

He kissed her. Lightly, not a romantic kiss. He stepped away quickly, but not before she felt him trembling.

"I told you I was working, that we'd talk later," he said. "Now is not a good time."

She sat in the chair across from his desk. She wasn't leaving without answers.

"Regan—" he began.

"Sit a minute," she said quietly. "Please."

He took his desk chair, his wide desk between them. Why did he seem nervous?

She noticed a photo of him and Chase on his desk. She picked it up, stared at it. She'd taken this picture after one of Chase's baseball games. He'd been eight here, grinning ear to ear and holding up the game ball because he'd gone four-for-four at the plate including an honest triple—no errors from the other team. She put it down as if it burned her hand, spotted another photo on the credenza behind the desk—of Grant and Madeline McKenna, his girlfriend, on a sailboat.

She motioned to that photo. "How's Madeline?"

"You don't really care, do you?"

"I'm being polite. I know you're seeing her—I'm not going to fall apart. Our divorce was mutual."

"Madeline is well, thank you."

Regan had known Madeline since she began working at Archer Warwick, and always suspected Madeline took advantage of Grant's vulnerability after Chase's murder. Regan sensed that the woman had been half in love with her husband for years. But as long as Grant was happy, that's all that mattered. She had never hated him.

"Good."

"Regan, I'm serious. I *am* busy, and now isn't a good time to have a real conversation. Like I said, come to my place tonight, we'll talk."

"I've been trying to talk to you for two days. Maybe it didn't sink in: Tommy Granger was murdered."

"You told me. I'm sorry." He sounded almost cold.

"Tommy was investigating Chase's murder," she said. "I believe it's why he was killed."

Grant jumped up. "I'm not going down that dark road with you, not again. *Never* again. Is that why you wanted to meet?"

He was practically shouting. His anger reinforced Regan's calm, but his reaction was over-the-top. The fury in his voice didn't reach his eyes.

"Sit down, Grant."

He didn't. He paced behind his desk, agitated. Very unlike the man she'd been married to for twelve years. "We're not doing this, Regan. The FBI did a thorough investigation and you damn well know that Adam Hannigan killed Chase because *you* killed his brother."

Grant's comment stung. First, because she knew it wasn't true, but mostly because he believed it—or she thought he had for the last ten and a half months. If he believed the FBI story, why would he be working with Tommy?

"Tommy left a message for me the morning he was killed. He had evidence—he was going to his boss, wanted to tell me. Then he was killed. And I know that you were—"

He cut her off. "You need to go." He strode to the door, but he didn't open it.

She rose, approached him. She touched his arm and quietly said, "What's going on with you, Grant?"

He didn't respond.

"I have Tommy's calendar, his phone records. I know you—"

He grabbed her by the arms, pulled her to him, and it took all her self-control not to bring him to his knees.

He practically growled in her ear. "Shut. Up. I think my office is bugged." Then as quickly as he grabbed her, he let her go.

She processed his words. *Bugged.* What in the world was going on?

"I'm really sorry about Tom," Grant said, "but we were never friends, you know that." Grant paused, as if waiting for her to respond, but she was still processing his previous comment. "When are you going home?" he asked.

"After his memorial. It's next week."

Grant nodded. "We'll get together before you go if you'd like. Dinner maybe?"

She narrowed her eyes. "Tonight?"

"Yes, tonight is fine, unless I'm running late with this case."

"Walk me out."

He stared at her, his eyes hollow yet full of emotion—confusion, anger, concern.

"Of course," he said as if they didn't just have a very odd exchange.

He opened his door, was about to say something to Jeff, when Franklin Archer walked into Grant's outer office.

"Regan! I heard you were here. I hope you didn't plan on leaving without saying hello." Franklin smiled broadly. Franklin was the same height as Regan—five foot eight—physically fit, with thick blond hair that didn't show much gray; light, intelligent eyes; and impeccably dressed, just like Grant.

She glanced at her ex. Grant was *usually* impeccably dressed, but today his belt was black on a light suit, and the white shirt didn't quite fit the overall look. Definitely preoccupied.

"Franklin," she said and smiled, letting him hug her. "It's so good to see you."

"Grant told me a friend of yours died. I'm so sorry to hear that."

What had Grant said about Tommy? And when?

"Thank you."

"Will you be here long?"

"A week or so."

"I hope you can join Isabelle and me for dinner one evening. She asks about you all the time."

Isabelle was Franklin's wife of twenty years. They had met in college, married after they both graduated from law school. She'd been a lawyer in the firm until she decided to stay home and raise their twin daughters after an unexpected pregnancy when she was thirty-eight. Their girls were now fourteen.

"How are Isabelle and the girls?"

"Amazing. Truly—you have to see them. Isabelle would never forgive me if I didn't make you come."

"You have my number. We'll try to make it happen."

During the entire conversation, Grant looked like a deer caught in the headlights.

Franklin said, "Are you going for an early lunch?"

"No," Grant said quickly. "I'm walking Regan to the elevator."

"I won't keep you. And I will have Isabelle call, Regan." Franklin squeezed her forearm and walked away.

Grant silently walked Regan down the long corridor to the lobby and the elevator bank.

She turned to Grant and asked again, "What is going on?"

"I can't talk about it here."

"Tommy is dead," she said quietly, even though no one else was around. "He was investigating Chase's murder. I've been putting some of the pieces together, and it's suggesting that Adam Hannigan was hired to kill Chase—or you. And, Grant—I know Tommy talked to you multiple times. You *met* with him."

"Shh." He closed his eyes, shook his head.

"Talk to me, Grant."

He whispered, "Everything we believed was a lie."

"What?"

"Everything *I* believed was a lie." Grant looked like a man tortured by demons he couldn't see or control. His office was bugged. He was working with Tommy, and now Tommy was dead. Was Grant in danger, or did he think he was?

"I'm busy, Regan," he said flatly as the law office door opened.

Jeff appeared. "Grant, Mr. Montebello is holding for your 9:00 a.m. Zoom conference. Do you want me to reschedule?"

"No," Grant said. "Apologize for my tardiness. I'll be right there."

"Of course." Jeff turned and walked back into the office.

"Tonight, your place," she said.

He nodded. "Seven."

"You'd better be there, Grant."

The elevator opened and two men exited. One looked familiar to Regan, but she didn't immediately place him. She was too preoccupied with Grant's strange behavior.

"Mr. Warwick," one of the men said with a smile. This man was sharply dressed—tailored gray suit, crisp white shirt, burgundy pocket square. Cuff links winked with a lone diamond in each and the monogram JS. He was in his fifties and tan, as if he'd just returned from a trip to a tropical island—or spent some time under a tanning lamp. "Are you joining us?"

Grant stuttered, "Uh—no—um—I don't have a meeting on my schedule. Did it get missed?"

"I wasn't expecting you to, but it's always good to have your input. Grant, this is our new in-house counsel, Anthony Vance."

"Good to meet you Mr. Warwick."

The two men shook hands.

JS turned to Regan. "Mrs. Warwick?" He smiled. "It is so good to see you again. I didn't know you were back—Grant, didn't you tell me your wife moved?"

"Ex-wife," Grant said automatically.

"We've met," Regan said, extending her hand. "I'm sorry I don't remember—"

JS took her hand, shook it warmly with both of his hands. "It was several years ago, at the Godwin Group's charity ball for pediatric cancer research. My company bought a table. James Seidel."

"Oh! Yes, I had forgotten. It was a successful event, if I remember correctly—at least for me. Grant bid a bit extravagantly on the silent auction for a week in Hawaii. But he won, and it was a wonderful trip."

It had, in fact, been a bone of contention between them because she thought it ridiculous to spend three times more for a trip just because it was for charity. It had been at a time when they hadn't been wholly comfortable in their finances, and she'd felt that Grant wanted to show off to his peers. Still…it had been a surprisingly relaxing week. The only vacation they had taken without Chase since his birth—her dad and sister had flown out and stayed at the house with Chase that week, happy to have the time with him.

"I'm glad you have fond memories. I'll make sure to reserve you a seat at my table for the next fundraiser. It'll be in September, at the Sofitel in Lafayette Square."

"I'm only visiting," she said. "I moved to Arizona."

"Oh, well, it *is* for charity if you decide to fly out for the event. It was good to see you. Grant." Seidel nodded to her ex-husband. "If I need your expertise, I'll have Franklin call you in."

"Of course. Anything you need, let me know."

Franklin's assistant stepped out and Seidel and Vance followed him into the main office. When the door closed behind them, Grant breathed easier.

"What was that all about?" Regan asked.

"What? Oh—nothing."

"You were nervous."

"They're our biggest clients. Seidel, and his company BioRise Pharmaceuticals. I didn't know Franklin was meeting with them today, I should have."

He kissed her on the cheek. "Goodbye, Regan."

Before she could respond, he left her alone in the lobby.

Regan stepped into the elevator, wondering what the hell was really going on.

Twenty-Three

Regan spotted the tail as soon as she left the parking garage. It appeared to be the same or similar black SUV that she'd eluded yesterday. This time, she wanted answers.

She called Charlie as she drove at the speed limit through Arlington. She wasn't an idiot; she didn't want to lose them, but she needed backup. Unfortunately headquarters was twenty minutes away, longer with traffic, and if they behaved like yesterday, they'd turn off before she got near the courthouse.

"The SUV that followed me yesterday is back."

"Where are you now?"

"On Glebe, turning north onto Wilson."

"Head back here, I'll come out front and—"

"No, they avoided the cameras at the courthouse yesterday. I need to find out what is going on. Trap them. How fast can you get out?"

"To Arlington?"

"I'll lead them to—" She thought. "I need a place where I can box them in, no civilians."

"The frontage road south of Reagan Airport," Charlie said. "The city maintenance facility."

"Right—the back of the yard is completely fenced at the dead end, perfect."

"There are security cameras all over that area. I'm already walking out—I'll meet you there. Don't confront them alone, Regan."

"Roger that."

Regan ended the call so she could focus on driving.

In the rearview mirror, she couldn't make out anything distinctive about the occupants in the car tailing her. Both males inside wore dark clothing. The passenger appeared Asian and the driver Caucasian. She tried to get a better look at them as she turned the corner, but tinted windows made a visual difficult. No front plate and the SUV looked like the same or a similar vehicle as the first that had followed her.

She turned onto the GW Parkway heading toward Alexandria, then took the airport access road away from the airport.

The SUV was still following her. Now no one was between them. They were staying back, approximately three car lengths away. Smart. If this was a two-car tag team she may not have picked them up.

She was forced to stop at a traffic light. She almost ran it but decided this was the best way to get a good visual of the occupants. Unfortunately the driver let a little Honda get in between them.

Still, Regan could make out two men in the car, both between thirty and fifty years of age—hard to tell because both wore sunglasses, but she'd put them on the younger side. She'd never be able to pick them out from a lineup or photos.

As soon as the light turned green, she crossed the intersection, then turned south down the industrial frontage road. The Honda went straight. The SUV followed Regan.

She had to time this perfectly. The road was narrow, two cars could barely pass each other. The dead end sign loomed, along with a chain-link fence that blocked the road about fifty yards down. She pulled over in front of a tall fence; on its other side was a refinery plant that took up the bulk of the block.

She looked at her phone as they passed, hoping they'd think she was lost or calling someone. They passed her and she glanced up, barely registered a license plate, but before she could repeat it to herself, they reversed the SUV to back up, immediately recognizing that she had tricked them.

Regan spun her vehicle ninety degrees and at a slight angle, blocking their escape. The driver slammed his brakes, barely missing her car. Charlie had texted her less than a minute ago that his ETA was three minutes. She didn't think she had even that much time, but she'd try to stall.

She jumped out of the car, wished she had her Kevlar vest, but kept her vehicle between her and the men.

"Why are you following me?" she shouted. "Get out, identify yourself!" She had her hand on the butt of her gun. In training, you never drew your weapon until you were ready to shoot.

It took the driver only seconds to make a decision. He sped forward, toward the fence, then did an expert three-point turn on the narrow road. Without hesitating, he sped toward her rental car. He slowed right before he reached it, and Regan knew exactly what he was going to do. A high-speed front-end impact could set off the SUV's airbags, so he slowed, turned the wheel to the right, and hit her car at an angle, pushing it out of the way rather than ramming it.

She ran to the side of the road to avoid being hit by her own car. She wanted to shoot at the vehicle, but that would be problematic. Yes, a vehicle was considered a deadly weapon and she would have cause to shoot at it, but she wasn't a cop anymore, and he had intentionally gone to the right, not to the left where she was standing, therefore not an immediate threat. Instead, she took out her cell phone and recorded them, zooming in on the driver, hoping that somehow she could get an ID if she had a good visual of his face.

As soon as her vehicle was out of the way, they sped up and disappeared back in the direction from which they'd come.

She phoned Charlie.

"They rammed my car and turned east on Westin, heading toward either the GW Parkway or the Toll Road. Dammit, my car is in no condition to pursue."

"Are you okay?"

"I'm fine. Pissed off. Can you spot them?"

"I'm coming from the west."

"I recorded it, but I don't know that I got anything we can use."

Charlie arrived a minute later. He took one look at her rental and said, "Did you call a tow truck?"

"I will."

"I'll call the police."

"They're not going to be able to help."

"First, you'll need a police report because of the damage to the vehicle. Second, they'll be able to access the security cameras faster than I can." He gestured to cameras on the maintenance fence. "Plus, there's cameras on the corner of the intersection to the east, and on the airport access road. Maybe we'll get lucky and get a decent look at the driver's face."

He'd been wearing sunglasses, so she wasn't holding her breath. But maybe another detail would stand out—a car pass, an employee sticker, something to identify who was following her and why.

After making their respective calls and waiting for law enforcement and the tow truck, Regan told Charlie about her odd meeting with Grant.

"He said his office was *bugged*? Like, a listening device?" he asked when she was done.

"Yep."

"You think he'll show up tonight?"

She nodded. "It's his house—he'll have to come home sometime. I'll wait all night if I have to."

"Do you trust him?"

She didn't answer; she didn't know. She didn't believe that Grant had known anything about the murder of their son last year. But what about now? He was paranoid, angry, worried…did he know more? Why wouldn't he talk to the authorities? Why wouldn't he tell *her*?

Charlie continued, "Meaning, you don't think he's somehow involved…"

"No." But maybe she spoke too soon. Grant was acting suspicious, and his comment about everything he believed being a lie? What did that even mean?

"Something is going on with him," she corrected herself. "But I don't have enough information to figure it out. I will, though. I'm not leaving until he talks to me."

"Tommy had a file on Grant's boss in his office. Maybe Grant gave it to him, helped him compile it."

"I certainly plan to ask him about it," she said. "I need to track down Jenna Johns. She hasn't returned my calls, but she doesn't know me. Face-to-face, maybe at her work, would be best."

"You think she has answers?"

"All I know is that Tommy talked to her nearly a dozen times in the last three weeks, and he believed that her sister was an accomplice in the Potomac Bank robbery."

They sat there and watched as a cruiser turned toward them at the end of the street. Charlie said, "Regan, why wouldn't Grant have told you everything he knows as soon as he found out that Tommy was dead?"

Why indeed.

Twenty-Four

Grant Warwick sat in his Mercedes in the garage of Maddie's condo. She wasn't going to like his decision. He didn't like his decision. But he *hated* doing nothing.

He closed his eyes and pictured his son. His head ached; for the last three weeks he'd been reliving Chase's death.

Over the months he'd been able to compartmentalize his pain. The bad dreams weren't every night; he could function day-to-day. He could focus on Maddie, fall in love. He needed that connection, needed to be held. He could remember Chase without a constant physical ache. Until Tom Granger called him three weeks ago.

Last night at Maddie's, he'd woken up at three in the morning in a cold sweat, still feeling his son's blood on his hands.

She hadn't wanted him to leave, but he couldn't stay, not when he had so much on his mind. He went home, showered, sat in his bedroom until dawn just staring at pictures of Chase. Trying to focus on the good times, and not that god-awful last day.

I wish it had been me. It should have been me.

It had been a Saturday night. Regan was working. She

didn't generally work weekends, but that night she and Charlie North were transporting a prisoner from New York to Cumberland Penitentiary and she wouldn't be back until well after midnight. Grant didn't like it, but it was her job. She had never complained about his long hours during the week, he could hardly complain when she had to work an occasional weekend.

They golfed in the morning with friends, another father and son from Chase's school, had lunch at the golf club, then Grant dropped Chase off at a neighbor's house to swim so he could get some work done at home.

"Dad! I'm home!"

Grant looked up from his work. Six thirty! Where had the time gone?

Chase walked into his office and said, "Sorry I'm late, I lost track of time."

"So did I," Grant said.

"Pizza?" Chase said, hopefully.

"I'll put the mac and cheese that your mom made in the oven." Regan wasn't the best cook, but there were a few things she did well, like homemade mac and cheese.

"When's she going to be home?"

"After your bedtime."

"Wanna play video games?"

Grant wasn't as interested in video games as his son, but he played because Chase loved them, and Grant wanted to spend time with him.

"After dinner."

"Great! When's the mac and cheese going to be ready?"

"Forty minutes. Go take out the trash, wash up, set the table."

Chase ran out of the room. He didn't do things slow. He

was a good kid—Grant knew it. He'd seen some of his clients' kids who were constant fuck-ups. He hoped, prayed, that Chase never went down the wrong path. He knew that even good parents could raise a rotten child.

Fortunately, though he and Regan had some problems in their marriage, they agreed about how to raise Chase. Good school, be attentive, follow up with teachers, homework, grades. Encourage outside activities, like baseball, which Chase loved. Know who his friends were, friends' parents. Keep an eye on him, but give him room to be a kid.

The video games were a bit of a sticking point—Chase loved them almost as much as he loved baseball. They agreed no games during the week—even in summer—but unlimited hours on the weekends, as long as he didn't let his responsibilities slide. Fortunately, they kept busy enough on the weekends—camping, baseball, day trips, sailing— that Chase only spent a few hours playing whatever new game struck his fancy.

Balance, Grant thought. He wished Regan would find more balance in their relationship. It had just become so hard to talk to her, because she didn't understand what he wanted, what he needed from her...and he had a hard time explaining. Anytime he had a problem and just wanted to talk, she would lay out his options. He didn't want another colleague; he wanted someone to listen. *Commiserate. Be there for him as a wife, lover, friend.*

He rubbed his eyes, wrapped up the memo he'd written, sent it to Jeff to proofread and edit, then shut down the computer. Enough work. Time to spend the evening with his son.

After they cleaned up from dinner, they settled in to the family room in the back of the house. It was a large room with a pool table, comfortable sofas, and a large screen television that Chase loved playing his games on. Tall win-

dows looked out onto their deck and backyard, which was thick with trees around a wide expanse of grass. Grant wanted to put in a pool; Regan thought that was impractical. Sometimes, he just wanted her to be a little less practical and a little more fun.

It was nine and they'd been playing for an hour—Chase kept beating him—when his phone buzzed. He looked down and frowned. *Dammit.*

"What's wrong?" Chase asked.

"Your mom is going to be later than she thought. They're still two hours out of Cumberland."

"What'd the guy do?"

"You don't want to know."

"Is it the guy who killed his wife or is it the pedophile that mom's been tracking for three months?"

Grant didn't like that Chase was so interested in Regan's job, or that he even knew what a pedophile was. He had agreed with Regan's advice that they shelter Chase until he started asking questions, then to answer honestly, with age-appropriate answers. He'd started asking questions early, and Regan answered them. Sometimes Grant thought she was too blunt and straightforward, but Chase seemed to respond better to a direct approach.

Grant was always uncomfortable with these discussions. Things had been...tense...between him and Regan for the last year. It wasn't the first time. Maybe going back to the marriage counselor was the answer. It had worked before, it might work again. Or maybe it was just him, maybe he was too fucking needy, wanting more of Regan's affection. She just wasn't an emotionally demonstrative woman, and it had been grating on him more now than when they first married.

"Dad?" Chase pushed. "Is something else wrong?"

He shook his head. "No, nothing, kiddo. Your mom is transporting the guy who killed his wife. He fled to avoid arrest, the marshals caught up to him in Albany, and she's bringing him back."

"Okay," Chase said. "Another game?"

"Sure. How about if I make some popcorn?" He started to get up off the couch.

"I'll do it," Chase said, jumping up.

Everything happened so fast, but Grant remembered it in slow motion.

The breaking of glass—a cracking sound. Chase falling to the floor. Grant thought he'd tripped.

"Chase? You okay?"

At first Grant didn't see the blood. Chase was wearing a red Nationals T-shirt with World Series Champs in bold white letters across the front. Then the letters started bleeding red. Blending with the shirt. Darker red, spreading, and Grant stared. His head was ringing and he could have stared at his son for one second or one hour, he didn't know. It was as if time stopped. That minute, that moment, lasted for eternity and disappeared too fast.

"Chase? Chase!" He collapsed to the floor, grabbed his son's body. Looked in his face, tried to figure out what was going on. He didn't immediately think that his son had been shot. He didn't immediately realize what had happened.

He felt the blood. On his chest. On his back as the bullet had ripped through his son's skinny body. And Chase's eyes. His green eyes, just like Regan's, open. Unseeing.

Grant screamed. Pain and rage and grief; he howled like an animal. He held his son's body close. Held him as every cell in his body ached in an unbearable pain as the truth hit him. That his son was dead. That his son was dead in his arms. He'd never hear his voice, his laugh, see his smile, *tell him to slow down as he ran up the stairs, or high-five him after a ball game.*

Chase was not just gone, he was dead.

In that moment, Grant wanted to be dead with his son.

Grant knocked on the door to Maddie's condo at twelve thirty that afternoon, then used his key to let himself in. She had arrived twenty minutes before he had; it wasn't that their relationship was secret around the office— Franklin of course knew, Jeff, Maddie's assistant, and probably most everyone else—but they nevertheless maintained a professional working relationship during business hours.

Maddie was everything that Regan hadn't been. She was passionate; she loved him and showed him every day that she cared. She sent him sweet texts, surprised him with dinner or a date night or with sex games. Spontaneous and bold and beautiful.

Grant had loved his ex-wife, but he needed more than she could give him. Maddie gave him all that he had wanted.

Only now, for the first time, he wished—for just this day—that Maddie could put her emotions and fears aside and assess this turn of events with a practical, clinical eye. His emotions were too raw, too troubled, and he needed someone to support his decision, not reinforce his doubts.

"Maddie, it's me," he called out.

She stepped from the kitchen into her living room holding a glass of white wine. She never drank during the day. Had he done that? Made her stress and worry so much that she was drinking alone at lunch?

She stared at him for ten seconds, shook her head, and gulped half her wine. "I knew it," she said, her voice cracking.

"Maddie, let's just talk this through again."

"We talked last night, and you agreed that you would

not tell your ex-wife anything. That we would just forget everything, and it will *go away*."

That was true, but when he went home after the nightmare, he couldn't sleep. After seeing Regan this morning, he realized he couldn't put everything in the past behind him. There were unanswered questions—questions Grant hadn't realized until now that he needed answers for.

If Tom Granger was right and Chase was murdered in his place—dead because the shooter missed Grant—then Grant needed to know who was behind it. Had Tom figured it out? Was that why he was killed? Would Grant be next on the list? If he learned the truth, would Grant be dead, too?

But then you would know. You'll be dead, but you'll know, and you need to know.

Grant didn't have a death wish, but he also couldn't walk away. The realization probably came too late, as everything seemed to be spiraling out of control. Tom hadn't shared with him a name, but Regan was a smart woman. She would learn what Tom did. Would she die, too? Could Grant live with her death on his conscience?

Yes…and no. He could live with it if he gave her everything he knew, so she went into this investigation, into Tom's investigation, with eyes wide open. She could take precautions. She was trained, she was smart, she was determined.

Granger was trained and smart and determined, too. And he's dead.

Grant said, "Regan came by the office this morning."

"I know," Maddie snapped. "Everyone is talking about it!"

Great, he thought. He didn't need the gossip, but mostly, he didn't need anyone to become suspicious. Franklin… Grant just couldn't believe his friend and mentor Franklin Archer was behind any of this. But one of his clients? Yes…

that Grant could see. Because Franklin had taken on some sketchy clients. Rich, powerful, but sketchy just the same.

"Grant, tell that nosy woman *nothing*!" Maddie pushed. "You have to just... I don't know, tell her that you don't know anything!"

"She knows Granger called me, that we met. Regan is not going to back down. Come with me tonight, talk to Regan with me. She can get you protection—"

"No fucking way am I saying a single word. I should *never* have helped you gather the information about Brock Marsh. *Never*. It's only going to hurt the firm. Do you actually think that *Franklin*, your closest friend and confidante, is somehow... I don't know...*privy* to what happened to Chase?"

"I don't know."

"You don't *know*? Don't you think you *should* know before you make accusations that will ruin his life, the firm, *you* if they are untrue?"

He had thought about that, which was why sleep was rare these last three weeks. "Fresh set of eyes..."

"No! You don't see it, Grant! I love you, I *love* you, more than I've ever loved anyone. You know that. So know that I'm telling you this as the woman who cares for you. You're going off the deep end. Granger—" she spat out his name as if it tasted foul "—was wrapped up in an insane conspiracy theory and used your pain and anger about what happened to Chase to get you to help him. Why? I don't know! But you saw the records, there's nothing there!"

"We think the records were coded. Tom was analyzing them, trying to figure out—"

"Do you hear yourself?"

He did hear himself, and he didn't know why Maddie was so angry.

"Regan will be discreet."

Maddie barked out a laugh, drained the rest of her wine, and for a split second, Grant thought she was going to throw the glass across the room. Instead, she firmly placed it on the table and paced. "As far as anyone is concerned, I know nothing. I will swear with my hand on the Bible that I don't know *anything* about *anything.* And if you were smart, if you cared at all about yourself—if you cared about *me!*— you'd do the same."

Last night Grant had been as scared as Maddie after hearing about Granger's death. Today, Maddie wasn't scared—she was enraged. Maybe it was a protective reaction to fear. That, he could see. But would she actually lie to protect Chase's killer? Would she claim she didn't know anything when, in fact, she'd helped him extract the files?

He didn't want to hurt Maddie. If this was about anything—*anything*—other than his son's murder, he would do exactly what Maddie wanted.

"Regan isn't going to back down. If I don't talk to her tonight, tell her why she found my number in Tom's files, she'll come back to the office, possibly make a scene. I need to tell her what I know."

"I'm a *junior partner*! You might survive the fallout, but I won't, I'll be fired, lose my license!"

"I'll do everything in my power to make sure that doesn't happen. I'll protect you." He paused. "I'll say, under oath, that I accessed the files using your password. I will swear that you knew nothing about what I was doing."

If that's what Maddie needed, he'd give it to her. He owed her that much, though it pained him that she wouldn't stand with him.

She didn't say anything. Did she not believe him? He moved closer to her. "I love you, Maddie. This isn't going away. Come with me tonight. United, we're stronger." He touched her cheek. Tears sprang to her eyes.

"Don't cry, baby," he said, kissed her lightly. Tasted the wine on her lips. "I'll pick you up tonight, six thirty? Pack a bag, you'll stay with me tonight. Longer, if you want. Okay? We'll talk to Regan together."

"I—I really don't want any part of this," she said, her voice cracking. She clung to him. "Tom Granger was *killed*. He was a marshal and he's dead. What if… God, what if Brock Marsh really is behind all this? And they know you were helping him? What if they come after the firm, if we expose them? Franklin? You? Me?"

The words were like a gut punch, but Grant had to stand firm.

"We have some of the pieces, Tom had other pieces, and between us, we'll get real answers about what happened to my son. I want you with me. Regan will have questions, and you understand the accounting better than me. Please. I need you on this."

She wiped away tears. "I really don't want to do this. I don't think there's anything here, but if I'm wrong, if Brock Marsh is who Granger thinks they are, we're all in danger."

"Trust me," he said. "I'll pick you up, we'll do this together. Then—we'll disappear for a couple of days, okay? Once this is behind me, I can finally move forward. Once I know the truth about Chase, I can breathe again."

He kissed her, hugged her trembling body.

He was just as scared as she was, but this was the right thing to do.

Twenty-Five

Jenna Johns thanked Lance for the hundredth time for letting her stay at his place last night, after she'd found her place ransacked. He'd even slept on the couch and given her his bed, which she hadn't wanted but couldn't deter him.

Now they ate peanut butter and jelly sandwiches for lunch. Lance had a morning class and came back to talk to her before he had to go back to campus. She'd called in sick at the hospital, which she hated doing, but her mind wasn't on her job and she didn't want to make a mistake that might get someone hurt.

"Stop," he told her. "I mean it. You needed help—I helped. End of story." He reached out and touched her hand. The gesture felt intimate, and she didn't know quite what to make of it. "Jenna, I'm going to help you get through this. You should never feel violated and scared like this. You can stay here as long as you need."

"I appreciate that," she said, picking up their plates and glasses and rinsing them in the sink. "But I need to go back. At least…for the afternoon. I told the police what I thought was missing—my laptop, my cell phone—but I need to go through more thoroughly and make sure that nothing else was taken. I didn't even think to check my jewelry box—my mother's wedding and engagement rings were there. They're not worth a lot, but…"

"They have sentimental value," he finished for her.

"Yeah."

"I'll take you, walk through the house, make sure it's secure. Okay? Then when I'm done with classes, I'll come back. You can decide if you want me to stay at your place or you want to come back here."

"You don't have to—"

"I *want* to."

She smiled. "Thank you."

Yesterday, Lance had stayed with her as she gave the police a report about the break-in. He'd driven her to his place because she was too jittery to drive herself. Now he took her back and like he promised, walked through her house and made sure all the windows and doors were secure.

"Don't answer the door. If anyone comes by that you don't know, call the police immediately," he said. "Okay? Better to feel embarrassed than have something bad happen."

"Okay," she said, and smiled to show him that she was brave. "Thank you."

"Stop thanking me!" He said it good-naturedly then he leaned over and kissed her lightly, quickly, on the lips. It surprised her and made her feel warm at the same time. "My classes are over at five thirty. Text me if you need me before then."

He left, making the kiss totally natural and not awkward, and she was grateful.

And she hoped he did it again.

Maybe *she* would kiss *him* next time.

After Lance left, she locked the door behind him, looked again at her house. The tears burned, but she did *not* cry.

She had chores to do—cleaning up the mess that the thieves had made, making sure that they hadn't taken anything else.

The police said that they suspected teenagers or young adults had grabbed the easy-to-fence valuables, then messed up her house because they were brats. She'd told them that she was worried because she might have information about the murder of a US marshal, but the officer started asking questions. Like if she'd been threatened, followed, had threatening emails or phone messages. And the answer was always no. He promised to add her house on the regular patrol, that the police would drive by every hour or two for the next couple days, but he didn't seem to be concerned. So maybe it was just a coincidence.

She didn't think it was a coincidence, but the more she talked, the more like an idiot she sounded because he was right—she hadn't been threatened. She hadn't been followed.

Jenna had a Find-Your-Phone feature and last night had logged in to her account on Lance's computer, but the phone didn't show up anywhere but her house, and she knew it wasn't there. Dammit. She erased the phone's contents remotely, so that when the jerks who stole her phone booted it up again, no one would be able to steal her personal data.

After she checked her jewelry box and determined that nothing had been taken, she breathed easier. The police were probably right—some teenagers taking advantage of the fact that she hadn't been home.

Jenna grabbed a garbage bag from under the kitchen sink and her tray of cleaning supplies and headed to her den to start cleaning. She worked fast and furious, getting her frustrations out at the thieves as she tossed papers, re-organized books, swept the hardwood floor, polished her bookshelves. Then the living room, which wasn't as messy, but she vacuumed and dusted and straightened the cushions. An hour later she headed upstairs to change the sheets on her bed and start a load of laundry. Then she would tackle the kitchen. The thieves hadn't made a mess there, but it needed a good wipe-down.

After she finished making her bed with clean sheets, she gathered the dirties in her laundry basket and heard a car drive up in front of the house. Looking out her bed-room window, Jenna saw two men in suits and sunglasses exit a black Suburban and slowly walk up the steps to her small porch.

FBI agents? They looked the part, she thought, though they also looked totally intimidating. She wished one of them was a female agent; it'd make her feel more comfort-able. She also wished Lance was still here for moral sup-port, but he was in the middle of class.

They knocked on the door as she was walking down-stairs. Jenna didn't know why she was nervous. *She* hadn't done anything wrong. She'd phoned the authorities because she thought she *might* have information that could help them find out who killed Deputy Granger. So she shouldn't feel nervous or worried or scared, right?

She said through the door, "Who is it?"

"Agent Richman from the FBI."

"Can I see some identification?" She looked out the side window. The men were crowding her door. Her deadbolt was already loose from the break-in yesterday. Why was she so damn freaked out?

One of the agents pulled out his wallet and flipped to a

shiny badge that he held at the window for less than two seconds, she couldn't even read what was on it.

"What about your FBI credentials?" she said.

The men looked at each other.

"Agent Wexford told me to ask for credentials," she stated.

Neither of them were reaching for their wallets again. Her heart pounded and she willed it to stop thudding, she could hardly hear herself think.

She was pretty certain these two men *weren't* FBI agents.

"We're here to discuss the call you made to the hotline, about US Marshal Thomas Granger and his unauthorized investigation. You wanted to speak to us."

She said, trying to make her voice light and casual, "I'll call Agent Wexford, just to check. I'm sure everything's fine. Hold on." Jenna was surprised that her voice was so steady.

She walked slowly away from the door, so they couldn't see her through the narrow glass window in the entry. She grabbed her purse from the dining room table and ran out the back door. Jumped into her car. Thanked God that she had bought a new car two years ago with a keyless fob that she always had in her purse. No fumbling with keys, and her Nissan hatchback started with a push of the button. She released the emergency brake and backed as fast as she dared down the long steep driveway.

Out of the corner of her eye she saw the two men running off her porch, down the stairs, and across the sloping grass. They were both fast and they looked angry. When she reached the end of her driveway and was backing into the street, the shorter, skinnier, faster man jumped on the hood of her car.

Jenna screamed, slammed on the brakes, and he rolled off and hit the pavement with a thud.

She released the brake and backed up again as the second, taller man caught up with her. He had a gun out, and she didn't even consider stopping or asking herself why. She turned the car around a complete one-eighty while backing up, almost hit a tree, then put it in Drive and floored it. Her car jerked at the sudden shift change, then responded.

In her rearview mirror, the men were getting into their SUV.

Their vehicle had no license plates. Didn't federal agents have government plates?

They're not FBI agents! Maybe they're the ones who broke into your house!

She knew this neighborhood better than anyone—she'd grown up here. Jenna sped down the street, not slowing at the stop sign after a quick look to make sure no people were around, then she turned right and sped up. Two blocks later she ran a red light, barely missing a minivan that was just starting through the intersection, eliciting the angry blare of horns.

She didn't care. Her heart thudded, her hands shook, all the way to the freeway. She spared one glance behind her; her pursuers had stopped at the light.

Thank God thank God thank God.

She went north on the interstate instead of south, because south meant she would have to wait at a light. North, she just turned and merged.

She got off at the next exit, only a mile down. She prayed hard that they were so far behind that they didn't see her exit.

Then Jenna drove under the Beltway and headed west,

taking a variety of turns through neighborhoods she was less familiar with, until she reached the nature center off Democracy Boulevard.

She didn't know exactly why she went there, except that she had volunteered there in high school for a semester because she had a crush on a senior named James. James had been her first real crush, her first kiss, and her first breakup, such as it was. But it wasn't a bad thing, and she and James still chatted on social media from time to time. He'd moved to England after college and had been living with a girl for the last three years, they both worked with the park system doing something outdoorsy, she didn't remember what.

But Jenna knew the center and its grounds well, and while most of the parking was in the front, employees parked in the back lot, which couldn't be seen from the road. She drove around and parked. The center was open only in the morning for school field trips, and on the weekends for the general public.

No one was there. But no one could see her if they were driving by, either. She didn't care if they had security cameras because she wouldn't mind talking to one of the nice officers from yesterday, telling him everything, and hoping he'd find her a safe place to stay. But she didn't see any on the building.

She turned off her car and sat, trying to control her emotions, figure out what was going on—and who she might call for help.

Not the FBI. How did those men know where she lived? How did they know that the FBI were going to send two agents to talk to her?

Maybe they really were federal agents...

No, they weren't. They didn't show ID and they jumped on her car then followed her! It was surreal.

She needed to call Lance, tell him what happened, tell him *not* to go to her house!

She searched her purse for her new flip phone. It wasn't there! She dumped the contents on the passenger seat, looked through all the pockets...and remembered she'd left it on her desk to charge.

She put her head down on the steering wheel and cried.

Had she actually run from FBI agents? Hit one of them with her car?

Who could she call? Who could she trust?

The only person she trusted was Lance, but she didn't want to get him in trouble or hurt for helping her. Still... she should wait until he got out of class, then talk to him in person.

She sat there, wiping the tears from her face, looking at her dashboard clock. She had two hours...how would she find him? She didn't know where he parked, what specific class he had, where he would be when he got out at 5:30.

The hospital! The hospital would be safe—Jenna knew everyone there; they knew her. She'd call him from there, tell him what happened. Then she'd call the Bethesda police and tell *them* what happened. They'd figure out if those agents were real or not.

Not real agents.

She liked having a plan. Resolved, she headed straight for the hospital.

But as soon as she turned down the street toward the employee parking entrance, she saw the black SUV. Inside were the two goons who had shown up at her house pretending to be FBI agents.

They spotted her two seconds after she saw them. Jenna

saw them looking at her car, and the passenger pointing right at her. The SUV engine roared, and their deathly black vehicle charged right at her.

Jenna spun her steering wheel while slamming on the gas, turning around her vehicle without hesitation, in the process almost sideswiping a car parked on the street. She floored it, hoping, praying, she could get away.

Twenty-Six

Regan really, really hated the traffic that now seemed to go in every direction, not just flowing out of DC and Arlington into the suburbs. Her GPS told her it would take more than an hour to get to Grant's place for a drive that should have taken thirty minutes. But there was no getting around it; she was going to see him tonight and not leave until he told her what he and Tommy had been doing.

Tommy was dead and she feared that Grant might also be in danger. She just couldn't figure out *why*. What had they found and why hadn't Grant told her immediately?

Her cell phone rang and it was Terri Granger, returning her call.

"I'm sorry I couldn't get back to you sooner," Terri said. "I had rounds all afternoon—this is my first real break of the day."

"I told you it wasn't urgent," Regan said. "And it doesn't really have anything to do with Tommy's murder. It's more about your line of work."

"Oh?"

"Are you involved in the Godwin Group?"

"Involved? No, but I'm very familiar with their work.

They raise money for pediatric cancer research. I believe they're the number-two-ranked private donor in the country."

"Do you know any of the principals? Someone I might be able to talk to about their donors?"

"Most charitable groups won't talk about their donors. Privacy rights and all that. But most of the donors are listed on their webpage. Why are you interested?"

"The name came up today, and I'm just crossing *t*'s. I was talking to my ex-husband at his office and the head of BioRise Pharmaceuticals came in, and I remembered meeting him at a charity event that the Godwin Group put on."

"BioRise? That's not surprising. They specialize in cancer research and therapeutics, and have done some groundbreaking research into actual cures."

"Curing cancer?" Regan asked, surprised.

"Not cancer as a whole, but specific cancers. They uncovered a gene that is involved in a rare cancer, and developed a screening test that is ninety percent effective. If we can prescreen for high-risk patients, we can intervene at the earliest stages."

"Like if a woman is at high-risk for breast cancer, we know because there's a history in her family?"

"Similar, but more focused. Soon, we'll be able to screen children for a large range of potential cancers and genetic disorders that don't manifest until later in life. Once we can identify the at-risk population, we can develop therapeutics to stop the cancers or disease before they develop. It's very state-of-the-art gene therapy and I'm cautiously optimistic."

Regan mulled that information over, but she didn't know if it was important. She might ask Grant more about BioRise and Seidel when she talked to him tonight.

"BioRise is a pioneer in this field," Terri continued, "and

I'm, personally, very excited by the early trials that they've conducted. Of course it will take years before we have answers, but I believe it'll be in my lifetime. They will save lives."

"Good to know," she said.

"How are you?" Terri asked.

"I should be asking you that question."

"I'm okay, and I have Grace. Are you sure you're okay staying at the house alone? Sometimes the memories—they can be haunting."

Had Tommy shared with his sister anything about his more personal relationship with Regan? That made her a bit uncomfortable. What could she say?

"Actually," Regan said, "it's been cathartic. I mean, I miss him—I'm always going to miss Tommy, he was one of my best friends and my mentor. But I feel… I guess… at peace being in his house, with his things, knowing that I'm going to solve his murder."

"You think you will?"

"Yes."

"Do you know—"

"No," Regan interrupted. "I don't have answers yet. But I'm making progress. I know what he was doing, what he was looking at, and I'm quickly retracing his steps. I'm not leaving until I know who killed him, Terri. I promise."

"Tommy is watching over you," Terri said. "I know my brother wasn't very spiritual, but he was a good man and I know he's in Heaven and I know that he's watching out for both of us. I can feel it. I can feel him. Be careful."

"Thank you. For what it's worth, I can feel him, too."

She ended the call and felt, oddly, at peace after talking to Terri. She had that way about her…her calm was contagious.

Regan decided she needed the rest of the drive to clear her mind so that when she talked to Grant, she didn't have any of the baggage rattling around. She pushed the CD button and listened to what Tommy had in his truck—it was Crosby, Stills & Nash. And she smiled, and remembered better times.

Shortly after Chase's murder, Grant had moved out of their house and bought the townhouse in Alexandria with a view of the Potomac River, just north of Founders Park. It was twenty minutes from his office in a quaint, exclusive neighborhood. Four stories, with the bottom floor being the tandem garage. Regan had been here a few times, but it had always been awkward—this was Grant, post marriage: sterile house, masculine furnishings, everything new.

She was only a few minutes early, but Grant wasn't home. She waited a minute, then decided she was too irritated—and yes, angry—that he was making her wait. That he was delaying the inevitable. And fearing he might not show up at all.

She didn't have the keys to his place, but there was an electronic keypad on his garage door. Grant was a creature of habit. She'd explained to him more than once the importance of not using key dates or names as his passwords. When they first met, he'd used his childhood address as his pin and the street and zip code as his computer password.

He hadn't gotten much better over the years. It took her two tries to decode the garage. Chase's birthday didn't work—that was too obvious, but one she thought he'd revert to.

Instead, he'd gone back to his childhood address. 9051. "Oh, Grant," she muttered.

She hadn't been able to shake how different he had

looked that morning. Scared, worried, almost...*lost*. Still, the idea that his office was bugged seemed nuts. Who wanted to listen to his conversations? A client or one of his partners? An associate? For how long? And why?

She made sure the garage door closed behind her, then walked up the stairs to the first floor. A small parlor in the front—not the main living room, but what could be used as an office or a waiting room if someone had a home-based business. Two narrow bedrooms in the back, a bathroom. Straight up from the front door was a wide staircase leading to the main floor, which had a living room, dining room, and a large gourmet kitchen. Neither she nor Grant had been great chefs, though she had a few things she cooked well. She was better at soups and casseroles than she was at four-course meals. But Grant didn't cook much at all. She opened his refrigerator and confirmed her suspicion that he hadn't become a gourmet chef after their divorce: wine, water, juice, fruit, and several boxes of leftover takeout.

Debating with herself for about a minute, Regan went up to the top floor to further explore. If he got home now, it would be difficult to explain what she was doing.

Yes, Grant, I'm snooping because you've been a dick since I came back to Virginia and I want to know what you're hiding.

But she pushed aside any residual guilt.

Everything in the house was expensive, well-appointed. Grant had always had expensive tastes. She didn't intend to go into his bedroom; it felt too intimate and personal. Odd, considering he'd been the only man she'd slept with in more than a decade, until Tommy six weeks ago.

What might be of interest to her was likely in his home office.

But something through the open bedroom door caught

her eye and she looked again. On a narrow wall to the left of a wardrobe cabinet were photos of Chase.

She couldn't *not* look at them.

The collection had been professionally framed, but—other than his grinning first grade school photo where he had no front teeth, which had always been both her and Grant's favorite—the photos were casual. Chase playing baseball. Chase at three with their family dog, who had died two years before Chase was killed. Chase at seven flying a kite in the park, his hair—a little too long back then—flying around his face as his wide eyes tracked the kite. Chase at Christmas opening a long, narrow box that had held a coveted bat. Because he would be playing with the older kids.

In his last Little League season.

There was even a framed selfie of the three of them camping in the Blue Ridge Mountains the summer after Chase turned eight, one of her favorite vacation memories. It had probably been the happiest year of their marriage. Grant had landed several big clients for the law firm, she was happily working in fugitive apprehension, Chase was doing well in school and excelling in baseball, they had friends and socialized often—something Grant enjoyed more than she did. He'd compromised by agreeing to small parties and dinners, not the big events that stressed Regan out. She much preferred talking with two or three couples in an evening than making small talk with dozens.

Her eyes burned. There had been so much hate and anger between her and Grant during the divorce, but it hadn't stopped him from at least reflecting on what had been good in their marriage, the times that had formed these wonderful memories...bittersweet as they were now.

The divorce had been nasty. Not because they fought

over the house or the things inside or money, but because of what Grant had said to her after Chase's funeral. That he blamed her for their son's death. His words more than anything had twisted inside her, dark and poisonous and painful. She knew he meant them. Her own guilt—of not being home when Chase was killed, of the possibility that he was killed because of her job—had most definitely contributed to her overwhelming sorrow and depression.

And then, six weeks ago, he said the three words she hadn't realized she needed to hear. As they sat at Chase's grave, he took her hand and she didn't pull away, she didn't flinch. He looked at her, waited until she looked at him, and said, "I am sorry."

She knew what he meant and why, and she had nodded, accepting the apology. She hadn't thought she needed anything from Grant, but she had. Maybe that's why six weeks ago she'd told Tommy she wasn't going to stay. Because *I am sorry* was the closure she had needed to bid farewell to this chapter of her life.

She walked away from the wall of photos. Regrets and what-ifs and anger and sorrow about Chase—none of it would help her find who killed Tommy.

Put it away. Put it all away and focus.

She went to Grant's office, grounded herself in the reason she was here: How was Grant helping Tommy in his investigation? Did Grant have the same information Tommy had, information that was now missing and presumably in the hands of his killer? Was the empty file labeled Franklin Archer important? If so, what had been in it? Was Franklin involved in any way in the death of their son?

She sat at Grant's tidy desk, nothing on it except his laptop, an attached mouse, and a photo of him and Chase at a Nationals game when Chase was six. That photo cut her—

it was a game she was supposed to be at but had missed because of a prison break at Lee Penitentiary and they'd needed all hands on deck.

She didn't attempt to access his laptop. That was crossing a line she wasn't ready to cross just yet. The top drawers were unlocked, but they didn't have anything of value—notepads, bills, pens. The bottom right drawer was locked.

Desk locks were notoriously flimsy; it took her only a few seconds to pop it using a letter opener. So maybe the lines for her were getting blurry, because she had no qualms about searching his desk.

Inside were files, including a file on Franklin Archer that on the outside was the same type of file that was empty at Tommy's house. But this file was full of court documents, lists of clients, financial sheets, and more.

She took a picture with her phone of a page inside the folder that listed many, if not all, of Archer Warwick's clients in Grant's small perfect printing. She saw Senator Burgess—she had met him many times over the years. BioRise Pharmaceuticals. A mining company in West Virginia, a host of other politicians and corporations—most of them on the larger scale. Corporations that would have their own in-house lawyers, like BioRise, but might need outside counsel for a host of other things.

On another sheet of paper were rows of numbers. She had no idea what the numbers represented—there were no dollar signs, they weren't addresses or phone numbers or anything obvious like social security numbers. She took a picture of that page, too. But there were too many pages to copy them all, and Grant could be home any minute. She would definitely be asking him about this.

She glanced at her watch. He was already ten minutes late. She texted him.

I'm here, where are you?

He didn't answer. She put the phone on his desk and looked through the rest of the drawer. Mostly there were legal notes from client meetings, and she didn't feel comfortable looking through them.

She closed the right drawer, opened the drawer on the left. Here were his personal financial documents—bank statements, tax records, receipts, the like. She almost closed it when she saw a folder with her name on the flap. It stood out to her in the sea of folders labeled Tax Receipts, Auto Insurance, Homeowners Insurance, Bank Statements, Regan Merritt, 401K Documents.

She pulled out the folder with her name and opened it. She expected their divorce papers, or maybe even a copy of their marriage certificate for nostalgia purposes. But all that was in the file was a square envelope with her name written in Grant's writing on the front.

Her stomach twisted. Shortly after she found out she was pregnant with Chase, she had written her unborn son a letter. It was short, full of hopes and dreams for him, talking about how she and his dad met, what they were doing in their lives, and why they were looking forward to his birth because it would complete their family. Grant had come in as she was folding it up, and she told him that her mom had written individual letters to Regan and her siblings after she was diagnosed with cancer. It wasn't until she died that their dad had given them the letters. Regan, who wasn't generally nostalgic, had wanted to do the same for Chase, but instead of a letter after trauma, she wanted to write a letter several times throughout his life.

He'd never read the seven letters she'd penned.

She steeled herself against the emotions threatening to unleash themselves.

She should put the letter back. It could be something he'd written in the event of his death, something that she'd get years from now, if ever.

Yet…why would it be here, alone, and not with his will?

She turned it over. It wasn't sealed. On the back there was a date.

May 1.

The day after Tommy and Grant had met in person, three weeks ago.

She pulled out the letter written on Grant's personal stationery, unfolded it. She'd always thought it was a bit old-fashioned to have personal stationery—she thought her mother was the last person to always send out personalized thank-you notes—but realized that the nod to the past built both personal and professional relationships, distinguishing Grant from his peers in a positive way.

In Grant's perfect, small cursive he wrote:

April 2

Dear Regan—

So he'd started the letter nearly a month before he put it in the envelope. She started with the main part of the letter.

Today at Chase's grave, I was reminded why I fell in love with you. And it hit me, everything that I said and did to you last year. Today, your quiet grief hit me, and I realized how cruel and selfish I was after Chase's death. You suffered as I suffered, but I couldn't see through my own rage and sorrow.

I am so, so sorry.

Together, we had Chase. For too short a time, we had a wonderful boy we both loved. I hope that now, after time and perspective, that when we see each other, we'll remember the good. Even if it's once a year, at our son's grave.

Grant had stopped there. Maybe he'd intended to write more, maybe he didn't, but an inch down he'd written *May 1*, followed by:

I blamed you for the longest time, as if it were your job that killed our boy. Even last month, when I saw you at Chase's grave, I thought that I could now forgive you. As if you had anything to be forgiven for!

I don't know what happened. But everything I believed then…it was a lie. Tom has a wild theory, and I don't know that I fully believe him…yet…something he said has me thinking, and I fear that he's right.

And if Tom is right, then I was very, very wrong.

—GRW

Regan frowned. What did Grant mean by that?

She remembered what he'd said to her at his office.

Everything we believed was a lie.

Regan put the letter in her pocket, looked at her watch. Grant was nearly thirty minutes late. He hadn't returned her text message.

She called him.

His phone went to voicemail. Her heart pounded as she feared for him. With everything going on, the risk to Grant had been in the back of her mind. She should have pushed him harder this morning at his office, made him leave the building with her, forced him to talk to her.

Where was he?

Madeline.

His girlfriend. Did he think he could hide there? That she wouldn't know where to look? Madeline McKenna had lived in a condo during the years that Regan knew her, before the divorce. She and Grant had even driven her home a few times after law firm social events.

A quick search on Google told Regan that Madeline still lived in the same place. If Grant was in trouble—in danger—Madeline might know where he went. But most likely, he was with her.

Twenty-Seven

Nelson Lee had survived in this business for years because he was shrewd and cautious.

He recognized the truck parked outside Grant Warwick's house. It was registered to the dead marshal, Tom Granger.

Nelson's interest was piqued; this was a turn of events he wasn't expecting.

He'd learned that Grant Warwick's ex-wife was staying in Granger's house; but after his employer analyzed Granger's laptop and cell phone, and Nelson reviewed the notes from his employer's surveillance of her, Nelson was convinced that Regan Merritt knew nothing of importance. She was suspicious, she was sniffing around, but she didn't have any useful information.

Grant Warwick was another story. He had outlived his usefulness, and any talk of working with the authorities was a big no-no. He'd learn that lesson the hard way, Nelson thought wryly.

At this point, he had a no-kill order on Regan Merritt, because her death would be too high-profile. One dead marshal could be explained away. But two? Even if he staged an accident, an unexpected death would bring in too many eyes, too many investigators. Of course, his orders might change depending on what she was doing here at Warwick's place, and if she made contact with Warwick. So far, Warwick had mostly avoided her for the last two days, but no one believed he wouldn't talk.

Ideally, the lawyer would show up here, and Nelson would take care of him before he even walked in the front door.

His assignment was clear. He'd taken care of part A. Now he had to take care of part B.

It shouldn't have been this difficult. What had spooked Mr. Warwick that he hadn't shown up at his girlfriend's place when he was supposed to? Why wasn't he here, at his house?

And what was Ms. Merritt doing here without him?

No one could run from Nelson for long. He had unlimited resources for this job, and he would use whatever it took to complete his assignment.

He desperately wanted to be back in South Carolina for the farmer's market on Saturday. If Grant Warwick delayed the inevitable, and Nelson missed the market, he would suffer the consequences. A little bit of torture before his death.

Wishful thinking, Nelson thought. It had to look like suicide.

At 7:26, Merritt left the house through the garage. Warwick's ex-wife had the code. Interesting. She walked directly across the street to Granger's truck, looking both ways, assessing the street. She didn't see him because he was far enough away, and he had no intention of following her.

She wasn't his to kill, not yet.

As soon as she drove off in Granger's truck, Nelson exited his vehicle and approached Warwick's house. The code would have been nice, but he had some skills in picking a lock and knew that Warwick had no security system on his house. With the porch light out, he could work in the dark unseen.

In less than a minute, Nelson was inside the house, waiting for Grant Warwick.

Twenty-Eight

Madeline lived in a penthouse apartment in Arlington one metro stop north of the Archer Warwick law office. Though the lobby was secure, requiring a card key or electronic code to enter, there was no doorman or security desk, and Regan didn't have to wait long to sneak inside behind a resident. She went to Madeline's apartment on the sixth floor—the top.

Regan knocked on the door, which to her surprise swung open on its own.

Instantly she was on alert. Maybe Madeline had run out to get her mail, or had forgotten to lock up, or she was just nearby at a neighbor's place.

Or she'd been robbed.

Regan pushed the door fully open, and called out, "Madeline, it's Regan Merritt." She then added, "Grant's ex-wife. Madeline, are you here?"

No answer. She probably wasn't home, but Regan couldn't in good conscience not check on her welfare.

"Madeline, your door is ajar, I'm coming in."

She heard nothing and proceeded with caution, identifying herself a third time.

Regan smelled blood as soon as she stepped into the entry. She pulled her sidearm and held it close to her body, beginning a search of the penthouse. On a small secretary-style desk in the entry was a cell phone, briefcase, and purse. Beige heels were kicked into the corner. Regan rarely wore heels, but when she did she couldn't wait to get out of them.

The condo wasn't large, but it felt spacious because of the spacious great room with windows that boasted a view of the lit city both to the north and east; to the left of the entryway was the kitchen. She couldn't see the bedroom doors and assumed they were also to the left.

Cautious, she walked through the main room and turned left. The kitchen was open here, with a counter and bar stools. A bright white kitchen. The dining table was on this side of the great room, and the hall that led to what Regan presumed were two bedrooms.

She stepped forward, stopped when she saw a hand on the white carpet, coming from the kitchen. She took another step and saw Madeline's body on the tile floor sprawled facedown.

Madeline wore beige slacks, a cream silk blouse, and was barefoot. The beige shoes would have matched the outfit. Her blouse was soaked in blood. A pool of blood spread out on the tile, had seeped partly into the white carpet where the kitchen met the dining area. So much blood that Regan didn't have to touch her body to know that the woman was dead.

The blood still appeared wet, and Regan avoided the wide circle as she quickly searched the rest of the apartment for an intruder—or another victim.

Grant.

Grant wasn't here, dead or alive. Neither was anyone

else, victim or killer. The blood appeared isolated to the kitchen and dining room. Regan didn't touch the body, glanced around for a murder weapon but didn't see anything in the area.

She pulled out her cell phone and dialed 911.

"My name is Regan Merritt, and I would like to report a homicide." She gave the address. Dispatch wanted her to stay on the line, but she ended the call and walked out into the hall. Stood sentry at the door as if she were guarding it.

Next she called Charlie, told him what she'd found.

"You were there looking for Grant?"

"Yes."

"And?"

"I don't know where he is."

"Text me the address. I'll be right there."

She ended the call, texted Charlie, then tried calling Grant again. He didn't answer his phone. Again. She left another voicemail message.

"Grant, it's Regan. I'm at Madeline's condo. She's dead." Damn, that sounded blunt. But right now she couldn't be worried about Grant's feelings; she was worried about his life. "You're not here, not at home, I need to know that you are okay. Call me immediately."

He didn't call, didn't text.

By the time the police arrived, Regan had run through every possible scenario, but none of them were good.

Grant was in serious trouble.

Twenty-Nine

Regan was going over her story for the second time with Arlington detective Kyle Quincy when Charlie arrived on scene.

Being his usual personable self, Charlie showed his credentials and chatted with Detective Quincy about people they both knew—namely, the assistant chief of police, who Charlie befriended on a task force where they'd both served. Charlie exuded authority without saying he had authority, which made him extra valuable in sensitive situations like this.

Fortunately, Quincy didn't think Regan had killed Madeline, though he hadn't said as much. It was during her second telling of her story that he seemed to relax, just enough to tell her that he didn't believe she was involved.

The crime scene unit had already arrived. They were doing their job—taking photographs, collecting trace evidence, waiting for the coroner in order to fully process the body and have it removed.

Regan, Quincy, and Charlie stood in the middle of the great room where there was no visible sign of blood or disturbance. The hall wasn't private—several neighbors were standing in their doorways watching the comings and go-ings of law enforcement personnel.

"Why did you believe that your ex-husband was here at Ms. McKenna's?" Quincy asked. She'd explained that she was supposed to meet Grant at his townhouse and when he was late and not returning her messages, she came here.

"I didn't know whether he was here or not, he hadn't returned my messages, but he and Madeline have been in-volved for some time, and I thought she might know where he was."

Another officer approached, whispered in Quincy's ear, then walked away.

Regan asked, "What?"

He hesitated, as if not wanting to share any information, then evidently decided it wasn't worth holding back. "I ran you, had to make sure there wasn't a restraining order. A domestic situation."

She didn't know why that bothered her—it was a logi-cal step in the investigation—but it did. She didn't com-ment on it, but instead said, "I'm worried about Grant. At first, I was irritated because he didn't show again, but—"

He arched his forehead. "Again?"

Damn, she hadn't meant to say that. "We were supposed to have dinner last night, he canceled last-minute, agreed to meet tonight at his place."

"Were you romantically involved with your ex?"

"No."

He stared at her, waiting for her to say more.

She had answered the question and didn't feel the need to elaborate.

Charlie broke the awkward silence. "Detective, since Ms. Merritt isn't a suspect, you wouldn't mind if we left." He said it as a friendly statement.

"I have your contact information," he said, looking at his pad. "Where are you staying while you're in town?"

She gave him Tommy's address.

Reluctantly—she didn't know if it was an act or not—he said they could go, and he'd contact her later. On their way out, she overheard Quincy ask one of the uniforms to get Grant's address and contact information.

She walked out with Charlie.

"Talk," he said when they were in the elevator alone.

"They're going to put a BOLO on Grant."

"That's what I would do," he said.

"Grant didn't kill Madeline."

When Charlie remained silent, she added, "I was married to him for nearly twelve years. I know him. She was stabbed in the back at least three times."

"You inspected the body?"

"Visually. I didn't touch her."

"How she was killed isn't proof that Grant didn't kill her."

He was right, but that didn't mean that Regan believed that Grant was capable of murder. She supposed that under the right circumstances anyone could kill, but her ex-husband? He would yell, he would definitely verbally attack someone, and—maybe—he could push or hit someone in the heat of anger. But in all the years that she had known him, the years she'd lived with him and shared his bed, she had never once thought that he was violent. He shied away from physical confrontations. He was a diplomat first and foremost; he could talk his way out of almost any situation.

She realized that's exactly what he had been doing with her for the last two days. He had avoided meeting with her because he knew she'd get him talking. There was something he didn't want to tell her. At his office, he had obfuscated, whispering there was a bug in his office. That implied someone in his *office* was bugging his office, because if it was an external source Grant would have it removed. Wouldn't he?

What was he keeping from her? What didn't he want to tell her?

They exited the elevator and walked out to the street.

"What are you going to do?" Charlie asked.

"Find Grant."

"How?"

"I'm going back to his place. If he's not there, I'll wait for Detective Quincy to show."

"You think he's going there."

"If I were him? It'd be my next stop."

Thirty

Grant circled Franklin Archer's Fairfax neighborhood for nearly an hour before working up the courage to confront him. Finally, he pulled up outside Franklin's gated estate. He'd been ignoring Regan's calls and messages; it was too much. He couldn't talk to her, not now. So he finally turned off his phone. He could hardly *think* and he didn't know what to do.

He should have gone to Regan when she was waiting for him at his house. More than anyone, Regan was calm under pressure—and this was pressure. Maddie was *dead*, and Grant was going to be next.

You were late. You would be dead, too, but you were late.

He'd walked in and saw her body and knew she was gone. All that blood on the bleached hardwood floors. He was supposed to be there at 6:30; he was late. He would have been dead; except that he was late.

Late because he was sitting in his car in the parking garage of the law firm, working up the strength to tell Regan everything. He knew he had to be resolved because Maddie was having doubts; he had to be strong. So he talked to himself, working through every argument Maddie might have, wanting her by his side but knowing that he might have to talk to Regan without her. Knowing that if he did that, Maddie might leave him.

He didn't expect to find her dead.

He'd lost his son, his marriage, and now his lover. He had nothing to live for. Everything he cared about was gone.

Maybe he wanted to die. The truth was becoming clear. Everything Tom Granger said was true. Knowing that he was indirectly responsible for Chase's death burned like acid in his stomach. Grant did not want to live with his son's death on his heart.

Was Franklin responsible? Could he have been? Grant had been thinking, thinking, *thinking!* all day, all night, and nothing made sense. Even if Franklin wasn't involved, he had to have known, right?

Brock Marsh worked almost exclusively for Archer Warwick…and in Grant's research, he realized the *almost* was only because some Archer Warwick clients hired Brock Marsh on their own—referred by Franklin.

Whatever proof Tom Granger had found was gone. Did Franklin know? Dammit, *did he know?*

Grant buzzed at the gate outside Franklin's estate. *Buzz. Buzz. Buzz.*

"Hello?" an irritated female voice said through the speaker.

"Isabelle? It's Grant. I'm sorry. I need to speak with Franklin, it's an emergency."

"Is he expecting you?"

"No. Please, Isabelle, I wouldn't be here if I didn't need to talk to him tonight."

A moment later, without comment, the gate swung open.

Grant drove in too fast, forced himself to ease up on the gas. He wished he had a gun. He'd confront Franklin, demand the truth. The *whole* truth. Ask if he was the one to bug his office.

When he told Regan that his office was bugged, he hadn't been positive. It was just that Tom Granger had gotten him paranoid, told him to be careful, and actually said he should sweep his office and house for listening devices. Grant had dismissed his concern, but Tom had been killed and Grant had spoken to him—on his cell phone—in the office. So after seeing Madeline at lunch, he'd bought a hidden microphone detector and searched his office. Found a bug under his desk. Almost couldn't believe it. He'd stared at it for so long—until Jeff had buzzed him that a client was holding for their scheduled call—uncertain what was going on. Had it been Franklin? A client? Jeff—who had full run of his office when Grant wasn't there? Someone else, someone hired to break in… His mind was going in every direction as the paranoia spread.

He would have to sweep Madeline's condo, his house, his car, everywhere he could think. If someone had bugged his office they could be listening everywhere.

The more he thought about the bug and Franklin's more unscrupulous clients, the more he thought that Franklin *could* be involved. He needed to ask him… *Franklin, did you hire Adam Hannigan to kill me? Did you hire someone to kill Maddie?*

Grant didn't want to believe it, but what else could be the answer?

Franklin met him at the front door. By his expression, he knew that Grant was angry and upset.

"Let's go to my office," he said and led the way down the hall. Dark double doors opened to a spacious library with high bookshelves, a rolling ladder, and three sets of double French doors leading out to an exquisite garden.

Franklin had always liked his *things*. He'd come from money, made money—too much of it from borderline il-legal activity. Borderline? Maybe he'd always been rotten.

Just confront him. You don't have to have the evidence, just tell him what you think and ask him for the truth.

"Why did you have Madeline killed?" Grant demanded.

Franklin stared at him blankly. "What?"

"*Don't.* Do *not* lie to me," he said. Swallowed. Dammit, he shouldn't be here. But he couldn't help himself. All his emotions that had been pent-up since Tom Granger came to him three weeks ago and said: *You were the target, not Chase. Adam Hannigan was hired by Brock Marsh to kill* you. *So the question is, Grant—who hired Brock Marsh to take you out?*

Neither Tom nor Grant knew who or why, which was the reason Tom wanted files from Archer Warwick. Files from every active client Grant and Franklin had worked during that window of time before Chase was murdered, and all Archer Warwick accounting records for the last two years.

"Grant, what on earth are you talking about?"

"I know you hired someone to kill us, it had to be you. And now she's dead."

"Maddie is dead?"

"Yes! Someone killed her!"

"How?"

Grant ran his hands through his hair. He really shouldn't be here, but he couldn't just walk away. What was he sup-posed to do? The guilt had been building, building, build-ing until he was about to burst.

"You know how! She was stabbed, Franklin."

"You sound completely unhinged, Grant." Franklin walked behind his desk, keeping distance between them.

"If not you, who? Who did it, Franklin? Was it Senator

Burgess? Was it BioRise? Why was James in the office this morning? No one else has the money to pull something like this off—no one else has as much to lose. Except *you*."

"You're wrong, Grant. Get a grip. I didn't have Madeline killed. That's—just insane. She called me last night worried about you."

Grant froze. He didn't want to believe it.

Why would Maddie call *Franklin* when she knew that Grant was becoming suspicious of Franklin's part in Chase's murder? Had she been working with Franklin all along? Had she hidden important information from him... information that would have implicated Franklin from the beginning?

Maddie loved him. She couldn't have been working against him, too!

He rubbed his eyes. His head pounded and he felt a scream building up in his throat. It didn't come out. He swallowed it.

"Your accusations are ludicrous," said Franklin. "I would never think of having *anyone* killed—much less our dear Maddie."

"How about me?" whispered Grant. "Would you *think* of having me killed?"

"Grant, there are things going on here that are above both of us. You wouldn't understand, and I can't explain. Just relax."

"Relax? Maddie was stabbed in the back!"

Franklin paled. His eyes were...concerned. Scared? Did he really not know?

"Who did it, Franklin? Who killed her? You started this chain of events, I know you did."

"Madeline was stabbed?"

"You wanted both of us dead. I see it now."

"I never wanted anyone dead," Franklin snapped, but the way he said it…his tone said it all. Franklin was scared. He knew who was responsible and he was choosing to remain silent.

"So things just got out of control, is that it?" Grant said with disgust. "Everything spiraled out of control, and you're now sorry. Just so very sorry that a ten-year-old boy was killed. Collateral damage? Is that what it is?" Then Grant had a revelation. Things shifted, became clearer.

He'd always known they'd taken some unscrupulous clients, but that was part of the business. Some of the businesses were…shady. Grant didn't always like the work, but some clients paid exceptionally well for discretion and legal sleight of hand, and he had never crossed the line, not in any serious way. He'd turned his back a few times…but he couldn't be accused of anything because he literally didn't know details because he didn't want to know.

Franklin crossed that line. Grant could see it now.

"You're being blackmailed, aren't you?"

Franklin stared at him, his mouth a firm line.

"Tell me the fucking truth! *Is my son dead because of you?*"

"You don't know *anything*!" For the first time, Franklin showed his temper. Then he startled, surprised at his own rage. He sat down at his large desk, clasped his hands in front of him.

"I will prove it," Grant said, his voice shaking. "I will prove that you were involved in the murder of my son. Maddie. I don't know what you did, what they're holding over your head—" *or who* "—but I will find out. Tom Granger learned the truth, didn't he—and you had him killed, too. If Tom could find it, I will."

Regan will.

Franklin shook his head. "There is no evidence. And your word will mean nothing."

"I've done nothing wrong."

"Keep telling yourself that," Franklin laughed humorlessly.

"I have never crossed the line."

"Oh, please. Saint Grant Warwick. You may not have got your hands dirty, but there are piles of *shit* that you helped create through your brilliant NDAs and protections for our clients. The shit they pulled under our legal umbrella? The shit we had to clean up with Brock Marsh? You think none of that will come back on you?"

"I never—"

"It doesn't matter what you did, your name is on everything. Grow the fuck up, Grant. When I'm through with you, no one you peddle your ridiculous conspiracy theories to will believe a single thing you say. I will accept your resignation."

"The proof is out there. The proof that Adam Hannigan was hired to kill me. Granger knew. I just want to know why."

"The evidence Granger had?" Franklin said it so quietly that Grant almost didn't hear him. "It's gone, Grant. Completely gone." He slowly rose from his desk. "I didn't want Madeline to die. I didn't ask for it. If she's dead...if... This is now all out of my hands."

He sounded resigned.

"I didn't hire anyone to kill you or Madeline," Franklin continued. "But... I knew it was inevitable when you started talking to Granger. You betrayed me, our firm, everything we worked for."

For the first time Grant realized how stupid he was. He should have a recorder on him, something to take to the police! Franklin knew who wanted Grant dead, who was responsible for Chase's murder. Who killed Madeline.

You are a fool, Grant.

"I'll tell you one thing, Grant, as a nod to our long friendship." Franklin forced a grim smile on his face. "I'm safe. It's a strategy of mutually assured destruction, and all my clients know it. I have dirt on everyone."

Grant believed him. Franklin may have been lying to him about his involvement—he may have more blood on his hands than he admitted—but right now, Grant believed him. Franklin Archer was a rotten criminal—dirty down to his soul. Worse, he enjoyed the game. The knowledge that he *had* information that could hurt powerful people.

But which of their powerful, corrupt clients was responsible for murder?

"What have you done?" Grant's voice cracked.

"I didn't start it. My father the bastard—yeah, get that look off your face, my father wasn't the man either of us believed him to be. My father started the firm, he built his empire with these corrupt corporate clients. Helped them, protected them, profited from them. And he walks away with a woman half his age only a year after my mom died… walked away with all the money and prestige and left *me* with this mess. But I made lemonade from his lemons, enriched all of us, built a legacy! But you—you never wanted to get your hands dirty. And because of that, because of your ridiculous *ethics*, you're *not* safe. You're a liability to some of our clients."

"Just tell me who is behind it. Who killed Chase?"

Franklin's arrogant smile disappeared. "Run, Grant. Or you won't live to see tomorrow."

Thirty-One

One in four murdered women were killed by their significant other, and more than half were killed by someone they knew. So logically, looking at Grant Warwick first, then Regan Merritt, was the logical way to proceed, followed by neighbors, relatives, and colleagues.

But Arlington detective Kyle Quincy didn't think Merritt was guilty. Merritt had seemed straightforward, but the deceased *was* the girlfriend of her ex-husband. That alone was enough to keep her at least at the bottom of Quincy's suspect list. First on scene, called it in, stayed on-site. She had no blood on her, and there was no sign that anyone had cleaned up in the bathroom or kitchen.

McKenna had been stabbed to death, so her killer would almost certainly have blood on them. There were pools of blood and spatter in the kitchen near her body, but the killer didn't step in her blood, and it appeared he'd bagged the weapon, taken it with him. No drops near the door. No prints on the door. He wore gloves. In and out, quick and efficient.

Not a crime of passion.

It *looked* like a crime of passion. McKenna was stabbed

in the back, which suggested she knew her killer. She had felt safe, turned her back on him. But the slaying also had all the earmarks of a premeditated murder: no visible evidence, no panicked attempt to clean up the scene.

Or maybe McKenna's killer snuck up on her, though that seemed unlikely. There was no sign of a break-in. No sign of struggle. Her phone was on the table inside the front door, with her briefcase and shoes.

Detective Quincy surmised that she came home from work, put her things down, took out a half-drunk bottle of wine, and poured a glass. It was sitting half-filled on the counter, a faint hint of pink lipstick on the rim suggesting she'd had a sip before putting it down. But she hadn't dropped it, broken it. She had sipped, put it down…on the counter not far from where she'd been stabbed.

One glass of wine…no other glasses or bottles. That suggested no guest. Yet, it was more probable that McKenna let her killer in. Maybe it was a maintenance worker, someone working on the condo, or someone she expected…

He looked around, trying to put himself in Ms. McKenna's shoes. Put the glass down, then head toward the bedrooms. If the killer came from down the hall, she would have seen him and run, knocked over papers, her wine, something. But nothing appeared spilled or disturbed.

There was no place to hide in the great room, but a large pantry off the kitchen could easily conceal a grown man. The way her body was positioned, the killer came from the kitchen. He'd either come in through the front door and turned into the kitchen through the side entry, or he'd been hiding in the pantry waiting to attack. No tampering of the door, so the door was unlocked or the killer had a key.

He'd need to talk this all through with the head of the crime scene unit once they'd processed the evidence and see what the forensic experts considered the most likely scenario.

He supposed Merritt could have killed her ex's girlfriend, left the scene, gone somewhere to shower, changed clothes and disposed of the murder weapon, then returned to "discover" the body. But if she was telling the truth about where she had been (her ex's house), that was more than thirty minutes round trip and if she was telling the truth about where she was staying (out in Reston), that was at least an hour round trip at the time McKenna was killed.

More likely, Grant Warwick killed his girlfriend and fled the scene. If Merritt was telling the truth that Warwick was supposed to meet with her at seven and didn't show, then she came here—arriving at approximately 7:45—he should be able to prove it.

Quincy watched as the coroner bagged the body, still running through possible scenarios in his head, while writing down information he needed to verify. Talk to her employer, people who knew both her and Warwick. Track down Warwick, interview him. Neighbors. Any friends? Someone she was close to, like a sister? Someone she would confide in? Were there any problems in her personal life? Professional life? What kind of clients did she serve? A quick Google search told him Archer Warwick Bachman was a civil law firm, not criminal. Did she have a stalker? Violent ex-boyfriend? All things he would learn over the next few days while waiting for the crime scene report, forensics, and autopsy.

But he really wanted to talk to Grant Warwick as soon as possible.

Officer Branson approached Quincy in the living room and said, "I talked to the building manager. According to security cameras, Merritt slipped in behind a resident at

7:42 p.m. this evening, came straight up to the sixth floor. There are no cameras on the resident floors."

That jibed with Merritt's statement.

"And Grant Warwick?"

"He's not on camera after 5:00 p.m. But that doesn't mean much. The parking garage is under the building, and if he had an access card he could have parked down there."

"Where there are no cameras," Quincy guessed.

"Correct. The manager is running all people going in and out of the garage, but it would be a card registered to Ms. McKenna we'd be looking for. Every resident is assigned two parking spots. We'll need to canvass neighbors, anyone who came in during our window—ask about Warwick's car."

"Did the manager recognize Warwick?"

"Yes, he knew him by name, said he had been regularly visiting for the last six months. He last saw Ms. McKenna at one fifteen this afternoon. She came down to pick up a package from the office, mentioned to him that she was home for lunch."

The lead crime scene investigator walked over and said, "Coroner is leaving. He'll do his assessment at the morgue, but my analysis says she was killed between six and seven this evening. Because her body was found quickly, I think the coroner can give a better TOD."

Still, an hour window to work with? That was good. "Thanks, let me know when you have a report."

"You'll be the first." The CSI walked over to where his team was taking more blood samples and packing up other items, like her wineglass, now that the body was moved.

Quincy asked Officer Branson, "Have you found Warwick?"

"No, sir," he said. "I put a BOLO out on him like you

said—wanted for questioning—and I have his contact information, employer, address."

"Let's start at his place. Maybe he showed up after Merritt left." Quincy glanced around. Two officers stood by the condo's front door. He told them to stay until the crime scene investigators were done, then seal the door before they left. He asked Branson to follow him to Warwick's townhouse in Alexandria.

And he was thinking how guilty Grant Warwick looked for murder.

By the time Quincy arrived at Warwick's pricy townhome in Alexandria, it was after ten. He was surprised to see an Alexandria police cruiser parked in the front of Warwick's house. Quincy exited his unmarked sedan and strode over, introduced himself.

That's when he saw Regan Merritt standing to the side.

"What's going on?" Quincy asked the cop.

"I was just about to call you. Ms. Merritt said you're investigating the murder of the owner's girlfriend, so would want to be here."

Did she now? "What happened?"

"Ms. Merritt said that someone broke in tonight. Said the front door has signs of tampering."

Quincy was more than a little irritated that Merritt had not only beat him here, to Warwick's house, but that she was inserting herself into this investigation. "Could Ms. Merritt have done the tampering?"

"Couldn't say, sir, but she called us."

"Have you gone in? Cleared the place?"

"No, sir. I'm waiting for backup."

"Is the house open?" Quincy asked.

"Ms. Merritt says she has the garage code."

If Warwick was a suspect, searching the house was problematic. But if he was another victim, they needed to do a welfare check.

Quincy motioned for Officer Branson to join the Alexandria officer. "Clear the house, welfare check only. I'm going to call my boss and see what we can do by way of a search."

"Roger that."

The officers walked over to Merritt, who led them to the garage access panel, where she typed in a code. The door opened.

Dammit. Something was fishy and Quincy couldn't figure out what. He went to call his sergeant.

Regan could tell the police detective was irritated, but she kept her face impassive and followed the barked direction of the responding police officers. She stayed outside, as told, though she itched to search Grant's house herself.

After she and Charlie left Madeline's house, she convinced him to go home. She went back to Grant's townhouse, hoping that Grant would be there or she'd wait for him. She walked around and noticed the front door keyhole had telltale scrapes that suggested someone had picked the lock—or at least attempted to. The marks hadn't been there earlier; she would have noticed. She called the police and waited.

She'd become more and more worried about Grant's safety as the evening wore on, and no one had been able to reach him.

Detective Quincy approached her before the officers were done in the house. He said, "Why are you here?"

"I wanted to see if Grant had come home. I planned to go inside, see if he'd been here since I left, but when I saw the front door was tampered with, I called 911."

"You can't see the front door from the garage here."

"I walked around the perimeter of the townhouse first."

"Why?"

"Looking for potential threats."

"You said you left the Marshals Service. Are you with another agency?"

"No. I'm currently unemployed, by choice."

"They must pay you a lot better than me if you can save up enough money to live for a year."

She bristled. She rarely let people get under her skin, but this cop was doing it. She wanted to explain—she had the proceeds from the house after her divorce, she had eight months of vacation and sick leave accrued that she cashed out, that she was living mostly free of charge with her dad. But she didn't say a word. It was none of his damn business.

The two officers exited the townhouse the way they came in. "No one is inside. No signs of violence. Should we lock up?"

"No, I'm going to do a walk-through, look to see if he took luggage or other signs that he is fleeing town, or any sign that he may have been threatened," said Detective Quincy.

Such a search was in a legal gray area, Regan knew. If Quincy found anything that might connect Grant to Madeline's murder, it would be thrown out as an illegal search.

"Let me help," Regan said. "I was here earlier, I'll know if something is out of place."

"No."

She raised an eyebrow. "I am allowed in. I'm the one who gave you access."

"It's not your house," said Quincy. "And I could have gone in on a welfare check, no questions."

"If Grant came in while I was at Madeline's, I'll know."

"Would you?"

She didn't comment.

Quincy scowled. "Stay with me. No wandering, no touching. If there's any sign that something is rotten, I'm calling in the crime scene investigators to do a full and thorough search and processing."

"In that case, you should know that because I was here earlier, my prints are going to be on doors, the refrigerator, his office."

"You had dinner?"

She shook her head, gave him a half smile. "You can tell a lot about a person by the contents of their refrigerator."

"What did his contents tell you?"

"That after we divorced, he still didn't teach himself how to cook."

Nothing appeared out of place until they reached Grant's office on the top floor.

"Hold it," she said.

The detective stopped.

If Regan hadn't been in this room only a few hours ago, she wouldn't have noticed what was missing.

"His laptop is gone."

"Are you sure?"

"I left here around seven twenty, seven twenty-five maybe. His laptop was on his desk, closed, plugged into the wall. The charger is gone. And his laptop case."

"He could have come home after you left, took his laptop."

"You cannot assume that it was Grant. The evidence at the front door suggests a break-in. Someone else could have taken it."

But it could also have been Grant, and they both knew

it. The break-in could have occurred before or after he stopped home—if he came home. Either Grant came back for the laptop and *then* someone broke in during the three hours Regan was gone, or Grant hadn't come home and a thief took the laptop.

"Do you have gloves I can use?" Regan asked. "My prints are already all over the desk, but I want to see if the files in his locked drawers are gone."

"Are the drawers locked now?"

"I don't know."

He hesitated, then handed her one glove. "I only have one pair with me. Use that."

She didn't put it on, only folded it between her fingers and used it to try the bottom two drawers.

Locked.

"You picked his locks," Quincy said, looking over her shoulder.

She didn't respond. "They're locked now, but I know what was in them, at least what the files looked like."

"I need a warrant to search anything that isn't in the open."

"You don't know Grant like I do. We were married for nearly twelve years. I don't know what's going on with him or where he is right now, but I can't see him stabbing a woman in the back multiple times."

"You were in law enforcement. You know that you can't always predict criminal behavior, especially a crime of passion."

"Maddie didn't fight back. There was no evidence of a struggle, no signs of a fight. You're suggesting that maybe they argued, she turned around, and Grant stabbed her in the back two, three times? Then he left her there, but took the knife? Didn't touch her, smear the blood?"

"I don't know what happened, but that's a plausible scenario. Do you have a better one?"

"An intruder. Lying in wait. Because there wasn't a struggle, no signs of a fight, one wineglass—not two."

"You're observant."

Regan hesitated, but she needed this detective on her side so opted for transparency. "I'm in town because my former boss, Deputy US Marshal Thomas Granger, was murdered on Monday morning. I have Tommy's personal phone records that show several calls between Grant and Tommy starting three weeks ago. Tommy's killer shot him at dawn, took his phone and laptop, and walked away. Now Madeline McKenna is dead, Grant is missing, and Grant's laptop is gone."

"Is your ex being investigated for Granger's murder?"

She didn't even know how to respond to that. "No. And Grant's not a sniper. The shot was approximately seventy feet from a slight elevation. Grant can barely hit a target fifty feet away on the range."

"Could you have made the shot?"

Of course she could, and he had to know that—she had been a trained marshal. "That's irrelevant. My point is, I believe Grant and Tommy were working together to solve my son's murder."

He stared at her. "I didn't know. I'm sorry."

She shook her head to dismiss any further condolences. She didn't want or need sympathy. None of this was a coincidence. Tommy's death, Madeline's death, the missing laptops, Grant's disappearance. She feared he was dead.

She had watched, assessed Detective Quincy and decided that she could trust him with what she knew. Not only was she worried about her ex-husband's safety, but she felt at a loss about what was happening around her. Death, violence, Tommy's investigation, all the pieces were here but she didn't know how they fit together.

But one thing was certain: the more people that looked for answers the better.

"Our son was killed at the end of June last year." She laid out what happened in a straightforward, matter-of-fact tone. Chase's murder, Hannigan's capture, his apparent remorse, and the FBI theory that he was avenging his brother's death—a brother he hadn't been raised with and wasn't close to.

Quincy was listening, didn't interrupt, so Regan continued. "I moved back to my hometown in Arizona, but three weeks ago, Tommy interviewed Peter Grey, the felon who killed Hannigan in jail. He'd been trying to talk to him for months, because we just didn't buy the FBI conclusion. Tommy went on leave, started talking to Grant, had planned to lay everything out for his colleagues the day he was killed. He believed he had enough information and discrepancies to start an official investigation."

"Let me get this straight—Granger did all of this without bringing you in? The mother? You didn't know?"

"I knew he was looking." Then, she added, "Losing my son nearly killed me. I couldn't go down that rabbit hole without something…tangible."

"I can understand that."

He said it matter-of-factly, no veiled sympathy. She appreciated it.

"Tommy was in contact with Grant. I don't know what they discussed, or what Grant was doing to help Tommy, but they had multiple conversations. His notes lead me to believe that *Grant* was Hannigan's target—not me, not our son. It was a theory I posited early on, after Hannigan told me he was sorry, he hadn't meant to shoot Chase. Now if I'm right and that is true, Grant is in danger."

"Nearly a year later?"

"I don't have all the answers, but I'm going to find them."

After a moment, Quincy said, "All interesting information, but none of it helps me find your ex-husband. I appreciate you letting us in, giving me your assessment, but I have to wait for a warrant before I do anything else here. Let's step outside."

Regan followed Quincy downstairs and back out the garage. As soon as they stepped into the cool May evening, a breeze picked up off the Potomac and Officer Branson approached. "Detective, a word?"

They stepped away and though Regan tried to eavesdrop, she heard nothing.

A minute later, Branson walked to his patrol car and Quincy approached her, saying, "Thank you for your assistance, Ms. Merritt. If you hear from your ex-husband, please let me know immediately." He handed her his business card. "I have your contact information if I have more questions."

"What just happened?" she asked. She didn't want to be shut out of this investigation but suspected Quincy didn't trust her objectivity—not to mention she no longer had a badge.

"I can't talk to you about this case, though I can tell you that your ex-husband is wanted for questioning in the murder of Madeline McKenna."

"You just put him to the top of your suspect list. Please be honest with me, Quincy. What do you have on him?"

She saw him weighing whether to tell her, and then he threw her a bone. "McKenna's second parking pass was used to access the condo garage at six fifty-one tonight. They don't require the pass to be used to exit, and there are no cameras in the garage. Our canvass, however, identified a security camera outside a restaurant across the street from the exit. We have Grant Warwick's vehicle exiting the parking garage at seven-oh-five. That puts him in McKenna's condo during the approximate time of her death."

"Or Grant found her body…" Fourteen minutes. *Maybe* two minutes to get up, two minutes to come back down, but what was he doing in her apartment for ten minutes?

"And he didn't call the police? A lawyer, not calling the police when they walk into a crime scene?" Quincy shook his head. "I need to talk to him. Right now, he's just wanted for questioning. If he reaches out to you, the best thing you can do is convince him to come in voluntarily. If he continues to avoid us and I find another piece of evidence that implicates him, I will get an arrest warrant. My boss is putting more people on this—pulling security, talking to neighbors, his staff, associates. This isn't going away."

Regan wanted to say, *But Grant wouldn't do this*… But she didn't. Because she was no longer one hundred percent certain he was innocent.

But why would he kill Madeline, his girlfriend and an associate he'd known for nearly a decade? Jealousy or a volatile lover's quarrel didn't fit Grant's personality.

Maybe Madeline's death had nothing to do with their relationship. Maybe it had to do with her place of employment, or with whatever Grant and Tommy were investigating together. Maybe it had to do with the information from Grant's files that Regan had taken photos of on her phone. Maybe…

"I'm willing to help if you want me," Regan said.

Quincy shook his head. "I don't want you anywhere near this case. I see a big red conflict of interest sign flashing above your head. If you don't see it, you're blind."

Thirty-Two

When Lance walked into the all-night diner at 10:30 that night, Jenna had never been so happy to see anyone in her life. She jumped up and hugged him tightly, not embarrassed, not worried about what he might think or if he thought she was crazy. She just might be crazy.

"You're shaking," he said as he took the seat next to her in the booth, not across from her. He clasped her hands in his. "I've been worried about you all day."

"I'm so glad you're here," she said. "I feel like I'm losing it, and I don't know what to do."

After she'd seen the two men who lied about being FBI agents outside the hospital, she'd driven for hours, heading *away*. Without a thought as to where she was going. But when she nearly ran out of gas, she finally stopped and practically begged the clerk at the station to let her use his cell phone. Maybe it was the tears that had him helping her; she didn't know or care.

She called Lance—and thank goodness he'd picked up even though it was an unfamiliar number. He told her he'd gotten to her house just after six and her car was gone and the back door was open.

Two men approached him, identified themselves as FBI, and asked if he knew where she was. Lance said no, he was supposed to meet her at her house. He went home and realized the men had followed him. Same two guys sitting in the same SUV. They'd compared descriptions; it was the same two men who had confronted Jenna earlier. They'd stayed outside his apartment for more than an hour before she called him.

"You weren't followed here, were you?" she asked, eyes wide. "I mean, you believe me, right?"

"Of course I believe you. They didn't show me their identification, they didn't act like FBI agents. They looked more like thugs."

"How do you know they didn't follow you?"

"I called the cops. It took like thirty minutes for them to show up, and as soon as the assholes saw the police car turn into my complex, they took off. I told the cops exactly what happened—that two guys without ID told me they were FBI agents looking for you, and that I couldn't find you anywhere. They said you should file a report about what happened; I wanted them to do something more. I didn't know who those men were, how smart they were, so I switched cars with my roommate."

The thugs might be smart, she thought, but Lance was smarter. She wished she could muster a smile for him, but she was so tense, so worried about what to do next.

The waitress appeared beside their table, and Lance ordered a burger and fries. Jenna just wanted more coffee. When the waitress left, Jenna told Lance everything, not holding back—about calling the FBI because of what she knew about US Marshal Granger and the FBI saying they'd send two agents to talk to her, so how did they *know*?

"Are you saying you have information about that guy's murder?"

"Not specifically. I told you that he was asking me a lot of questions about Becca."

"Yeah." He squeezed her hand. "And the marshal was looking into whether she might have been involved in the bank robbery."

She nodded. "I realized I knew a lot more about the bank robbery than I thought. I hadn't put it together at the time. I mean—okay, there were some weird things going on with Becca back then, but I didn't think about it because she had been killed." She swallowed uneasily.

"Hey, just tell me. I'm not going to judge you, or her. You know that."

She nodded. "I told you that she had all this money and everything…but there's more. Like, she was driving around this supernice car and told me it belonged to a corporation that she was working for part-time. I mean—that's weird, isn't it? To be working for someone part-time and they give you a supernice car to drive around? It was a brand-new Malibu, or something like that. And I saw her with some people—people that didn't seem like her friends. Becca had a way, that if I asked her anything about what she was doing, to turn it around as if I was prying or judging her or, I don't know. She was always so defensive. But I really didn't think about any of this after Becca was killed because she was dead and I had her funeral and…and stuff. I missed her."

"Why would you think about it? It wasn't like she told you she was going to rob a bank."

She nodded. "Yeah. And Tommy wasn't victim shaming her at all, so I opened up. Gave him everything—copies of her tax returns, her employment slips, her bank statements, everything I had. She had an apartment, but she used our house as her mail drop because she was always moving around. I don't like to throw financial things away, and I didn't know if I'd need them later." She looked down at her hands, frowned.

"Hey, it's going to be okay. I'm here now—we're going to get to the bottom of this. I promise."

She looked at him again, tears in her eyes, nodded.

"And the FBI didn't ask you about any of this? After the robbery?"

"No. When the FBI showed up at my house and told me Becca had been shot during a bank robbery, I just…fell apart. I didn't ask a lot of questions, because it seemed so cut-and-dried. There was so much to do after with her funeral and all her financial stuff to deal with. Becca didn't have a will, she didn't have a living trust, and my house was put into probate—I had to pay her debt otherwise the bank might have sold the house to pay for her taxes. It took me over a year to settle everything. And when that was done I just didn't think much more about it." She paused. "I miss Becca, she was fun and smart and happy—but she was irresponsible. It's why I'm sometimes a spoilsport and don't go out a lot. I never want to get in over my head like she did. I mean, I just turned twenty-six. I have a will and everything. Then I feel bad for criticizing her because she's dead."

"Hey—none of that. Family is family. We love them, warts and all. I love my brother and sister more than anything. We were very close growing up, but they've both made decisions I think are foolish. So you can love Becca and recognize she made mistakes."

Jenna was so glad that Lance understood. "Whatever she did I know it wasn't because she was mean or a bad person or anything. Mr. Granger thought that Mike Hannigan, the robber, hooked up with Becca because she worked at that bank branch. That either he paid her or promised to pay her to help him. Mr. Granger thought that she got the box numbers of the customers that he wanted. But he didn't know why Hannigan killed Becca. Maybe it was always part of his plan, so there were no witnesses to what he took. But they're both dead."

"Why are these guys after *you*?" Lance asked. "What do you know?"

"Deputy Granger had me write down everything I remembered—her friends, what she said, what she did. She'd met with one of her old employers—whose company had a box in the bank. He thought that was interesting, he said it was suspicious. Told me not to say anything, but that I may be asked to give an official statement, under oath."

"We need to go to the authorities—"

"Who? I called the FBI, and then two *not* FBI agents came to my house specifically saying they wanted to talk to me about Deputy Granger. How did they know? I haven't told *anyone* other than the FBI agent on the phone—and I called the hotline number from the news. I didn't just call anyone. I called the number on the news!"

"Granger was a marshal, right? We go to *his* office. They'll have known what he was doing."

"He was on leave, investigating on his own time." She sighed and let out a sob. "I know what you're thinking. I'm a total idiot."

"I wasn't thinking that."

"Mr. Granger said that the Potomac Bank robbery is connected to a death of a child, and he was going to prove it. That, I know nothing about—he didn't talk about it.

But I believe him. He was good man, Lance. I'm not a bad judge of character."

Lance still didn't say anything and Jenna bit her lip, worried that maybe she had read Lance wrong, that he didn't believe her, or thought she was foolish.

"I'm sorry—I shouldn't have dragged you into this."

"Stop. You didn't. I'm glad I'm here—I'm just thinking. You did the right thing helping the deputy and now we have to make sure that right thing doesn't get you hurt."

Lance picked at his food. Jenna stared out the window, worried about her safety, Lance's safety, whether or not she'd ever be able to go home or back to work or see her grandma.

"I have an idea," he finally said.

"Anything." She was desperate.

"We're going to find a hotel, go off the grid. We'll use my credit card so no one can trace you there. Then tomorrow morning, I'll go to the Marshals office, alone. I'll tell them what happened to you. And then when it's safe—when they can guarantee your safety—you can go in and tell them everything you know."

"I can't ask you to do that."

"You didn't ask. It's my idea. Those two guys looking for you are *not* FBI agents, which means they lied to you and to me. We don't know what they want, but you can't go anywhere until we know you are safe. And the US Marshals protect people—it's what they do. They probably know more about what's going on than you do at this point."

She spontaneously hugged him. "Thank you."

He hugged her back. And for the first time since she heard that Tommy Granger had been murdered, Jenna felt that everything might be okay.

Except there was one not-so-small detail that Jenna had

not told Lance. She feared that what she knew, what Tommy Granger had confided in her, was the reason she was in danger now. She didn't want to put that on her friend.

She wished that she didn't know the truth, but you can't *un*know something that important.

FRIDAY

Thirty-Three

Regan had stayed up until the early hours to put together all the information she had, then went to bed before dawn. After only a couple hours sleep, a shower, and strong coffee, she stepped into Tommy's library at eight and looked at the wall she had created so she could visually assess everything she knew.

She knew a lot—and still, nothing made sense. She had also made several logical deductions but didn't have proof.

But the biggest outlier—the one thing that frustrated her because Grant *must* have the answers and he wasn't talking—was what did the Potomac Bank robbery have to do with Chase's murder?

She went back to the safe deposit boxes that Michael Hannigan had broken into. A cursory look into them hadn't yielded anything of interest; now she needed to go deeper.

But before Regan could really dive into it, Charlie phoned.

"The FBI has arrested Roger Valera for Tommy's murder."

She frowned, remembering the name. "Valera? He's in prison. He has to be—he was given twenty to life."

Valera had threatened Tommy years ago in court.

Tommy had been part of a special US Marshals task force at the time investigating child trafficking. It was a difficult assignment, and most deputies rotated in for no more than a two-year stint. Valera had been found with more than one thousand kiddie porn videos on his computer. Three of the children in the videos had been recovered, thank God, based on digital geotagging. Tommy's testimony and the FBI cybercrime experts had helped put Valera away for a minimum of twenty years.

Clearly, that hadn't happened.

Charlie sighed. "Valera was granted early release—don't ask me how, who, why, I don't know. But he was set loose two weeks ago. The FBI followed up on a tip that led to his arrest. He wasn't supposed to leave the state of Pennsylvania, but they located him in Richmond. They couldn't find the rifle he used to shoot Tommy, but they have newspaper clippings, internet search history, and GPS on his vehicle—which puts Valera in Tommy's neighborhood a week before his murder. They're still putting together details, but they're positive it's him."

Valera had threatened Tommy in court and accused him of planting the videos that were found on his computer—including, not incidentally, videos of Valera himself with minors. The court didn't buy it.

"It can't be Valera," said Regan.

"I'm passing on the information. O'Dare just called me, said she'd send over the documentation. They're positive they have the right person."

"They're wrong."

"Tommy's investigation into Chase's murder could simply be a coincidence."

"You do not believe that any more than I do," Regan said irritably. "Grant is missing, his girlfriend is dead, I was followed—and I guarantee you that it was not Roger Valera who followed me. He's a convenient scapegoat."

"Regan—"

"GPS on his vehicle? What about on Monday morning, the day Tommy was killed? Does he have sharpshooter skills? Because to make that shot, the guy would have to be way above average."

"You can come in and read the file when I get it."

"O'Dare has her head up her ass if she can't see the whole picture here!" She was angry and raised her voice— something she rarely, if ever, did.

Charlie didn't speak. She rubbed her eyes. "Charlie," she said after a moment, "we need the rifle and proof Valera could make the shot. Proof he was even in Reston on Monday morning. This seems too easy. Who called in this tip? Anonymous? Isn't *that* convenient."

"I'll admit, it seemed to fall into place a bit too neatly," Charlie said cautiously, "but it is also true that Tommy made a lot of enemies. Mostly bad guys, but when Tommy had a bone, he didn't care whose hand he bit in the pursuit of justice."

Charlie was right about Tommy—but Valera? Regan couldn't see it. *Especially* in light of everything else going on surrounding Tommy.

"Keep me in the loop," she said.

"What are you planning to do?" Charlie asked suspiciously.

"Find Tommy's killer."

"Regan—you're swimming in rough waters. Grant is missing. His girlfriend is dead. If you're right—"

"I am right."

"Then you really have to be careful here. The FBI has their bone, they're going to push on Valera and he probably has something illegal going on. Pedophiles like him don't change. So the FBI is going to be all over that, and they want to believe he killed Tommy."

"And they will be wrong. Again. Something big is going on. Either the FBI is incompetent or they're corrupt. They got the wrong guy. Tommy was bringing in evidence related to Chase's murder and that evidence is missing. Was Tommy's laptop and phone found with Valera?"

"O'Dare didn't say."

Too easy, too convenient. Diverting the FBI's attention away from other avenues.

Just like Adam Hannigan's murder. He was a convenient scapegoat, had motive—chalk it up to revenge. And never look beyond the obvious.

"Did you get anything from the security cameras at the maintenance lot? When the men who followed me trashed my rental car?"

While there had been no plates on the first vehicle that had followed Regan, she had caught a glimpse of a rear plate on the second.

"Swapped plates—assigned to a different make and model. I'm asking the team here to track them down, talk to who they're registered to, find out when they could have been switched, but we don't have the resources to get this done quickly. I want to pass them along to the FBI."

"Maybe you should."

"O'Dare isn't going to be happy."

"Her joy is not my concern."

"I have one good image of the passenger, at least in profile. I'll send it to you. Not excellent—he was wearing sunglasses—but he has a distinctive mark, either a birthmark or scar right above his collar."

"That's better than a sharp stick in the eye," she muttered. "Thanks, Charlie. I know I'm asking a lot."

"Tommy was my friend, too—as well as my boss. I'm worried about you right now. Let's say the FBI is wrong—"

"I can buy into that."

She heard Charlie snicker. "Okay," he said, "the premise is that they are wrong and you are right. Hannigan was hired to kill Grant. Chase was an innocent bystander. Now—look at the fallout. Hannigan is dead. Tommy is dead. Grant's girlfriend is dead. Grant is missing. A child molester is being framed. What does that tell you?"

She wasn't certain what Charlie was getting at. When she didn't respond, he continued. "It tells me that someone with a lot of money and human resources is working hard to hide the truth about Chase's murder. Or—Chase's murder and Michael Hannigan's motivation behind the bank robbery. If they don't care about killing a kid or a US marshal, they're not going to care about killing anyone. Including you."

"I need to tread carefully. Got it. Have you heard anything from Detective Quincy? Anything about Grant? I've put feelers out, but so far—silence."

"Nothing," Charlie said.

The fact that his body hadn't been found overnight was a good sign: he might still be alive. But being alive had its downsides, too: it also made him appear more guilty.

"Hold on," Charlie said. "Lee's calling." He didn't wait for Regan's assent before putting her on hold, but she didn't care.

Lee Penitentiary. Where Peter Grey was currently behind bars.

Nearly five minutes later, Charlie came back on the phone. "Grey has agreed to talk to us."

"Let's go."

"Six-hour drive? I got something better—the warden agreed to let us video conference with him. Grey agreed. Can you get here in an hour?"

"I'm leaving right now."

Thirty-Four

"Thank you for agreeing to speak with us," Charlie said.

Regan and Charlie were in the small conference room in the US Marshals office, where a large screen on the wall currently showed them Peter Grey, convicted murderer, in prison orange. Grey sat at a metal table in a drab room, a microphone in front of him.

Grey, fifty-eight, was a large man with a short military-style haircut—mostly silver—and sharp, cold blue eyes. His hands weren't cuffed, and rested on the table in front of him. The short sleeves of his prison orange shirt revealed two complete tattoo sleeves. Some of the tats were elaborate and well drawn, some cheap and faded, the blue ink bleeding into his skin.

"You put three hundred in my account, I'm yours for the next fifteen minutes."

Regan hadn't known Charlie paid to talk to Grey. They couldn't give money directly to the prisoner, but people were allowed to put money into individual commissary accounts to be used for extras, like toiletries, snacks, MP3 players, shoes, aspirin, and more.

"Then we'll get right to the point," Charlie said. "You

pled guilty to the murder of Adam Hannigan, who you killed while in holding last year."

"I didn't so much plead guilty as not argue about it," Grey said, leaning back in the chair. There was a sparkle in his eyes, as if he now realized exactly why they had called him and he was looking forward to the conversation.

"A half dozen people saw me, and it wasn't like I could take care of all witnesses," Grey continued. "Four murders? Five?" He shrugged. "I was already in for life, what's another lifetime for whacking a scumbag child killer?" He laughed, then abruptly stopped. "You should be giving me a medal, Ms. Merritt. Justice has been served. You're welcome." He winked at her.

She forced herself not to react.

Charlie said, "Three weeks ago when you were housed in Cumberland, Deputy US Marshal Thomas Granger talked to you. Tell us what you told him."

The truth dawned immediately on Grey. "I told him he was a dead man."

Regan kept her face impassive. She said, "Why?" Her voice was as tight as her hands clasped in her lap.

"Do you have a death wish?"

Charlie said, "Mr. Grey, what did you tell Deputy Granger?"

"Nothing."

"Bullshit," Regan said. Losing her temper was not going to get them answers, but she was angry. When he killed Hannigan he stole answers from her—he would damn well give her answers now. "Tommy went to you, you gave him information that he pursued. Did you lie? Is that why he was killed, because you sent him down the wrong path?"

Grey half smiled. "If he's dead, it wasn't the wrong path."

Charlie said, very calmly, "Mr. Grey, no games. When Deputy Granger met with you, he was on a leave of absence and had been investigating the Potomac Bank robbery from two years ago. Nothing was taken, but a victim and the suspect were both killed."

"Michael Hannigan," Grey said with a grin. "Adam's idiot brother."

"You're familiar with the case, even though you were in prison at the time?"

"I know a lot of things," Grey said.

"Then what did you tell Deputy Granger?" Charlie pushed.

"Nothing."

"I don't believe you," Regan said. *Be calm. Don't react. He wants you to react.*

Grey shrugged. "I don't care."

"Mr. Grey, you must have said something that led Deputy Granger down this path."

"I didn't tell him anything. He had a theory—I played the game."

"What does that mean?" Charlie demanded.

"I wasn't going to give him anything. He knew that. Shit, I don't have a death wish. Tommy was an interesting guy. Real smart. He'd been doing his research, came to me, and we played twenty questions. It was fun. Yes, no, yes, no. Anything can be learned if you ask the right questions."

Regan said, "So you only answer yes-no questions?"

"Bingo."

"What did Tommy ask?"

"That's not a yes-no question."

Asshole. He was having fun with this. Tommy was in the morgue and Peter Grey's cold eyes sparkled in enjoyment.

What *had* Tommy asked him?

Charlie started. "Were you hired to kill Adam Hannigan?"

"Yes."

Her stomach fell. She had known it, but she didn't *know* it.

"Who?" she asked.

"Tsk-tsk," Grey said.

She took a deep breath, realized that if they were going to get the answers they needed, she had to play the game. "Was Adam Hannigan going to tell me who hired him? Is that why they wanted him dead?"

"Ummm…rephrase the question."

"This is ridiculous," she muttered.

Charlie, however, was calm, and his even temper helped her keep her head.

"Mr. Grey," Charlie said, "was Hannigan hired to kill Grant Warwick?"

"Yes!" Grey lit up as if Charlie was his star pupil. "Very good, Deputy North."

"Did Hannigan have remorse for killing Chase Warwick, a minor?"

"Yes."

Not as enthusiastic. Regan asked, "Was Hannigan's murder a fait accompli? He was always going to be silenced, wasn't he?"

Grey leaned forward, a gleam in his eye. "Yes."

Regan dug deep into what Tommy had written down. The names, businesses, what was he most interested in?

He had a question about Adam Hannigan working for Brock Marsh.

"Did Brock Marsh hire Adam Hannigan to kill Warwick?" she asked.

He laughed. "What do you think they are? Assassins for hire?"

"Adam Hannigan had at one point worked for Brock Marsh."

He shrugged, didn't comment.

"Was Brock Marsh as an entity—or an individual inside the organization—primarily responsible for hiring Hannigan?"

He shrugged.

"They were tasked with the assignment, correct? Hired?"

"You're making this so much harder than it needs to be, Regan. I can call you Regan, can't I?"

Charlie put his hand on her knee under the table where Grey couldn't see him. He squeezed, then asked, "Yes or no, did Granger ask if Brock Marsh was involved."

"Yes."

"Did he know who was behind hiring Adam Hannigan to kill Warwick?"

"No."

"Did he have a list of names or businesses and ask you if they were responsible?"

"Yes."

"Was one of the names that he mentioned to you involved?"

Grey grinned. "Yes. You're good at this, Deputy North. This is so much fun."

Charlie nodded at Regan. "Regan?"

She quickly caught on to Charlie's plan. She asked Grey about each of the businesses that had been accessed in the Potomac Bank heist.

"Novak Construction?"

"No."

"Delarosa Equity?"

"No."

"Legacy CPA?"

"You're boring me," Grey said.

"That's not a no."

"No." He sighed dramatically. Appealing to his humanity wasn't going to work; she doubted he had a conscience.

Tommy reached out to Grant immediately after he talked to Peter Grey. Something Grey had told him—or something Tommy suspected and Grey confirmed through his ridiculous Twenty Questions game—had Tommy going to Grant.

If Grant was the target, it was most likely related to one of his clients. She didn't have his client list—that information wasn't easily accessible. But Tommy could have been reviewing court cases, newspaper articles, other resources to build a list of Archer Warwick clients.

Grey had already confirmed that Grant was Hannigan's target. So she asked, "Have you heard of the Archer Warwick Bachman Law Offices?"

"Yes."

"Did one of their clients put the hit out on Warwick?"

"Took you longer than Tom to figure it out, but you get some credit for finally getting warmer."

"Is that a yes?"

"That is a yes."

"Which client?"

He laughed, didn't answer.

"I don't have their client list," Regan said. "And other people are going to die if we can't stop them."

"So?"

Then suddenly, she remembered the photos she'd taken from Grant's desk. Inside a folder was a list of names.

She looked at it more closely, skimmed it. "Senator Clarence Burgess," she said.

"No."

"Hank Burgess."

"No."

"Bruce Rockford."

No answer.

She looked at Grey. "Well?"

"Not the question you want to ask."

What the hell did that mean? But she didn't show her frustration. Instead, outwardly calm, she asked, "Is Rockford involved in any way with the assassination attempt on Grant Warwick?"

"Yes."

"But he didn't order it."

"No."

"A middle man."

"Yes."

"Does he work for Brock Marsh?"

As she said it, before Grey responded, she realized *Brock* stood for *Bruce Rockford*.

"Yes," Grey confirmed.

"Is he the contact person who makes it happen? He's *Brock* in Brock Marsh."

"Bingo."

Rockford runs Brock Marsh and he must have known Hannigan from way back. Used him for this job. Had him killed to cover their tracks because he hadn't been on their payroll for a long time.

She asked, "Did Tommy have a name other than Rockford?"

"Your friend didn't even mention Rockford."

She looked back down at the list that had been in Grant's files. Tommy didn't have this list when he talked to Grey. But he had known that everything revolved around Grant.

"Franklin Archer," she said quietly.

"You're getting warmer."

"Did Franklin Archer put out the hit on Grant?"

"No."

"But he knew about it," she said.

"I couldn't say." Grey looked at his hands as if inspecting his nails.

She went back to the list on her phone. "West Valley Mining."

"No."

"BioRise Pharmaceuticals."

Silence.

She looked up.

"You have your answer."

"BioRise hired Brock Marsh to kill Grant Warwick?" she said. "Why?"

"Your guess is as good as mine."

"But you know."

He shrugged. "I don't care."

Nothing he told them—or that they guessed—was going to get them a warrant. Nothing was going to get them a foot in the door of a multibillion-dollar pharmaceutical company.

But it *would* get her in the door to talk to Franklin Archer.

And now…she understood why Tommy reached out to Grant. It wasn't because Grant was Chase's father, it was because Grant had access to Archer Warwick client files.

Someone had to pay Brock Marsh. Perhaps it was those records that Tommy needed to make the connection.

But what did any of this have to do with the Potomac Bank robbery?

"Thank you for your time, Mr. Grey," Charlie said.

"One more question," Regan said. "Did Brock Marsh hire Michael Hannigan to rob Potomac Bank two years ago?"

It made sense. They hired his brother to kill Grant; they hired Michael to rob the bank. It was the why that eluded her.

"Wrong question."

Too specific? She asked instead, "Was Michael Hanni-gan hired to rob Potomac Bank?"

"Yes."

"Did Brock Marsh hire him?"

"No."

That surprised her.

"Did BioRise hire him?"

"No."

What the hell? Who else?

Charlie asked, "Did Franklin Archer hire Michael Hannigan to rob the bank?"

Grey smiled. "Yes, yes he most certainly did."

"And," Regan said, "Becca Johns was his inside person at the bank."

Grey shook his head. "She wasn't Hannigan's inside per-son." He put his hand over his mouth. "Whoops!"

"Who was she working for?"

"Your dear friend *Tommy* figured it out. I'm sure you will, too."

"Was it someone we mentioned?"

"Yes."

"BioRise?"

He sighed, didn't answer the question. "Honestly, if you don't figure it out soon, you'll be joining your friend in the morgue."

"Is that a threat?" Regan said.

"Not a threat. Just a fact. Your fifteen minutes are more than up. I'm ready to go back to the rec room now."

Regan paced the conference room once they shut down the video chat. "I don't know where to start with all that."

"He's bored. He's playing games."

"So you don't believe him?"

"I didn't say that."

"Then what?"

"Tommy went into his meeting with Peter Grey with some different information than we have, but we have more—we got more information because we had more questions to ask. I think we're almost there," Charlie said. "Tommy went back to the Potomac Bank robbery because of the Hannigan brothers. Two brothers, no criminal records, each committing a violent act seemingly out of the blue."

She stopped pacing. "Do you think they were blackmailed into committing these crimes?"

"Blackmailed or needed the money, I don't know. But both were outliers."

"Becca Johns—she wasn't his accomplice? Tommy thought she was, at least that's what I got from his notes. Maybe I misunderstood."

"I don't know that I completely trust him with that information," Charlie said cautiously.

"If we believe anything he said, we should at least take everything he said as a possibility until we can disprove it. Tommy was interested in Becca Johns. Maybe not because she was Michael Hannigan's accomplice, but because she was working for someone else."

"For what? To steal from the boxes before he got there?"

"What if...what if Hannigan *was* working with Becca, but she was playing sort of a double agent?" Regan prompted. "If she alerted someone that the heist was imminent."

"That would suggest that one or more of the five box owners had something to hide. They would have removed the information prior to the robbery."

"Maybe Hannigan figured out Becca double-crossed him and killed her. Jenna Johns hasn't called me back. I want to drive up there today, but first I'm going to talk to Franklin Archer."

"Are you sure that's wise?"

"Very sure. I'm not going to tip our hand—but I need to feel him out. And in light of Grant gone missing, now's the perfect time."

"Then let me track down Jenna Johns," Charlie said. "I suspect she'll be able to fill in some of our holes."

Thirty-Five

Regan had known Franklin Archer almost as long as she'd known Grant. While she couldn't think of a viable motive for Grant's longtime friend and colleague to be behind any of this, she couldn't discount what Peter Grey had said. That, coupled with the empty file with his name on it and Grant's fear that his office was bugged, suggested that Franklin Archer was involved in something nefarious.

She would need to tread carefully, she knew. No overt questions. Perhaps just express concern over Grant. It was no secret she'd found Madeline's body last night. It would be natural for her to talk to Franklin.

It was after ten by the time Regan arrived at the Archer Warwick Bachman Law Offices. The receptionist looked up with red, weepy eyes.

"I don't suppose Grant is in," said Regan.

"No, he isn't." She sniffed, wiped her nose with a tissue.

"I know about Madeline," Regan said. "What a loss for everyone."

"It's awful. And the police want to talk to Grant. I know he couldn't have done anything to Maddie. He loved her. Oh—I'm sorry."

"I know they were involved," Regan said. She also agreed with the receptionist, but she had other fish to fry. "Is Franklin available?"

The receptionist seemed surprised by her request. "I'll check. Can you wait here?"

Regan gave a nod, and the receptionist left her desk. There were two women posted at the counter; the other was answering phones and typing, not paying any attention to Regan. She was new, hadn't worked here when Regan was still married to Grant.

A moment later Franklin came out of the main offices. Looked like he hadn't slept much, Regan thought. He put his left hand on her arm when he approached, squeezed it.

"Regan, I just spoke to the police. It's awful. Let's go to my office." He escorted her down the hall, past Grant's wing, to the larger spread in the far corner. Franklin told his secretary no interruptions, then motioned for Regan to take a seat while he closed the door.

"Oh—I should offer coffee. I'm not thinking."

"I'm good, Franklin. Thank you."

She sat on the leather sofa; Franklin took a seat on the leather chair across from her.

His office was twice the size of Grant's and beautifully decorated. Its pristine bookshelves had perfectly aligned law books; expensive oil paintings featured under accent lights on the walls; a prominent portrait of his father, the founder of the firm; and an amazing view of downtown Arlington with the river beyond. If the day was clear, they would have been able to see DC in the distance, but gray skies hadn't lifted this morning, suggesting rain later today.

It had been his father's office before the old man retired from the law, remarried a woman half his age, and moved to Florida. It sounded cliché, but anyone who knew the elder Archer saw his midlife crisis coming a mile away. She had wondered, perhaps a bit cynically, that if Mrs. Archer hadn't died of cancer if Franklin's father would have left her for a trophy wife. She had never particularly liked the older man.

But she'd always liked Franklin. Until the last few days and her suspicions of him blossomed.

"I know you're busy," Regan said. "Thank you for taking a few minutes."

"For you and Grant? I'd do anything."

"You spoke to the police?"

"A Detective Quincy called the office right after I came in this morning. Told me that Madeline McKenna had been stabbed to death in her own home. They want to talk to Grant. They wanted to know if I knew where he might be. I tried calling him a number of times, but he doesn't answer."

"I tried as well."

"The police contacted you?" he asked, apparently confused.

"In a manner of speaking. I found Madeline's body."

His eyes widened. "How?"

"Grant and I were supposed to meet last night at his place. When he was late and didn't answer my calls, I went to Madeline's."

Franklin sighed, rubbed his eyes. "I can't imagine Grant doing such an awful thing. I'm certain you can't, either."

She sensed a *but* in his tone and didn't comment.

She wanted information, but she wasn't about to put her trust in Franklin. Regan had never been good at deception or game playing. She preferred straightforward questions and answers, but asking Franklin direct questions would tip her hand.

The idea that he knew about the plan to kill Grant—a

plan that ultimately killed their son—had her seeing red, but she maintained a straight face. She had no proof, no evidence, just the word of a convicted killer who enjoyed playing games and vague references to Franklin Archer in Tommy's notes.

Franklin said, "Grant has been preoccupied lately."

"How so?"

"Moody. Quiet. Then he'd snap at his assistant or the receptionist for no apparent reason." He paused, then added, "His assistant overheard Grant and Madeline arguing last week in a conference room."

"Did you tell the police that?"

"No. I should have, but Grant's my friend, above all. I said *I* never heard Grant and Madeline arguing, which is true." He leaned forward, looked earnest, worried. "Regan, Grant came to my house last night. He was very agitated."

"What time? What did he say?"

"Late, after ten. He was in a full panic, wasn't making much sense. You can ask Isabelle. She was worried about him, too, how frazzled and out of sorts he was. Ranting about Madeline, told me she'd been stabbed. He said he was in trouble."

"Did you tell the police that Grant came to your house?"

"I did, but I played it down, said it was business related, that he seemed preoccupied. I mean I had to tell them he came over—if I didn't and they found out, they'd think I was trying to protect him, or helping him. In fact, I don't know how much I helped, because Detective Quincy informed me that he would be coming by the offices later today, and that I should make myself available. I would do anything for Grant, but if he and Madeline were in a fight— it must have been some sort of accident. Grant would never hurt anyone on purpose."

Regan didn't know how much she believed of what Franklin told her. And the way he was speaking—it was clear he either *thought* Grant was capable of killing Madeline, or he wanted people to *believe* that Grant was capable of killing Madeline. Neither gave her comfort—and both made her suspicious.

It was only a matter of time before Detective Quincy issued an arrest warrant for Grant.

"Tell me," Franklin said. "Do you know what happened between Grant and Madeline?"

His eyes were wide, questioning, and she felt it was all an act. She'd arrested, interviewed, observed enough liars in her life that she could see it, plain as day. She wanted to confront him, but didn't.

She stated, "I want to find Grant. I'm worried about his safety."

"Do you think—that he would—no, he wouldn't—*hurt himself*?"

Suicide? That's where Franklin's mind went? Did he honestly believe that Grant killed Madeline and planned to kill himself?

"No." If she was being honest, the lowest point of their lives was after Chase was killed. Neither she, nor Grant, had become so depressed that suicide was ever on the table. Not for her, at least. She didn't *think* Grant would contemplate it, but sometimes you didn't know what the people you loved were struggling with, deep inside. And the murder of a child…grief was debilitating. Grief could drive even the strongest down a dark path of despair.

She dismissed the thought, though she would consider the possibility later. Right now she had the distinct impression that Franklin *wanted* her to believe that Grant was suicidal. Out of actual concern for his safety? Or because he was planning something nefarious?

"*Someone* killed Madeline," she continued, "and the police are looking at Grant because they were romantically involved and they can't reach him. I would like to find him first—convince him to come in and answer their questions." She didn't state whether she believed in his guilt or innocence, wanting to watch Franklin's reaction, listen to his explanations.

"I'm so sorry you have to deal with this. I don't know what's going on with Grant. I cannot for the life of me figure out why he would run like this."

One thing had bothered Regan ever since Detective Quincy told her last night that Grant had been seen leaving Madeline's condo within the timeframe of her murder. Why didn't he call the police when he found her body? Why didn't he call Regan for help? He knew she wanted to talk to him about Tommy's investigation. If Madeline's murder was connected to Tommy…it would benefit Grant to talk to her. Running was a sign of guilt.

Or of fear.

Dammit, Grant! What are you doing?

"I don't want to take up your time, but I stopped by to see if you might have any idea where Grant might go, who might help him," Regan said.

"The police asked, and I really don't. You, of course. His family? Possibly. He's not particularly close to his family, though, as I'm sure you know."

Grant had a cordial relationship with his parents. They never talked about anything substantive. Not because there was anything wrong with his parents—they were good people, upscale, from Boston. They had two sons—Grant, then eight years later, his brother, Richard. There was too large an age gap for Grant and Rich to have been close growing up. They were friendly, but didn't see each other much outside of the occasional holiday.

Regan didn't think Grant would reach out to Rich. Rich was in the military, stationed at the naval airbase in Pensacola, last she heard. He might be deployed now, but she hadn't kept up with him since she last saw him at Chase's funeral. He was a good man, dedicated to his career, married to a career naval officer, no kids. He wouldn't help Grant evade the law.

Regan, as a marshal, had an uncanny way of finding people who didn't want to be found. Right now she was still churning over possibilities, but the idea about his family tickled a memory in the back of her head. Where would Grant go to think? To consider his options? To make decisions?

Where would Grant go to hide?

She thought hiding from the police was secondary to hiding from a threat—and everything about Grant's behavior over the last few days told Regan he was scared. He'd hunker down in a place that felt secure and comfortable. Some place remote.

She had to find him before the police. It would be a million times better for Grant if he came into questioning voluntarily, and Regan could convince him to do just that.

"Was Grant working for any clients who bothered him?" Regan asked Franklin.

"I don't understand what you mean."

"Grant didn't work criminal cases, but I know he had a few civil clients that were less than squeaky clean."

"Regan, you know I can't talk to you about any of his clients."

"I'm just spitballing here, Franklin. Just wondering if

Grant might have uncovered something more criminal, or something that disturbed him, conflicted him."

"If that were the case, he would have spoken to me about it. We've discussed numerous ethical issues in the past. We've turned down clients we didn't feel comfortable working for, and if Grant didn't want a client, he would decline their business." Franklin cocked his head and eyed her. She couldn't read him, but he had always had a good poker face. "What are you really getting at, Regan? Do you honestly believe that Grant or Madeline were working on something that put them in danger?"

"I couldn't say," she said. "Grant and I haven't talked much since the divorce. I was hoping you might know more about his work life. It would be better if I found him first, convinced him to talk to the police—before this gets out of hand."

Franklin nodded solemnly. "Do you have any idea where he is?"

"If I did, I wouldn't be here," she said. "If you hear from him again, would you call me?"

"Of course. I promised the police I'd contact them, but I'll call you as well."

"I appreciate it."

She rose, and Franklin jumped to his feet. "Let me know if I can do anything for you," he said, reaching for the door.

"Oh—I almost forgot," she said, even though she hadn't. Regan turned to him, looked him directly in the eye. "When I came to see Grant yesterday morning, he said something totally weird to me. I really didn't think much about it after everything that happened last night, but I just remembered. He said he thought his office was bugged."

"As in, someone planted a listening device?"

"Yes. Did he express that concern to you?"

"No. I think you must be mistaken. Are you certain that's what he said?"

"I am."

"I will have our IT unit check at once. That would be—shocking, to say the least. He must have checked himself, because our clients expect privacy and loyalty. If a rival or competitor was listening in on confidential conversations, that would be disastrous." Franklin's eyebrows tilted up. "Perhaps Grant was a mite paranoid lately. That would not be the first odd comment."

"Oh?"

"He was tired, late to important meetings. Mis-dressed—not his usual self. Perhaps he had something serious weighing on him."

Maybe something like finding out that someone you trusted killed your son.

Ice ran through her veins. She had no proof that Franklin was involved. But watching him now—his manner, his words, his tone—Franklin Archer knew more. Far more. About Grant. About Chase's murder.

Knew and said nothing.

She wanted to take him down. Demand answers, force him to tell her what had happened that he would steal from her the brightest light in her life.

But she didn't.

Regan thanked Franklin for his time and walked out.

He would pay for his crimes. She would make sure of it.

Lance Martelli was nervous but determined when he walked into the US Marshals office for the Eastern District. He approached the woman at the front desk, cleared his throat, and said, "I need to speak to someone about Deputy Thomas Granger."

The woman, who initially smiled, froze, assessed him critically.

"Your name?"

"Lance Martelli. I'm a nurse at Bethesda General Hospital. I work with Jenna Johns. She asked me to come in."

A tall, slender black man with broad shoulders wearing a shoulder holster over a gray button-down shirt approached him. "I'm acting chief deputy Charlie North. We've been looking for Ms. Johns. I just got off the phone with her employer who said she's called in sick for the last two days."

"Yeah. I need to make sure you can protect her. Before I tell you where she is, you have to promise me you'll protect her."

"Come into the conference room and tell me what you know. Then, I'll tell you what we can do."

Thirty minutes later, Charlie said, "I'm going to call a colleague of mine. When she gets here, we'll go talk to Jenna."

"So you'll protect her."

"I need to hear from her exactly what she knows about Deputy Granger's investigation and a statement about the two men she saw who claimed to be FBI agents. But yes— if her story holds, we can and will protect her."

Thirty-Six

Regan and Lance drove with Charlie in his truck an hour south to a nondescript suite-style hotel off the interstate. Regan was finally going to have answers. Maybe not all of them, but Jenna Johns had been threatened and she was in hiding, which told Regan that she knew something important.

Though Lance had been uncomfortable at first, he seemed to relax as they drove and talked. It helped that Charlie had a similar military background as Lance and Lance was naturally predisposed to trust law enforcement. Regan let him and Charlie talk about the army, tell stories, become familiar with each other, while she considered what the connection was between the bank robbery and Chase's murder.

She still didn't see it. But there had to be *some* connection, otherwise why would Tommy have been so involved in tracking Becca Johns during that time? Why would he have reached out to Jenna?

The answers were in those safe deposit boxes. What if... one of those companies was affiliated with the law firm? Or with Brock Marsh, the security company? Perhaps it had to do with the financing of crimes—crimes like taking out a hit on a lawyer. Because Grant wasn't the first target of these people.

Once someone got away with murder, they'd do it again… and again.

Lance introduced Charlie and Regan to Jenna. "You can trust them," he told her. "I do."

Jenna was a cute, muscular girl with dark blond hair she had loosely braided down her back. She had the ruddy skin of someone who liked to be outside when she could, wore no makeup, and had intelligent brown eyes that looked at all of them warily. Except for Lance—when she looked at Lance she relaxed.

He went to her side, took her hand. "Tell them everything, Jenna. They both knew Deputy Granger. They're investigating his murder."

"Full disclosure," Charlie said. "The FBI is investigating Tommy's murder, but we haven't talked to them about you or anything Lance told us. Why don't we start with why you called the FBI in the first place?"

The "suite" was really an oversized room divided by a half wall. Two queen beds were on the sleeping side of the room, and a couch and desk were on the living side of the room. Lance and Jenna sat on the couch and Charlie motioned toward the chair for Regan, but she shook her head. She wanted to stand, observe. So Charlie took the seat and Regan leaned against the door, waiting for answers.

Jenna's story was very believable, Regan thought, and Jenna herself a credible witness, even though she was nervous. She recounted that when she hadn't heard from Tommy she'd called him and a stranger answered his phone, a man who wanted to meet with Jenna in person to discuss Tommy's unauthorized investigation.

"Those were his words," Jenna said. "He said, 'unauthorized investigation' and I hung up. It didn't sound right. He called back, but I didn't answer. He left a message, saying that it would be beneficial for me to call back and talk to him, but I didn't. I panicked, left at ten o'clock at night. Packed a bag and left my phone because I thought someone might be able to track me."

Lance said, "You should have called me."

"I know. But I had a couple days off, so went to this family camp I'd gone to as a kid. They have individual cabins and I thought it would be far enough away—near the Pennsylvania state line—that I could figure things out. I planned to call Deputy Granger's office in the morning, not his cell phone, but then I learned that he'd been murdered. The news reported it, and had a number to call, the FBI hotline."

"You called the number on the news?" Charlie clarified.

Jenna explained how she called the number, talked to several people before Agent Wexford called her back on Wednesday. "She didn't think I had any important information, but I told her I was scared because of the stranger who answered Tommy's phone. I must have sounded scared, because she said she'd have two agents come to my home or work to talk to me."

"Did you tell the FBI, on the phone, anything about why you were working with Tommy, or what he was investigating?"

"No. I'll admit, I was really nervous and didn't know what was important, and I didn't like how Agent Wexford kind of, I don't know, dismissed my concerns."

"And Tommy reached out to you, correct?" Regan asked.

"Yes," Jenna said. "He was so nice to me, so patient even when I got upset—he didn't judge my sister, anything. Just listened and helped me figure everything out. I knew he was on leave—he told me. He was building a case, but he said he needed to devote all his time on it. Then he called me last Sunday and said he was going to his boss because he needed a warrant, and he felt he had enough evidence to get it. A warrant for Legacy CPA."

One of the boxes in the bank.

Before Regan could ask Jenna about it, she said, "When I got back from the camp, I found out my house had been robbed. My cell phone and laptop, gone. My place was a mess. I called the police, and Lance let me stay at his place because I didn't want to stay home alone."

"Did the police arrest anyone?" Charlie asked.

"No. At least, not that I know about. Then the next day, Thursday, I went to clean up—it was the middle of the day, I thought it would be safe. Lance was going to come over after his classes. I saw an SUV drive up. Two men in suits got out. They looked like FBI agents, and because Agent Wexford said they would be coming, I thought they were FBI, but I asked to see IDs before I opened the door and they didn't show me. One of them flipped open a badge, but I couldn't read it. Something about them felt...I don't know, off. So I ran out the back. They chased me. I hit one of them with my car, but he was okay, he got right up." She spoke faster as she got going.

"I know the area well," Jenna continued, "and drove to a place I didn't think they could find me, waited awhile. Then I went to the hospital, because I wanted to call Lance, tell him not to come over, but I'd left my phone, the new phone I got at Walmart, at the house. And I saw them there, at the hospital, like they were waiting for me! I bolted, just kept driving until I almost ran out of gas, contacted Lance... and that's it. Oh—and the two men at the door? They mentioned the phrase *unauthorized investigation*. Just like the guy on the phone. That freaked me out."

Charlie said, "Lance, you saw them, too?"

"Yes. Before I knew where Jenna was, I went to her place and they confronted me there. Then I saw them outside my apartment. So I called the police, and they disappeared. But I didn't take any chances, I swapped cars with my roommate."

Regan said, "Tell me more about what you and Tommy were working on, what he needed from you."

"A few weeks ago, I think May first, Tommy came by the hospital. He waited until I was off shift, then told me he was looking into reopening the Potomac Bank robbery investigation, and he wanted to ask me some questions about it. He showed me a photo of my sister, Becca—you know about the robbery, right? She was a teller and she was killed."

"Yes," Regan said.

"The photo was of Becca and Michael Hannigan, the man who killed her. I had never seen it before. Tommy told me that he found it on social media from more than ten years ago. Becca and Michael had known each other in college. I hadn't known—no one told me, and I was still in high school. Tommy said he thought that Becca might have been Hannigan's accomplice. He wanted to talk to me about her finances, her state of mind, her friends, her history—anything I knew.

"At first, I said I wanted no part of it. Denied everything. But the next day, I realized I was being willfully blind. I mean, Becca was killed so I didn't want to believe anything bad about her. But I realized I knew a lot of stuff about Becca and not all of it was good. So I called Tommy and we met. He listened to everything I had to say, even stuff that wasn't relevant. And I'll never forget what he said. He said, 'Everyone makes mistakes. Your sister didn't deserve to die for hers.' And I knew he would do everything he could to find the truth. And I wanted the truth."

"How did you and Tommy come to the conclusion that Becca was an accomplice?"

"Becca had an influx of cash in the month before the robbery. A car she drove that she said belonged to her second job, and she refused to tell me what it was because they were paying her under the table. She made some comments to me about how everyone had secrets, and some people even kept their secrets in safe deposit boxes.

"But, it wasn't until the second time we met, when Tommy asked me to look through some information he'd compiled—this was a week before he was killed—that he realized something else was going on."

"What was that? Did he tell you?"

"He asked me to review the evidence logs and witness statements from the robbery to see if something stood out to me. One thing did. Legacy CPA. Becca had worked for them for several years, back when I was still in high school. I told him that and he got quiet. Said he had to research something, but this might be the connection."

"The connection to what?" Charlie asked.

"To the murder of a little boy."

Regan's heart tightened. "How so?"

"I don't know. He asked me for any of her personal financial information, so I put that together for him—I had handled her estate and debts after her murder. I've always been a bit anal-retentive about tax things, so I had all her tax information, which included W-2s. She worked for Legacy as a receptionist for more than two years."

"Did Tommy indicate what he thought about this information? Whether she was involved because she knew Legacy had valuable information in the box, or for another reason?"

"He thought that Michael Hannigan had been hired to get information from one or all of the boxes. But when he learned about Legacy, I don't think he thought quite the same thing—he didn't give me details. But he was very interested when I told him I'd seen Becca and her old boy-friend."

"Who was?"

"A CPA at Legacy. Chad Rockford."

"Rockford?" Regan and Charlie said simultaneously.

"Tom had the same reaction," Jenna said, wary.

"Is he any relation to Bruce Rockford?"

"I don't know. I'd only met Chad a couple of times, when Becca was still living with me in Bethesda. He'd pick her up, so I didn't really talk to him much. He was older than her—like she was twenty-two when she was working there, he was thirty, maybe older. I mean, I guess there's nothing wrong with it, but he was just very different than Becca. Anyway, they'd broken up—Becca didn't lose sleep over him. At least not that she told me. Then I saw them having brunch. And I thought that he had gotten married, so that made me sad and angry at the same time."

"When and where?" Regan asked.

Her abrupt tone seemed to startle Jenna.

Charlie smoothed things over. "We're in the process of investigating a man named Bruce Rockford, a principal with a security firm, Brock Marsh."

"Oh, I've heard of them."

"The firm?"

She nodded. "Tom mentioned them several times, but

in passing. Like he was trying to figure out their angle—
something like that."

"Rockford is not a common name," Charlie said. "So
now I'm thinking Bruce and Chad are related. Regan?"

Regan did a quick search on her phone. "Yep. Looks
like they're brothers."

"You saw them at brunch," Charlie said. "Was it spontaneous? Why were you there?"

"This was a week before the robbery. Like I said, Becca
was acting all strange, like she was rolling in money. I
wasn't happy because she owed me money for the property
taxes on the house."

"She owned the house with you?"

"It was left to us when our parents died. Their insurance paid off the mortgage, but we still have to pay property taxes and maintenance. I handled it, because Becca
was never that responsible with her money. I had covered
her for the taxes, but I needed her to pay me back. She told
me to meet her at her apartment—she had an apartment
in Arlington because she didn't want to live with me, even
rent-free." Jenna looked at her hands.

"Jenna, it's okay," Lance said. "Whatever you're feeling
about your sister is okay."

"I didn't understand why she just threw money away like
that. It wasn't like she couldn't get a teller job in Bethesda.
Anyway, she told me to stop by her apartment Sunday
morning—the Sunday before she was killed. She'd have
the money for me. I did—she wasn't there. I called her,
she didn't answer. I was so mad—I usually either work or
visit our grandma on Sundays. I left and a couple blocks
from her apartment, I saw her new car parked in front of
a breakfast place. So I pulled over and went in to look for
her. She was having brunch with Chad."

"Did you confront her?"

"Of course. I went up and said did time get away from her? That we were supposed to meet an hour ago. She was really mad that I interrupted them."

"Were they romantic?" Charlie asked. "Or did it seem like a business meeting?"

"Kind of both? I mean, they were sitting close together and Becca was being flirty and wearing a knockout sundress. Becca was beautiful. I mean, gorgeous. Petite, but without the big bones that I have. What people call vivacious. And I knew when she was being flirty. Chad's a good-looking guy, but I couldn't tell what was going through his head.

"Anyway, Becca pulled me aside, away from him, and said I was going to ruin everything and to go away. I reminded her she still owed me fifteen hundred dollars, and she said she'd be making fifteen *thousand* this month and there was more if she got 'the job.' I asked what job would pay fifteen thousand a month? She didn't answer. Told me to go away, she'd call me later. I was angry and left. She never called me...and then she was dead."

Tears sprang to her eyes and she wiped them away. "I hate that the last conversation I had with my sister was an argument. I *hate* it."

"It's okay," Lance told her quietly. "You didn't know."

"Did the FBI ask you any questions about Becca at that time? After she was killed?" Regan asked.

Jenna shook her head. "Nothing. And to be honest, when they told me she was killed in a bank robbery, I didn't remember, at least not to bring it up, not until Tommy asked me questions."

"I'm going to show you some pictures," Charlie said. "Tell me if you recognize these men. The photos aren't great—they're from a security camera—so if you don't know just say so."

"Okay." She took a deep breath as Charlie turned his phone around. "Oh. My. God. That guy. That guy there— he was the one who came to my door. I swear to God, that's him. The other—it could be the taller guy. Could be, I'm not sure. They were both wearing sunglasses just like these. But the shorter guy? I hit him with my *car*! I wouldn't forget him, or that scar on the side of his neck."

"Okay. That's good."

"Do you know who they are? Are they FBI agents?"

"They're definitely not FBI," Charlie said. "Can you sit tight in here while I talk to Regan in the hall?"

Charlie and Regan stepped outside. "Wow," he said.

"That's why Tommy thought she might be in danger," Regan said. "Jenna saw Becca with someone from Legacy CPA the week before the bank robbery. Why was she with him? Because she was working with Hannigan to rob the bank? Tipped them off? We now know there's a connection between Legacy and Brock Marsh—the Rockford brothers. Did Tommy find it? And if so, how does it connect to Grant?"

"Why didn't Tommy bring this to me sooner?"

"He wanted proof." Regan turned the new information over in her head. "He had some of the information, but we have more. Grant has the rest of it. He knows. And he ran instead of telling me."

"What are you going to do?"

"Find him. Can you put Jenna into protective custody?"

Charlie nodded. "I'll bring them to a safe house in Alexandria. Then I'll talk to Lillian O'Dare. Find out what the hell is going on—not just with the Valera arrest, but the fact that a caller's information got out of the building.

They have a leak—a major leak—and they need to plug it now. Hopefully, they'll be able to trace it and find the mole."

Regan and Charlie walked back into the hotel room. Jenna had her head on Lance's shoulder, and practically jumped up as if they'd been caught in a compromising position.

"What's happening? Can I go home?"

"I'd like to bring you back to Alexandria for a few days," Charlie said. "Put you in a safe house for the weekend while we follow up on the two fake FBI agents. You could go home, and I would contact the local police to have them keep an eye out for you, but it wouldn't be 24/7. The safe house is near our headquarters, in a secure building. You won't need a marshal on-site, but we can be there quickly. We have some rules for your safety, but there's a television, cable, lots of movies and books and games. It's not the Ritz, but it's a nice enough place. There's an approved list of places you can call for delivery—places we vet regularly. Ultimately, though, it's your choice."

Jenna looked at Lance. "I can't ask you to take the weekend off."

"You don't have to ask. I'm doing it. Until we figure out what's going on, and know that you'll be safe, I'm not leaving."

"Thank you," she whispered. She turned to Charlie and Regan. "Thank you."

"How fast can you pack up here?"

"Five minutes. I only have an overnight bag, then need to check out."

"I'll take care of that," Charlie said. "Regan, you good here?"

Regan nodded. She itched to look for Grant—but first things first. Get Jenna Johns safe, then find her ex.

She had two ideas where he might be, but she needed to do some research to make sure the property was still in his family. She'd leave first thing in the morning—before dawn.

The faster she found Grant, the faster she'd have the final piece of the puzzle. And then—maybe—she'd get justice for Tommy.

And Chase.

Thirty-Seven

Franklin Archer canceled all his appointments after Regan Merritt left his office.

If she found Grant first, he would tell her everything he knew. If Regan had half a brain—and she did—she'd know how to put all the information together, there was no doubt in his mind. And then he would be ruined.

Franklin was stuck. And scared—though he shouldn't be. As he'd told Grant last night, mutually assured destruction meant that he was safe. Except that tickle of fear that he may have been overconfident.

Brock Marsh should have handled the problems before everything got out of control!

Madeline was dead…and that meant that his client had taken matters into his own hands. It meant that his client didn't trust him to keep his people quiet. He had Madeline killed and Grant would be next.

What did that mean for Franklin?

He needed to run.

Just like he told Grant to do.

No. You can't run. You have the law firm. Your wife, your daughters.

A chill ran down his spine.

He called Isabelle on his private cell phone in his private bathroom. He knew Grant's office was bugged—he'd had it bugged, because he needed to know how much Grant knew and what he'd been telling that damn marshal. But what if his client had *his* office bugged? What if they were listening to his conversations?

"Honey, I hit a snag here at the office, and I need you to take the girls out of town for a while."

"Out of town," she said bluntly. "How far out of town?"

Isabelle didn't know everything about his clients, but she knew enough.

"Switzerland. Head to New York tonight and stay in a nice hotel. I will join you there tomorrow if I can. If I can't, then I'll meet you in Switzerland."

"We have to leave that quickly?"

"I think it would be best."

"What happened?" she whispered. "Does this have anything to do with Grant's visit last night? With Madeline's murder? What is going on?"

"We'll talk later," he said emphatically. "Just do what I say, Isabelle. I love you."

"You had better be safe, Franklin. I'm not going to lose you over this…this unfortunate business."

He ended the call because Isabelle wasn't stupid. She would figure out that everything had gone off the rails, and if he couldn't put the pieces back together, he didn't want her to suffer. She had access to enough money and resources to take care of the girls for the rest of their lives. That was all that mattered to him. And she didn't know anything specific about his dealings, so if she was questioned, she had nothing that would incriminate him—or her.

All she knew was that some of his clients were not quite...*ethical*. That was a tame word for criminal.

His other cell phone rang and he jumped, as if the caller was going to tell him he'd heard everything.

But it was Bruce Rockford with Brock Marsh.

A man who Franklin was beginning to believe was playing both sides.

"Report?" Franklin answered crisply.

"Jenna Johns is in the wind. Hasn't used her credit cards, no toll roads. Our inside man in the FBI may be compromised if she talks to anyone."

"He doesn't know anything substantive, does he?"

"He won't talk."

Rockford's specialty was gathering dirt. Gathering dirt on federal agents was difficult, but very lucrative.

"I pulled the team from her house, the hospital. We have another problem. Regan Merritt."

"I'm aware."

"I have orders."

"Not from me."

"I don't take orders from you, Archer. I never have. You just never realized it until now."

His blood ran cold. "Bruce, I *made* Brock Marsh. I took you from a small two-bit security company babysitting spoiled brats like Hank Burgess into a state-of-the-art security and surveillance company."

"I appreciate the boost, but I know what side my bread is buttered, and I know when the ship is going down. Your ship. I've been ordered to take care of all loose ends, starting with Ms. Merritt. I suggest you get your affairs in order."

Bruce hung up on him.

Franklin stared at his phone. His hand was shaking.

What about *mutually assured destruction* didn't they understand?

Everything had gotten out of hand over the last three weeks. When Regan Merritt left Virginia, everyone breathed easier—no one was looking too closely at Adam Hannigan's death. Until Thomas Granger started stirring the pot.

Franklin hadn't wanted to have Tom Granger killed; killing a federal agent was dangerous. But he had compiled far too much evidence and Franklin panicked. They acquired Granger's evidence and destroyed it. No one else should be able to figure anything out because Granger pulled together facts from multiple sources. And Grant? Well, now Grant was suspected of murder, so he wasn't exactly trustworthy.

Killing Madeline was not Franklin's idea. He hadn't even known, but he should have. He should have known that his clients had recalled Nelson Lee to handle it.

Without telling me. They did it without telling me. Am I next?

That was a problem.

While he believed his information would keep him safe, he had that niggle of doubt...that fear that maybe, just maybe, they didn't care. Or they thought they could withstand the release of their dirty secrets.

But there was so much at stake. Billions of dollars. *Billions.* With that much money, they might just cut him loose and deal with the fallout.

He could only hope he lived long enough to see his family again.

Thirty-Eight

Charlie North walked into FBI headquarters at four that afternoon. Lillian O'Dare made him wait fifteen minutes; his temper was on a slow boil. When she finally sent for him and closed the conference room door behind them, he snapped.

"I told you this was a major security issue, and you made me wait?"

"I can't drop everything every time the Marshals Service throws a tantrum. You had the deputy director call my boss over Valera? And then expect me to be at your beck and call after I had to jump through a hundred different hoops to prove I had the right man?"

"You don't," he said through clenched teeth. Charlie prided himself on keeping his cool in all situations, but he was furious with how the FBI had treated this case from the beginning.

"I know," she snapped.

Okay, that was a surprise.

"You know Valera didn't kill Tommy?"

"He had a rock-solid alibi. And unless he hired someone,

of which we can find nothing, he's clear. Not innocent—
we have him on a bunch of other crimes. But not murder."

"Why didn't you tell me?"

"Because you went over my head! Embarrassed me. Because I don't subscribe to your out-there theories?"

"I'm going to tell you something, and you have to listen with an open mind. Because you have a security leak in this office."

"I doubt that, but I'm listening."

She crossed her arms and glared at him. Neither of them had sat down.

Charlie told her everything Jenna told him, but left her name out of it.

"You have a witness you're keeping from me?"

"Didn't you hear what I just told you? Two men showed up at her house, said they were FBI agents, refused to show credentials. This was twenty-four hours after she called the FBI hotline and told Agent Wexford almost everything she knew about Tommy Granger's investigation into Chase Warwick's murder."

She frowned. "I didn't hear about us sending anyone out to talk to a witness." She motioned for Charlie to follow her to her desk.

They wound through cubicles and office doors until she sat in a cubicle on the far side of the room. It was cluttered, but not messy. Pictures of two kids took up much of the desk space and were pinned into the cloth frame of the cubicle. He asked about her kids.

"They're good, thanks. Both in high school. One day sweet as molasses. The next day I'm ruining their lives. Trevor made the varsity football team as a sophomore. Scares me to death, to be honest, with all the reports of head injuries. But my husband thinks it's good for him, team building and all that." She typed on her computer, glanced at him. "You have a couple kids, right?"

"Two girls and a boy. Not teenagers yet, but middle school is bad enough."

"Honestly, high school is better than middle school."

"I have something to look forward to."

She peered at her screen. "I have the log here. Agent Natalie Wexford spoke to forty-seven people this week who called the hotline about Granger's murder. Nothing panned out with any of them." She scanned the computer. "Two agents were sent out to a neighbor of Granger's, a Mrs. Abigail Frieze, who said she saw a car in the neighborhood that matched the description we had of the suspect's vehicle. She didn't have much information, but gave us a firm time. Nothing more came from that. And…well there's a Jennifer Johns who Agent Wexford spoke to on Wednesday at 11:58 a.m. I have her phone and contact information. No agents have been sent to follow up. She indicated low priority—that the witness had no first or secondhand information about the shooting and did not claim to witness it. Her contribution was that she was privy to Granger's activities leading up to his death."

"If agents were dispatched, it would show in the log."

"Yes. If there's one thing the FBI excels at, it's our bureaucracy."

Charlie smiled. "May I sit?"

He motioned to a chair against the wall, and she nodded. He pulled over the chair and said quietly, "The two fake agents that showed up at Jenna's house had information that she'd only given to the FBI the day before."

"Are you certain? Do you trust that she didn't tell anyone?"

"I debriefed her myself. Does your log indicate that she

said a stranger answered Tommy's cell phone *after* he was killed?"

Lillian looked at the report. "Yes. That's—odd. We've put a trace on his phone and the GPS isn't popping."

"You and I both know that a marginally competent tech person can disable or bypass GPS tracking. And," Charlie continued, "the individual who answered used the same phrase as the two fake agents. That Tommy was conducting an *unauthorized investigation*."

"What you're suggesting is that someone with access to the FBI log system—someone who understands how it works—gave private information to an outside party and found a way to cover his tracks."

"Yes. Not only an outside party, but to Tommy's killer."

He slid over the file he'd brought. "That's your copy. Jenna Johns's statement, signed. A photo of two men—one indistinct, she couldn't positively ID him, the other she ID'd as one of the two men outside her house. These two men also followed Regan twice this week, totaled her rental car the second time when she attempted to confront them."

Lillian looked through the information. "You're bringing this to me, and not my boss?"

"Yes. I sent the file to *my* boss and he may go directly to yours, but we've known each other for a long time. We have different styles, but you've always been straightforward. Until last year and Chase Warwick's murder investigation, I never had a problem with you."

"We're not going back to that, are we?"

"Unfortunately we are. Tommy was investigating Chase's murder. While I know you won't take the word of a convicted killer, I talked to Peter Grey, just like Tommy did three weeks ago. Grey plays games—he excels at the bullshit—but in his own way, he confirmed that Adam

Hannigan was hired to kill Grant Warwick, accidentally shot his son. Tommy believed that the assassination attempt on Grant was connected to the Potomac Bank robbery in Arlington—how, I still don't know. But Jenna confirmed that—it's in her statement. Read it."

"Where is she?"

"We're not sharing that information at this time. Only my office knows, and it ends there."

"I mean, I'll want to talk to her."

"I can make that happen. But first, you need to find the mole."

Lillian didn't say anything for a moment as she scrolled through the log, then looked again at Jenna's statement.

"I'll find him—or her. Every file that's accessed is logged by the system. If someone found a way to bypass it, I'll know—because other than bureaucracy, the FBI excels at redundancy. It's impossible to fully erase a digital trail. It's a pain in the ass to pull anything out of the master file, but I can do it."

"Keep me in the loop. If your mole is working with these people, he's an accessory to murder."

"If anyone in my office has compromised my investigation? I'm going to get them on a lot more than accessory. I promise you that."

Thirty-Nine

Regan talked to Charlie while he was driving back from DC in peak Friday commute traffic. He told her that O'Dare was on board, then said, "You're lucky I just started a good book on tape or I'd be a basket case by the time I get home in what looks like *two hours*."

"Sorry about the traffic, but good that O'Dare isn't the mole."

"Definitely not her—at least, I'm ninety-nine percent positive. She's a bureaucrat not a traitor. She'll find him."

"I have some news for you," Regan said. "I just got a call from the rental car company. Their mechanics thoroughly went over the car and they found something unusual in the wheel well—they think it's a tracking device, though it was damaged in the crash. I told them that a US marshal would pick it up, sent the information to Maggie. I hope I didn't overstep."

"No, you didn't. You're sure?"

"Positive. So I checked Tommy's truck. There was a tracker in his wheel well."

"Damn."

"Whoever was tracking me knows exactly where I've

been and what I've been doing. It looks high-end. I've bagged it—I'll leave it in Tommy's top desk drawer if you want to pick it up tomorrow. You should check your car, personal and work."

"We're clean," he said, "we regularly go over the vehicles because of witness transport. But I'll have them do a deeper sweep, just in case. Do you think Tommy's house is bugged?"

"No—I invested in a little bit of spyware this afternoon, swept the place. Nothing in his den or bedroom. I doubt they bugged any other rooms."

"You're going after Grant?" Charlie asked.

"Yes. I've researched likely hidey-holes. Two places are high on my list—I'll send you my itinerary when I know exactly where I'm headed and when, but I'm going to leave before dawn. Both are out of state."

"Do you want company?"

"Thanks, but I need to do this myself. Grant isn't going to talk to anyone but me. He'll tell me the truth when I find him." If he tried to lie or obfuscate, she would bring him in, even against his will.

"Keep in touch, or I'm sending in the cavalry."

"Thanks, Charlie."

She ended the call and finished making her dinner. She wanted to leave by four in the morning, which meant getting to bed early.

She had two places in mind.

Grant's family owned a second home near Olivebridge, in New York's Catskills. It was a good five-, six-hour drive, but it was very private. Grant's parents bought it when he was in high school, and she and Grant had spent at least one weekend a year there, sometimes more. Chase had loved running through the woods or hiking to the lake. In the winter they skied and built snowmen. They roasted marshmallows and barbecued steak and played board games every night. It was a wonderful place with good memories.

The other possibility Regan considered was another Warwick house—this one on Lake Champlain and owned by a family trust. Grant's grandparents put all their children and grandchildren on the trust, and the family agreed to never use the place as a vacation rental—only family and friends could stay there. Grant loved it there because some of his best childhood memories were on that lake.

If Regan wanted to disappear or lie low for a while, she'd opt for the Catskills. It was more remote, no direct line of sight to any of their neighbors from the house. Also, given the two locales, that one was safer, with more ways to get out. While the benefit of Lake Champlain was that it was closer to the Canadian border with multiple ways to cross, there were more people in the immediate area and the lake house was visible to multiple neighbors. Being spring, there would be a lot of activity at the lake.

Nope, she put her money on the Catskills. If Grant wasn't there, she'd head up to Lake Champlain. But she didn't think she'd have to.

Regan ate, cleaned up the kitchen, then called Terri and told her she'd be gone for the next day or two. Terri informed her that the memorial service would be Thursday evening, if that was acceptable to Regan. Of course it was—she would stay for it. And, hopefully, have found justice.

Her cell phone rang as she prepared her overnight bag. It was her dad.

She winced. She'd promised to keep him in the loop, but hadn't called him.

"Hi, Dad."

"You didn't tell me there was an APB out for Grant. That he's wanted for questioning in a murder."

"Word travels fast."

"What is going on, Regan? Don't sugarcoat it."

"Grant's girlfriend was stabbed to death. Grant's on the run. But he didn't kill her."

"Why is he running?"

"My guess? He thinks he's next. So do I. I'm going to find him, bring him in."

"You're too close to the case. Can't Charlie do it?"

She sat on the edge of the bed and realized she was going to have to tell her father everything.

"Dad, I have a lot to tell you."

She went through everything she knew—Tommy's investigation into the Potomac Bank robbery, her conversation with Grey and his ridiculous Twenty Questions game that confirmed that Grant had been Hannigan's target—and that Hannigan had been hired to kill him. She even shared her theory that Franklin Archer knew who wanted Grant dead.

"And, Dad? He may have known before."

"Before Chase was killed?"

"Yeah."

"Bastard," her dad whispered.

"Charlie and I haven't figured out the connection between the robbery and the attempted assassination of Grant, but Peter Grey indicated that the same people were responsible for both crimes."

Her dad didn't say anything.

"Dad? You there?"

"Yes."

His voice was clipped. Worried. She didn't want to worry her father. But he'd asked, and she wasn't going to lie to him.

"Well?"

"You're positive they're connected?"

"Tommy was."

"That means these people...they'll kill to keep from being caught. A bank teller, a child, a lawyer, a marshal? Regan—"

Now she heard the fear in his voice.

"I'm okay."

"For now!"

"Dad, don't do this to yourself, or to me. Every day you went to work, I knew you could be hurt. Don't put an added burden on me because I'm no longer a marshal. I'm still trained, I'm still prepared, and I'm still a better shot than you."

It was a running joke between them, but her dad didn't chuckle. He said, "I trust you implicitly, Regan. But in this case—there are emotions in play."

"I'm on top of them. I promise you, I'm not reckless. I have a good idea where Grant is, and I'm going to talk to him, bring him in, figure out what's going on."

"You think he knows."

"I think he has the final piece of the puzzle."

"Then why the hell didn't he turn these people in? If he knew that they killed his son, why didn't he do something?"

Yes, her father was angry. She didn't blame him.

"I don't think Grant knew until Tommy contacted him three weeks ago. Grant was helping him."

"And he still didn't come forward after Tommy was killed. That's a weak man, Regan. You can't trust him."

She trusted Grant—to a point. But she wouldn't be able to convince her father. "He panicked by running, but he'll talk to me. Grant grieved as hard as I did, Dad."

"Grant treated you like shit," he grumbled.

"I told you he apologized. And I've forgiven him. I can't live my life with a heart full of anger, resentment, hate. I had to let it go. And now—I'm ready for the truth, wherever it leads. Trust me, Dad. Okay?"

"I do." His voice was raw with emotion and she hated that she'd put fear in his heart. "I love you, kid. Don't get dead."

"I love you, Dad."

She ended the call and sat there, feeling all the pain that her dad had in his voice. Her dad wanted to fix everything.

Some things couldn't be fixed.

At nine thirty she finished with her overnight bag, showered, and slid into bed before ten, her hair still damp. She set her alarm for three thirty, would be on the road by four. It would be Saturday, so she shouldn't have too much traffic—most people heading up to the mountains for the weekend would have left today, but she might encounter a few slow spots. Still, she hoped to reach the Catskills in less than six hours.

And prayed Grant was exactly where she thought he was.

A noise woke her. For a split second Regan thought it was her wake-up alarm, then she realized the sound had been farther away, downstairs.

The room was completely dark. There was no light from the clock on the nightstand. The power was out.

She reached for her gun under her pillow.

She normally kept her firearm holstered in her dresser, but after all the events of late, it had seemed prudent to keep it closer. She was glad she had it in hand now.

She listened. Why hadn't the alarm gone off?

She slid out of bed in sweatpants and a tank top—her

version of pajamas. Light *plonks* of rain on the windows
and roof accented the silence.

She focused on downstairs. Heard movement. At least
two sets of footsteps.

The intruders moved slowly, steadily, methodically. She
heard no voices, but Tommy's old floorboards creaked. No
matter how quiet they were, they couldn't be completely
silent.

Upstairs, the floors were carpeted, so Regan could walk
silently—at least quieter than the intruders. She crept barefoot to the bedroom door, which she'd left ajar. Listened.
No voices. Through the crack in the door she saw a dull
beam of light—then another. Two people...

No, three, she realized as she heard a footstep on the
stairs. Then another. Another.

She hit the panic button on the security panel in the
bedroom. The alarm should scare the living shit out of the
intruders.

Nothing. It was dead.

That wasn't supposed to happen; if the power went out,
it would alert the security company. Unless, as she now
suspected, the power was out in the whole neighborhood.
Had these intruders blown a transformer or interrupted the
power supply another way? That would take considerable
planning and skill. Maybe it was simpler than that—maybe
they'd found a flaw in Tommy's security system and then
disconnected it.

Even if the police had been dispatched, response time
could be up to fifteen minutes, depending on where the
units were in the town.

She couldn't worry about any of that.

Assess the threat, stop the threat.

Regan walked back to her cell phone that she'd left

charging on the nightstand; it wasn't charging—the power was definitely out—but there were bars. She took it into the closet, wincing at the idea of being trapped in here. But she could see the door open from this angle, and she needed backup ASAP. She could take on any one man. She could take on two.

Three? In the dark? That was stretching even her skills.

Though she had the element of surprise. They thought she was sleeping.

She hit 911 and waited as it rang, clicked, rang, clicked, then the dispatcher picked up.

Regan interrupted the dispatcher's spiel, immediately whispering, "This is former deputy US Marshal Regan Merritt at 1616 Nance Road—three, possibly more, home invaders in house, likely armed. I am also armed, currently in the master bedroom. Need immediate response. I'm leaving the line open, mute."

She muted the phone because she didn't want the intruders to hear the dispatcher speaking but left the phone on a shelf in case they needed to trace the call. She'd given the address, but law enforcement could also track an open phone line.

Regan stepped out of the closet and walked to the door, standing behind it. If the door opened fully, they'd see her.

She listened. One of the men was on the landing right outside the door. She heard a whisper, but not what was said. Though no lights were on, just enough outside light came through the windows to cast shadows and give her marginal visibility.

Her eyes locked on the door as it slowly opened, a slight creak to the hinges.

She couldn't see the intruder, but his arm came up. He

wore gloves and held a gun. The gun was aimed at the bed where she had been lying just minutes ago.

He stepped in, lowered the gun slightly when he didn't see her in the bed.

Her breathing was calm, her heart rate steady, her training kicked in as she watched and listened. A man was coming down the hallway outside her room.

Correction: there were two of them upstairs.

Regan couldn't safely shoot at what she couldn't see. She entertained the hope that they might see her bed empty and believe she wasn't at home...or that she was sleeping in another room. She stood silently.

The intruder stepped forward. Because she was standing in front of the wardrobe cabinet, she couldn't fully hide behind the door.

He turned toward her, saw her, his posture tensing as he raised his gun.

Regan got off two shots in rapid succession, the bullets hitting him dead center in the chest. He went down.

A second man stood in the threshold, but he immediately turned and ran back down the hallway. She aimed and fired. Hit him in the upper shoulder, but he only grunted and continued to run. He shouted, "Go, go, go!"

She checked the pulse of the man at her feet: faint. She kicked his gun away and ran out of the room. As she stood at the top of the stairs, the man she'd shot was joined at the bottom by someone coming out of Tommy's office, and they ran out the front door.

She almost pursued them. She had the right, they had broken into the house, had come up to her room, and aimed a gun at her...but shooting a man in the back, even armed, outside of the house would cause more complications than she needed.

She bolted down the stairs to the front door just in time to see them barreling down the driveway to a car that was blocking the circular drive. The man she shot would need medical attention. A fourth man was behind the wheel.

The vehicle drove off almost before the two men jumped in.

Four men were sent to her house to kill her, she realized.

She had definitely kicked the hornet's nest. She only wished she knew who was the queen bee.

SATURDAY

Forty

The intruder died before the cops or the paramedics arrived. Regan figured he died within minutes of being shot; by the time Regan got back upstairs to restrain him, she couldn't find his pulse.

She waited on the front stoop for the police. Her adrenaline was still high when they arrived. She gave her statement—clear, concise—and when she was finished, the paramedics declared the intruder DOA. Charlie arrived moments later and sat with her while the crime scene investigators processed the scene and removed the body.

Based on not only the location of the body in Regan's bedroom, but Regan's 911 call and her clearly defensive shooting, she was all but cleared. Still, jumping through the hoops of a lawful shooting as a civilian was just as much a pain in the ass as when she had been a marshal. They took her gun—her favorite .45. Standard procedure, and she'd get it back in a few days, but it irritated her.

She would have to borrow one of Tommy's guns.

Finally, she and Charlie were alone. It was after two in the morning. They sat in Tommy's fancy kitchen, drinking coffee.

Charlie said bluntly, "They planned to kill you."

"I know."

"They broke into the house and tried to kill you."

He was angry and worried; she didn't blame him.

"Didn't even get a shot off," she said, trying to lighten the mood.

"They killed a marshal, probably killed that lawyer, and tried to kill you. All for what? What the fuck is going on here, Regan?"

Charlie was angry—he rarely swore.

"It's spiraling out of control. They're panicked and reckless. They want everyone who might know something dead."

"We don't even know who *they* are. We *think* Brock Marsh, but what if we're wrong?"

"Go after them. Raid them. Do anything necessary to light a fire under their asses."

"It's already in the works. Joint operation with the FBI."

"Did they find the mole?"

"No—Lillian knows when it happened, but it was from a dummy terminal not assigned to any agent. But she said she can find the culprit, and I'm going to trust her on this."

"Franklin Archer," she said.

"You think he's behind this?"

"I had a feeling that he was scared when I talked to him yesterday. I didn't tip my hand, but I asked some pointed questions. He doesn't have the balls to kill anyone, but he could have reported to someone who does."

"I'll get a warrant and bring him in."

"Good luck—he is a lawyer. My gut feeling isn't going to be enough for a judge."

"I'll find something. And Lillian is a damn good bureaucrat who knows the laws inside and out—she'll think of cause if I can't."

"Wow, you and *Lillian* have really become besties, haven't you?"

He ignored her. "You should be in protective custody."

She shook her head. He didn't argue with her.

Charlie took her hand. "You know, Regan, you've always been the rock of the office. But this case is different."

"I don't know the truth, but I *need* to know it. I have to find Grant. He's the key to all of this."

"You know where he is." It was a statement.

"I have a good guess. And I'm going alone—I know that's your next ask. He'll talk to me because we have history. I bring in the cavalry, he'll clam up, get defensive, and this won't end soon. Tommy was killed because he had *proof.* He had something tangible, a piece of evidence. It can't just be what Jenna knows about the safe deposit boxes, or that Becca had worked for Legacy CPA or was seen with Chad Rockford. That's all circumstantial. Maybe enough to open an investigation, maybe not. I think he had something that would compel the Marshals to open the case—and I think it's something Grant gave him. Files from the law firm, a money trail, accounts, I don't know. But *something* that told Tommy now was the time to push. Grant could have been planning to blow the whistle—or turn state's evidence. Maybe—just guessing here—Tommy was going to put Grant into WitSec."

As she said it, she believed she was right about most of it. She continued. "Information might be missing, but Grant knows what it is."

"You need to be careful with him."

She did. But not for the reasons Charlie's tone implied. He said, "Did you hear Arlington PD put out an APB for him? They have an arrest warrant—or will have one first thing in the morning."

"I'm surprised it took so long."

"I avoided Detective Quincy's calls this afternoon."

"Me, too." She smiled at him, picked up the mugs, put them in the sink. "I'm going to sleep for a couple hours, then leave."

"I'm staying." He walked back to the sink, picked up the mug he'd been using, and poured himself another cup of coffee.

"You don't—" Then she stopped. "Thank you, Charlie."

"You'd do the same for me."

Forty-One

Regan left Reston at eight in the morning and arrived at the Warwick family vacation house outside Olivebridge, New York, nearly eight hours later. A stop for gas and food then an accident outside Philly had delayed her.

She drove up to the two-story house—three stories if you counted the garage and storage room that took up the ground floor—off Lower Sahler Mill Road at four Saturday afternoon. If she was wrong, she'd wasted a day driving. Either way, she'd stay here tonight; after her busy night and broken sleep, she was too tired to make the drive back or tackle the five-hour drive to Lake Champlain, especially when she had increasing doubts that Grant would have gone there.

She parked Tommy's truck—which she had thoroughly checked for a tracking device, and it was clean—in front of the closed garage and looked out into the woods that surrounded most of the house. From the deck they'd have a view of more trees, an endless landscape of green that was even more stunning in the fall when the leaves changed into glorious colors. A bubbling creek right out of a storybook ran year-round, visible only from the deck. With her engine off, she could hear the fresh water flow. It was now suitable for easy rafting and in the summer it would be only ankle deep, but it was always moving.

Chase had loved coming up here. He'd reveled in any outdoor activity, just like his mom. Together they hiked and climbed trees. They drove to the lake to fish. Fishing wasn't Chase's favorite—he got bored sitting still for too long—but he humored her, chatting about baseball and the Washington Nationals, and his nerves when he was pulled up to a higher age group for Little League. The coach had moved him from center to second base, and he was worried he'd fail. He was the smallest on the team, younger than the others by a year or more, and he was going from best player on the team to middle of the pack.

But Regan reminded him that he'd worked hard to get this slot, that they didn't pick him because they were being nice, but because he fit the team and a need they had. That as long as he gave one hundred percent on the field in practice and in games, listened to the coach, and was a good teammate, he would have nothing to regret.

He'd had one season with that team, but that year Chase had bonded with the boys more than with any other team he'd been on. But it was here, in the Catskills the fall before he was killed, that Chase shared his hopes and fears with her, at the lake, fishing rods in hand.

She closed her eyes against threatening tears. Chase had been gone ten months, three weeks, and six days. She didn't know when she'd stop counting, or if she could, if the passage of time would always be marked in the days since her son died. She'd thought returning six weeks ago for Chase's birthday would give her that push to move forward, but haunting memories still crept in.

Sensing someone watching, she opened her eyes. She looked up at the deck. Grant stood rigid, watching her.

She'd been right.

She exited the truck, grabbed her go bag—which included two guns and extra ammo that she'd selected from Tommy's gun safe—and walked up the stairs, tense, weary, needing answers. Grant didn't move. He watched her walk toward him, his handsome, chiseled face drawn, pale, unshaven. His conservative haircut was rumpled, sticking up as if he'd just gotten out of bed. He looked older than thirty-nine, as if he'd aged even in the two days since she'd seen him.

"Are you here to arrest me?"

"I'm not a marshal."

"I didn't kill Maddie."

"Good."

She believed him. He was no saint, but murder wasn't in him.

"We need to talk," she said.

He stared at her; she stared back. Was he going to make this difficult?

"Yeah," he said softly and walked into the house.

The place was a fishbowl. She didn't know how safe or secure he was here. As soon as the sun went down, anyone with a visual of the house would be able to see inside. She didn't know if his car had also been tracked, or if the tracker could work from a distance. She would assume if Grant had been tracked, it was the same type of device that she'd found on Tommy's truck, which Charlie was having analyzed.

She worried about Grant's safety—and hers—but she was also concerned that he might try to lie, obfuscate, ignore the obvious.

But if he was innocent, someone was framing him for murder.

And they planned to come after him next.

Grant knew enough to damage the people behind Chase's murder. The people behind Tommy's murder. Of that, Regan had no doubt.

More pieces started to fall into place. The only real questions she had—aside from a few nagging details—were *who* and *why*. Who was behind these crimes and why had they targeted her family?

Regan followed her ex inside.

Though the sun was a few hours from setting, she didn't like how open the house was—two walls of windows that overlooked the creek and the valley. Definitely the fishbowl she imagined when she first drove up.

She walked over to the wall panel that controlled the blinds and pressed the button to lower them. Slowly, quietly, they descended. The house grew dim, so she turned on the kitchen light and made a pot of coffee.

The house had a two-story great room and the kitchen was in the center. A master bedroom and den were behind the kitchen, along with a powder room and large linen closet, plus access to the garage below. She checked the doors and made sure they were all locked. Upstairs were three bedrooms, each with their own bathroom. Two bedrooms accessed a balcony facing west, perfect for sunsets. She made a quick sweep of the upstairs. Grant wasn't staying up here; the rooms were closed up, the vents closed, the beds stripped.

She went back downstairs and poured two cups of coffee. Sipped hers, put one in front of her ex.

Grant sat slumped at the kitchen table, staring into an empty cocktail glass of melting ice. It was not even the dinner hour and he was drinking. When did he start? She took the glass from him and put it in the sink. He'd been drinking Scotch. Grant wasn't a big drinker, but when he did drink, it was always high-end Scotch.

She pushed the cup of coffee in front of him. He wasn't drunk yet, but it looked like he was nursing a hangover with more alcohol.

She leaned against the counter. "I found Madeline's body."

Tears sprang to his eyes. He pinched the bridge of his nose hard, squeezing the inside of his eyes so hard it had to hurt.

"The police issued an arrest warrant for you. They wouldn't tell Charlie what evidence they have, though there is evidence that you were in Madeline's apartment building during the window she was killed. They'll find you here…a day, maybe two. All it takes is calling your parents and finding out what other property you have access to. It would be best for you to go in on your own. With a lawyer."

"I didn't kill her."

She didn't say anything.

"Dear God, Regan! Do you actually think I could kill anyone?"

"You don't have to convince me—you have to convince the police. Possibly a jury."

"How can you sound so cold, so…fuck!" He turned his back to her.

It burned her, what he said. But she didn't react. She needed answers.

Grant walked over to the bar on the opposite side of the dining area, pulled out a fresh glass from the cabinet, and poured himself a double shot of Scotch. He drank half in a gulp, didn't bother with ice.

"That's enough, Grant," she said, her voice calm, collected, and yes—cold.

He didn't return to the kitchen but watched her from the other side of the dining table.

"I found the letter you wrote to me in your desk." She hadn't meant to say that, but it came out. She didn't apologize.

"You searched my house? How'd you get in?"

"You're not all that original with your passcodes," she said, perhaps a bit snarky. "You were supposed to meet me for dinner at your place. Instead, your girlfriend is killed, and you ran."

"I didn't kill her!"

"So you've said. Three times."

"You don't believe me."

She did, and she hoped she wasn't wrong. But she needed him to be as forthright as possible, and that meant not coddling him. She said, "We'll talk about Madeline momentarily. First, I need to know what got Tommy killed and why you didn't tell me you were working with him."

He snorted. "Working with him?" Grant was angry, bitter, grieving.

She waited.

He finished his Scotch but didn't pour another. If he had, she might have dumped the bottle down the sink. She needed him sober because his life was in danger, and that meant hers was, too.

He swore under his breath, ran both his hands through his disheveled hair, and sat down at the dining table.

She brought him the coffee she'd poured, put it in front of him, and sat across from him with her own mug. When he didn't immediately speak, she said, "Tommy called me the morning he was killed, left a message that he had evidence pointing to someone hiring Adam Hannigan. Since I've been here, I've learned Tommy believed that Hannigan was hired to kill *you*." She couldn't quite bring herself to say that Chase was collateral damage. Her emotions were still too raw when she thought about her son. Remaining calm was the only way she would learn the truth from Grant, the only way she could protect him.

"I didn't want to believe it," Grant whispered.

She waited. He didn't say anything else.

"I talked to Peter Grey," she said. "He told me, in his own twisted way, that Brock Marsh, a security company, was behind it. And the more I dug around, the more I realized that Brock Marsh is connected to you—through your law firm. Connected to Franklin.

"I don't have all the answers yet," she continued, "but I'm close. I will learn the truth. It goes back to one of your clients, doesn't it?"

He didn't say anything.

"I'm your best bet right now of not only staying out of prison but staying alive," she said, her anger rising. "But dammit, you owe me. You owe me because Chase was our son and you put his death on my shoulders. You blamed *me*." And it had hurt. She hadn't wanted to admit it, but it had been so intensely painful to have the man she once loved, the man she shared a bed with, raised a child with, blame her for their son's murder.

As if the pain of losing Chase wasn't enough.

Grant finally spoke. "Tom called me three weeks ago. He wanted to meet. I said no. I couldn't imagine what he wanted, and I don't like him. Didn't like him. He went out of his way to make me feel like a lesser man, and I knew it was because he was half in love with you."

"He wasn't, Grant," she said.

"Bullshit, Regan. You can't be so blind as to have missed the signs." He paused. "Or maybe you did. You certainly missed all the signs that our marriage was dead in the water."

Though what he said was partly true, it still hurt.

"Our marriage is over. I'm not talking about it." She'd missed a lot of things in their marriage, but she couldn't go back there, allow Grant to drag her into an argument. He always wanted to argue. He always wanted her to admit that she was in the wrong.

She waited for Grant. He had to drive this conversation; if she started asking questions, she'd go back into marshal-interviewing-a-fugitive mode, and he'd clam up or pick a fight. He was already starting with his snide comment. He hated that she could remain impartial in the face of high emotion. What was she supposed to do? Fall apart? She'd already done that after the murder of her son; she did not intend to do it again.

There was no one on the planet she loved more than her son.

"I tried to avoid Tom," said Grant, "but he kept texting me. Said that Peter Grey was hired to kill Hannigan by Brock Marsh Security. It wasn't in any records, nothing Tom or anyone could prove. I thought he was making it up. He had to have known that my law firm used Brock Marsh as legal investigators and negotiators. But Grey said the evidence was the fact that his daughter won the lottery."

"Won the lottery?"

"Not literally. But Grey killed Hannigan and his daughter received a two-hundred-and-fifty-thousand-dollar trust from a private partnership, ostensibly for college. She doesn't know it was payment for murder, but I don't know if she asked too many questions. Her daddy is in prison for life, and he was happy to do it. That's what Tom said."

She ran that through her head. Nothing in Tommy's notes pointed to Grey's daughter, so she hadn't asked those questions. But if Tommy had learned it...if that information was with him when he was killed...it stood to reason it had jumpstarted Tommy's investigation.

"Explain," she said.

"Brock Marsh arranged the trust for his daughter. And as soon as Tom told me, I knew exactly how it happened. Franklin and I have done the same thing many times for our clients. You need to pay off a mistress, you arrange a trust, something that on the surface raises no flags. The firm puts it all together—our accountants create the trust, we take care of the legal paperwork, and Brock Marsh is in the field working with the beneficiary. Their team convinces the subject to sign on the dotted line, take the money, abort the baby, leave town, whatever it is that's needed. And—according to Tom—pay for murder."

"Accountants," she murmured. "Let me guess: Legacy CPA."

"Yeah. So you put it together, too. Just like Tom."

"Partly."

"It was a nasty part of our business, a gray area, but not overtly illegal. I mean—I'm not talking about Brock Marsh contracting to kill anyone, that I didn't even suspect until Tom came to me—but all the rest. No one had to agree to the terms, they were free to pursue lawsuits or go to the press, but everyone took the money." He said it wearily, like he had no faith in human nature. "Everyone," he repeated. "Mistresses. Whistleblowers. Victims. Didn't matter who, with enough money, our firm could make problems go away. And all our clients had enough money to make it happen."

"Who hired Adam Hannigan to kill you?"

"I didn't believe it," he said.

"Answer the question, Grant! We don't have the time for you to wallow in self-pity or guilt. I don't know how safe this place is, I don't know if Madeline's killer tracked you here. What I do know is that a marshal is dead, a woman you loved is dead, and someone tried to kill me last night."

That brought Grant out of his stupor. "What? Where? How?"

"Three men broke into Tommy's while I was sleeping. Would have killed me in my sleep if I hadn't woken up. I killed one, shot another, but he and his two partners escaped. They're not going to be able to hide for long. We finally have the FBI on our side with this, and the FBI knows they have a mole. Between Arlington PD, the sheriff's office, the FBI, and the Marshals—we're going to stop this insanity. But I need you to start talking. Now, Grant."

He looked her in the eye for the first time. Not her hair, not her shoulder, but directly in her eyes when he said, "I didn't know, Regan. I swear to you on our son's grave, I didn't know I was the target. I didn't know that Hannigan was hired to kill me. Not until Tom Granger told me. Then… I didn't want to believe it…but I helped him. I had doubts when he laid it out, and I desperately wanted to prove him wrong. But I helped him."

"Okay," she said. Maybe that was the truth. Sounded true.

When he didn't say anything else, she gave him a bone. He needed it, she realized. He needed her faith in him. She might not have much—but she could at least give him what she had. "I believe you."

His eyes watered. He looked down at his coffee, picked

up the mug, sipped. Grimaced. "You always loved your coffee strong."

"I love the caffeine that comes with strong coffee."

She waited. He was ready to talk; he had to do it at his own pace. She couldn't yell at him, browbeat him into speeding things up…though the longer they sat here, the antsier she became.

"Brock Marsh gets the job done," Grant said after a minute. "That's what Franklin always said. We come up with the plan, Brock Marsh implements it. Generally to pay people off, a mistress or a disgruntled employee. But this time—it was one of our clients. Tom didn't know which one—he only had some pieces; I had some pieces; a girl Tom was working with, Jenna Johns, had some pieces. But we didn't know who was behind it. That's why Tom needed me—to go deep into Archer Warwick files and find out who might have wanted me dead then, but not now. I went back to what I was working on at the time Chase was killed, to try and figure out what I might have known that made one of my clients nervous. Nervous enough to put a hit out on me."

"And they hired Hannigan because of me," she said flatly. "So that investigators would look at my job, my actions instead of your law firm."

Grant nodded his head once. "That was Tom's theory."

"You know about the Potomac Bank robbery," she said. "Tommy was investigating the robbery as well, because he believed it was connected to Chase's murder."

"Indirectly, it is. But—well, let me lay it out for you. Once you see it, it's obvious, but it's complicated. It took me a while to accept it." He paused, sipped more coffee. "I've done a lot of things for my clients that I'm not proud of, but I've never crossed the line. Rode it damn hard. Immorality, however, is not a crime. Paying a consenting adult to abort their kid is not a crime. Paying a mistress to leave town is not a crime. Paying an employee an ample severance package if they accept a gag order, not a crime."

Immoral and unethical, but probably not against the law, Regan figured. Didn't make it right, and her respect for her ex fell. She'd known he'd done things he didn't like. But where do you draw the line between personal ethics and professional? Just because something is legal doesn't mean you should do it.

Grant continued. "Franklin crossed a lot of lines. I knew, I turned my back. Franklin was my best friend, practically family. I didn't realize how far he'd gone. When Tom came to me with Peter Grey's confirmation about Brock Marsh, I started looking. Madeline helped me because she understands our accounting system. We found files hidden deep in the system. Nothing overt—if someone found them, they wouldn't know what any of it meant, but she and I did. They were coded, but Tom was working on figuring out the key. But then I started to think about what was going on in the weeks before Chase was killed. I had a lot of cases then, but most were straightforward contract law. Except…"

He fidgeted with his mug. Grant was working through things in his head, but she was losing patience. Time was not on their side here.

"The week before Chase was killed I had a list of questions related to two NDAs. In hindsight, I should have seen it, shouldn't have asked…"

He cleared his throat and said, "Several years ago, we took on BioRise Pharmaceuticals as a client."

Regan remembered. They were a multibillion-dollar pharmaceutical company with labs in four countries and a DOD contract. Grant's firm had to hire additional staff in order to take on such a large company as clients. The company had their own lawyers, but hired an outside firm as well—Archer Warwick.

And they were still clients. She'd seen James Seidel this week. In hindsight, she realized that Grant had been nervous around him. Suspicious?

BioRise. She'd also asked Grey about them. He hadn't directly answered. Who was Peter Grey and why was he still alive if he had so much information about a company that ordered hits on people?

"Franklin was the primary," Grant said, "but I also worked with them because my specialty is contract law. I handled contracts and NDAs for their employees, Franklin took care of legal settlements and disclosures in their drug trials, working with their in-house counsel. It was lucrative. God, was there so much money involved. If we dropped every other client, we'd still have been flush."

He stopped talking, looked beyond her. She had to keep him focused and on track. She prompted, "And?"

"Eighteen months ago, there was a particular drug trial that went real bad, real fast. It was supposedly a mistake, and two employees were blamed and terminated. These two threatened to sue because they claimed they hadn't made the mistake—that it was the product itself, which is how Franklin became involved. The NDAs are ironclad—even if it was the product, they weren't allowed to speak. Even if they quit or were fired, they couldn't talk about *anything* related to BioRise or their drug trials. BioRise would have tied them up in court for years to come. It would have cost them millions to defend themselves against the NDA violation. They may have won—but they didn't have the money to take it on. Who does? And few lawyers are going to work something like this pro bono, especially against a company the size and scope of BioRise. BioRise would bury them financially, destroy them personally, they have no scruples."

Neither did Grant, Regan thought, though she didn't say it.

Regan had always been frustrated at the system where the government or big business could essentially sue citizens into compliance. It didn't matter if the individual was on the right side of the law, they rarely had the time and resources to fight back.

"One of the two employees in question died in a car accident, and the second took an obscenely large severance package. The case went away." Grant snapped his fingers. "Disappeared, poof.

"But I started asking questions. The medical trial was on teenagers, and according to a statement by the two employees that I was privy to, three of the 210 test subjects died almost immediately after taking the test drug. The families were paid large sums of money—and signed NDAs. The official clinical paperwork indicated that the three subjects received the placebo—a sugar pill—and thus the trial drug wasn't responsible. But the results were falsified; I saw the original paperwork. They buried it."

"The employees could have turned whistleblower," she said. "Gone to the DOJ."

He laughed. Actually laughed at her, and she bristled.

"It happens. I've protected whistleblowers before."

"Yes, it happens," he said snidely. "But when there is this much money at stake? If it got out, just the rumor, it would have jeopardized a major, *multibillion*-dollar contract for BioRise. If anyone hinted at being a whistleblower, the company would have destroyed them. If you destroy someone's reputation, no one believes them. The whisper campaign becomes truth, accusations become truth, social media spreads the new truth, and people are destroyed. I've seen it happen, Regan, more than once."

"Okay," she relented. He might be right.

"I was curious, but I wasn't looking to be a whistle-blower. I was trying to understand the process so that we could develop contracts and legal protections for our client. But my questions made BioRise nervous. I didn't know at the time—I swear I didn't. If I had, if I thought they were capable of…any of this, I would have come to you, Regan. And after Chase was killed, I didn't even *think* about Bio-Rise or anything I was working on. I couldn't think about any of it because… I couldn't get it out of my head. The blood."

He let out a small cry, from deep in his throat, closed his eyes.

Quietly, she asked, "Did Franklin know?"

He didn't answer her question, instead said, "They thought I was going to expose them. I wasn't. I didn't even really know what I knew, and when Chase was killed… nothing else mattered. I blamed you. And I guess they left me alone because I wasn't asking questions anymore."

"Until Tommy."

He didn't respond to her statement. "You read the letter," he said softly. "I treated you like shit. I really thought it was your job. *Your* threat. Not me and mine. I wish they had killed me. I would do anything to bring Chase back."

"I know," she said. She reached for his hand across the table. He clasped hers as if he was a drowning man, so tight it hurt, but she didn't let go.

Grant was suffering as much as she had. And she would never wish what she suffered on anyone.

Yet in the back of her mind, in the darkest place that she rarely accessed, she wondered how he could have been so blind, so ignorant, of what was going on in his office. That he so easily blamed her without even considering his criminal clients.

She closed down the dark anger, worked through what she felt was the most logical chain of events. "BioRise had Franklin put the hit out on you, because they didn't want their hands dirty. Franklin used Brock Marsh Security as the intermediary."

"That's what Tom thought, and everything I learned in-house brought me to the same conclusion, but we couldn't prove anything—the accounts were coded. We were stymied. And I couldn't see Franklin wanting me dead. Maybe he'd known, but I just didn't see him acting on it."

Willful ignorance, she thought bitterly. "So you and Tommy investigated BioRise."

"I was looking into Brock Marsh, specifically jobs we'd hired them for in the past. I initially was looking for evidence that they negotiated the deal for Grey's daughter that Tom uncovered. I could find nothing that showed that Brock Marsh hired the Hannigan brothers at any point in the past. In my search, I realized Brock Marsh worked for no one *other* than us and our clients. This isn't unusual, because we have a large client pool, but there were some questionable invoices. Then I realized that we'd started paying them less over time, and I suspected they were bypassing Franklin and primarily working for *some* of our clients."

"Because they didn't trust Franklin?"

"I don't know. They didn't trust me, so maybe they were pulling the more blatant criminal jobs from the firm and putting them in-house. They had two of our lawyers move over to work in *their* legal department."

"And they bugged your office?"

"I thought it was Franklin, but after talking to him the

other night I don't think so. I think it was BioRise. And they may have all of us bugged, to make sure that we're not going to expose them. They're cocky and arrogant, but they're also smart."

She could see it as clear as day. But nothing that Grant said explained why Tommy was looking at the Potomac Bank robbery.

She said, "Jenna Johns saw her sister—the victim in the Potomac Bank robbery that Michael Hannigan orchestrated—with Chad Rockford. Charlie confirmed that Chad is the brother of Bruce Rockford, the principal of Brock Marsh. Chad is a CPA for Legacy. That's *your* CPA firm, correct? Tommy didn't think this was a coincidence, he must have been looking at the robbery from the beginning."

"Adam Hannigan was hired to make it appear that you were the target, or revenge was the motive," Grant said, "so Tom went back to the bank robbery and realized there were several anomalies. I don't know what he found, specifically, except when he showed me the list of safe deposit boxes that were accessed, I told him that Legacy was our law firm's CPA, about how they handled trusts when we had people paid off. Tom learned that Legacy was keeping evidence of all Archer Warwick payments to Brock Marsh and other entities, plus details of some of Franklin's less than ethical dealings. If the details became public, our firm would be destroyed. Franklin in prison, possibly me—even though I swear to you I never crossed the line. But it looks bad. I would be disbarred at a minimum. Not to mention our clients..."

Regan didn't care. She didn't care about the fallout, all she wanted was the truth,

"Why would Chad go against his brother?" she asked.

"He wouldn't. I think he was tracking these payments *for* Bruce, to make sure that Bruce and his business were protected. Blackmail if necessary."

"Peter Grey said that Franklin hired Hannigan to rob those boxes."

"I don't know."

"Are you sure?"

"What do you mean am I sure? I told you I don't know!"

"Do you think that Franklin was behind it? Knowing that Grey said he was, do you believe it?"

Grant shrugged, weary. "At this point, I'd believe anything you told me."

"Becca Johns had once worked at Legacy and she had also been romantically involved with Chad Rockford. A week before the robbery, Becca had brunch with him. They were chummy."

"I don't understand what that means," Grant said.

"Becca betrayed Hannigan. He must have told her who the target was, and she went to Chad Rockford and told him. Why? Maybe to ask for more money. Maybe to get her old job back. Maybe because she was still in love with him. I don't know. But Rockford retrieved whatever was in the box *before* Hannigan accessed it. Could Legacy have promised her something for the information? To the tune of fifteen thousand dollars?"

"Pocket change for these people," Grant said. "Becca may have warned Legacy, and they removed the evidence. I can see it."

"And when Hannigan didn't find it, he realized Becca must have betrayed him. Killed her in a spur-of-the-moment act of retaliation. But why would Franklin hire him? For BioRise? Or for his own reasons?"

"Franklin," he said quietly. "I'll be damned."

"What are you thinking?"

"Franklin trusted Brock Marsh and Legacy…but he must have known they were keeping blackmail information on him and his clients. Their security blanket, in case Franklin screwed them, or to use as a get out of jail free card."

"Not if they committed a felony."

Grant laughed. "Noble to think that, but it's all a matter of who you go to and what cards you have to play. Franklin wanted information, either to prevent them from using it or to use it himself. I don't know. But he understood the value of leverage." He paused. "I suspect he had extensive files on BioRise, Brock Marsh, everyone. Franklin wouldn't leave anything to chance."

"Yet, the blackmail materials were there, and everyone who knew about the actual target—Hannigan and Becca—is dead, Chad and Bruce keep their respective businesses moving along." But something didn't quit fit. "If Legacy was keeping information about Archer clients—like BioRise—why would BioRise want you dead, Grant?"

He shrugged, rubbed his head.

Regan got up, grabbed two water bottles from the empty refrigerator—had Grant even eaten since he arrived here?—and put one in front of Grant. She drank half of hers, then switched back to coffee.

"So," she said, "to get this straight, Franklin hired Hannigan to retrieve evidence that incriminated *him* and the law firm. But they'd already moved it. And you think, because of this evidence of Franklin's wrongdoing that Legacy and Brock Marsh has, that he went along with the assassination attempt against you."

It was wild but checked all the boxes.

"Franklin didn't say anything. Not about the blackmail, not about BioRise, not about Brock Marsh. Even after

Chase was killed, he *didn't tell me he knew who hired Adam Hannigan*!" Grant slammed his fist on the table, his face red, his eyes wet. "He commiserated with me, cried with me, sat with me at the funeral—he was my fucking *friend* and he told me your job was too dangerous, and this proved it. He helped sell my fears, by agreeing with me that it was your fault. God. *Dammit.*" He sobbed once, put his head in his hands. "Fuck," he croaked.

Franklin was in over his head. He'd done something illegal—something that would put him in jail, cost him his law firm, his family, his freedom. Every step further into corruption took him deeper. Killing Grant…dear Lord, he had gone along with the plan to kill his best friend in order to protect himself and his clients…and when Chase ended up dead, Franklin remained silent.

The *bastard*.

"Tommy was killed by a professional," she said. "A sniper who went in and, even though Tommy was already dead, put a bullet in his head. His laptop, files, and cell phone were taken."

Grant's hands were trembling. He opened his water bottle, drank heavily.

"Tom had everything—our emails, messages, documents I sent him. If Franklin didn't suspect I was helping Tom before, he knows now. And that's why Madeline was killed."

"Franklin had her killed?"

Grant shrugged. "He said no. He said it was BioRise, cleaning up after the mess that Tom Granger made. But he must have known."

Unless Franklin was one of the messes that BioRise planned to clean up.

"Why Madeline and not you?" she asked bluntly. "You're being framed for murder—but you can still speak to the truth."

"I was late."

"What do you mean, late?"

"I was supposed to pick up Madeline at six thirty, but I was late."

"Why were you at her condo for ten minutes, Grant? They have you on surveillance."

"I didn't realize I was there so long. I couldn't believe she was dead. I just stared at her—I almost called the police, but I knew how it would look."

"It looks worse that you *didn't* call the police. What did you do in her apartment? Do not lie to me, Grant. You didn't just stare at her body for ten fucking minutes. If you didn't kill her, *what were you doing*?"

"If? You don't believe me?"

"Do not change the subject, Grant. Tell me the truth. Right now. If you lie to me, if you try to handle me, I will take you down and bring you to the closest police department and let them deal with you. I'm willing to help you, Grant, I'm trying to save your life. But not if you lie to me. Do you understand what I'm saying?"

He took a ragged breath, then said, "I did not kill Maddie. I walked in, called out for her, started down the hall toward her bedroom. She was there, in the kitchen, dead. So much blood..." He stared at the table, then shook his head and continued. "I stood in the hall a minute, two maybe, in shock. I didn't think about an intruder right away, then I turned around, as if someone was behind me. No one was there. I realized that if I hadn't been late, I also would have been dead. I don't know if it was Franklin who ordered it or BioRise, but because Maddie helped me, she was killed.

"I didn't know what to do. I had to think. You texted me, said you were at my place. I almost called you then, but..."

"But what?" She wasn't in the mood for obfuscation.

"You never make mistakes. If I came to you and admitted all this, everything I've done, what I've allowed to happen, what I turned my back on, what I didn't know but should have, I didn't want you to look at me like I was... stupid."

"I've never thought you were stupid, Grant. Until now. Until you fled a murder scene!"

"Not everyone is as calm, cool, and collected as you, Regan." His voice was snide, snippy, mean. She ignored it.

"After you decided not to call me," she said slowly, forcing her anger down, "what did you do?"

"I looked for her laptop. It wasn't there. Someone took it."

Like they took Tommy's. And Grant's. And Jenna's. They were trying to destroy any evidence outside of their control. And they didn't care who they killed to do it.

"When I couldn't find her laptop," Grant said, "I went down to the garage and searched her car. It wasn't there. Then I left."

That could have taken ten minutes. But the fact that Grant had the wherewithal to look for Madeline's laptop after finding her dead body wouldn't go over too well with the authorities.

"And then?"

"I drove around for an hour, maybe two," said Grant, "before I ended up at Franklin's. Confronted him."

"I talked to him. He said you were half-crazy. He's building it up to seem like he cares about you, he's your best friend, but yes, you may have killed Madeline. Shit."

She could see it all now. It would be hard for Franklin to get away with it because of what she knew...which was why someone came after her last night.

Damn damn damn!

"Franklin denied having Maddie killed, but I didn't believe him. Then he said I should have expected it from *them*. He didn't say their name but I knew he was talking about BioRise and Brock Marsh. Maddie and I were the dangerous loose ends, after all."

"Why didn't you tell me this Wednesday?" Regan snapped. "You've been avoiding me since I came to town, and you knew what was going on! I told you I was looking into Tommy's death—you had answers."

"I didn't know anything for certain."

"Bullshit. I said don't lie to me!"

He didn't say anything for a second, then said, "I didn't want to believe what Tom told me, and he didn't have proof, but there was a lot of circumstantial evidence. Then I found the bug. I didn't know what the hell to do, and Maddie was scared and angry. She talked me out of meeting you for dinner, but I should have gone. If I had been stronger, she'd still be alive."

"How could Madeline talk you out of telling the truth? Tommy was *killed* by the same people who killed our son! You had to have known you were in trouble—and in danger. Only the truth will keep you alive."

She couldn't believe Grant would ever be hesitant when he possessed information about their son's needless death.

"Maddie helped Franklin on some of these questionable cases," he said. "She was afraid of being disbarred. She pulled the accounting files and could have been arrested."

"Chase was *murdered*!" Regan didn't mean to shout, but that her ex-husband could be so easily manipulated into indecision was beyond her.

"Maddie was going to come with me on Thursday, to talk to you. She was scared, but she was also right in that we didn't have any hard evidence of anything. And I didn't, even then, believe that Franklin was involved."

"Then you're an idiot."

"Always so certain of everything, aren't you? I went to her condo to pick her up, she was dead. Stabbed in the back. I was supposed to be there at six thirty but was late. She was already dead!"

So he'd said. She glared at her ex-husband. She'd married him, slept with him, had a child with him.

"You're not the man I thought you were," she said.

Her insult made him cringe, but she didn't care about his fragile ego. She was angry and deeply sad.

"You should have come to me," she said evenly. She rose, walked to the kitchen, poured more coffee.

Think, Regan.

She had to figure out how she could expose the truth about Franklin Archer and BioRise. How she could make it stick. Brock Marsh were enforcers, they did the dirty work, but they weren't ultimately the ones calling the shots.

She had a headache. They had all the pieces, but to prove anything—to gather the evidence that they needed for prosecution—they had to build a case. Physical evidence, witness statements, hard proof. That took time. And one by one, BioRise and Brock Marsh were killing off witnesses. Covering their tracks. Hiding—destroying—evidence. Soon, there would be no evidence and no one left to tell the truth.

They'd get away with everything.

They'd get away with murdering her son.

Jenna's fear and subsequent flight after she learned that Tommy had been killed had likely saved her life.

Regan pulled out her phone and sent Charlie a text.

Jenna is in grave danger. Double up security on the safe house. Do what you can to get her into full protective custody, I'll explain soon.

She didn't tell him she'd found Grant; she didn't want to put Charlie in that position. He'd already deflected Detective Quincy's inquiries, and Regan would have to deal with the police as soon as she got back to Virginia. But for now, she had to figure out what was evidence and what was conjecture.

They needed hard evidence.

Her phone beeped.

Already done. Me, O'Dare, and SWAT are about to raid Brock Marsh offices. Holy shit, Regan, it's been a wild Saturday. Stay safe and call me when you can.

Forty-Two

While Regan was on the road to the Catskills, Charlie had put an extra detail on Jenna Johns and her friend Lance Martelli. After the attack on Regan last night, Charlie wasn't taking any chances with an untrained nurse and her former military nurse boyfriend. Well, maybe not *boyfriend* yet, but Charlie was a romantic at heart and he saw the signs.

He touched base with Lillian O'Dare, fully briefed his boss, then slept a couple hours on the lumpy couch in the Marshals break room. At two that afternoon O'Dare called him.

"Donald James Portman," she said in lieu of *hello*. "That bastard. He's been on my team for two years, and he's the mole who sent those goons after your witness."

"Is he in custody?"

"No. He left the office at five last night and no one has seen him—not his wife, not his *mistress*, not his neighbors or friends. He must have known the gig was up. We'll find him. He's not smart enough to run for long."

"I talked to my boss. He said I'm on your team when you're ready to go."

"I'm working on it. About to debrief my boss, just waiting for him to get in. He's pissed about everything—but he'll authorize it. We need warrants, and that might take a couple hours. Hell, maybe longer because we have to convince a judge that our circumstantial evidence is enough. You good for a night raid?"

"I'm good for a raid anytime."

Four and a half hours later, they were in Arlington staging out of line of sight of the Brock Marsh offices. That wasn't as easy as it sounded—the security offices were in a dedicated building in the middle of nowhere, complete with security cameras, gates, a loading dock, more. They'd be able to see anyone coming *literally* a mile away.

The FBI had a search and seize warrant, and they were going in, but they didn't want to give anyone inside time to destroy evidence.

O'Dare was not SWAT and she was manning the tactical van with the communications officer, while letting the head of FBI SWAT, Bob Dodge, coordinate the raid. Charlie had trained and worked with FBI SWAT many times over the years, and he fell seamlessly into the structure.

"Everyone has their assignments," Dodge said. "This is a security company. Tactically trained. We secure the facility, disarm and detain anyone inside, lock it up. Everything inside is covered under the warrant—full sweep. Once it's clear, B team comes in to start the evidence collection—document everything, bag and tag it, prepare for transport to headquarters for review and analysis. This is the fun part, we'll leave it to the nerds and lab rats to find the smoking gun."

Charlie grinned. Yeah, this was the fun part.

They drove to the gate in a half dozen SUVs, each with four agents, Dodge in the lead vehicle. He showed the guard the warrant and told him not to contact the building. The guard didn't object, and volunteered that there were only two janitors inside the building.

They couldn't trust the information, not without verification, but by the time they swept and cleared the facility, they knew the guard hadn't been lying. Two janitors were detained, questioned, ID'd, and released. The B team came in and started processing documents.

O'Dare followed them in. "We're looking for financials to tie Brock Marsh to Legacy CPA, Archer Warwick Bachman Law Offices, or BioRise Pharmaceuticals. Names, money, accounts, papers, contracts; if any of those names are on it—or the names of the principals that are listed on the warrant—flag them. We can't touch any records unless they have one of those names."

She turned to Charlie. "Building secure, shall we track Bruce Rockford at his house?"

"We need a team. These people are trained security."

"I have one. Dodge is giving me two of his people for the night. And I have you."

"True, I'm worth at least three FBI agents."

"And here I was beginning to like you," she said, rolling her eyes.

Bruce Rockford lived only five miles from his office; he wasn't home. O'Dare flagged his passport and put out an APB on him.

"Let's try his brother," Charlie said. "We can at least question him, right?"

Chad Rockford wasn't home, either.

"Oh, this isn't at all suspicious," O'Dare said. "APBs on everyone. When do I get to talk to your witness?" she asked Charlie.

"We'll arrange it, handle security. She might be in the

clear if everyone's on the run, but I don't want to take chances since she can identify too many of the people involved. One itchy trigger finger, dead nurse. I'm not going to let that happen."

"Where's Regan?"

"Looking for her ex-husband."

"The lawyer? Who's wanted for killing his girlfriend?"

"Don't think he did it."

"You don't? Or Regan doesn't?"

"Neither of us. Regan plans to bring him in to talk to Arlington PD. When she finds him," he added.

O'Dare didn't say anything.

Charlie said, "News on the warrant for Franklin Archer's house?"

"We're working on it. He's a lawyer, so we need a clear path to get the warrant, and without a witness statement, we're going off conjecture and thirdhand information."

As soon as O'Dare walked away, he sent Regan a message.

FBI secured Brock Marsh. Rockford brothers in the wind. No warrant for Archer, FBI will talk to him on Monday, sooner if you find Grant and he can give a statement? Our girl is secured. FBI is looking for evidence that can get them a warrant on BioRise. Be safe.

His phone rang. It was Anna Lujan. "Is everything okay?" he immediately asked, worried. Had people from Brock Marsh found her?

"On this end, yes, we're all secure. Carl took over for me an hour ago."

"Why aren't you sleeping?"

"I came by the office, wanted to check on something.

Remember when Jenna said Chad Rockford might have been married, and that's why she was upset that her sister was flirting with him?"

"Yes." He didn't see the relevance.

"I talked to her more about it, and then came here to dig deeper. Chad Rockford married Ashley Seidel a year before the robbery. They'll be celebrating their third anniversary this summer."

"Seidel—the daughter of James Seidel, the CEO of Bio-Rise?"

"Yes. I don't know if this helps—I don't see how—but you said if there were any connections between these people, to let you know."

"I'll tell Regan. Maybe she can make sense of it. Thanks, Anna. Great work. Now get some sleep."

Forty-Three

Grant had been fading—too much alcohol, too much emotion—and she had become angry at his comments. Yes, she could be cold and clinical—she had to be at times. But that didn't mean she didn't feel; it didn't mean she didn't care.

She took a break, checked the perimeter now that the sun was setting and she'd lose visibility. Checked the garage—Grant had driven her old truck, a Ford Ranger she had left behind when she moved to Arizona. Maybe he had thought his Mercedes was being tracked. She'd almost forgotten that Grant had been storing her truck. Still, she checked the wheel wells and the engine for any tracking device. It was clean. Good.

She'd loved this little truck. It was a basic four-door midnight blue Ranger. Washington Nationals decal on the back left window. Fairfax Little League decal on the right. Great for camping trips, though not as comfortable as Grant's Mercedes for everyday driving.

Regan went back upstairs and made dinner. There wasn't much in the house to eat—nothing fresh at any rate—but there was a bag of pasta that hadn't expired and a jar of spaghetti sauce. She whipped up a meal and put two plates on the table.

Grant was sitting on the couch, not looking at anything.

"Eat," she said. "We both need our strength."

He slowly rose, walked over to the table, sat down as if he was an old man. He was drinking again. She took the glass away from him, poured it out, and he didn't object. She put water in front of him.

"I get it. Your best friend betrayed you. Had our son killed. Your girlfriend. Lied. You're feeling the brunt of that betrayal. But I need you sober, alert, listening to me. Understood? The Rockfords are in the wind, the FBI has raided Brock Marsh, and they are pursuing a warrant for Franklin Archer. They'll get it eventually, but it would help if you could make a statement about what you know as *fact*."

"That's the thing—what facts? Do we have any proof? Or is this all…just theory?"

"That's up to the FBI. All you can do is speak to what you know."

She dug into her spaghetti. It was after eight and she hadn't eaten since a breakfast sandwich this morning. She needed the fuel.

Grant drank his water, stared at his food. She motioned for him to eat. He picked up his fork and played with his food.

"Someone broke into your townhouse after I was there Thursday night," she said. She was the calm one, rational, organized. She had to keep that perspective now. Prepare, plan, execute. She didn't have the luxury of anger or grief—not tonight.

She swallowed more spaghetti. "They took your laptop. Maybe took files from your drawers, I don't know—the detective wouldn't let me look when we returned later."

He stared at her. "You're working with the police?"

"I found Madeline's body, Grant. Which you know because I called and texted you enough times."

"I turned off my phone, took out the battery. I didn't know if they were tracking me that way."

"Someone was tracking me," said Regan. "They had a tracker on my rental car, another on Tommy's truck. I don't know for how long." She paused. "I saw that you are driving my old Ford Ranger. I thought you'd sold it."

He shook his head, took a small bite of food. "Too many memories. The good kind." He shrugged. "I kept meaning to sell it, but never got around to it. I had it in the parking garage and no one cared because the lot was never full. Took it out every now and then to keep it running. We used to take it to Chase's baseball games. It was our fun car, and I guess I equated it with the best of times—when you, me, Chase were happy. A family."

That got to her. Dammit, it got to her.

She closed her eyes, willed herself to focus on the here and now. After a few deep breaths, she had herself under control. Turned back to Grant, eyes dry.

"You realize leaving your car in Arlington or Alexandria makes you seem guilty."

"I don't care!"

"You need to care." But the fact that he had driven a different car, not easily traced to him, and that he had his phone off, battery out, gave them a little more time to plan. "It's too late to drive back tonight. Not on these roads, not when I only had a few hours of sleep. We leave early tomorrow morning—like 3:00 a.m. early. You need a lawyer, and you need to turn yourself in to the police. Let them question you. Tell them the truth. They have no hard evidence—not that I could see—but your visit to Franklin's house isn't going to do you any good. What is he going to say to them? He could tell them that you confessed, that you were distraught. Hell, I don't know. But it could confuse the situation. Still, they'll need something physical, like the murder weapon." Which could have been planted in his car or his townhouse, but she didn't say that. A good frame job would have it found, but not in an obvious spot. "Being here isn't going to do you any good. I'll help you, but you need to turn yourself in."

Grant stared at her. "If I'm in jail, I will be killed. Didn't you hear what I said? I was *late*. If I had been on time I would have been dead with Maddie."

She believed him.

What Grant knew was dangerous. He might not have physical proof, but he was a well-known civil law lawyer and his testimony could take down BioRise as well as Franklin Archer.

"Do you know who killed Tommy?" she asked.

"Not for a fact."

"But you suspect."

He nodded. "BioRise uses a man named Nelson Lee. He doesn't work directly for Brock Marsh. I think he's hired on a case by case basis. BioRise has more money than God, so that's where Bruce Rockford will gravitate." He finally took a bite of spaghetti.

"So Lee is BioRise, but it's Brock Marsh who is targeting me." She thought about the men in her house, the men following her.

"Lee comes in when no one else can get the job done. I know the law firm has hired him before."

"You know for a fact that Archer Warwick hired an assassin?"

"No—a fixer. Someone that comes in and—"

"I know what a fixer does. But you just said that you suspect Nelson Lee killed Tommy."

"Just…well, something Franklin said a while back. Something about how not every problem can be fixed in the traditional manner."

"And your mind went to murder."

He didn't say anything. "I fear I know a lot more than I should."

He probably did, information that would get him killed or imprisoned. And if he was imprisoned, he wouldn't be alive for long, considering the reach of these people. "I have a coded sheet of payments from BioRise to Brock Marsh, Nelson Lee, others. Payments that Brock Marsh made that they wanted hidden."

Her head jerked. "Was it in your desk?"

"Yes. I guess it's not there anymore."

She opened her phone. "This?"

She turned to show Grant the photo she'd taken. "I didn't take the file but wanted to study these numbers again."

"You broke into my desk?"

"Tommy had been murdered and you were avoiding me. You want to press charges? Go right ahead. But this probably isn't there anymore. I told you, when I went back with the detective, your laptop was gone."

Grant looked at the image on her phone. "This is the top page. I coded it but it's simple. The first twelve numbers relates to our internal client code, the next eight are the date, the next six are what we paid—so zero one five zero zero zero means fifteen thousand. The last numbers are an alpha numeric code—zero one is *A*, zero two is *B*, one one is *K*, two six is *Z*. Anyone can crack it, but at quick glance it's not easy."

"And that was for?"

"The job. Paying off a mistress, negotiating a settlement, whatever it was. But Franklin added in another code—these last three digits which don't seem to mean anything. I think those were the illegal items. I never asked. Maybe I didn't want to know. I pulled them manually because I didn't want Franklin to know what I was doing, hoping I could crack it. Madeline was helping until she got scared after Tom was killed. I should never have included her in this mess."

"Enough with the regret and guilt. Right now, the information you have is extremely valuable. Franklin could be, as we speak, shredding documents, destroying anything that incriminates him. You may be the only person who knows this." She considered her options. "You need a lawyer, someone you trust—someone above reproach. He can negotiate the terms of your questioning. We'll have you in the Marshals office and put you in federal protection. Arlington PD can't easily null a protection agreement."

"They'll never go for that if they think I killed Maddie."

"But you didn't, and they don't have proof." She paused. "Is there anything you're not telling me?"

"I'm sure there is. But what? I don't know. My head is pounding, the woman I love is dead, my best friend killed my son. He didn't pull the trigger, but he might as well have. And I'm a dead man. I know it, Regan. They aren't going to stop."

"I'm not going to let that happen."

"They'll kill you to get to me."

"They already tried and failed. Eat, Grant. Then go upstairs. I made a bed for you. I'm staying down here. I need to think." And she needed sleep, but she didn't completely trust Grant not to bolt. She'd taken his keys, but he could go out on foot. She wanted to be able to hear doors opening.

Both going out and coming in.

Grant ate in silence. He could only get down half the plate of food. When he pushed it away, she took his plate and her empty plate and did the dishes while Grant stared at nothing in particular.

Then he rose and headed for the stairs. At the base of the staircase, he turned back to look at her, as if he wanted to say something. Then he didn't, and she was relieved.

She needed to figure out what she was going to do, and the last thing she wanted was another argument with Grant.

Forty-Four

Late Saturday night, Franklin Archer walked into his empty house. His wife and daughters were in New York City for the weekend; Monday morning they would be flying out to Switzerland. He'd moved money around, but most of it Isabelle wouldn't be able to access until she arrived in Europe.

His family was safe. That was all that mattered.

Now he could focus on damage control. First things first: figure out what the fuck was going on.

Bruce wasn't returning his calls, and the Brock Marsh offices had been raided by the FBI. None of that was good.

He sat down at his desk and his house phone rang, startling him. He immediately thought of Isabelle. The girls. He answered.

"Archer."

"It's James," the voice said.

James Seidel. The CEO of BioRise. Franklin's most valuable client. Half his legal billing was from BioRise.

"You have a problem," James said. "Several problems."

"We need to sit down. Talk about this. Come up with a plan, a strategy. That's what I'm best at."

"Brock Marsh has been compromised," James said. "That doesn't make me happy."

"That's on them. They fucked up."

James grunted his displeasure. Franklin swallowed heavily.

Why are you scared of him? You have proof they're corrupt. Mutually assured destruction.

"First thing tomorrow, James," Franklin pushed. "I fear you have made the situation a thousand times worse. You killed Madeline. That's going to have repercussions."

James laughed but without humor. Franklin sensed the underlying anger. A rough bark around the edges. Franklin probably shouldn't have pushed him, but he couldn't help it. Having Madeline killed? Framing Grant? It was beyond the pale. It brought undue attention to the law firm at a critical time. They had just conspired to kill a deputy US marshal! They needed to keep a low profile. Franklin understood that better than anyone. Why didn't James?

"You would be wise, Franklin, not to test me."

"You would be wise, James, to treat me as an equal, not an underling," Franklin snapped.

He sounded a lot braver than he felt. Franklin did not want to go to prison. He had an escape plan. But if he was caught, he would turn state's evidence so fast James Seidel wouldn't know what hit him.

Mutually assured destruction.

"I want the files. *All* the files," James repeated. "Including the recordings you made."

How did he know about the recordings? *How?* No one knew...well...maybe his assistant. And Grant's assistant. Dammit, could he trust *no one* anymore?

"And give up my security?" Franklin said, feeling hot and cold at the same time. "It's not going to happen."

James ended the call. Franklin frowned, almost called him back, but his phone vibrated. He pulled it out of his pocket, looked down as a text came in from an unfamiliar number.

He clicked it.

A photo loaded onto his phone. His blood froze and he began to shake.

Isabelle. The girls. In the lobby of their hotel in New York City.

His house phone rang again, and he answered.

"Bastard," he managed to say.

"We are terminating our business relationship with Archer Warwick effective immediately," James said. "You will prepare all the files and keep nothing. And I mean *nothing*. You had better take care of your associate, because if he says a word about our business, it's *your* family who will pay the price—since he has no one left he cares about. You have twenty-four hours to comply."

James hung up on him.

Franklin couldn't stop shaking.

This was Grant's fault.

Grant needed to be gone. All this—because Grant had betrayed him. Worked with the damn marshal! Gave him confidential files and information. This mess could all be laid at Grant's feet.

Franklin wiped sweat off his forehead with the back of his hand. He had to fix this. Somehow.

Franklin called Nelson Lee. It was a risk, because Nelson worked for BioRise. But they had a common enemy here, and Franklin needed to just make everything *go away*.

The phone kept ringing and ringing.

Franklin almost threw his cell phone across his library. "Dammit! Dammit!"

He pulled himself together. He had a plan. Twenty-four hours? Screw that. He'd leave tonight.

James thought he had the upper hand? Bullshit. Obviously, his pet assassin Lee had killed Madeline and framed Grant. What had they planned, to fake a suicide? Grant kills his girlfriend, then kills himself. It might be believable on the surface—to anyone who didn't know Grant Warwick well.

Franklin would just let that play out. Grant made his fucking bed. And he'd already started the ball rolling by what he'd told the police and then Regan.

Grant was paranoid. Grant was arguing with Maddie in the office. Grant came by his house, hysterical. Yeah, it might work.

Would Regan buy a suicide? That was the million-dollar question. Her leaving Virginia had saved Franklin last year. Once Adam Hannigan was dead, the answers to her questions died with him. With Granger gone, a fall guy firmly planted, and Grant on the run… Regan would do well to return to Arizona and never darken Franklin's door again.

And if she didn't, if she stayed, he wasn't responsible for what happened to her.

Franklin called his wife. He wasn't surprised she was wide awake; she knew how deep he'd gotten in with Bio-Rise. She didn't know everything—certainly not about the accident with Chase Warwick. But she knew enough. Isabelle was a tolerant, understanding woman with ample business sense who understood the gray areas very well, but she wouldn't have been able to live with knowledge of murder.

"It's bad, isn't it?" she said.

"They know where you are. I'll be there first thing in the morning. I'm going to wrap up our contingency plan and drive up there. Stay in the hotel room with the girls until I call you. We'll go to Canada, fly from there. It'll be fine, but we have to be careful."

"I already sent the girls to Monica and Kevin."

"What? Why?"

"Because I sensed someone in the lobby watching me. The girls are fourteen, they're innocent."

Monica was Isabelle's sister, and she and Kevin were the only people Franklin might trust with his daughters. They lived in Canada, on a farm outside Edmonton. Where everyone knew everyone, and strangers stood out.

"You should have gone with them, Isabelle. Why didn't you?"

"Because I love you, Franklin. We're in this together. I'll wait for you. When it's safe, we'll send for the girls."

"I've made mistakes."

"We both have. But *we* are not a mistake. I'll wait. Don't be long."

"I love you."

He ended the call, sat at his desk for a long few minutes, listening to the night around him. The house was quiet, too quiet, without his family. The grandfather clock ticked in the foyer—his great-grandfather had brought it over from Switzerland more than a hundred years ago. That was the only sound.

His father…his father had started this. He'd brought in BioRise. He'd created the monster. Then he left, turned everything over to Franklin and at first, it had been a gift. A bright, shiny, moneymaking gift and he'd been grateful.

Now he was paying the price. Not his father, no—he was still happily retired in Florida with all the money in the world. But he, Franklin Archer, the good son, the son who wanted to please his father, who built on what his father created, was now at risk of losing it all because of Grant Warwick.

The lawyer he'd brought in, cultivated, educated, treated like a brother.

Franklin never wanted his life to come to this…to running away. He'd always taken risks in his business, but it was both thrilling and rewarding. Until two years ago, he was on top of the world.

Then one thing and another and another, and now he was on a slippery slope down to hell. He walked over to the minibar hidden in his bookshelf and poured himself two fingers of whiskey. Drank it in one long burning gulp.

"You were looking for me."

Franklin choked, gasped, turned around and saw Nelson Lee in the doorway.

He'll kill you when you turn over the files. It's a lose-lose.

But Franklin couldn't show fear.

"I want to make this right," Franklin said calmly. He was surprised he sounded so nonchalant. He didn't want to die. He didn't want his family to die, but showing weakness now would be the final nail.

The girls are safe. Remember that. The girls are safe.

"I have not been able to find Mr. Warwick," Nelson said. "He didn't go home. He left his car at the law office. He hasn't used his credit cards. He's not where his ex-wife is staying. Where is he?"

Franklin was flustered, tried to bury it with the fear.

"James told me to handle Grant." His voice was strong, even though he was very afraid.

Nelson smiled, a quiet evil hiding behind his grin. He held up his phone. "And you called me. Why did you call me, Mr. Archer? Perhaps to take care of your problem for you?"

Nelson stared at him, his pale brown eyes almost yellow. Franklin didn't speak, trying to see a way out of this mess.

"Where is Grant Warwick?" Nelson demanded, his voice both calm and terrifying at the same time.

Franklin found his voice. Forced himself to sound braver than he was. "I don't know, Lee. If I knew, I'd take care of it."

"He hasn't rented a car. Did he borrow one of yours?"

Franklin shook his head. "He came here, as I told James, and he was a mess. I thought for sure the police would catch up to him."

"Does he have another car?"

"No." But… "His ex-wife had a Ford Ranger truck. He kept it in the garage this past year. The firm's garage."

"Details."

"Dark blue, five, maybe six years old. How are you going to find it? He could be anywhere."

"Now that I know he had access to a vehicle, I suspect he went to his family home in the Catskills."

How the *hell* did Nelson Lee know about Grant's second home?

The weight of everything that had happened over the last two years hit him hard, starting with Franklin's attempt to protect his family by hiring Michael Hannigan to obtain the blackmail documents in Legacy's safe deposit box.

"The Catskills?" Franklin squeaked.

"You should have thought of it, Mr. Archer."

He'd gone up to the Warwick family vacation home a few times over the years. The rural mountains weren't Franklin's idea of fun, but his wife and girls had enjoyed it.

"I can find the address for you," Franklin said.

"I have it." Nelson hadn't moved from the doorway. He said, "I'll be back tomorrow for the files that my employer wants."

Franklin breathed easier. He still had time to get the hell away. No way was he turning over the files if his daughters were safe. He just had to make sure that they were, then he'd make the move.

"I will be here."

Nelson smiled. "Yes, you will."

Franklin hadn't seen the gun; it had been in Nelson's pocket but then it wasn't. He was fast.

Nelson fired twice before Franklin registered that Nelson was going to kill him. His chest burned as the bullets hit in rapid succession. He staggered, fell to his knees, his vision turning black.

He sensed Nelson standing over him. Franklin couldn't see him, he could barely hear him.

"I already have the files, you fool."

The third bullet went into Franklin Archer's skull.

Nelson Lee stared at Archer's corpse. Good riddance. This man was partly responsible for Nelson missing the farmer's market today. He now had to wait a full week to enjoy the freshest, most flavorful produce on the East Coast. He was angry and, he could admit to himself, quite a bit sad.

However, there was one bright spot in this whole miserable week: Franklin Archer hadn't been lying. He *did* have files. Five flash drives containing every recording of every client in the law firm, including BioRise. A file listing what was on the drives. And papers documenting the specifics of what Brock Marsh had done for the law firm—and, surprisingly, for BioRise.

Sure, this all might not be admissible in court. But the recordings would still destroy the company, and James Seidel personally, if they ever got out.

Now they were *his* insurance policy.

He called his employer.

"Is it done?" Mr. Seidel asked.

"Yes."

"Do you have the recordings?"

"No, sir," he lied smoothly. "He denied having anything, said they were a bluff."

"Do you believe him?"

"No. I'll find them."

"Good work. Now take care of the rest. We launch the new product next month. Generational wealth, Nelson. Once in a lifetime. Enough to set my children and any children they have for life. And I will not allow Grant Warwick to destroy my legacy."

SUNDAY

Forty-Five

Regan slept only a couple of hours in the great room on the couch, restless because she was half listening to the quiet. Finally, at 3:00 in the morning, she got up and made coffee. There was little food in the cabin, but she found an unopened box of Cheerios that was only a month past the expiration date. She opened it and ate from the box.

She texted Charlie, told him to call her when he was up. A minute later, her phone rang.

"It's early," she said.

"Light sleeper," he said.

"Join the club. How's Jenna?"

"Holding. Carl is with her now. Anna will take over in a few hours. I have her under a forty-eight-hour watch. After that, we'll need to do it official, but that's not going to be a problem. She wants to go back to work, she misses her job, her grandmother—but she understands that right now things are dicey."

"And Lance is holding up, too?"

"Yep. She told him he could leave, but he's sticking. Good guy. Detective Quincy is looking for you. I've been avoiding him, but he's tenacious."

"I'm bringing Grant in. I told him to get a lawyer, and he's just not thinking straight, so I reached out to a friend of mine in Arizona who is referring a top defense lawyer here. I want to wait until the lawyer arranges the surrender, but I'm getting antsy. I want to move him."

"Can I tell Quincy? It might settle him down."

"Tell him to expect a call from Grant's lawyer sometime today to arrange the terms of his surrender. Good?"

"Perfect. Are you in a secure location?"

"I thought so, but now I'm having second thoughts." She didn't tell Charlie where she was, and he didn't ask. Better to protect him. "Grant confronted Franklin Archer Thursday night. Franklin knows Grant. He might be able to figure out where Grant went. Did you get my memo?" She had emailed him everything Grant told her.

"Yep. Sent it to the boss and O'Dare. She's been good, real pissed about the mole, wants to make it up to us. I'm taking advantage of that generosity to get everything we need."

She laughed. Couldn't help herself, and that felt good.

"I'm going to get an apology out of her, too," Charlie said. "For you. About Chase."

"You don't have to do that."

"I know, but might as well get her when she's feeling guilty that the agent she trained is a bastard mole."

"Franklin Archer knows everything," Regan said. "I don't want him to get a deal; damn, I want him in prison for the rest of his life. But..." She didn't finish her thought.

"I know," Charlie said quietly. "We're working on getting a warrant to search his house, but it's touchy. He's a lawyer. He's avoiding calls, not answering the door. The law firm is going to be tough for a search, but O'Dare is good—she's talking to the AUSA and her boss and my boss and something is going to give."

"They'll have everything destroyed before then."

"Possibly, but this is going to be a major investigation for months. Anything financial can be tracked, it's just a matter of time and resources. And because there was an FBI mole and a dead US marshal? They'll have all the resources they need."

That made her feel slightly better.

"Knowing the truth—it helps," she said.

She wasn't lying.

"Justice is better," Charlie said.

She certainly didn't disagree with that.

"Keep in touch," Charlie continued. "I need to hear from you often so I know you're okay."

"I'll let you know when we're on the move. I want to be out of here before sunrise."

"How far out?"

"Six to eight hours depending on traffic, roads, which way I go."

"If anything changes on my end, I'll tag you."

"Thanks, Charlie. For everything."

"Be safe."

She hadn't been lying to Charlie; she *was* feeling antsy about their location. Too many people knew about this house—including Franklin. She should have left last night, but after driving all day, a broken sleep the night before because of the attack, then the emotional conversation with Grant, she needed time to recover—proving to her once again that she was right to have left the Marshals. She couldn't think and plan properly anymore, she'd lost her edge, her ability to be a good protector. Because that's what the marshals did: they protected people.

She walked upstairs into Grant's room—the one bedroom that had no balcony, no access to the outside. He was still in bed, but not sleeping.

"We leave in fifteen minutes."

"Maybe we should stay. It's safe here."

"It's not. The deed is in your parents' name, easy to find. By the time we cross the Virginia line, you'll have an attorney working on your behalf. We're going to get out of this. The Marshals office and the FBI are already executing warrants, they raided Brock Marsh, they're going to get to Franklin as well."

"Brock Marsh? They have people everywhere. Half its staff are former cops, feds, military."

"I don't care—they're going down. At least Bruce Rockford is—and he's in the wind. And possibly Chad Rockford considering his connection to BioRise. Through James Seidel's daughter."

Grant didn't say anything.

"You didn't think that was important?"

"When did you find out?"

"Last night, but that's beside the point."

"I didn't think it was relevant."

"BioRise is behind the murder of our son. James Seidel is the CEO of BioRise. And I fucking *shook his hand* on Thursday!"

"I didn't know then…"

"Dammit, Grant, I can't help you if you don't tell me everything."

"What do you want from me? I don't know what's important and what isn't. I'm not keeping secrets—I just don't know what to say or do."

"Get your stuff together, Grant."

"I think we should stay," he said again.

"I can't protect you here. I trust Charlie—I trust the team he's put together. My job is to keep you safe until you're in police custody."

"You think I killed her, don't you?"

"Dammit, Grant! You keep saying that, and I keep telling you I believe you. Do you want me to say yes? Yes, Grant, I think you killed Madeline? If I thought that, you'd already be in police custody—I would have called the state police, had them haul your ass down to jail. If I thought you were guilty, you would already be behind bars."

"Wow."

"You're pushing my buttons like you want a fight. Don't do that. I need a clear head so I can get you out of this mess. The circumstantial evidence is damning, and the police have an arrest warrant. You left a crime scene. You didn't report it. You fled the state. None of that looks good. But no—I don't think you killed her. I think you made a series of bad decisions out of fear and panic and grief. But what matters now is that you're going to tell the truth, the whole truth—but first we have to get you to safety. We're too isolated here."

"Great that you have so much faith in me."

"Just stop." She rubbed her eyes. She wasn't going to do either of them any good if there was this tension between them. "You fucked up. Is that what you want to hear? I'm at my wit's end. My best friend is dead. Killed because he was investigating *our son's* murder. Something I should have been doing, but my emotions were too raw, and after Hannigan was killed, I lost hope. Tommy didn't. And Tommy is dead because of it. Are the answers worth it? Worth losing a good man? I don't know. I honestly can't tell you if I'm happier knowing the truth than the uncertainty I've lived with for the last eleven months. So I'm not okay, but I'm going to be okay. Getting you back to Virginia in one piece is all I can do right now. Then I'm going to find a way to bring every person involved in Tommy's death to justice. If I have to take down James Seidel and BioRise itself, I will."

She turned around, worked to tamp down her anger, the rage, the deep depression that threatened to overwhelm her at all she had lost.

And she did it. Because that's who she was.

"Ten minutes," she said without looking at Grant.

Ten minutes later, the house was locked up and they were in Tommy's truck. It was newer and had a full tank of gas—she'd filled up at the last gas station she'd seen, knowing a full tank was essential if she had to make a quick getaway. She'd looked at the Ranger's gas tank—less than a quarter. Grant rarely followed her advice to not let the tank fall below half-full.

It was still dark, though a faint, thin glow crept up to the east. Official sunrise was still thirty minutes from now.

Almost as soon as she turned onto Lower Sahler Mill Road, Regan suspected they were being followed.

She called Charlie. Now wasn't the time for heroics; she needed backup.

"Charlie, it's Regan."

"Regan? You're breaking up."

Dammit! This windy mountain road messed with cell service.

"I'm going to text you where Grant and I were staying, the direction we're heading. We're being followed."

"What?"

"We're being followed."

"Followed?"

"Yes. I'll text you, send you my location via GPS. I need backup."

"Text?"

Argh. She ended the call and handed her phone to Grant. "Text Charlie. Tell him where we were, that we're heading north on Lower Sahler Mill Road toward Krumville, then east toward US 209."

Grant didn't argue. He sent the text.

"Now tell him we're being followed. If I can't get to the highway, we're going to double back to the house."

When Grant just looked at her, she said, "Do it, Grant. Then go to location services and share my location with Charlie."

He complied.

She kept her eyes darting from the road to the bright lights behind her.

The area was remote with few homes, and most of the houses were well off the road.

Regan couldn't risk turning down a driveway. Some of the houses might be unoccupied, but others could have people, families, inside. She wasn't bringing violence to the innocent.

No, she needed to get to the highway—five miles away—then to the interstate—another five miles. Find a police station or highway patrol.

If she had the time.

But the way their pursuer was following them, on this narrow, winding road?

She didn't think they had the time. She was fast running out of options.

She had to slow at Krumville, but she didn't stop at the stop sign. She saw no lights coming toward her—not at 4:30 in the morning on this remote country road. But she had to slow to make the turn. As soon as she pulled out of it, she put on the gas.

Her pursuer did the same.

Grim, jaw tight, she continued increasing speed. She knew the roads, but not well—and in the dark, they were a death trap for speeders. Trees towered above her as she wound around the mountain, needing to focus on the road more than the person behind them.

The lights were coming at her fast.

"Brace yourself," she told Grant.

She barely got the words out when she felt the violent impact of their pursuer ramming the back of the truck. Her seatbelt tightened around her chest as she lurched forward. Grant automatically put his hands up in front of him, and she wanted to tell him no, he'd break a wrist, but no words came out.

She managed—barely—to keep the truck on the road. Her alignment was off, but she compensated with her steering.

They were rammed again from behind, and this time, the other vehicle accelerated, pushing her truck forward as they were approaching a sharp turn.

She had only one option. And if she didn't do it now, they were dead.

Regan turned her wheel sharply to the right. Her truck went hard into the ravine next to the road, the front end slamming into the ground, her rear wheels up in the air as the truck was almost at a ninety-degree angle.

Their pursuer didn't expect the move and the momentum took him forward, forcing him to spin out as he clamored for control of his own vehicle.

The airbags inflated, slamming into Regan's face, and she momentarily saw stars. But she couldn't be sidetracked. Their attacker would be back any second.

"Grant!" she shouted as she used all her strength to push open her door. "Grant!"

He was disorientated, but she had to get him moving. She was out of the truck, her feet sliding on the steep slope. They were on the edge of a small lake. The ground was soft, muddy, and their truck was sinking.

"Grant, move it!"

She grabbed her go bag from where it had slid onto the floor of the truck; pulled it over her back. Every muscle ached and blood dripped down her face. She wiped her nose and winced. Broken nose. Not the first time, she knew exactly how it felt.

She pulled at Grant, and finally he slid over the bench seat and out her door. He fell to his knees, coughing from the airbag powder.

"We have to go."

"Where?" he gasped, trying to catch his breath.

"Back to the house. Through the woods. It's two miles as the crow flies. We'll make it because it's dark. But he's coming back, so we need to move fast."

As if to accent her point, the light from their pursuer's truck whipped around down the road. Solo light—he'd broken one of his headlamps.

"Okay," he said. "Okay."

He followed her, and Regan set a brisk pace. She looked at her watch to get her bearings, mentally thanking her dad for teaching her to not only wear but use the military-grade compass watch. Her muscle memory kicked in as she looked at the small compass on the watch face to make sure she was heading in the right direction.

"We should get help. There's a house over there." Grant, panting, pointed up the slope to where a house was nestled among the trees. A porch light was on.

"And bring a killer to their doorstep? No."

Too many people had died. She wasn't going to risk a civilian.

She saw the light of the truck turn brighter, as their attacker looked for their retreating forms. Fortunately, the thickly leaved birch and maple trees shielded them.

But she had no doubt that he would pursue.

If he didn't—if he drove away—she wouldn't go to the cabin. He might expect them to return. But there was no way he could know this area as well as she did. He hadn't explored it; he hadn't walked through the woods, played hide-and-seek, taught his son how to use a compass to find his way home.

Regan had done all of that, and more.

In minutes, she knew she was right. The light went off, but the truck didn't drive off.

"He's following on foot," she told Grant. "We have to move faster."

"I can't make it."

"Yes you can."

"My head hurts."

"You're going to make it. You're going to follow my lead. You're the only one who can get justice for Chase."

He was silent, but he kept up with her fast pace.

She hoped the text Grant sent on her phone went through. That Charlie contacted the authorities and they would find the wreck, track them.

The slope was steeper, and while she could manage it thanks to years of hiking in Flagstaff, Grant was struggling.

Their pursuer was gaining on them.

This wasn't going to work.

"Okay," she whispered, "we're going to backtrack to the road."

"I can do it," Grant said, breathless.

She couldn't use a light, that would make it much easier for them to be tracked.

Just as she turned west, so they could walk around the mountain rather than over it, a voice shouted at them. He was close, but not too close.

If this is the same man who killed Tommy, he can shoot. He can't know where you are.

She worked on being as quiet as possible.

"You're not going to get away," the voice said. Regan gauged him to be between thirty and forty yards away. Too close. He had a light.

He had a light.

She needed to take the shot. It might be their only chance of getting away from this.

"Grant," she whispered, "keep in the ravine. Don't go on the road, stay in the ravine. Keep walking west. Avoid houses, move as fast as you can."

"What are you going to do?"

"Buy us time. Go. Don't hesitate, no matter what you hear."

"Regan—don't do this."

"We don't have time to argue. *Go!*"

He finally went.

She headed up the slope, and then flattened herself against a tree, gun out, waiting.

The pursuer was making good time. His flashlight cutting swaths of light among the trees.

"Grant, you know what you did—you need to face the piper," the man called out. "Come out and I'll make it quick."

And still, Regan waited. She had to aim at the light. She couldn't risk missing and having him take cover, or worse, trap her. But she could take out his flashlight, and if she was quick enough, hit him. Slow him down, kill him, she didn't really care.

She needed to protect Grant. Because she hadn't been lying to him; he was the only one who could give Chase justice. The only one who had answers—or could turn the FBI toward the truth.

If Grant died, the truth died with him.

So she waited. Her heart rate slowed, her eyes sharpened, her hand was steady.

She only had one shot. Shoot and move. Because if he had a gun in his hand, and was a good shot, he could turn and hit her, especially at this short distance.

She didn't have her favored .45, but she'd picked a .45 Sig from Tommy's gun safe that had a similar weight and feel and fit well into her holster. But she hadn't practiced with it, didn't know how it fired. She assumed, because Tommy took care of his guns, that it would function as intended.

"I'm going to find you, Grant."

He was closer, both his voice and his light.

The light stopped moving. Did he sense her watching? She aimed.

The light went off.

She fired three times in rapid succession to where the light had been. The .45 had a kick; she was used to it. She heard a grunt. Not waiting to find out if he was down, she bolted.

"Regan!"

Grant's voice came from a distance. Dammit, why couldn't he just do what he was told and remain quiet? Hadn't she told him to keep going, not look back? Wouldn't that imply not to shout and give away his location?

She ran over the rocky soil, sliding on the slope, but moving forward. Toward Grant.

She could hear him coming back toward her.

"Keep moving, Grant!" she ordered. Dammit, she didn't know if their pursuer was dead or had a flesh wound, and she wasn't going to stop and find out.

"Move move move!"

He didn't. He was standing in the ravine waiting for her.

"Did he hit you? Are you hurt?"

"I hit *him*. Now move, dammit!"

They ran together.

She picked a route from the intersection of Krumville and Lower Sahler Mill Road that mostly ran parallel to the road.

"He's not following," Grant said, winded.

"He's not giving up."

"He could be dead."

"I don't think so."

She wondered if the police had been called. Charlie would have…if the message had gotten through. If not Charlie, then a neighbor?

Except this wasn't New York City, this was rural New York, and maybe people here in the mountains didn't think twice about gun fire. There were black bears and bobcats and other wild animals. A lot of farms here. Even in New York, farmers had a right to protect their horses and chickens and sheep from four-legged predators.

Her guess was that if the shooter was injured, he'd go back to his truck, patch himself up, and beat them to the house.

She needed to get to high ground and get a call out.

"We need backup," she said.

"Do you have a signal?"

"Not here. I need to get back to the house. I can get a good signal from there. But that could also be where the asshole is headed."

"If he's alive."

"We have to assume that he is," she said.

They also had daybreak to contend with. Dawn was rapidly falling into the valley, and that meant real quick they wouldn't have the cover of darkness.

"We're going to cut through here." She motioned to the forest and a path that was barely a path that wound through it.

"We'll get lost."

"I don't get lost," she snapped.

He didn't say anything, just followed her.

Ten minutes later, she turned south again and then west ten minutes after that. She didn't see anyone in the woods, didn't hear anyone, didn't even hear a vehicle—though they were pretty far from the road.

Soon, she stopped. "The house is through there," she said.

Grant stared. "You were right."

"I need to check it out—see if he doubled back. Stay here."

He looked around. "If he's following us—"

"He's not."

"But—"

"He's not, Grant. Stay by this tree—it'll shield you. I'll whistle if it's clear."

"And if you don't?"

"Just stay put."

She reached into her go bag and retrieved the 9mm backup piece. "Take it."

"I really don't—"

"Take it," she repeated. "To protect yourself."

He reluctantly took the gun, held it awkwardly at his side.

Regan ran toward the house, staying close to the trees.

She didn't see another vehicle. But he could have parked on the road or down the driveway. He might have assumed they would be coming from the road, or if they came from the woods, he didn't want them to see his vehicle.

She looked at her phone. One bar. The house was elevated and she'd have more bars, but she should be able to call out now.

She texted Charlie, he immediately responded.

I got your message! Called the police.

She acknowledged it. Called 911. Informed them that she had been run off the road by a man with a gun. Charlie could give more details. She gave her exact location and said they were heading for the house to barricade themselves because she didn't know where the attacker was.

Then she walked back to Grant.

"Stay behind me, do exactly what I say. Understand?"

"Yes."

Dawn was breaking, but it was still too dark to really see more than shadows and light. She ran low, tree to tree, toward the house. When they reached the carport, she had Grant squat, between the pillar and the truck, and she checked out the immediate area.

Silence. Birds. A rodent scurrying. No cars, no voices, no breathing other than Grant's.

"Okay, we're going up the stairs. It will expose us, but you stay between me and the house."

"He's a sniper. He could be anywhere."

"Then being out here is foolish," she said. "We need cover. The police are on their way."

Grant didn't immediately follow her.

"Come!" she hissed.

"I wasn't completely honest with you last night."

Her stomach fell, her heart constricted.

"Later."

But he kept talking. "You asked what I was doing in Maddie's apartment for ten minutes. I retrieved evidence that I had hid there. Printouts, documents. After Tommy was killed, I feared I was going to be next, and I thought if Maddie found it, she'd do the right thing. So I hid it. I had to get to it. I then mailed it to you in care of the Marshals office."

She was stunned. "Why didn't you tell me?"

"Because I did it with Maddie's dead body right there! I felt cold and unfeeling and just... I couldn't process everything that had happened. I thought I was going to die, and I needed you to have what we had. It's not everything, but it'll give the white-collar crimes division of the FBI a lot to sort through. I couldn't crack all the codes, but they probably can."

"Okay. That's good. Now we just have to wait for—"

She heard something—not sure what. A branch? A rock?

"Go! Now!" She pushed Grant up the stairs as a bullet hit her old Ranger right where they'd been squatting.

She couldn't see the shooter.

"Thought you were so clever," he called out from the thick trees.

Close, too close. She didn't have a vest, and Lee was a good shot.

"You've been a fucking thorn in my side, Merritt. I was supposed to be back home before today. You've ruined my plans. But you and your ex just don't play by the rules."

She gauged where the voice was coming from. She had one shot to do this, to get Grant to safety.

"Grant, get to the door, get inside. Don't hesitate. On three."

A bullet breezed by her, clipping her arm. It didn't hit her, not exactly, but her arm stung. Lee swore. Good thing the lights were off and the sun wasn't fully up. He didn't have a good visual; the truck and part of the house were in the way. But as soon as they ran up the stairs, he'd have a shot.

She couldn't let him take it.

She said to Grant, "Three. Two. One. GO!"

She stood fully and fired repeatedly in the direction Nelson Lee's voice had come from, near the largest pine tree to the east of the house. She counted down her shots while Grant ran up the stairs. She switched to her nondominant hand—which she was almost as good with as her right—and ran up behind Grant, still firing in the general direction of their pursuer.

Grant fumbled with the keypad but got it open when she had one bullet left. She pushed him inside, slammed the door, dropped the magazine, and slammed in another. She wanted Grant the farthest away from the shooter, which meant upstairs—but the shooter would also expect that, and that's where he would go if he could get in. So she'd keep Grant on the main floor.

She said, "Go to the back bedroom, barricade yourself in until I give you the clear."

"He's going to come after you."

"Do it, Grant."

"When are the police going to be here? How long will it take?"

"Stop talking and do what I said!"

Grant had information, he was a witness, he was going to need to testify. Without Grant, she didn't know if they would be able to shut down Franklin Archer or BioRise. She wanted BioRise most of all. She would destroy them.

Grant ran down the hall while she locked and bolted the front door. Shoved a chair under the knob to delay him. Then she went into the kitchen and crouched behind the butcher block counter. Checked her gun again. She'd given Grant her backup and she hoped if Lee somehow got past her that Grant would use it and protect himself.

She waited, her training taking over and keeping her as calm as possible. Her heart rate was elevated, but she had a clear head. She listened.

She couldn't hear anything outside. Not Nelson Lee, not the police.

She pictured where he might come in. They'd secured the sliding glass doors, and it would take a lot of bullets to break the windows, which would alert her. She had to assume he was wearing some sort of body armor. Probably a vest.

She didn't hear him on the stairs or deck. Was he waiting for them to come out? No…he would know by now that she'd called the police. He would know that time was not on his side. She could wait him out here, she had the upper hand.

But the man wasn't stupid. What was his plan? Take out the first officer? Buy himself time?

The garage.

The Ranger was parked in the carport, but there was also a garage and basement. Shit, she should have thought of that!

Then she heard a loud shotgun blast in the hall. He'd blown open the lock of the door coming up from the garage.

She prayed that Grant stayed put. That he did what she told him!

She moved around the counter, staying low, because the kitchen was too open, too exposed.

She had to buy time. Keep him from finding Grant.

"Nelson Lee!" she shouted. "The police are on their way. You won't get out of this." She knew she was exposing her location, but better her than Grant.

"Don't underestimate me," he said. "There's too much at stake."

He was in the hallway that separated the kitchen from the garage door and downstairs bedroom. The stairs were to her left, closer to the front door. Getting him up the stairs would enable her to, hopefully, trap him up there until the police came.

She maneuvered herself through the kitchen and to the dining table, which she immediately pushed over to give herself a shield. The shotgun pellets hit the table just as she dove for cover.

She caught a glimpse of his weapon before she shielded herself—a tactical shotgun, pistol grip. Nice piece. Likely seven shots. He'd fired two.

Wouldn't kill her at this range, but the closer he got, the more damage it would do. And if he hit her head, even forty feet away, she'd be toast.

"Nelson, the truth is out there," she called out.

He laughed. "You're an *X-Files* fan?"

"Not really, but in this case, it's the truth. Tommy Granger had enough evidence in his house that we were able to piece together his investigation. We know about Legacy, we know about the Potomac Bank robbery. We know about BioRise and their clinical trials. We know James Seidel is behind it all and his connection to Legacy through his son-in-law. When I say we, I mean the US Marshals, the FBI, the AUSA. It's all coming down. Your only chance to escape is now—because you will be brought down when the net falls."

"No proof," he said. He was coming closer. She crawled to the edge of the table, her head close to the floor, and looked out. She didn't see him. The house was dark, though the windows showed some light from the rising sun. But he stayed in the hall, where she didn't have a clear shot. She could see the tip of his shotgun.

"No evidence," he continued. "It's all hearsay. And trust me—these people will fight with every fiber of their beings. They have more money than anyone on earth. They'll win. You won't break them."

"Brock Marsh was raided. It's shut down. The Rockfords are on the run. The FBI found their mole. I sent a recording of Grant's statement to the Marshals. He already turned over all the evidence he has."

That wasn't true, the part about her recording Grant's statement, but she wished she had. She hadn't thought about it when she finally got Grant to talk to her last night. That was stupid on her part. Just plain stupid. She'd been so drained, physically and emotionally, but that was no excuse.

"You know, I almost believe you," he said. "But even if I did believe you, I was paid to kill Grant Warwick, and I will kill him. I always live up to my commitments."

He was moving as he talked. He didn't know where Grant was, but he was also an operative, and would have expected she'd send Grant upstairs, the safest place.

And that's where he was moving. And that's where he was wrong.

"Fool me once," he said, then stepped out of the hall and fired his shotgun repeatedly at the dining table, shattering the wood. She scrambled away as splinters and shards flew everywhere. Something cut into her cheek and she winced, but still moved back to the counter while counting his shots. He had one more.

She rolled as she was trained and then positioned herself, gun out, prone on the floor, and fired at center mass. He stumbled back, grunted, but she was right—he had on a vest. He slowed, the wind knocked out of him, but he wasn't injured.

She aimed higher, fired three times at the meaty part of his shoulder, hoping to hit around the vest. You always aimed center mass to take out the threat, but making him bleed from a non-fatal injury would also work.

The third shot hit flesh. Blood spattered behind him. She fired again at his other arm as he moved behind the wall again. Then she heard him on the stairs.

She jumped up and, cautious, approached the hall. He was standing on the third stair and when he sensed or saw that she was nearby, he fired his last shotgun pellet into the drywall next to her head. Her ears rang.

Then he was running up the stairs.

She ignored the throbbing from the close blast, and ran after him, firing, hitting his thigh. He fell to his knees on the landing. Crawled up the stairs. He had left his empty shotgun at the bottom of the stairs, but she saw one holstered gun on his hip, another in his hand.

It was now or never.

Regan moved quickly up the stairs as he turned and aimed at her. She fired twice, hit one into the vest and one into his arm, and he jerked, dropped the gun. She couldn't risk crossing his body to retrieve his gun—he could have a knife, stab her in the thigh. Pull his other gun. Tackle her, even though he had several holes in him and was bleeding. None of them were fatal, if he got medical attention.

But if he made a move, she would shoot him in the head.

"Don't move," she said.

She wanted to kill him. The urge was overwhelming, to put a bullet in his head. He had killed her best friend, her one-time lover. A good man who had sacrificed himself to give her peace and justice.

She itched to kill him. Her hand twitched.

"Let me go," he said. "Let me go and I will hand you BioRise and James Seidel on a silver platter. There is so much more you don't know."

He'd nearly killed her and Grant. She would get away with it. Kill him, end it.

She wanted to. God, she wanted to.

He killed Tommy. He sat in a tree and waited and killed him.

But she couldn't pull the trigger. She would never be able to live with herself if she killed a man in cold blood—no matter how much he deserved it.

"You go for your gun, I will kill you," she said.

He knew she was stuck on the stairs. They were at a standoff, but she had the upper hand.

She knew it; he knew it.

She just had to wait him out.

She had never been so relieved as when she heard sirens a minute later.

Behind her, where the stairs curved, she heard something else. She didn't want to take her eyes off Lee, but she had to assess the potential threat.

She turned her head slightly and saw Grant out of the corner of her eye.

"Go back!" she ordered.

Grant wasn't looking at her, he was looking at Nelson Lee.

He had the 9mm she'd given him aimed at the killer. Rage and pain twisted his face.

"You killed Maddie."

Without thinking, she pushed Grant's arm up as he pressed the trigger and the bullet went high.

"Stop!" she cried. "You don't—"

"Yes I do!"

He tried to aim again, and she elbowed him in the gut, disarmed him of the weapon.

But in the split second she was forced to turn away from Nelson Lee, he had pulled his second gun from his holster and aimed it at Grant.

She saw him raise the gun, blood still pouring out of his wounds onto the carpet. His face drawn, white, determined.

Grant standing there, screaming at her, screaming at Nelson, but she didn't hear his words.

Nelson's hand was shaking as he pressed the trigger at the same time she fired her .45 three times at his head.

Nelson's bullet missed Grant, but grazed her arm. She bit back a cry as a burning sensation coursed through her body. She'd never been shot in the line of duty, and now this.

But Nelson Lee was down. And he was never getting up.

THURSDAY

JUNE 1

Forty-Six

Tommy's memorial service was attended by three hundred people. Friends of Terri and Grace—mostly from the hospital and their church. Dozens of cops, a few FBI agents, and fifty marshals. Friends and neighbors. Former and current military—two of Tommy's closest friends were career military who had been given three-day's leave to attend his service.

And Regan's dad.

She sat with her dad, surprised at how emotional she'd been when he showed up yesterday at Tommy's house.

"You will never say you need me, but you needed me," he said.

"Yes, Dad, I need you."

He sat with her in his suit, still looking like a cop though he'd retired four years ago. Terri's minister gave a nice sermon, about duty and honor, loyalty and hope. About how Thomas V. Granger had lived up to the code of the United States Marines, and then the United States Marshals Service. But mostly, he'd lived up to the code in the Bible: to love your neighbor as yourself.

Terri said a few words, stories about Tommy when he

was younger, including one where he nursed a stray cat back to health. One of his Marine buddies told stories about Tommy in basic training, including one where he broke curfew because he was helping his bunkmate propose to his girlfriend.

And Regan spoke.

It was difficult, but not as hard as she thought it would be. All she could think about was that Tommy should be alive, Chase should be alive, and the greed and selfishness of others took what was good and right in the world and destroyed it.

But saying goodbye—that, she needed.

At the end, she slipped out, needing a moment alone. She was surprised when her dad followed her.

"I thought you were having a nice chat with my old boss."

"He's an interesting fellow," John Merritt said. "He's coming to Scottsdale for a charity golf event for fallen officers in the fall, one I'm involved with. We plan to catch up more then."

"Good," she said, and meant it. She watched people from a distance. She couldn't hear any one conversation, but imagined that they all had stories about Tommy. His legacy. "Thank you for being here, Dad."

"Any word on when you can return home?"

"Saturday, I hope, but it might not be until Monday."

"Monday is good," he said. "I agreed to adopt a couple horses from the Rickmans. They're moving, won't have room for them. I could use your help getting them settled next week."

She loved horses; they'd had them when she was growing up.

"I guess I'd better get started on that apartment over

the barn." She'd already paid for remodeling plans for the apartment her grandfather had lived in for years before he died. All that was needed was her signature and a down payment to get started. "Are you sure you won't get tired of me being around all the time?"

"No promises, but I'll tell you this—after having you back for a few months, when you were gone this last week, I missed having you around. Maybe I'm just getting sentimental in my old age."

She laughed. "You? Old? Sentimental? I don't see it."

"You're right. I just like the company."

"Me, too, Dad." She swirled the beer around in the bottle, not really wanting any more. "I need to find a job."

"I thought you had a nice nest egg."

"I do. And it'll last a bit longer. But… I need a purpose. Now that I have closure here, I feel I can finally move forward."

John nodded. "I think you can. Do you have some ideas?"

"Can you get me in touch with your friend in security? I think my skills might benefit his business."

"I know they will," John said with a smile. "I'm glad. And I'm especially glad that you're returning to Flagstaff."

"Honestly, Dad—there's no place I'd rather be. Flagstaff is my home."

Regan managed to eat a bit, talked to some of her old colleagues, spent a few minutes with Terri and Grace. There was a peace in the air, a sense of closure. She grabbed a second beer when her first became too warm. They were serving Samuel Adams, which was Tommy's favorite beer. He used to toast, "Brewer, Patriot," with a grin whenever they had a barbecue, back before her life had turned upside down. "Maybe that's what I should do, open a brewery when I retire," he would say.

She tilted the bottle to the sky. "Goodbye, Tommy."

Charlie sat down across from her. He looked worn out. "You okay?" he asked.

She nodded. "I should be asking you the same. It's over, at least for me."

"Yeah, it'll be a roller coaster here for a few months."

He opened his own bottle of beer, clinked the neck against her bottle, and they both drank.

"Jenna is back at work," he said. "We did a threat assessment and she's not in danger. Between the evidence you found in Nelson Lee's truck and the evidence Grant has plus his statement, there is more than enough to take down BioRise, Brock Marsh, and Legacy."

"And James Seidel? Is he in custody?"

"It's going to take time, but he hasn't fled the country and the FBI pulled his passport."

"He has the wealth to fight us every step of the way."

"Us?"

"You know what I mean."

"We have enough against BioRise that he's going to have to pay his fortune to fancy lawyers to keep him out of jail, and even then I don't know if that'll work."

"So you think Jenna is okay, then," Regan said. "Because if Seidel thinks that killing her gets him off, he'll do it."

"Jenna's statement is small potatoes compared to those documents. She's the icing on the cake, and pulls a lot of it together, but even without her they're going down."

"Okay. Good. And Lance?"

"I think he's in love with her."

She smiled. "Trial by fire."

"Grant's going into WitSec until the trial, if there's a

trial," Charlie said a moment later. "I went over the contract with him yesterday."

"Good."

"He leaves tomorrow morning. Because we haven't located the Rockford brothers, it's best that we get him out quickly and quietly."

"Okay."

"You should say goodbye."

"I don't have anything to say."

She was angry that Grant had forced her to kill Nelson Lee, and she was angry at herself that she didn't feel remorse for it.

"I think you do. Closure."

She looked into Charlie's dark eyes, saw the friendship, the affection, the concern on his face.

"Maybe you're right."

Regan was cleared to enter the hotel room where Grant was being housed. She didn't know where he would be going when he boarded a plane tomorrow morning; Grant probably didn't know yet, either.

He was surprised to see her.

"I didn't think I was allowed to see anyone."

"You're not. But I have friends in high places. After tomorrow, though, we won't be able to talk. You know the rules."

He nodded.

"I wanted to say goodbye," she said.

"I'm sorry."

"About what?" She didn't mean to sound bitchy. She didn't want an argument. She was so weary, so tired, and all she wanted was to go home. But she was stuck here in Virginia for another couple of days because of the shooting in New York. Statements, reports, more statements. She would be cleared, but they were hoops she had to jump through. She'd told her dad they'd probably be able to leave on Monday, but that might have been a bit optimistic.

"You should have let me kill him, so you didn't have that weight on your soul. I have no soul."

"That's not true, Grant."

She sat across from him on the couch. "I don't know what happened with us, other than I wasn't the wife you needed. But I loved you once, and I loved our son, and I'm choosing to remember that."

When he didn't say anything, she continued.

"I drove back the old Ranger after I gave my statement to the state troopers up in New York. I'm going to give it to Charlie. The stickers on the back reminded me of simpler times. That we had Chase, and he was loved. There was never one minute of doubt in my mind that you loved our son as much as I did."

"Will you visit his grave? For me?"

"I'll visit his grave for us. On his birthday, every year."

Tears welled in Grant's eyes. "I hope you find peace, Regan. I really do."

She nodded. She was on the road to peace, but it was a journey, with ups and downs. "I have my dad. My brothers and sister. I have a home in Flagstaff."

"You have a foundation I never had. I mean, my parents are good people and all, but it wasn't the same as yours."

"You can't compare them, but I know what you mean. Are you going to be okay? I mean, really, Grant, have you even processed everything that's happened? With Franklin?"

"He's dead. Sometimes, I think that's the easy way."

"Don't—"

"I'm not. I'll be okay. Do you know what's going to happen to his wife, his daughters?"

"They're with family out of state, and Isabelle is talking to the FBI. I don't know what she knew or how she might help the investigation, but she's cooperating. His estate is tied up now, but I suspect she's going to do just fine."

"Franklin would have set her up with separate accounts— money the government won't be able to touch. Trusts, in the kids' names, I don't know—but Franklin had been brilliant."

"Franklin was a corrupt, unethical bastard and I'm not going to shed a tear over his dead body."

Grant didn't argue with her.

"Seriously, Grant—witness protection isn't easy."

"I think," he said after a moment, "being able to create a new life, at least for the time being, will give me the chance to find out who I am." He laughed without humor. "I'm thirty-nine and still need to figure out my life."

She rose, then sat next to him. She hugged him.

He hugged her back, tightly. His body shook with sobs. "I'm sorry for everything, Regan."

"So am I, Grant."

But it was over. She had justice for their son, answers to her questions, and her future…well, she would take it one day at a time.

She was okay with that.

* * * * *